About the Author

For most of World War II, the author lived with his family on the outskirts of London and, like many others, he witnessed the Battle of Britain in the bright, blue skies of late summer 1940. As a young boy it seemed like fun rather than the deadly killing game that it really was. But it was not fun later when, night after night, the sirens wailed and the bombs whined down, and the house shook. It was not fun to see the devastation: the piles of rubble that hours before had been some family's home, or the tall skeleton that had been the local church. Nor was it fun to say goodbye to older brothers as they went off to fight for their country, or to his father as he went to his daily work in the shadow of St. Paul's, perhaps not to return. Especially, it was not fun to watch as the Doodlebug Flying Bomb plummeted towards him and he vainly cowered for protection behind the garden fence.

Now, almost 70 years later, these memories and visions are still so powerful, so etched in the mind, that he has felt compelled to turn them into this, his first novel.

James Brown was educated at private school in Surrey. There followed two years National Service in the Royal Artillery and then a career in Electronics Manufacturing where he became Director of Sales and Marketing. Now retired, he lives with his wife whom he married in 1957, in the remote and beautiful isles of Scilly.

Currently he is writing his second book. He thinks he will call it "Stories to Send My Grandchildren to Sleep". But who knows – it may give them nightmares instead!

Dedication

This book is dedicated to my darling wife Susan, who has been my lifelong friend and inspiration. Her love, patience and devotion have been a blessing, a miracle I have not deserved. All thanks to her, and to my God for sending her to me.

Acknowledgements

I should like to express my deep gratitude to Margaret Gill for her invaluable encouragement and help in writing this book.

I am grateful for the factual information provided by: *"The Encyclopedia of Military Aircraft"* by Robert Jackson, *"World War II"* by Ivor Matanle and *"World War II – Day by Day"* published by Dorling Kindersley.

Cover design from an original watercolour painting by Jennifer Johnson.

CHAPTER 1

The Browning family were gathered round the old wooden radio. The voice they heard seemed weak, quavering, defeated. Finn Browning, the youngest of the family and only eight years old, would never forget the words that were spoken. The man they were listening to was the British Prime Minister, Neville Chamberlain. At this time, Sunday morning on September 3rd, 1939, he was seventy years old. Not really old, but too old for the trial that lay ahead for him and his country. It would not be his war.

Few who listened would be surprised by the words he spoke. For many months he had struggled to avoid the need to utter them. The grim shadow of war in Europe had been growing more inevitable day by day, darkening the hearts of all who were old enough to understand the terrible realities of what war would mean, for it was scarcely twenty years since the end of The Great War, "The War to End All Wars" they had called it.

"…and in consequence I have to tell you that we are at war with Germany. God save our country. God save the King."

The broadcast ended. In millions of homes throughout Britain and in free Europe across the English Channel, radios were switched off and women stared silently at their menfolk and children. They all knew what was to come. At least, they thought they did, for in truth it would be more dreadful than could ever be imagined. Men slumped in their chairs, or left the room so that their women and children would not see the fear in their eyes. Some sought a bottle for comfort, for was there ever a moment when a stiff shot of whisky or schnapps would be more welcome.

Claud Browning, like the others in his family, sat motionless. He had been in the trenches twice, in 1915 and again in1917. The second time he had been gassed, the ghastly mustard gas, that blinded and choked, and burned the lungs. He had been lucky though. At least since then he had been able to work, and marry and support a family, even if his health had never since then been robust. Not like his brother Eddy, who was buried in the mire somewhere near Ypres.

At last, Claud's wife Bobby broke the silence. "Well, Claud, at least YOU will not have to go this time. They won't need a man of forty-six."

"No, dear, I suppose that's a consolation, but Clive is nearly seventeen and if the war goes on for any length of time, as surely it will, then he will have to fight. And Douglas is sixteen soon, so who knows, it could be him in uniform too."

The Brownings had four sons. Besides Clive and Douglas, there was Kenneth, born in 1926 and Finn, born five years later. "Worm" his brothers called him. Mrs Browning had always been called Bobby, but her full name was Roberta. She had been born Roberta Finnebraaten in Moss, a little town south of Oslo. She had met her husband in 1921 in Dublin. Like many Norwegians, she had mastered English at school, and was now employed as a governess to Crispin Lampart, the young son of Lord and Lady Lampart. She had met Claud at a Ball the Lamparts had given one April weekend. Claud had ended the war as a Captain in The Royal Naval Division and had stayed on in uniform and was now in Ireland as a member of the hated Black and Tans, an armed British police force trying to control the renegades of the Irish Republican Movement. There and then that April night, Claud had been fascinated by this blonde, slender and very beautiful young Norwegian girl. The rapport was mutual. The wedding took place only a few weeks later in the Chapel of the Lamparts' estate. Outside, a Company of Black and Tans kept guard, rifles fully loaded. The risk of attacks by the IRA was very real indeed.

Soon after they were married, Claud brought his bride back to England. Before the Great War, Claud had been a reporter on the London Evening Gazette. He came from a journalistic family. His father had been Editor of the Stoke on-Trent Tribune. Claud now returned to Civvy Street, to his old job as a crime reporter for the Gazette, and he and Bobby rented a semi-detached four bedroom house in Barnes, a south-West London suburb bordering the Thames, and an easy journey for Claud into Fleet Street. The Browning house was in Nassau road, with the river at one end and Barnes Common at the other. In later years, the whole family would troop down to the river to watch the Oxford and Cambridge Boat Race.

For a time, Claud's career went well. Frequently one of his reports would be on the front page. Not surprising, perhaps. After all, as a fledgling correspondent, he had written brilliantly at the trial of the infamous Dr Crippen. Bobby was happy in Barnes. Her English was near perfect, and she was soon accepted by neighbours, who would ask her out to tea or invite her to an afternoon playing bridge. With her statuesque figure and long, blonde hair falling below her shoulders, she was regarded as an enhancement of the local landscape in this quiet, conventional scene that was Barnes SW13.

In November 1922, Claud and Bobby's first child was born, a healthy seven pound, seven ounce boy. He soon displayed an angelic smile, which he never lost. They christened him Clive. Bobby was a devoted and sensible mother. Claud was doting – more than he should have been. He could not see that pampering a child could do any harm. Perhaps it was to do with losing his brother Eddy in the mire of Flanders. Clive grew well and showed his kind nature when, two years later, Bobby gave birth to another fine boy, whom they named Douglas. Clive adored little Doug. and spent hours just watching him, trying to talk to him, or cradling him in his little arms.

There are moments in a reporter's life, especially in crime reporting, when excitement is high, the adrenalin flows and the rush is on to be first with the story. But there are other moments too. Times when you have to stand in the rain hour after hour, drenched and shivering. Or spend lonely nights in some dreary provincial boarding house. Leisure can seldom be planned. Not for the reporter the certainty of being home by six, of playing with the children and tucking them up with a bedtime story, or taking the wife out to dinner, or to the cinema. The phone rings and off you go, catching the night train to Bradford, where some demented man has stabbed his neighbour to death.

Doubts grew in Bobby's mind, too. Although she said nothing, her mind was troubled. Work was taking precedence over their private, family life. She loved him passionately, and knew that he loved her. But he was chained to his other life, his other love it seemed, almost. She hated the long nights when he was away, and even their rare evenings together, in case the phone rang to disrupt their privacy, even sometimes their very intimacy. Claud was not insensitive to this gradual change in their relationship; he saw her growing frustration and sadness.

In January 1926 a third child was born – yet another boy. Kenneth was a little chubbier at birth, and into boyhood, than either of his elder brothers, but like them he was healthier enough and showed a greater aptitude for sport than either Clive or Douglas. The three of them got on well. "The Three Musketeers" they were called by the Ashworth family opposite.

Bobby became more subdued after Kenneth's birth. It may have been Post Natal Depression (a condition that was not even recognized in those far off days), but more likely it was the growing effect of her husband's absences and unpredictable job. By now, Claud had switched from the evening Gazette to its sister paper, the Sunday Gazette. And he had "come off the road", no longer reporting, but helping to edit the paper. He had done this primarily for the sake of his marriage. For national "Sundays" the busiest day of the week was Saturday, when the paper was "put to bed". The afternoons and evenings became ever more busy and frenetic as the deadline for going to print got nearer. On Saturday nights Claud rarely got home before midnight, and then in an exhausted state. Sundays became largely a day of recovery: late up, and then pottering about in the garden. To compensate for working all Saturdays, he had Monday off. But it was not the same. Suburban social life just did not happen on Mondays. Mondays were Washing Day, and getting the kids off to school.

Bobby tried hard to maintain a warm and loving relationship with her husband. Their determination that the boys should have a private education soaked up the money that Bobby would much have preferred to channel into the purchase of their own home. But that apart they managed comfortably enough, running a small, second-hand Austin car and having an annual summer holiday on the south coast.

Then, in 1930, two events occurred that changed the Brownings' lives. The first was that Bobby found she was pregnant again. She and Claud had always wanted a daughter, but that hope had evaporated when number three had turned out to be a third son – Kenneth. Four years had elapsed since then. The passion that had ignited the couple's marriage had faded. Claud's long absences away and his weariness on his return home, had taken their toll. They still loved each other, but sex happened rarely, more out of habit than as an expression of passion. The fourth pregnancy breathed new life into their relationship. Perhaps, at long last, they WOULD be granted a daughter.

The second event took place in late October. Normally, Claud went to his office in Fleet Street on the No.9 bus, but on this particular day he had driven the car for a routine service to the garage in Hammersmith and finished his journey by Tube to Chancery Lane. The day had been routine. For once, not much was happening, so he left the office early at about 4.30 pm. This would allow him time to pick up the Austin from the servicing people before they shut for the day. The escalator at Hammersmith Underground Station had broken down, so passengers were compelled to climb the stairs from the platform to the street above. As Claud emerged, the pain struck him. During his time at The Front, as well as being gassed, he had received a bullet wound in his right calf. It could have been much worse. The bullet had missed the bone and travelled straight through the flesh at the back. But the pain had been excruciating. Like the thrust of a red hot poker. The pain Claud now felt in his chest was as agonising as had been that bullet wound. It was as if his chest had been struck by a cannon ball. He fought for breath, but his lungs would not fill. Perversely, nor would they empty. Claud collapsed on the pavement. The light faded and he collapsed into unconsciousness. Claud was lucky – if having a heart attack can ever be called lucky. Emerging from the Underground just behind him was a doctor. As Claud slumped to the ground, the doctor ran to him, tearing off his jacket to make a pillow for Claud's head and loosening Claud's collar and tie. For Dr. James Lumley, the diagnosis was not difficult. He had dealt with scores of similar cases and knew exactly what to do. One, pinch the earlobe to establish the depth of unconsciousness. Two, check the tongue has not been swallowed and the airway is clear. Three, check the patient is breathing. No breathing? Start resuscitation: two mouth-to-mouth breaths, then commence compressions: fifteen at the rate of one hundred per minute. Depress and release the breastbone.

To Lumley's relief, Claud stirred and opened his eyes. Very slightly, Claud's pain had eased a little, and he could breath more normally again.

They took him to Hammersmith Hospital, just up the road towards Kensington, where he was kept for two weeks. Bobby and the three boys visited him every day. Dr. Lumley, though he had no connection with Hammersmith Hospital, came to visit him too, and Claud was able to thank the doctor for certainly having saved his life. "There is no reason" Dr Lumley told Claud, "Why you should not make a good recovery. It depends on you. You are still a comparatively young man and should have many years of active life left in you. But I should qualify the word active. It would be most unwise, for instance, to go mountaineering or to take up squash. On the other hand, a round of golf, plenty of steady swimming and regular walking would be excellent. Do you like gardening? Well, that's alright, but try to avoid the heavy digging, or lifting. May I ask what you do for a living?" "I'm a journalist on the Sunday Gazette."

"That's fine, but try to avoid stress"

It was six weeks before Claud returned to work. He and Bobby went to Torquay for ten days without the children. "To take the sea air" they told friends. It did more than allow him to recuperate; it gave him and Bobby time alone together. Their relationship recuperated too.

Nine weeks later, Bobby went into labour. This time it was Claud who did the hospital visiting, and on January 3rd Bobby gave birth to their fourth child. They had only talked about girls' names and had decided on Marcia. They need not have bothered. It was a fourth boy and they called him Finn.

CHAPTER 2

The eight years between Finn's birth and the outbreak of war were spent contentedly enough by the Browning family. Claud's experience as a field reporter bore him in good stead in the Editorial Department. He got on well with The Editor in Chief, Gordon Johns, a man of similar age. Circulation of the Sunday Gazette grew steadily. In no small measure Claud's ability to insert "oomph" into some of the factual stories contributed to this. He turned his hand too to improving some of the Regular Features that the paper already ran and instigated the introduction of two new ones: a Health Page, which had as one of its contributors James Lumley, the doctor who had helped to save his life at the Underground Station. The other feature focused on humour, under the title "A Laugh a Minute", running amusing anecdotes sent in by readers.

Away from the office, Claud took life carefully. He wanted no recurrence of the heart attack that had nearly ended his life. He took up golf. Not only did the game take his mind off work, but more importantly gave him steady and regular exercise, so vital to men at his stage in life. He used to say to Bobby "swinging that club rids me of all the angst I incur at work – even when I hit the wretched little ball into the gorse bushes!"

They both adored little Finn, but Bobby, in contrast to Claud, realized the danger of devoting too much time and love to one child. The older three boys were being educated at Glengylmer Preparatory School in Putney and in 1936 Clive went on to St Paul's in Hammersmith. Apart from caring for Finn, this left Bobby time, at least in term time, to pursue her social life, especially Bridge. Now in her 40s, she was still a very beautiful woman, gracious in movement, charming in manner, and an excellent hostess. Long gone was her depression of the days when Claud had been a reporter. So faultless was her English accent and vocabulary, that few ever suspected her Norwegian background. Occasionally she missed her family and friends back in Moss. Her mother and father were in their seventies by now and loath to travel to England, involving a long overnight sea crossing. Air travel in the 1930s was still a rarity, mostly practised by the wealthy, or businessmen. Once, in 1937, Bobby did make the journey back home, but it was to be the last time she did so before the outbreak of war.

Clive was a gentle young man and, unlike Douglas and Kenneth, or indeed his parents, had firm religious beliefs. There were few Sundays when he did not go to Church and he was a diligent reader of the Bible, both Old and New Testaments. He was not academic, and only scraped through his

Common Entrance to St Paul's. He was considerate. He cared terribly for his mother and for his young brothers. His smile was dreamy, some thought almost saint like. Although perfectly fit physically he had little aptitude for sport, the one exception being that he loved fishing. He was never happier than when he could sit on his little three-legged stool by Barnes Pond, or better still, when the family holidayed by the sea, when he would spend happy hours sitting on a rock, casting and re-casting, in the hope of catching a mackerel.

Douglas was quite different. For a start, he was a little more academic, though by no means a scholar. Taking after his father, Douglas was an adept writer, and an avid reader of newspapers. He dreamed of becoming an ace reporter, like his Dad. To practise, he "invented" murders and wrote sensational reports on them, which he kept in a lockable file. Douglas never lacked for friends, and passed many happy hours with the Ashworth boys across the road. They were fascinated by Flight. They took every opportunity to cycle out to Hendon, in North London, to watch the planes landing and taking off, and Douglas used to go with them. In those days it was safe for young boys to cycle anywhere, even in London, for there was only a tiny fraction of the cars and lorries that you see on the road today. Douglas also liked to model aircraft, usually out of balsa wood, and these he would hang from his bedroom ceiling. Other models would actually fly, by means of a propeller which you wound up with a long elastic band. At games, the Sports Master at Glengylmer referred to Douglas as a "Dash and Crash" player. Plenty of energy and enthusiasm, which were not matched by his skill. Thus, he was best suited to Rugby, where he found some fulfilment in the darkness of the front row of the scrum.

Kenneth was the brainy one of the three. Exams at school held no terror for him and he would always sail through with ease. Also he was diligent: no need to badger him to do his homework. He had a serious disposition, though not without some sense of humour as well. He liked to set himself challenges, both physical and cerebral. One such –physical- took place when all the family were walking in Richmond Park. When faced with a ten foot wide stream, discretion dictated a walk along its bank until a bridge was reached. But not for Ken No, Ken was sure he could leap across it. The inevitable happened. It was a great jump, but not quite great enough and he landed in the sludge at the foot of the far bank, and toppled backwards into the stream itself.

At sport, too, although not blessed with exceptional speed or strength, young Ken would practise for hours on end. He loved tennis and, especially, rugby. His kicking skills with a rugby ball were prodigious, be it kicking for goal, or clearing in defence. A born full-back.

He also developed at an early age a money-sense. Mental arithmetic was child's play to him and even before he reached the age of ten, he could quickly add up the cost of a shopping list. By a long stretch, the Brownings were not affluent, but each of the boys was given pocket money each week. Only Ken was able to save any, the others headed straight to Turner's The Confectioners, or Vermont the Toy Shop.

And so the pre-war years drifted by. In September 1936, aged five, Finn started school at the Convent in Barnes, just round the corner from Nassau Road. The nuns were very kind, the gentlest people on God's earth, and Finn soon settled into life there. One of the highlights he remembered was one day in the Convent playground, when he looked up and saw brother Ken waving to him over the wall that divided the Convent from the end of his family's garden. He did not dare wave back, for fear of one of the nuns scalding him. There were low moments too, especially when spinach was on the lunchtime menu. Finn just could not stomach the stuff, but, gentle as they were, the nuns were quietly insistent that he should at least eat some of it. "It puts iron into your little body, Finn" Sister Marina used to say. Poor Finn could never understand why, then, he would not go rusty inside his small frame.

It meant little to Finn one evening, when Dad came home with a worried frown. There was no tuppenny chocolate bar, and no hug. Claud Browning went straight upstairs, beckoning Bobby to follow. The older three boys were not there; they were at the Ashworths opposite. He could hear his parents voices from their bedroom, but could not make out what they were saying, only that they sounded unhappy about something. It was the Summer of 1938.

In March of that year Germany, led by Reichschancellor Adolf Hitler, achieved union with Austria, his southern neighbour, by peaceful, unresisted invasion. Western Europe, mainly France and Great Britain, stood on the sidelines and watched warily. After the devastation of the 1914-18 War, these countries were weakened. Weakened in armed manpower and equipment, and in the will to go to war again. And least of all to fight other peoples' battles. Then Hitler turned his attention to Czechoslovakia, a country "created" from the turmoil of the Great War, and which contained a sizeable minority of German-speaking people. But the Czechs wished to continue as an independent state. They had no desire to be annexed, least of all by Hitler and his Nazis. Throughout the Summer the tension grew.

14

British Prime Minister Chamberlain flew to meet Hitler, to dissuade him from his course, and to buy time for Britain to re-arm.

Claud Browning, and all the other survivors of that terrible conflict of twenty years ago, were reading the signs. The clouds over Europe were darkening for a second time in the Twentieth Century. It was this menace that Claud wished to discuss with Bobby, out of earshot of little Finn. Claud had not been taken in when Chamberlain returned from Munich waving a paper and saying "There will be peace in our time".

But peace there was – at least for another year. And although Hitler's ambitions remained undiminished, there was breathing space in England, in which rearmament and preparations for war could be accelerated. Life continued more or less normally for a time and the Brownings planned a summer holiday at Middleton-on-Sea for mid-August of 1939. Young children do not think a great deal about war, nor any world events much, and the Browning children were no exception. Thus, Hitler forcing the Czechs to become a "Protectorate" of Nazi Germany made little impact on them. It was March 1939.

The Summer Term at St. Paul's and at Glengylmer and at the little Convent in Barnes, came to an end and the Brownings prepared for their holiday. Bobby retrieved the suitcases from the attic. Swimming costumes, and beach towels were pre-washed and ironed. Wind breaks, Lilos, picnic baskets, buckets and spades were checked. The Austin was packed and on Saturday 19th August the Brownings set off for Middleton-on-Sea.

They did not know, they could not know, that they would never return to Barnes.

CHAPTER 3

This was the third time that the Brownings had rented Mimosa Cottage for their summer holiday. It suited all of them, for varying reasons. Mimosa Cottage nestled in a private estate in Middleton-on-Sea, just east of Bognor Regis. There were four bedrooms. Kennneth and Douglas were happy to share, which meant that Clive and Finn had one each, with their parents occupying the fourth. Finn was more than happy to be on his own, because he knew that the other three boys looked upon him as a "Very Junior Person", best referred to as "Worm". They were not really meaning to be unkind; it was just that he WAS to them a rather insignificant and very spoilt nuisance.

Apart from its privacy, surrounded on all sides by high box hedges, the Brownings liked it because it was spacious, with a large garden for the boys to run around in, and far bigger than the garden at Nassau road. The owner was a London businessman, with children of his own, who used it as a weekend retreat, but was happy enough to derive some income from it by letting it out for a few weeks in summertime. And because he had children there was no shortage of toys and sports equipment, which he was happy to let the Brownings use. Best of all was a model racing car, which actually had a small petrol engine and could be driven on the gravel track that ran round the perimeter of the large lawn, and in and out of the flower borders.

At the end of the garden was a gate that let out onto a private road leading down to the beach, no more than a minute or two's walk away. Every morning, Clive, Douglas and Kenneth would get up early and go for a pre-breakfast swim, but Finn, being only eight, was not allowed to go unless either Bobby or Claud went too. To Finn this seemed terribly unfair, but was nonetheless a sensible precaution. He did not see why his older brothers could not keep an eye open for him, little understanding that to them this would be an annoying curb on their freedom to do as they pleased.

Finn felt this "juniorness" intensely. He had a sensitivity that the others lacked, a sort of inferiority that would cloud his childhood and early youth for years to come. If his mother was aware of this resentment she did nothing to ease it. Meanwhile, his father just continued to spoil him, totally failing to perceive the effect this had both on Finn, who recoiled from it, and on the other three, who looked upon this favouritism with disdain. Despite this, by and larger the Brownings were a happy lot, not short of friends and, whilst not affluent, then certainly better off than most people.

So in the family sense, there were no looming clouds on their horizon. But beyond this cosy environment, the shadows of war were lengthening.

Hitler's ambitions had not stopped with the annexation of Austria and Czechoslovakia. Poland was in his sights. Britain and France had signed a treaty with that country under which they were obligated to come to her defence should this be needed.

On September 1st 1939 Hitler's army marched across Germany's eastern border with Poland. Chamberlain made a final appeal to Hitler to withdraw, or else a state of war would exist between them. Hitler's answer was silence. Nothing. And so, two weeks into the Brownings holiday at Mimosa cottage, that dreadful, fateful announcement was made. The morning sky was blue at 11.00a.m. but by five minutes past, a dark cloud veiled the sun.

"Well, Claud, at least you will not have to go this time, they wont need you now you are 46."

After Bobby had spoken those few words, the family were silent. Silent with their thoughts. Numbed. For Claud it was bitter memories of twenty-two years ago –1917 at Ypres. Memories of the mud above all. Squelching, stinking mud even though it was Summer. Claud remembered the sight of fragmented, decomposing bodies, both German and British; rotting and bloated. Dead horses, abandoned rifles, the smell of cordite, the sound of shells whistling overhead (if you were lucky!) and the Crump as they exploded, the sharp thump of grenades and the crack of rifles, the screams and cries of the wounded and the dying. The agonisingly slow advance from Ypres towards Passchendaele had been the worst and it was here that Claud had received the wound that ended his direct involvement. Would this be the fate of his son Clive? This time would the Germans succeed in occupying not only the Low Countries, but France as well? Worse still, would the Fuehrer's grey hordes cross the Channel and take revenge for their defeat 20 odd years ago?

If anyone in England was close to the news, it was those who worked in journalism. Claud had heard terrible stories, as yet unpublicised, of the atrocities the Germans were committing in Czechoslovakia. He had heard as well of the build-up over the last ten years of the Luftwaffe, the German Airforce. Already, hundreds, probably thousands of their bombers were pounding the Poles: Dorniers, Heinkels, Junkers, the dreaded Stuka Divebomber. The names were already familiar. Would they now turn their attention to London?

The peace was over. Laughter would give way to tears. There would be fear and apprehension. There would be heroes and cowards. Pain and sacrifice and loss.

Over, also, was this carefree holiday at Mimosa Cottage. In a year, or even a few short months maybe, the garden of Mimosa cottage could be a battleground, the hedge flattened and the lawn churned by unstoppable tanks, the pretty thatched roof ablaze from grenades or flamethrowers.

Claud realised he had to make plans...

Bobby knew little of war, at least at first hand. Norway had been a bystander in the last great conflict. Whilst Claud had been fighting in France and Belgium, Bobby had spent her summers on the beaches near Moss, or on outings with her folk to Lake Vansjo a little way inland. One thing Bobby had missed terribly by living in England was her childhood winters skiing in the mountains. At this moment, her thoughts were far from there. Uppermost in her mind was Clive. Clive would be eighteen in November next year, the age at which men would be called to arms. The thought of him facing the enemy, of killing and worse still being killed, or maimed was horrendous for her to bear, and impossible to accept. Worse might follow: Douglas might also be dragged into the fighting if the war dragged on.

It did not occur to her that she, and all the family, could be in danger if London came under aerial attack like Warsaw. But it had already crossed Claud's mind.

In one corner of the room stood a cocktail cabinet. Claud had had the permission of Mimosa Cottage's owner, to help himself to its contents, but respectfully had refrained to do so. Now, though, he needed a drink. He poured himself a large measure of Scotch and added a dash of soda. Without asking her, he poured Bobby a sherry and then, turning to Clive, who had never in his life touched alcohol, he said "Clive, this is the moment in your life when you leave youth behind and become a man. From now on, life becomes deadly serious. Start adulthood with this." He handed Clive a small tumbler and poured a small measure of whisky into the glass. "Sip it. It will probably taste foul and burn your throat, but after a bit you will be glad of it. Trust me."

Then he turned to his other three sons. "You are too young. Especially you little Finn. But we all have to think what may happen and what we should do.

The first thing is this. It is clear that Hitler will overrun the whole of Poland, and quickly. They can not resist for long. Hitler's army is probably the biggest in the world, even bigger than America's, and the best armed and equipped too. Not only that. For years, we know that he has been building up his air power. He has thousands of bombers and squadrons of the fastest, best armed fighters to protect them. When he has dealt with Poland, he will turn his attention westwards. That means France and us. We are now committed, which means we will be sending such forces as we have across the Channel, as we did in 1914. But there is a fair chance that we will not be able to hold him back for long. We are totally under manned and under equipped. And if he overwhelms our army in France, and takes the whole of France, it will leave this island as the only important country in Western Europe that is not in his hands. And we will be virtually defenceless. Especially so here in the South and South-East of England, only 22 miles from France. He could be here in days. I hope to God I am wrong, but this is what I think is the situation. OUR situation. Yours Finn, yours Kenneth, yours Douglas. All of us."

Claud paused. No one spoke. The first tremors of anxiety began to course through them. Clive sipped his whisky. It WAS vile and it DID burn. But the bitterness and burning receded and he felt a strange warmth that was in some way reassuring. So far, Bobby had not spoken. She sat in an armchair, her face ashen. As Claud paused, Bobby stirred, and stood up.

"I would like to say something. Two things. First, pour me another sherry, please Claud. The second is this. If I was alone, with no family, I would now return to my homeland and my family in Norway. But I am not alone. Even if it were possible to go home it would not be right to leave England. This is my home and my loyalty is to you and to England. But how will it be if we stay living in London, in Nassau Road? I ask myself that, knowing the way Hitler has used his Stukas on those poor people in Poland. Claud, I do not think we should stay in Barnes. It is too near central London, I feel. We will be in danger. We must go somewhere, anywhere that will be away from the threat of bombs."

"The likelihood, darling, is that if they attack London, they will concentrate their attacks to the East of the City: Dockland and the factories along the Thames Estuary. But you are right. They may well use terror as a weapon and bomb residential areas as well. We should not take risks with you and the boys. What do you think we should do? We can't just go and camp in a field somewhere, can we?

And anyway, where ever you go, I shall still have to be in London, that's where my work is for Heaven's sake. I think I had better ring Gordon Johns to see what the paper is planning to do. No, better still, I will drive straight up there now. I should be up there by mid-afternoon. You stay here all of you and I will phone you tonight. We still have this Cottage until next weekend. Nothing much is going to happen before then."

Bobby gulped the last of her sherry. "I'll make you some sandwiches for the drive. Then you won't need to stop on the way."

Finn listened to all of this with little real understanding. "War" was not a concept he could really grasp. He knew that people, nations, were always fighting each other, and there was nothing he liked better than to play with tin soldiers the others had passed on to him. But that was all. Thankfully, he had not had to witness, or yet even read of the wretchedness of war. For the other three, it was real enough, even for Kenneth who was not really yet a teenager. And they had a solid idea of what had been brewing, especially since Chamberlain's meetings with Hitler. Clive, in particular, had had to study the Great War as part of his History project for Schools Certificate at St. Paul's. He shrunk at the thought that this time it would be he, not his father, who would be holding the rifle. And using it. That it might be he who would have to kill. Or be killed.

An hour later, Claud bade them goodbye and left for London.

CHAPTER 4

Gordon Johns seemed surprised to see Claud. He had not phoned to say he was coming up to Town, but Claud knew he was nearly always there on a Sunday. It was the quietest day of the week for a Sunday paper, when he could assess quietly the edition that had just come out, and consider the week ahead, without a lot of interruptions from the rest of the Editorial Staff. It was a little after 4.00pm.

"Claud, what are you doing here? I thought you would be basking in the sun with your family at Middleton! Still, I imagine this morning's little bombshell has something to do with it. In fact "bombshell" is probably an apt word. Right?"

"Yes, Gordon. Family IS what it's about. Them and this damned war we've let ourselves in for.. You and I have seen before the misery to families losing loved ones, and that was without a single Hun even crossing the Channel. I have a nasty feeling that this time we will be less lucky. The bastards have a sky full of bombers and we have precious little defence against them. A few Hurricanes and even fewer of this new Spitfire. And that's assuming they don't parachute in a few thousand Stormtroopers as they have in Poland and Czechoslovakia."

"I know" Johns replied. "We must just hope it never happens. Hitler has enough on his plate in the East for the time being.

Perhaps that will give us time to get our act together. Build a few more squadrons of Spitfires, always assuming we can train enough pilots to fly the things. Anyway, you did not come all this way just to discuss that did you?"

"No I wondered if you could help Gordon. Bobby and I have had a discussion and we are of one mind that it is not wise for them to stay in Barnes, at least not for a while until we see how things pan out. Of course, I'll stay, but I want to get Bobby and the kids as far away from London as possible. It's bound to get a pasting from the Luftwaffe, and probably pretty soon. I know you have connections in the West Country and wondered if you knew of a country cottage somewhere we could rent for a time."

Privately, Johns had been thinking along the same lines. He, too, had four children. Over the years, he had seen little enough of them, having been ambitious and dedicated, working far into the night to ensure the paper got to press on time, without any slip-ups. This did not mean that he was neglectful of his family, nor that he would fail to do his best for them.. Even better than Claud, he had known war was looming. As Editor-in-Chief he had channels into the corridors of Westminster, and these contacts had given him early and detailed information on what was going on. His wife, Sofia, had made clear her intention to stay in their lovely home in Esher, at least until they all had a better picture of how the war was progressing. But this had not prevented Johns from planning for the worst.

A major shareholder in the paper's parent company was Richard Hannah. Hannah had made his fortune investing in rubber plantations in Malaya in the 1920s and 30s. He was the son of General Sir Henry Hannah, who had had a distinguished military career, starting as a young 2nd. Lieutenant in the Boer War in 1881 and ending with his retirement in 1918, after commanding a Corps in France and winning the DSO and Bar.

Johns had discussed the gathering clouds with Richard earlier in the summer and voiced his fears for his family living so close to the capital. Although semi-estranged from his parents (due to his failure to follow a military career like Sir Henry), Richard had nevertheless responded immediately by contacting his father to ask if there was any empty accommodation somewhere in the grounds of their large country estate in Dorset that they might care to let out to the Johns family on a temporary basis. Sir Henry had responded promptly but gone one better and offered them the whole of the attic floor of the main house, Rosedown Manor. But if Sofia Johns was determined to stay on at Esher, then maybe- just maybe Sir Henry would agree to accommodate the Brownings instead. After all, apart from Finn, the other boys would be away boarding at school for much of the time and Finn himself would go to the local village school in Marshwood. So they would be little trouble. Rosedown was a beautiful Tudor mansion. The main accommodation was on the first two floors, with most of the attic floor devoted to staff quarters. But Sir Henry had cut back on house staff in recent years and the space was largely unoccupied. It included a small kitchen and bathroom, as well as four bedrooms and a sitting room. It would be ideal for the Brownings.

There and then, with Claud still sitting in his office, Johns picked up the phone to Richard Hannah and explained the Brownings' anxiety. Did he think his father might agree to one of the Paper's key manager's family billeting at Rosedown for a time instead of the Johns family? At least until it was clearer which way this ghastly war was going? Richard Hannah promised to call his father and get back to Johns as soon as he could.

It was barely quarter of an hour before he rang back to Johns. Lady Hester and Sir Henry would be more than willing to take in the Brownings, and there was no question of their paying any rent. They would welcome their company, and could come immediately if they wished.

That first day of the war it was barely 6 pm when the air-raid sirens began to wail in London. Even then, before an enemy plane had even entered British airspace, the very sound sent shards of fear piercing the hearts of every Londoner. Later, the shards would not be fear, but real - shattering glass, tearing through flesh, as windows and mirrors imploded from the blast of German bombs.

Claud Browning picked up the phone on John's desk and dialled Mimosa Cottage.

"Bobby, I have made arrangements for you to go to Dorset. I want you to go immediately, first thing tomorrow morning. There has already been a siren test here in London. You probably think I am panicking, and maybe I am being hasty. But better safe than sorry. No, you are not going back to Nassau Road. Just pack the things you have down there. I will follow at the weekend with the Austin and bring anything else you may need from the house." He explained the extraordinary offer that the Hannahs had made. "These are the train details for you and Finn. The three older boys have their bikes down there and they will enjoy the cycle ride to Dorset. It will be a great adventure for them."

The war – Finn's War, had really started.

CHAPTER 5

For Bobby, the sudden uprooting from their sweet Mimosa Cottage was a crude shock. Yes, she had agreed with Claud that it might be dangerous to stay living in Barnes, but from DAY ONE. Surely, a few days to get back to Nassau Rd. and pack properly would not matter? Days in which she could pack some of her more personal possessions and some warmer clothes for herself and the boys, for Autumn was not far off? And how about a few toys for Finn? But Claud was adamant there should be no delay.

Clive, Douglas and Kenneth could not decide whether they were pleased or disappointed. On the one hand, they were going to be cheated out of the last part of their summer holiday at Middleton. They loved it there. Always had. And what was going to happen to their schooling? Autumn term would be starting in two weeks time. On the other hand, Mother had said that to save the rail fare to Dorset, they could cycle there. What an adventure! None of them. Not even the eldest Clive, had attempted anything as long as that.. Rosedown was near the village of Broadwindsor and this was a distance of about 150 miles from Middleton. For safety's sake they would have to avoid the major roads as far as possible and this might add 20 or 30 miles, so a total of maybe 180 miles. The most Clive and Douglas had done at a stretch was the fifty miles from Barnes to here at Mimosa Cottage and Kenneth had not even done that. His bicycle had been strapped to the back of the Austin.

Clive and Douglas spent that evening poring over the map of Southern England and choosing the route. They had to choose carefully, and not be too ambitious, because Kenneth was only twelve and a half and could never cover the daily distances that they could. Also, they had to check the location of Youth Hostels for overnighting. They reckoned the journey would take three days, so involving two night stops.

Then there was Finn. Unlike his older brothers, Finn was not at all in two minds about what was happening. He was going to be ripped away from his favourite place, the beach, and from this lovely garden, three times the size of the garden at home. Here he could kick a football and ride the miniature car to his heart's content. The idea appalled him. And that was not all. He had come to enjoy the Convent, and the nuns were really nice to him, and he had even come quite to like spinach. Where would he go to school in this awful Dorset place. And what would it be like living with this ancient old soldier man? And what about friends? He would know nobody. And he would have few if any of his things – his tin soldiers and Meccano and all his other toys and books and so on. He had heard his brothers talking about some rambling old place, buried deep in a strange countryside. What would one do all day in the countryside? The only good thing was that he had his Teddy with him. He could take that to Dorset, at least. With this thought Finn went to bed. For the last time at Mimosa Cottage. Cuddling Tiny Tim, his Teddy, he fell asleep.

They were met at Crewkerne Station. It was not the General who met them, although it was the General's car. That was obvious because it was a Rolls-Royce, and who else would have such a regal car? Naturally, it was black. Most cars were in those days, but this one's coachwork was gleaming just that little bit extra. Standing beside it, as Finn and Bobby emerged from the station, stood the General's chauffeur, Herbert. He was very old, or so it seemed to Finn. He wore a dark uniform – jacket and breeches all in dark grey, and a shiny- peaked cap. A great shock of white hair bulged out of the side of the cap, and his nose was bulbous and purplish. But he had a friendly smile, and saluted the pair smartly. There were few passengers that Monday evening, and Herbert had had no difficulty in picking out this tall, fair-haired woman and her young son.

"Evenin` ma`m, be you Mrs Browning, and is this your young son Finn? Here, let me help you with them cases. They baint for you to lift any further, ma`m."

He smiled at Bobby and patted Finn on the head. Finn usually hated this sort of treatment. He had recoiled from it many times from silly old people, and it reminded him of the soppy way his Dad had treated him so often. But there was something slightly different about this old man. There was something warm and friendly about him and, without being conscious of it, he just knew they were going to be friends.

"By the way, ma`am, my name be Herbert." He announced, touching his peak respectfully.

The distance to Rosedown was only about eight miles, but it took all of twenty minutes along the narrow, tortuous country lanes. Herbert was not one to hurry. Nor, it seemed, was he in a hurry to change gear. To ease the agony, Bobby engaged the old man in conversation. Finn had fallen asleep almost immediately they started the drive.

"Have you been with the General a long time?" She asked.

"Meanin` no disrespect, ma`am" came the reply, "I bin wi` `im for longer than you bin on this planet, I suspect . I were wi` `im in Africa back in 1881 and I been wi` `im ever since. He never let me down, nor I `im I like to think, and that includes some not very nice times fightin` them Boers and them Fritzes. I dunno which were the worst, the heat and flies in Africa, or the mud and lice in them trenches in France, beggin` your pardon, ma`m. Anyways, that's all behind now, an` I'll be happy to end me days wi` `im here in Rosedown, wi` `is permission, o`course."

"Well Herbert, you must have had some terrible experiences. My husband was in the trenches in the Great War, though he says little about it, like most men. But sometimes in his sleep he has tormented dreams and I know that they stem from that dreadful war. He was shot in the thigh – a high price to pay for a little respite from the fighting, and he was back at the Front inside two months."

"I'll be pleased to meet him then" said Herbert "we'll have a few notes to exchange, I daresay."

The evening light was fading as they turned off the narrow lane into the long driveway to the great house. Just inside the gate, the driveway divided to form a large, sweeping horseshoe, each arm meeting at the house., which nestled a hundred yards or so from the road. Inside the tree-lined oval, a small herd of fallow deer were grazing. Finn stirred and Bobby gently shook him into wakefulness. "We're here, darling, and it is far past your bedtime. We'll just let you meet the General and Lady Hester, and then a glass of milk and it's off to bed with you."

Finn had never seen such a vast residence. Immediately in front of him was a huge studded oak door, set in a protruding stone porch. On either side of the door stood a stone lion, life size, with a snarling face. The house was built in red brick, a warm rust colour, weathered through the centuries. There were four large bay windows on either side of the porch. Immediately above the porch, which had a flat roof, was a pair of French Doors. Finn could imagine kings and queens walking out on this balcony and waving to "their people".

Standing in the open doorway was a short, bald man He could not have been more than 5ft 6in. He had a florid face, with bushy white eyebrows and a white, waxed moustache, which had sharp-looking points. He was dressed in a hairy brown tweed jacket and matching "plus-fours".

Beside him stood the most enormous lady Finn had ever seen. She was at least six feet tall and very fat. She, too, had a rather red face, and she, too, had a white moustache, though not waxed and pointed. Finn was petrified.

"Let me introduce myself" said the man. "I am General Sir Henry Hannah, and this is my wife Lady Hester. Welcome to our home Mrs Browning. And this must be your youngest son. Welcome to you, too, young man." He bent and gently shook Finn's hand. You must both be very tired. Do come inside. Herbert will take care of your bags, though I notice you have not brought much. I take it the rest is being forwarded."

Lady Hester had preceded them, and vanished from view. To Bobby she looked a very daunting lady. Inside they found themselves in a vast, panelled hall, at least a cricket-pitch from end to end. In the middle was a huge banqueting table, enough, Bobby thought, to seat eight or more on each side. It gleamed with decades of diligent polishing that was exceeded in brilliance only by the four silver candelabras that stood upon it. Along the walls hung trophies of the General's gaming expeditions: the roaring head of a lion, a leopard's head, a gazelle and mounted in a glass case, a preserved and dainty dik-dik. In the centre of each end wall was a large oil painting. At one end Sir Henry in full dress uniform and facing him at the other end Lady Hester in a white ball gown. Both had been painted a good twenty years earlier, as Sir Henry was depicted with a full head of black, wavy hair, and distinctly slimmer than now. Lady Hester, also, was seen as a slimmer, elegant and graceful woman, certainly no more than forty years of age. "We use this hall rarely for dinner parties these days, and I imagine it will be even less from now on, but one exception is Christmas. It will be marvellous to have the Browning clan to join us this year. We turn out all the electric lights and illuminate the room only with candles. They must be red. It makes a fine sight Mrs Browning."

If Finn had been sleepy on arrival, he was wide awake now . He was in awe of these fine surroundings and this oddly mis-matched couple of old people. He bustling but jovial, she so commanding. Shouldn't have been the other way round? But was Lady Hester so commanding? Was it actually that she was just HUGE. With this thought running through the boy's mind, Lady Hester appeared from a doorway at one end of the Great Hall. "Mrs Browning", she called, "Mrs Browning, I believe you come from Norway. A very picturesque country, I'm told, though I have never visited it. One day you must tell me all about it and how you came to settle in England. Not now, though, you must be very tired. I have arranged some sandwiches and coffee for you, and some warm milk for Finn. Nothing like warm milk to settle a child down for the night.! Follow me, and I will show you the Small Dining Room, where we take virtually all our meals these days. Henry, would you kindly ensure Mrs Browning's guest room is warm please. It may still be early September, but the nights can be chilly, especially in the attic. Mrs Browning, may I call you Roberta? I have taken the liberty of putting Finn in the same room as you for now, at least until he feels fully settled in. We can re-allocate rooms once the rest of your clan arrive." Her forbidding face dissolved into a warm smile. "Oh, and I think it would be best if you called me Hester. But Henry, I think, would prefer you to address him as "General". He tends to live in the past I'm afraid". She chuckled.

It was a long while since Bobby had been referred to by her full Christian name, but she did not suggest "Bobby" to Lady Hester, thinking this might be thought as over-informal.

The coffee was steaming and strong, just as she liked it, and the sandwiches delicious. Before she had finished there was a slight thud across the table. Finn's head had slumped onto his forearm and he was fast asleep. His glass of milk was still half full.

The Second World War was a day and a half old. At Rosedown there was no indication it had even started.

CHAPTER 6

Lady Hester rang the small hand bell on a side table and after a short interval, old Herbert appeared. "Herbert, the boy is fast asleep and we do not wish to wake him. Do you think he is light enough for you to carry him upstairs?"

Yes, milady, straight away. I'm sure the boy is as light as a feather." And so saying Herbert bent down and gently lifted Finn into his arms. For a man of his years, for he must have been at least eighty, Herbert moved with remarkable ease.

"Roberta" Lady Hester spoke firmly, "I think perhaps you would like to see your quarters and you too, I suspect, would like to retire. Please follow me."

The room allocated to Bobby and Finn was in the servants quarters in the Attic suite. It was quite spacious, with twin beds set well apart, either side of a large dormer window. Between them was an old chest of drawers, with an alarm clock and a small table lamp. The only other lighting was a single ceiling bulb, with an opaque white glass shade. At one end of the room was a round table with two small chintz-covered armchairs.   At the other end a huge mahogany wardrobe with a full length mirror. On the floor there was brown linoleum and a very old and worn Persian rug. Until recently, it had been occupied by Mr and Mrs Compton, who had been respectively, the handyman and the cook. But Mr Compton, Bobby learned later, had acquired another female interest in Broadwindsor, which immediately prompted Mrs C. to leave Mr C. and return to her mother in Dorchester. This had happened quite recently and there had been no time to replace them – very fortunate for the Browning family. This news left Bobby wondering what quarters would be found for them, should new servants be engaged. All this Bobby learned from old Herbert, for whom, as the days passed, she developed a growing admiration. Herbert seemed to know about everything, from fighting the "fuzzy-wuzzies" in Africa, to knowing the best places to catch trout in the nearby river. Not overlooking all the local gossip, either. But he was never indiscreet. Bobby suspected Herbert could have relayed a large fund of stories about the General, especially when he was serving overseas, but he never did so.

For now, though, she was content that Finn was safely tucked up for the night, and she herself could settle for a long night's sleep. She bade goodnight to Herbert and thanked Sir Henry and Lady Hester for taking her and the Browning family into their home at such very short notice.

It was soon after Lady Hester had departed, that Bobby realized she had no idea where the bathroom and lavatory were. By now, the landing outside the room was in total darkness, except for the dim light from her open bedroom door. Bobby groped along the wall for another door, or at least a light switch. There was neither, only the stairs down to the floor below. It was one thing to go to bed without washing or cleaning one's teeth, but another all together to last through the night without "spending a penny". She sat down on her bed, wondering what to do. As she did so she felt her heel kick up against a cold something under the bed.

It was a chamber pot, an object she had not seen since childhood. There was nothing for it: raising her night dress, she squatted down......

In the bed was a warm hot water bottle. She held it to her stomach and wondered what tomorrow would bring. Through the open window stars twinkled, but no moonlight. She could almost hear the silence. There was silence inside the room, too, except for the Finn's gentle breathing in the bed beside her. Suddenly, there was a cough. It was a hollow, unearthly cough. Outside. It was not human. Echoey. She heard it again. This time it was answered by the unmistakable "wooing" of an owl. Lying still in the darkness, she wondered who or what was making that coughing sound. She wished Claud was here, instead of hundreds of miles away in London. For a moment, her mind wandered away to London. What was happening there? Were bombs dropping already? Her fretful mind drifted round and round. The coughing had stopped. But the owl still hooted. At last there came that slowly swirling mist when thoughts drift and then sink into unconsciousness. Blessed oblivion. Sleep.

"Mummy, I need the toilet." Finn had slept for ten hours and was bursting. "Where is it Mummy?"

At that moment there came a knock on the door. Old Herbert entered holding a small tray, upon which was a large mug of steaming tea, and a glass of cold milk. "Oh, Herbert, how kind, but please, can you show Finn where the lavatory is?: I am afraid he can't wait any longer." Old Herbert grinned from ear to ear. "Why, Mum, it's right here. See, there next to the wardrobe. You'd be forgiven for not noticing it, seeing as its papered to look like the wall its let into". Finn made a dash towards it and vanished inside.

Old Herbert turned to leave the room. "Oh, please Herbert, don't rush off. I would like to pick your brains for a moment or two, if you don't mind" Herbert laughed. "I'm not credited with having much in the way o' brains, ma'm. I'm happy enough just to do as I'm bidden", he replied. "But izal help as best I can. What is it you'm would like to know, mum?"

"Well, really, there's so much I don't know, Herbert, and I'm afraid that whilst Lady Hester was very kind yesterday evening, she was not terribly informative. I think that when you know everything about something, you tend to assume everyone else knows to. I could start by asking you what time it is; I forgot to wind my watch yesterday. Next, when it would be courteous to appear downstairs. And will we be expected to take breakfast in the kitchen, wherever that is, or with the General and Lady Hannah:"

"Oh, don' fear ma'm. the lady may look fearsome sometimes, but she's a fine woman, and you'll get on fine with her, I've no doubt. No, the only person who has to watch out for her is the general hisself. She can be a scourge to him. He's terrified of her and she knows it. But what he doesn't know, and I does, is that when she's given him a right ticking off about summat, an' he's gone off with his tail between his legs, she grins like one o' them hyenas we used to see in the svelt! And doan you dare let on I told you so, mum or I'll be on the receiving a rap on me knuckles meself! Oh, and by the way, it'll be eight o'clock in five minutes, which is when the General and the Lady sit down in that little dining room you had your nightcap in.. Shall us let them know you and the boy have overslept a little and will be down in a trice or two?" Soon, Bobby and Finn were dressed and washed and had made their way to the dining room. In such a rambling house, they had lost their way twice: once into what was clearly the general's study, and the other into a ground floor cloakroom.

Lady Hester greeted them. "Good morning Roberta. Good morning Finn. I trust you slept well. The General will join us shortly. He has been out with Francis, the gamekeeper and hopefully will be able to top up the larder with a few brace of grouse or partridge! Now then, young Finn, when did you last have a proper meal? I rather think you could eat a horse. Right?" Finn nodded and grinned. "How about bacon and eggs, then. Unless, of course you really could eat a horse. There are one or two in the stables. Of course, the bacon and eggs are from our own animals, too."

Finn settled with two large fried eggs and two rashers of bacon, topped up with mushrooms and fried tomatoes. Bobby was more restrained and settled for toast and marmalade, and black coffee. It was during breakfast that Bobby remembered the strange coughing sound in the night. "Lady Hester, I wonder if you could tell me what was that strange, hollow coughing that I heard. It seemed to be coming from the parkland in front of the house. But it did not sound at all human. Do you know what it may have been?" Lady Hester laughed. "Oh, yes, dear lady. It was not something that should alarm you. We don't have any poltergeists as far as I know. It was the deer. The fallow deer. You will get used to it, I am sure." They were just finishing when Sir Henry appeared. He was dressed much as he had been the evening before, with the addition of a deer-stalker hat, plus a 20 gauge double-barrelled shotgun, broken for safety, and slung over one shoulder. "You are late, Henry, but will be forgiven if you have stocked the larder" announced Lady Hester.

"Then Madam, I AM forgiven. It was a fine shoot. Francis and I are more than satisfied, except for the inner man. I have left Francis in the kitchen with Mrs Hardy and the fruits of our labour."

Bobby had not heard of Mrs Hardy before, but soon learned that she had lived in Broadwindsor all her life, had recently been widowed, and glad to have been hired to replace Mrs Compton. She needed the work to keep her mind off her loss, and the money to keep her head above water. She had known three generations of Hannahs, having served as an undermaid to the General's father.

Sir Henry was left alone to breakfast in peace and reflect on his successful bag with the gamekeeper, whilst Lady Hester showed Bobby and Finn the lie of the land. Rosedown was constructed in the shape of the letter E. The "upright" of the E faced East, and was dominated by the main entrance and the Great Hall. At each end a curved staircase led up to the first floor. At the South end a door led though to a small Lobby room and then to the Main Drawing Room. This was on the corner of the building, with windows facing East on to the entrance drive and deer park, but with the main view to the South, over a lush valley towards the tiny village of Pilsdon and beyond to Lyme Bay, Bridport and Seatown, guarded by the majestic cliff called Golden Cap.

Envy of others' good fortune was not something that troubled Bobby, but it would have been hard for anyone not to marvel at this beautiful room. Already the morning sun was flooding in, gleaming on the newly polished tables and sideboard, and casting a glinting sparkle on the fine silverware. On the walls, oil paintings of English rural scenes hung side by side with scenes from Africa: great plains teeming with antelope and zebra and giraffe, and one stunning portrait of a charging bull elephant. Finn, meanwhile, stood transfixed by the sight of peacocks and peahens strutting on the lawn that sloped away to the right, to what appeared to be a high-walled enclosure. Later, Finn found that this enclosed the Walled Garden, with peach and apricot trees trained along its South Face and beds shaped like a Union Jack, stocked with red and white roses amidst a haze of blue delphiniums.

At the far end of this Drawing room, a glass door led to the Music Room, totally dominated by a baby grand piano. No ordinary piano this: it was completely covered in a scarlet and gold Chinese Lacquer design, depicting mountains and trees and mandarins with long beards. "Do you play, Roberta?" asked Lady Hester. "Oh, I used to a little. Mostly when I was a governess in Ireland in the early Twenties. But I am afraid once Claud and I started a family, we could not afford a piano, nor lessons for the children. So I am afraid I would be very rusty now." "Then we will have to let you practise my dear. Please feel free to come in here whenever you wish. Now let me show you the Conservatory. It is just through here."

This was the end room of the South Wing and on one side looked out on to the Walled Garden, on to a large vegetable garden to the West and to the centre wing of the "E" to the North. The centre arm of the "E" was shorter than the other two, and housed the billiard and games room. The third, North Wing of the "E", Bobby later learned, was devoted to Services: the Kitchen, Scullery, Laundry and a small sitting room for Staff. And of course, the Dining room where she had just breakfasted.

"It is hard to take it all in", sighed Bobby, "It is all so beautiful, and so peaceful here in this heavenly countryside. Do only you and Sir Henry live here?"

"Yes, I am afraid so now" Lady Hester replied. Of course, when the children were young, the place was bedlam, and I suppose it will be again if we ever have any grandchildren! But we were late in life being given the gift of children. Neither our son nor our daughter are married yet, so we will have to be patient and keep on hoping." Bobby noticed a little sadness in the great lady's eyes. "Of course, we have many friends who visit. Some are Sir Henry's old Army friends, but even they are fewer now. Tempus fugit. Of course there is always old Herbert, and Mrs Hardy for company, plus Findlay, the gardener. They are good souls and companions too. You haven't met Findlay yet. You may well spot him though – a very small man, with rather a bent back. That's what digging and cultivating do for you!" She laughed. "Do you have a taste for gardening, Mrs Browning?" "Yes, indeed, I love it. We have a pretty little garden in Barnes. It abuts the convent where Finn goes to school. Perhaps I can give Mr Findlay some assistance, if you and he would like it."

"Absolutely. I am sure if you are here for any length of time, you would want to find a useful form of occupation, and Findlay would love some help. He may be old, but he still has an eye for pretty ladies, too, I should warn you!"

Finn had been faithfully following the two women on their tour, but saying little. Now he took courage in his hands. "Lady Hannah, I wonder if I may go outside and look at the peacocks, Please."

"Of course, Finn. Of course. You can do better than just look. See that little wooden cabinet over there. You should find some food for them in a tin. Go and give them a little. You'll be their friend for life."

"Strutting their stuff" is a term in common use today, but in 1939 it was unknown. But how apt it is to describe the male peacock. Finn had never seen peacocks before, and here were six of them on the lawn; three males and three females. Two of the males were putting on a full display of their tail feathers, arcing like a huge and brilliant fan of dazzling blues and purples and shimmering green. Oh, how proud they were, head erect, surveying the ladies as if to say "Ladies, am I not magnificent. How can you possibly resist my beauty and charm? You are mine to command."

For several minutes Finn stood entranced. Finally, he remembered the handful of food he had taken from the cabinet and sprinkled a little on the grass. Well, if the peahens were fascinated by Lord Gorgeous, they were much more beguiled by Plain Old Food. Nor was it long before the boys succumbed to the temptation of this unexpected bounty.

From somewhere behind him, Finn heard a gruff voice. "Don't you go spoiling them now, lad, it's bad enough the General and Lady Aitch indulging them. I suppose you are one of the boys I hear is coming to live her for a time. I'm Findlay the Gardener. Pleased to see you, young fella. I'll be glad of some company. Maybe even a little help once in a while, if you've nothing better to do. And what's your name, young man?"

"Finn, sir, and I am eight years old. Actually eight years and eight months, so I'll soon be nine. I've got three older brothers who will be here soon. They're cycling all the way from Sussex."

"That's fine, then" Findlay replied, "You'll soon settle in here the lot of you. Brighten the place up a tid, maybe. Tis a bit quiet these days with only the General and his missus around. Perhaps your big brothers will do a bit to help, as well as you. There's a lot for an old 'un, and me back's not what it once was, and all the young fellas in these parts doan want to know about gardening, or they're all going to get caught up in this damned war, 'scusing my bad language. I was in the last lot, and lucky to be here to tell the tale, I suppose. 'Twere no picnic out there in France, and this 'un will be no better, mark my words. That's if that Hitler beggar doan hop across the water and finish us here in our own back yard first. Now, how about I show you round the rest of the estate? Would you like that? I'm sure the General won't mind me taking a little time off for that."

So Finn's first day soon passed. A whirl of memories. A blur of new places, new sights, new people. Much later, when he looked back upon it, he remembered a day of warm sunshine, a smell of roses, the sharp cry of the peacocks piercing the silence of the Dorset countryside, the sound of Findlay mowing the grass. Dear old Findlay, so bent and yet so strong still. Old Findlay had shown him the outbuildings. There was a huge grain store, a barn twenty-five feet high, packed with the new harvest – tons and tons of it. And for the first time he had seen a family of rats gorging themselves, until Findlay chase them out. A second huge barn had been converted into a squash court. Finn had never seen a squash court before, indeed had never heard of the game. Then there was a third store for the winter feed for the small flock of sheep that was the General's hobby. Sussex Southdowns they were.

The first day had ended with high tea with The General and Lady Hester. The talk was all of war, though most of it was over his head, beyond his comprehension. His young mind was too full of peacocks and rats and a peculiar game called squash

CHAPTER 7

Finn's brothers arrived early next evening. They were exhausted, especially Kenneth, but exhilarated too. It had been their biggest adventure, their first real act of independence. It had been especially hard for Kenneth, still short of thirteen, and the other two had had to slow down or stop frequently to let him catch up.

Though not showing it, Bobby was hugely relieved to see them safely there, and to have them all together, unharmed, under the same roof. All three were given a hug (too old now, she thought, for a mother's kiss) They spotted Finn, standing a little to one side, with Old Herbert. "Hello, Worm" they called in chorus. "What a fantastic place. Done any exploring yet?" "Don't be silly, I've only been here two days. But I can show you round the grounds here. You wouldn't believe it: they have sheep and peacocks, besides the deer out front here. And they grow peaches, and there are tons of grain in a barn, and an indoor haystack, and a funny sort of barn, only with white walls and red lines painted round it, and on the floor, too, and its called a Squash Court. Oh, and there's a full time gardener called Mr Findlay and he has promised to take us up into the hills over there to show us how to trap rabbits. And he's going to show me how to skin them and cook them as well, if I wanted. He says Findlay's Rabbit Stew is the best dish in the whole of England! Oh, and this is Herbert, who does practically everything. Actually you say to call you OLD Herbert, don't you, but I think that's rather rude, so I am just going to call you Herbert, if that's alright."

"Phew, Worm, that's quite a speech" Douglas laughed. I wonder if there's anything left for us to find out."

At this point Sir Henry and Lady Hester appeared from the garden. They had been checking the peaches, which were nearly ready for plucking. One of the general's hobbies was to make Peach and Apricot Wine. "Well done , lads. That must have been quite a ride. I am General Hannah and this is my wife Lady Hester. Welcome to Rosedown. I hope you will be happy here, and we will do our best to make you feel at home, won't we Hester? And I daresay you are ready for some liquid refreshment. Roberta, is your oldest boy old enough to try a glass of last year's Peach Wine, or would he rather devour a beer? There is still some sun round in the walled garden. Shall we all repair there and let the boys recover a little?"

And so Wednesday the 6th of September 1939 drew to a close. The war was three days old. In beautiful Dorset, Thomas Hardy's country, it seemed to belong to another world.

But to the Northwest, far away in the North Atlantic, it did not seem so, when a German U-Boat's torpedo struck the liner S.S. Athenia, on her way from Glasgow to New York. No warning was given. The great ship sank in a few agonising minutes. One hundred and twelve passengers and crew were lost. Actually, the disaster had taken place on the <u>first</u> day of the war, three days earlier, but the news was withheld for fear of demoralising the public, already stunned with the announcement that Great Britain was once again at war.

Before September was over, the German fleet of submarines had struck again. This time to sink a British aircraft carrier, HMS Courageous. By mid-October, U-Boats had penetrated the Royal Navy's so-called "impregnable" anchorage at Scapa Flow, in Scotland, and had sunk at anchor the British battleship HMS Royal Oak.

And yet, very strangely, this Autumn in Britain became known as the Phoney War, a war where little happened. The nation as a whole saw little to disturb their normal lives. Oh, it was true that an Expeditionary Force left for France, and that in the streets more men and women were to be seen wearing military uniform. It was true also, that the public were ordered to fit blackout screens to all their windows, and street lights were extinguished for fear of German bombers being shown the way to their targets. The public were issued with gas masks, for fear of poison gas attacks. Many that Autumn began to construct air raid shelters in their gardens, buried deep and concreted over. Cellars were reinforced, to withstand falling masonry and many public buildings were barricaded with high sandbag walls, to protect them from bomb blast.

Meanwhile the Brownings were settling into their new lives at Rosedown, far from all this disturbance. Clive, Douglas and Kenneth were enrolled at Beaminster Grammar School. Finn began the new term at the Primary School in nearby Broadwindsor. Now together at the same school, the three older boys became even closer pals, especially as they weekly boarded. Of course, they cared about their younger brother, but the age gap was too great, and they were preoccupied with their own interests and activities to spend much time with him. But there was a compensation. Findlay was true to his word about showing Finn about how to snare rabbits, and in his spare time would take him, rather than the other three, into the woods or up Pilsdon Pen. Findlay had been married, but Mrs Findlay had died some years ago. Their two daughters were both married now, and living in London, but so far had not given their father any grandchildren. So perhaps unwittingly he saw in Finn the grandson he would so dearly love to have had. Finn felt a growing attachment to him, too, especially as his own father was seldom able to visit from London, and when he did, it was to be with his wife for much of the time, rather than his four sons.

Bobby had fallen in love with the magnificent gardens, and together with Lady Hester and the General (when he was not out shooting, or seeing to his sheep) spent long days tidying up before winter arrived, and propagating in the huge greenhouse. So when Findlay had his day off on Sundays, off he and Finn would go. At first, Finn was appalled at the sight of rabbits dying in the wire snares. It was cruel, a terrible death for the poor creatures, trying desperately to pull themselves out of the looped wire, only to tighten it even further round their necks, until their eyes literally popped out of their little skulls. But in time, Finn became accustomed to it, and was reassured by Findlay stressing that rabbits destroyed the vegetable crops, and themselves provided good food for humans, especially now at a time when meat was becoming short in supply. Occasionally, the pair were joined by Old Herbert, who would bring his shotgun. There was no shortage of game in these woods and hills, and the General turned a blind eye to what was going on. Francis the Gamekeeper was less sanguine. "Bloody cheek you got Herbert, and you Findlay, taking all those birds. I sweated my guts out raising them." "Yes, Francis, and isn't it true that you yourself snaffle a few for your own dinner table, and I wouldna put it past yer to sell a few in the village, too." In the end Francis would quieten down and get off his high horse. After all, they were the General's property, and he wasn't complaining.

Finn liked his new school, and soon made friends with the boys from Broadwindsor and the surrounding villages, who were his classmates. They took to him, too. They'd never met a Londoner before, and were fascinated by what Finn told them of life in Barnes. Things like the red double-decker London Buses, the Varsity Boat Race, Convent Schools, the London Underground and visits to the Hendon Air Display. They would be wide-eyed to think Finn had actually seen Clem Sohn, the Bird Man, who leapt from an aircraft and glided to earth safely on his silver fabric wings. Until it went wrong one day and he plunged to his death to the horror of thousands of spectators. But likewise it was fascinating for Finn to hear about haymaking, milking cows, learning to plough the fields, not with a mechanical tractor, but with a horse-drawn, hand-held plough.

Finn was bright in class. Most of all, he enjoyed words. He had a natural aptitude for the English Language and even at his tender age, was developing a vocabulary beyond his years. He had a vivid imagination, and liked to write stories. They were simple in concept and execution, but they had a defined beginning, middle and end, and a clear plot. He even found he could make a little pocket money by selling them to the other children at a penny a time. Of course, in those days, there were no photocopiers, so he borrowed an ancient typewriter and laboriously produced carbon copies.

There was no playing field attached to Finn's school, but every Friday afternoon, Mr Royston, the Head Teacher, took the boys to Broadwindsor Football

Club's ground on the outskirts of the village and there he began to teach them the game. Mr Royston soon recognised that Finn was both a fast runner and light on his feet, and had a flair for ball control. He was a "natural" centre forward. Up until now, there had been no organised inter-school matches for juniors, but Royston knew the Heads of other schools in the district and by November had arranged a triangular match between Broadwindsor Primary and the Primary Schools at Stoke Abbott and Beaminster.

Finn was an easy choice for the Broadwindsor team, and the contest took place on Saturday Nov.11th. Claud Browning was down for the weekend from London and all the family turned out to watch their youngest member. So did the General. And so did Old Herbert and Old Findlay. All games were limited to 20 minutes each half. In the first game Beaminster played Stoke Abbott, and the former won easily 3-0. This was followed by Stoke Abbott playing Broadwindsor. Stoke were badly stung by their defeat and, fully warmed up, tore into the Broadwindsor team who had stood shivering in the cold November air. There was little Broadwindsor could do to hold them at bay, and before ten minutes had passed, they had scored twice. Finn did his best, but his opposite number was at least a year older, three inches taller and clearly faster. By half time they had scored again. Stoke Abbott 3 – Broadwindsor 0. A massacre seemed inevitable. The Brownings and the General and all the Broadwindsor supporters watched with sinking hearts. Worse, they knew that Broadwindsor had to play Beaminster next, who had thrashed Stoke Abbott. The outlook was desperate. The whistle blew for the second half and Stoke kicked off. Fortunately for Broadwindsor, instead of the kick going to its intended left wing, it curled to the feet of Broadwindsor's inside right. A quick pass to Finn and he was through the Stoke defence and had only the goalie to beat. As he readied himself to aim at the gaping goal, he was tripped from behind. A penalty!

Finn made no mistake. The goalkeeper never saw the ball whistle past him. 3-1. The Broadwindsor team took new heart and the touchline support redoubled its roar of encouragement. Two more goals followed to level the score. 3-3. Stoke Abbott were tiring. Two matches, with only a few minutes breather between them, was taking its toll. With a minute left, once again Finn weaved his magic, leaving his big opposite number floundering like a beached whale. Peter, Finn's outside left, screamed for the pass, dribbled to within feet of the Stoke full back, slipped the ball neatly back to Finn, who drove it past the outstretched goalie's left hand. Broadwindsor had won 4-3.

The final match was between Beaminster and Broadwindsor. But this was November and the clouds were dark and low, and the light was fading. No score in the first half; somehow, Broadwindsor held Beaminster at bay. It was announced that the match would have to be shortened to Sudden Death – the first goal would end the contest. The rain began to fall. Heavily. Soon the pitch turned into a mud bath, and it was hard to tell who was who. The last but one kick of the game followed a failed Broadwindsor attack that missed the goal my a mile. The Beaminster goal keeper took the goal-kick. It was intended for his centre –half. But in the gloom, he mistook him for the Broadwindsor centre- forward. Finn. Finn needed no further invitation. Neatly trapping the ball, he was off in a flash. Only the goalie to beat and he was not even back in his goal mouth. The goal yawned empty. Finn couldn't miss. The game was theirs. Finn was the toast of the school. Not bad for a "townie."!

And the Phoney War continued.

CHAPTER 8

Bobby's activities working with the General and Findlay in the garden and greenhouse were curtailed with the approach of Winter. Long since picked were the peaches and apricots, and the apples and pears. Together with the masses of blackberries in the hedgerows, the apples had been turned into delicious pies, cooked to perfection by Mrs Hardy. As for the peaches and apricots, they had either been packed into preserving jars for winter consumption, or turned into wine by the General. So Bobby began to look for a new occupation.

For a long time she had been intrigued, as were the boys, by the Squash Court converted from one of the barns. The game of Squash was in its infancy; hardly known to the country at large, and played by only a tiny minority of people who had access to the very few courts that existed. These were almost wholly in London and the affluent Home Counties. A few Tennis clubs had had the funds to build a court, and some of the English Public Schools had installed them. That was where Richard Hannah had learned the game and become so enthused that he had prevailed on his father to convert one of the barns. Unfortunately, Richard was a rare visitor to Rosedown now that he had settled in Canada, and Sir Henry and Lady Hester were far too old to take it up. So the court was rarely used.

Although forty-two, Bobby was still fit and agile, and the idea of a form of exertion that could be undertaken in all weathers had a strong appeal. In London, Claud made enquiries and found that there was a body controlling the sport, the Squash Racquets Association. They were not only happy to mail a copy of The Rules of Squash to Rosedown, but also provided two second-hand rackets and two balls. Bobby began to practise, soon mastering the correct grip and basic strokes, and working up a good sweat even though she had no partner to play a match with. But at weekends, the three older boys, back from school, would join in and soon all four of them were enjoying the game. At only eight, Finn was considered too young. He would just get in the way and prevent the others from practising and playing matches against each other. Bobby, because she could practise all week, could thrash any one of them at first. But after a time, it became clear that Kenneth had the greatest talent of the three boys and would soon challenge his mother on equal terms.

Finn was deeply disappointed not to be included. It seemed totally unfair to him that his three brothers and his mother should have all the fun, and he should be confined to watching from the gallery at the back of the court.

Finn made up his mind to practise in secret, when Bobby was busy elsewhere and the boys were at Beaminster. Old Findlay agreed he would not let on to Mrs Browning or the General and his wife what was going on. Better still, he promised to sneak in a pal of Finn's from school and they could play together. Peter Partridge was in the football team with Finn and they got on well. More than that both boys had an unusual gift in children of eight or nine, the determination to practise and practise, and not accept second-best.

Normally, the General was too busy to go near the Squash Court, but one morning happened to hear the unmistakable, echoing sound of ball against wall, and ball against racket. From the gallery he watched astonished as Finn and Peter stroked the ball around the court. He soon realized they were doing so with extraordinary accuracy, the ball inching above the tin, and dropping delicately deep into the front corners of the court. They could crack it hard too, when the occasion arose, to the rear corners. Clearly, the boys had done their homework, and although they could not hit the ball with the same ferocity as adults, their subtle skill was beyond doubt.

"Boys", he called down to them, "Please stop for a minute, I want to have a word with you both." Finn and Peter were startled. They had been oblivious to Sir Henry's presence, and wondered if they were in trouble. He soon reassured them. "I am delighted that you are using this court." It sounded a bit pompous, but not ominous. "It's not much use if it's not being used and I was very pleased when your mother, Finn, took up the game. She's teaching your brothers, isn't she? Does she and they know you are playing, too?" "No, sir, my mother felt I was too young to play, but I thought I might manage it a bit when she wasn't around, and Mr Findlay thought it would be alright and got my friend Peter, here, to come and learn too. I hope you don't mind sir. But please, don't tell her, or my brothers. I want it to be a surprise in the Christmas holidays. My mother thinks I am off exploring up on Pilsdon Pen with my pals." The General laughed: "Don't worry, Finn, I won't spill the beans. But more important than that, you are learning the game extremely well. Both of you. Clearly you have been taking it very seriously and I've half a mind to say that you would give your elders a run for their money. I promise it will be a secret – but on one condition." "What is that sir? I'll do anything I can" "The condition is this, Finn. You MUST promise me that when you decide which day to tell them you want to challenge them, you let me know. Because Lady Hester and I would be desperately disappointed to miss the fun. Agreed?" "Yes, sir, of course I will. I promise." "Righto. Carry on with your game. I have business to attend to. Oh! I tell you what. My son Richard still has some kit here. I'm sure he would not mind me lending you a better racket, and one for you too, Peter. By the way young man, what's your surname?" "Partridge, sir. I live with my parents in Brodwindsor.". "Oh" said the General, "Is your father Frank Partridge? If so, he served with me in France in 1916. He was a good Sergeant. A fine sniper, too. He killed scores of the blasted Germans! Give him my best regards." "I certainly will, sir, and he will be pleased when I tell him that I have met you, sir. He often talks about you and says what a fine Commander you were." Smiling quietly, but proudly, to himself, General Hannah left the two boys to their game.

Claud Browning was not a happy man to be away from his wife and sons for such a long time, and was only too pleased to walk out of his Fleet Street office on December 16th, take a taxi to Paddington station and catch a train to Dorset, to spend Christmas with his family. It was three and a half months since the war had begun and he had shipped them away from danger. Of course, there had been no danger. Not yet, anyway. Nassau Road, Barnes was a cold and lonely place to be on one's own. Especially as the Hannahs had let him know how happy they were to have the Browning family living with them, and that they could stay as long as they wished.

Not only was it "doing their bit for the War effort", but it gave Rosedown and their lives a joyous fillip, an injection of youth and vitality that had been lacking since Richard had departed to Canada, and their daughter Philippa had joined the WAAF the very week after war was declared. Thankfully, she would be down for Christmas. It promised to be a great occasion. An enlarged family, plus their devoted staff – Herbert, Findlay, Francis the gamekeeper, and the newest "recruit" Mrs Hardy. Then on Boxing Day friends and villagers would join in for a glass of mulled wine and mince pies. Yes, reflected Sir Henry, it might be wartime, but we can still manage to do that much for the neighbourhood. And how magical they would make the Great Hall look, with holly and mistletoe, and a gigantic Christmas tree from the park, with a small gift for everybody present hanging from its branches. And, best of all, a hundred or more red candles casting a shimmering, twinkling light all round the room.

Finn was more excited than anyone that Christmas at Rosedown. But not just because it was Christmas. He had kept secret the fact that the regular squash practice with Peter was paying rich dividends. At Beaminster Grammar School, the term ended on December 11th, and his own term at Broadwindsor Primary the following day. The three older boys spent the next few days, exploring the countryside side on their bikes, and making a trip to Crewkerne for the day. Together with Bobby, they also managed to play a Round Robin squash contest, each of the four playing a best-of-three match with the other three. A little to everyone's surprise, because he was the youngest, Ken came out on top, and was rewarded with a new ball as his prize. Finn kept quiet until the prize had been awarded and then boldly stepped up to his older brother, in front of his parents, and Clive and Douglas, and said in as firm a tone as he could muster, "Kenneth, I would like to challenge you to a game, and if I win you give me the squash ball." Finn had let the General know that this was his plan and unnoticed, he and Lady Hester had crept up into the gallery to join the others. Quietly, the two of them smiled at each other.

"Worm, don't be ridiculous. You can't even play. Go and play with your marbles or something." Clive and Douglas joined in. "Come on Worm, this isn't for you. Wait until you're older." Mr and Mrs Browning, whilst not wishing to ridicule their youngest son, gently assured Finn that when he was older he could play with Bobby, who would be glad to teach him.

"No, I want to play Kenneth NOW" insisted Finn. "I think I could beat him NOW"

At this moment, the General cleared his throat audibly and said: "Mr and Mrs Browning, I really think you should let him try. You might be surprised, I think."

"Yes", Finn joined in. " I WILL give Ken a surprise. Now come on Ken, get back on court and let's see who really is the family champion. You or me. Best of three games."

It was not a challenge Kenneth could refuse. Honour did not allow that. And in any case he knew it would be a farce. As far as he knew, Finn did not know which end of the racket to hold. Slipping off his outdoor shoes, Finn entered the court, followed by his smirking brother. He had no gym shoes, so would have to play in bare feet, as he normally did. Ken won the toss and elected to serve first. He had developed a cunning lob serve, which fell right in the back left hand corner, a serve which both his mother and brothers had found almost impossible to return. But Finn had a flexible wrist action that enabled him to extricate the ball from low in the corner and drive it low, and hard, to the front corner. Ken was wrong footed, and the ball was dead before he had even left the serving box. 0-1 to Finn. "A fluke" Ken thought to himself. The spectators, or at least the other Brownings, thought the same. The General thought differently. He had watched Finn a number of times, without Finn even knowing he was watching in the gallery shadows. Ken's next serve, from the left hand box, was fast and low and he was quick to follow up to the centre of the court for Finn's return. The return by Finn whistled past his left ear, but struck his racket's frame and flew out of court. Another fluke? Ken was a little less sure. So were the spectators. 0-2 to Finn. Ken won the next four points, but still went down 4-9. In the second game, with Finn serving his favourite lobbed serve high, then dropping into the corner, Ken managed to return a few, but not enough and Finn ran out that game 9-5, and thus won the contest by two games to nil.

Ken was humiliated and furious. To be thrashed by his kid brother who was only eight years old, was hard to bear when he was soon to be thirteen, and not only that, knew he was no slouch at the game, having beaten his two elder brothers. Ken ran off trying to hold back anger and tears. Clive, Douglas and both parents were just open-mouthed with astonishment. Not so the Hannahs, They knew just how talented this small boy had become at this odd sport. Sir Henry spoke first: "I thought you would be surprised. The boy has been playing when you were not present at the house. He has been learning and practising with a pal from school, Peter Partridge. They have read all the rules thoroughly and I managed to get them an Instruction Manual. Finn is the better of the two, but Peter is not far behind. It is all the result of starting really young. Is that not true of many things in life? You should be really proud of him, though I can readily understand his brothers being a bit peeved. But they should come round to realizing that he has had far more opportunity to practise than they have, and that he has a very special talent for this odd game. If I may dare to make a suggestion, why don't you go and talk to young Kenneth. It is no good him sulking about it. Far better that he accepts the situation and helps Finn to become even better by practising with him. His own game will improve in the process. Oh, and I happen to have found a hardly used racket amongst my son's things that you could give to Kenneth as a consolation. The one he's got is really rather ancient; this one will serve him much better.."

It is true of all happy events that with time the thrill subsides. And so does the pain of disappointment diminish. For a day or two Ken could hardly bear to set eyes on Finn, let alone speak to him. But Finn came to him on Christmas Eve and looked up to his stony-faced brother and said: "I'm sorry, Ken, I really did not want to hurt you. Please be friends again. Now you have a new racket from the General, would you please, please come and play a game with me?" Kenneth stared at his little brother for a moment, and then his round face broke into a grin: "Oh, alright, Worm. Maybe you can teach an old dog new tricks. I'm still better than Clive and Douglas and I can beat nearly everyone at School. So come on, then. I'll play you. P'haps I'll even beat you."

It was a happy start to a happy Christmas, that year of 1939. Finn would never experience another quite like it, and it would remain emblazoned in his memory. But not merely because of Squash.

Far away from peaceful Dorset, far from England itself, the German pocket battleship "Admiral Graf Spee" had been hunting British and Allied merchant shipping in the South Atlantic. Ship after ship, all unarmed, were consigned to the sea bed, together with hundreds of helpless seamen. But in December she was detected and attacked by three British cruisers: HMS Ajax, HMS Achilles and HMS Exeter. Though far inferior in firepower, these brave ships were implacable in their determination to destroy "Graf Spee". A fierce battle ensued off the coast of Uruguay. HMS Exeter suffered terrible damage and casualties and was forced to limp away to seek refuge in the Falkland Islands. But HMS Cumberland joined Ajax and Achilles and together these three forced "Graf Spee" to take shelter in Montevideo Harbour. Her Captain pleaded with the Uruguay Government to grant asylum. But Uruguay was a neutral country, taking no sides and no part in this dreadful war, and insisted that "Graf Spee" leave port after 48 hours, to face the waiting British warships. Rather than face further destruction and defeat and loss of life, Kapitan Ludendorf sailed into the River Plate estuary and scuttled the huge battleship in full view of thousands of onlookers.

For Britain, this was the first victory of the war, and whilst it would not change the course the war took, none the less it brought a much-needed lift in the British public's morale. On the Western Front by that first Christmas of the conflict, little had happened. German was preoccupied with its occupation of Poland, and was not yet ready to push into France. Equally, Britain and France seemed reluctant to attack Germany from the West, perhaps because they were wary of Germany's vastly superior airpower. At that time it was estimated that the Luftwaffe had almost 5,000 military aircraft, against little more than half that number in the RAF, many of which were inferior or obsolete.

And so the Phoney War continued.

But there was nothing phoney about Christmas at Rosedown. For Finn, the mere sight of the Great Hall being dressed for Christmas was enough to make him almost sick with anticipation. In those early months of the war, and especially in the heart of agricultural England, there was little shortage of good food. What was not grown on the Rosedown Estate was easily obtainable from local farmers. Finn was awake that Christmas Day by 5.30am. In the dark, he groped his way downstairs to the kitchen and watched Mrs Hardy preparing not one, but two huge turkeys for the range.

On the Welsh Dresser stood an enormous side of beef, still on the bone. A mountain of potatoes a foot high were piled in the sink waiting to be peeled: There were cauliflowers, brussels sprouts, parsnips, bowls of cranberry sauce and chestnut stuffing, and over all the pervading and delicious aroma of Christmas Pudding, slowly heating on the Aga. In those days, every family made its own Christmas Pudd, and this was traditionally prepared weeks before the great day when it would be consumed. And being liberally doused in brandy, it would keep for a year or more if needs be – though it seldom was.

"That's enough of you spying on my handiwork, my lad." cried Mrs Hardy. "Off you go and see if Father Christmas has brought you any presents. Not that you deserve any , you cheeky young scamp!"

But as he departed, she slipped into his hand a still-warm mince pie.

CHAPTER 9

After he left Mrs Hardy's kitchen, Finn crept back upstairs, to find that his mother and father, and all three brothers, were still asleep. Well, it was very early, and not yet fully light. Finn could see the first glimmer of day, clouds tinged pink by the distant rising sun. He had noticed the bulging, pale green pillow slip tied at its open end with red ribbon, at the foot of his bed. His mother had always said that It Would Bring Bad Luck to open Santa's sack before every member of the family was awake. "Open it too soon, and Father Christmas might never come again" had been her warning. But that was hard to do. To resist temptation. But surely it would not hurt just to lift it up to see how heavy it was, and perhaps to feel some of the bulges?

Bobby in the next room was a light sleeper. She heard the rustling and little bumps next door. Silently, she crept to Finn's door, which was slightly ajar. She watched as her youngest son, her only baby now, gazed longingly at the sack and ran his hands over it: feeling, prodding. What a wonderful, precious moment this was! Not just for the boy, full of hope and excitement for the treats in store, but for herself, who had given birth and life to this child. She stood there, remembering her own childhood, in that little seaside town in Norway, where she had been born and raised. Moss seemed as far away as the stars now, some forty years later. Her parents were getting old now, both in their Seventies. She wondered if they had stood and watched her, as she was now doing with little Finn. Seeing if she would resist the temptation to open the stocking that hung on the end of her bed. Quietly, she returned to her room and gave Claud a gentle nudge, then signalled him to keep very quiet and follow her.

They watched Finn for a time. "Ahem" coughed Mr Browning. Startled, and realizing abruptly that he was not the only person now awake, Finn hurriedly tried to hide the pillow case beside his bed. "I saw you, Finn! You know the rule: every member of the family must be up and about before you can open your stocking." Claud looked and sounded stern. "But Dad, I thought it would be alright because this is a sack, well a pillowcase, which is not a stocking, is it? The rule says you must not open stockings, it doesn't say that you can't open sacks or pillowcases."

Bobby laughed. Claud smiled. "Oh, go on then, you clever child. You can open it, but before you do, you can go downstairs and ask Mrs Hardy if you could bring up two cups of tea. And after that you can give those brothers of yours a shake,"

Well before breakfast time, Finn had opened every parcel. There were several different board games, including Monopoly, L'Attaque, and Tri-Tactics. A box of coloured pencils, a diary, a football and two new squash balls, a kite, some chocolate, a book called "Swallows and Amazons" by Arthur Ransome, a tin of Nestlé's Condensed Milk, and an orange. Attached to the orange was a label, which read: "Enjoy this orange. With a war on, it may be the last you get for a long time, because the ships that bring them from the hot countries where they grow, must bring more important things for the war effort. Signed Santa Claus".

And it <u>was</u> the last orange Finn enjoyed for five years. Very soon, many commodities that had until now been freely available, vanished from the shops, as strict rationing was imposed. Every man, woman and child was issued with a Ration Book, containing a series of coupon exchangeable in shops for the food, or clothing that the individual wished to purchase. Without these coupons, the goods could not be purchased, at least legally. There did develop a Black Market – mainly food – which could be obtained "under the counter." Of course, many people, including townspeople, began to produce their own in back gardens or on allotments. People who before the war would not have dreamed of keeping pigs and chickens now began to do so. Others took to the countryside and hunted or shot anything that ran or flew.

The Browning family were joined for breakfast by their hosts. Their daughter Philippa would arrive by car in late morning from London. Soon into the New Year, petrol would be rationed, too, and supplied only to those deemed by Authority to be essential users, such as doctors. Everyone else would have to lay up their vehicles for the duration of the War, including the Brownings.

"Good morning to you all and happy Christmas" exclaimed the General. "And may I say what a delight it is to have you with us at this special time. As a token of our pleasure, we have a gift for each of you", Sir Henry announced. His tone abruptly became more serious. "You may think that some of them are odd choices, but this is wartime, and there is a need to recognize what that may mean for each one of us."

To Finn, the General presented a catapult, with a small carton containing solid steel balls, about the size of marbles. "Young man, I would like you to practise with this. If you become half as good at its use as you have with a squash racket, you might be able silently to fell any German soldier that comes your way. God forbid that you should ever have to set eyes on the devils, but if you do it is better to be armed, and to shoot before he does!

Failing any   Germans appearing on the doorstep, you might manage to despatch the odd rabbit for supper, ha-ha!" To each of Douglas and Kenneth the General presented Air Pistols. Though not lethal against humans, they could nonetheless cause a nasty wound, especially if the target was the face or eyes. To Clive, he handed a 0.22 Air Rifle. "This, young man, will penetrate the skull of a cat or small dog and would kill it. If fired at a man at close range, it might do the same. It will certainly shatter bone and is especially effective if you hit the enemy in the knees. He certainly would not run after you very fast!"

The General turned to face Bobby. "Madam, I do not think your needs would be served by handing you any kind of firearm. I think you are far too kind and gentle a person ever to use such a deadly weapon. However, that might just be an occasion when self-defence is unavoidable, especially at very close quarters. Some of the Huns are no respecters of women, and it is by no means beyond them to attempt a certain form of violation. The General chose his words with delicacy, but Bobby, indeed all the Brownings, except Finn, knew what he meant. To Bobby he presented a dagger, about eight inches in length, sheathed in a brass and leather scabbard. "I took this off the corpse of a Boer. I never thought I would be giving it to such a beautiful and charming lady. I am sad, but it is a sign of these dreadful times." Bobby could scarcely believe what was happening. Here, on Christmas Day. In place of laughter and joy, this old man was handing out Christmas Gifts that at best would injure and at worst maim and kill, another human being. Was this the Season of goodwill? Where was this world heading? She trembled, and moved closer to her husband.

As she did so, the General turned to Claud. "I must apologize to you, Claud. Perhaps I have chosen an ill moment. Our hearts at this moment in the Christian Calendar should be full of elation. The baby Jesus was born this day. But for an old man such as myself, who has seen so much horror and cruelty in his life, it is hard not to see such things occurring again, but this time here on our doorstep. Maybe literally so. And very soon. It is my sincere belief that the enemy will soon overrun France, and then he will be a mere twenty miles from our shores. Who, or what, is to stop him crossing the Channel? Good God, you can see France from the cliff tops at Dover. An aircraft can cover that distance in a few minutes. The Germans could be here in Dorset in a day or two, and we must be ready for them, as best we can. In France in 1917 I was present at the storming of a German stronghold near Ypres. Most of the Germans were killed, but amongst those who were taken prisoner was a Colonel. He saw I was of senior rank, and as he gave himself up he bowed deeply to me, and unbuckled the revolver he was wearing, and which he had just used to try to kill me. It was a fine weapon. Beautiful, if you can call any destroyer-of-life that. I have kept it as a trophy ever since. But I think it would be poetic justice if it was now turned against those who once held it in their grasp and pointed it at us. I hope you never need to use it. But if you do, I know that you will know how to use it, and would not hesitate to do so. After all, you have already had practice twenty years ago! Please take it."

There was silence. It was a long speech, on the face of it totally inappropriate to the occasion. But this was no ordinary Christmas Day. Claud took the revolver. Instinctively, he inspected the chamber. It was fully loaded.

The General spoke almost in a whisper. "All those years ago I had the foresight to ensure I had some ammunition for it. A sixth sense, perhaps. A feeling of foreboding that this business was not yet finished." The General slumped into his chair. For a moment he was pensive. No one spoke. Then his face lit up again. "Now let us enjoy our breakfast, and put aside these dark thoughts. Happy Christmas to all of you!

The day passed all too quickly for Finn's liking. He spent an engrossed morning with all his presents. Much practice with his sturdy and potentially lethal new catapult. His brother Clive set up a target for him to aim at: the head and shoulders of a Wehrmacht trooper drawn on cardboard and pinned to an easel erected in an outhouse. He sampled his Condensed Milk – deliciously sickly and sweet – but only a little. It had to last. The games he kept for later, as he did the orange. Bobby took away the chocolate bar, rationing him to only three small squares so as not to spoil his appetite.

Just after noon, Philippa arrived and was introduced to the new house guests. She had come straight from her War Office posting in Whitehall and was still in her smart blue-grey WAAF uniform She was tall, slender and very beautiful, with long, straw coloured hair. She was not unlike Bobby, except that her eyes were olive, not ice blue. Though seven years older than Clive, he immediately fell in love with her and knew that he would never love anyone else. First love is often like that. Time would tell if it would be transient or enduring. Such sweet agony!

After a light lunch, everyone went their separate ways. Douglas and Kenneth played squash "to work up an appetite for the turkey." Claud had a nap and did a little reading. Bobby and Lady Hester spent the afternoon together in the Music Room, Bobby playing for her hostess on the gorgeous red-lacquered piano. It was a dry and bright afternoon so Sir Henry inveigled the Gamekeeper Francis to join him for a shoot on the sheep leas. To his immense surprise and delight, Philippa asked Clive if he would go for a walk on Pilsdon Pen.

At 6-00pm Sir Henry and Lady Hester, accompanied by the divine Philippa, greeted their house guests in the beautiful Drawing Room, adjoining the Great Hall. Old Herbert stood just inside the door, smart in his butler's uniform holding a tray of champagne. None of the boys had ever tasted champagne before, and Claud and Bobby only rarely. Finn had to make do with lemonade.

"Here's to a happy Christmas" toasted the General, "And to a quick and successful prosecution of this second war against the Bosch. Perhaps we will do the job properly this time, and finish him for good." All agreed, and then to everyone' surprise, the General turned to Finn and handed him a sealed envelope. "Finn, young man, I have been impressed with the ability you have shown at this game of squash. I think we all have." Everyone murmured assent – even Ken a little begrudgingly. "So, I have a small extra gift to give you." Finn thought to himself "Goodie good, perhaps it is a ten shilling note – or even a pound if I'm really lucky". The General hadn't finished: "It is a gift I give to you, but it is not all for you. Open it and the mystery will be quickly solved." Finn's hand was shaking a little as he tore open the envelope. Inside were two Junior Membership Cards for Dorchester Tennis and Squash Club, plus voucher for 24 lessons from the club Professional Coach. One of the cards was in his name, the other for his friend Peter Partridge. "Finn, Peter's father served with me in France. He was a fine soldier and on at least one occasion actually saved my life. I thought it would be fitting to give his son Peter the opportunity to improve his squash skill, too. So you can both go to Dorchester together. Herbert can drive you there and back, at least as long as we can get petrol to run the Rolls. There, what do you think of that?" Finn was speechless. He felt he would like to hug the old man, just as he would have done his father, but thought better of it, and, blushing, shook his hand.

"Thank you, sir. It is very generous of you. I-I will always be grateful." "Ha!" replied the General, "Just show your thanks by becoming a champion."

Much later, Finn would remember that when he won his Half-Blue for Squash at Cambridge University.

The party moved into the Great Hall at 6.30pm precisely. Sir Henry, a soldier to the last, considered promptness a virtue that should be practised at all times. The myriad of red candles burned and glowed all around the vast room – on shelves and tables and on the high mantelpiece above the roaring log fire. The whole room shimmered, a sea of light. The long table was set with fine silver and porcelain and two immense candelabras, each with five white candles. The candlelight reflected into the eyes of the trophies on the wall – the tigers and lions, the gazelles and the impalas, until it seemed that they had come alive.

Everyone wore their best clothes. Lady Hester and Bobby in long gowns. The General in full dress uniform – scarlet and blue. It looked a little tighter round the middle than once it had, but still was a fine sight. Philippa wore an off-the-shoulder yellow satin cocktail dress. Clive was intoxicated by her alabaster skin, so liberally revealed, a glowing sheen in the candlelight. Mrs Hardy, Old Herbert, and Old Findlay were invited to join the party and drink a toast to the New Born Child Jesus, and then Lady Hester sprang a surprise. Rising to her feet she declared rather grandly: "We are all about to enjoy a sumptuous feast. It may well be the last such Christmas for some time, and I do not think it is right that Mrs Hardy, who has toiled so nobly all day to prepare it for us, should have to clear it up afterwards. Are we all agreed?" "Yeeesss" came the cry from the whole table, and Mrs Hardy blushed to the roots of her grey hair. "Oh, madam" was all she could stutter. "Hush, Mrs Hardy. Say no more. It is decided. Furthermore, rather than delegate anyone for the task, we will draw straws. The two people who draw the shortest straws shall do the work. Finn, you are excused. You are too young to be up that late. Besides, I do not wish to see my best porcelain chipped or broken! We will delegate you in a few years time, perhaps."

Straws were drawn. The losers were Clive and Philippa. Clive could not believe his luck! He would be alone in the kitchen for half the night with his Goddess. Philippa did not look half so pleased, but managed a weak smile.

It was a great meal and after it was over, joined by Herbert and Mrs Hardy, and Old Findlay, they all move back into the Drawing Room where they played charades, whilst Bobby entertained on the piano, from the Music Room nearby. All except Clive and Philippa, of course. They had other things to do in the kitchen, but Finn was allowed to stay up to the bitter end. Well, until he fell asleep on a settee just after 11pm.

At 11.30 all the Hannahs and all the Brownings left Rosedown and drove the short distance to Broadwindsor for Midnight Mass and Carols.

And so ended the first Christmas of the Second World War. There would be five more before the world was at peace again.

CHAPTER 10

The year 1940 began quietly in Dorset. On January 3rd, Finn became nine year old, and a few days later the new term began, both for him and his brothers.

Claud Browning had returned to London, but remembered to send Finn a birthday card and a balsa wood construction kit of a Wellington bomber. Finn and Peter began their squash lessons in Dorchester. Britain had not been invaded, so there were no Germans for Finn to shoot with his catapult. But elsewhere the war raged.

Crucial to Hitler's ability to command the seas around Britain, and thus starve its people and war machine of food, oil and munitions, were those northern European countries with long seaboards, in particular Norway. Here were important naval bases: Narvik, Trondheim and Bergen in particular. The nation who controlled this coastline controlled the North Sea and the North Atlantic Ocean, and also the Baltic. It was Hitler's fear that the weak Norwegians would not resist being occupied by the Allies and so he decided to strike first. Early in April Germany invaded with a naval task force and a large force of paratroops.

The attacks on Bergen and Trondheim were brief and successful, though not without German casualties. Most notable was the sinking of the German cruiser "Konigsberg" by aircraft of the British Fleet Air Arm. Although suffering further losses, notably at the capital Oslo, the German forces forged ahead and it was not many weeks before the remnants of the Norwegian army were forced to flee to England. Bobby was inconsolable. Her family in Moss were now under the Nazi fist, and would remain there for the duration of the war. She would not know if they were dead or alive.

The British, although they did not stand idly by (hence the sinking of the Konigsberg), reacted too late. An Expeditionary Force was despatched, together with a strong contingent of Royal Navy warships. Some progress was made in central Norway, and several more German warships sunk, but Hitler was determined and finally sent sufficient reinforcements to force the British to retreat and evacuate the country. It was a sad and humiliating episode. And it marked the end of Neville Chamberlain's time as Prime Minister. He was forced to resign.

In May 1940, his place was taken by Winston Churchill, who was to be Britain's leader all the way to the defeat of Hitler and final victory five years later. Churchill would go down in history as the greatest of all Britain's leaders. Claud tried hard to raise Bobby's spirits, but it was difficult, being away in London most of the time. The Hannahs tried to occupy her mind, and her time, in various ways, such as involvement tin the local Women's Institute, the Church, and helping the elderly with their shopping and meal preparation. Her sons did their best, too, especially Finn, who was there with her every day. There was one activity that really did raise Bobby's morale, and this was playing squash. By now, she and Finn were a good match for each other, and had titanic struggles which left them both tired, but elated. Nothing lifts sadness and depression from the human mind quicker that violent, physical exertion, and so squash achieved what no acts of sympathy and consideration could accomplish.

Winter finally gave way to Spring. Snowdrops gave way to crocuses. Daffodils and primroses appeared in the hedgerows. And along the country lanes the sun renewed its brightness and its warmth. And the rabbits! The rabbits produced their young and the young were everywhere, and all the farmers cursed and swore at the robbery being committed in their fields and on the cabbage patches. To augment food supplies, gardens and allotments were not enough. Now, every piece of spare land was ploughed and planted: parkland, commons, playing fields, nothing was immune. People could grow whatever they liked, as long as it was edible! Much of the beautiful lawns at Rosedown were ploughed up and were soon producing vegetables of every kind. Old Findlay, helped by Bobby, constructed a fruit cage for growing raspberries and strawberries and gooseberries and red currants, which if not essential would none the less be very welcome come the summer. Gradually Bobby's spirits rose, as she dedicated the lengthening days to producing food. And not only for the occupants of Rosedown, but also for the folk in Broadwindsor who were too old to manage an allotment of their own.

Bobby warmed to the task of distributing food. The Rolls-Royce had by now been laid up for the duration of the war, but out came the old farm cart. A carthorse was purchased from a local farmer and Bobby would load it up with F and V as they called it and off she would go every Friday to Burstock and Broadwindsor. She became a familiar and welcome sight in the country lanes and villages. Dorset folk were not used to seeing beautiful Norwegian women, with flowing blonde hair, driving an old cart around the countryside. But the bounty she brought soon drove such thoughts out of their heads.

Finn was very proud of what his mother was doing to help the War Effort, and she was often the object of chatter amongst his chums at school. "Not bad for a townie lady, your mum, Finn" they would say. "And a foreign one at that" It was very good natured. Their parents admired what Bobby was doing, even though they knew it was Rosedown's produce, not hers personally. Finn had become increasingly popular amongst his peers, and not only because of his success in the football team. And they were curious about his prowess at this strange game of squash. And Peter's of course. Now several others had nagged their parents into letting them play at Dorchester at weekends, that Club having had the enterprise to start a Junior Section. Sometimes, Finn would accompany Bobby on the horse and cart, and became quite proficient at driving it himself, though only with supervision. Finn loved the old horse, whose name was Winnie. A funny name for a stallion, but this fellow was forever baring his teeth and whinnying, especially at the sight of Bobby or Finn approaching with a haybagful for him. Besides, the country's new leader's nick name was Winnie, so what could be more appropriate?

Old Herbert had at one time been a cavalryman, and had forgotten none of his horsemanship. "Now then, young Finn, baint it time for you to learn to ride this animal. Your brothers, too, if they have the inclination. But seeing as that they are away at school much of the time, I'll show you the hang of it first. It baint difficult once you have the knack, and once you stop feeling scary at being so high off the ground. Anyways, if you do take a tumble, why at your age you should bounce right enough. Probably bounce right back up into the saddle, wouldn't wonder. And whilst we're at it, perhaps your ma would care to try also."

And so they did. And they both did bounce, though neither was worse than bruised a bit, in both body and self-esteem. Claud on his rare visits from London, was astonished and delighted that Bobby had been able to calm her anxiety about her kinfolk back in Norway, though there was still no news of them, nor likely to be. The older boys had settled well at Beaminster Grammar School, and were enjoying their time there. Not that they were not pleased to be back at Rosedown at weekends. Now that Spring was here, they would often be off on their bikes, roaming far and wide. Sometimes they went down to the coast some fifteen miles away. The nearest point was Bridport, but usually they would cycle on to Lyme Regis, where there was more going on, perhaps stopping for a quick dip in the sea at Seatown, on the way. Clive, though not the other two, could pass for being eighteen and would buy himself a glass of beer or cider, which he preferred. He had enough sense not to drink more than one glass, nor to allow Douglas and Kenneth any alcohol.

On the fateful day that Churchill became Prime Minister, Adolf Hitler invaded the Low countries, Holland Luxembourg and Belgium, and the

German offensive against Western Europe was launched. For the second time in the twentieth century, the peace-loving people of these countries lost their freedom. But this time, many were to lose their lives at their enemy's hands as well. They did not know it at that moment, but tens of thousands would be transported to the East, to forced labour and to concentration camps. Germany's military strength was overwhelming. Not only did they outnumber their opponents on the ground, in both men and equipment, but also in the air. The German airforce – the Luftwaffe – was able to put into the air three and a half thousand front line aircraft. Against them was a small fraction of that number, and many of these were inferior in speed, manoeuvrability and armament. The RAF could do little to help these small countries. Such air defence as they possessed was being held back awaiting the inevitable attack against Britain itself.

The German advance through Holland and Belgium was terrifying in its speed and ferocity, and despite sturdy resistance, especially by the Dutch, the German army reached France inside two weeks. The occupation of France itself became inevitable. It only remained for the British to withdraw its defeated and bedraggled Expeditionary Force as best it could. It was a dark hour, and it was only then in the months that followed, that raw Fear and Danger confronted the Brownings, the Hannahs and all the people of the United Kingdom.

CHAPTER 11

On May 22nd, German forces attacked the encircled British troops on the Channel coast. Like some gigantic beached whale, the British Army had nowhere to go. They were completely trapped on the sand dunes at Dunkirk, and along to the west as far as Boulogne. Their situation was desperate. A flotilla of British destroyers managed to evacuate some four thousand troops from Boulogne under heavy German fire, but several thousand others were taken prisoner.

There then followed, during the ensuing days, one of the most extraordinary seaborne rescues ever. Every seaworthy vessel, however large or small, and some were tiny, crossed the English Channel to collect these desperate men. It was an extraordinary feat, and an extraordinary sight. There were river paddle boats and Royal Navy ships of every description and size. There were small fishing vessels, Thames barges, yachts and pleasure cruisers. They were shelled by German artillery, and were bombed and strafed by the Luftwaffe. But time after time they returned to pick up more men. Many were sunk. Many lives were sacrificed. Nevertheless, between May 26th and June 4th, no fewer than 330,000 men were brought back to England, to fight another day. It is a matter of record that in excess of 850 vessels took part. 240 or more were lost to enemy action.

The episode became known as "The Miracle of Dunkirk".

It was a dreadful shock to the British people, and no less to the Browning family and to Sir Henry, and all those at Rosedown. How could we have suffered such a defeat, and in so short a period of time? It was an appalling humiliation. And yet, perversely, it gave everyone hope. One third of a million men had cheated Hitler, and escaped his deadly net. Deep down there was a feeling, no, a conviction that these men and many more with them, would return across that strip of water and would ultimately defeat this evil monster. Not yet awhile. But in time.

For Finn, a much greater shock was the news that Bobby imparted one Saturday morning at breakfast. "Finn, your father and I have been discussing where we should go to live. Sir Henry and Lady Hannah have been very generous and kindness itself to let us stay here with them at Rosedown, for nearly a year. But we think it would be wrong to expect them to accommodate us indefinitely. We should have a home of our own, with all our own things in it. Whilst we have been here, our father has been on his own in London, and that is not very nice for him; he would like to be with his own family day by day."

"So why he can't he live here at Rosedown?" cried Finn. "I love it here and I never want to live anywhere else. Not ever."

"No, Finn. That is impossible. That is just thinking of what you want. Your father cannot work in London and stay here; it's totally impracticable, I'm afraid. We will stay here until the end of the summer Term and then we are going to a new house. Not the one in Barnes, which is very near Central London, and might be bombed. We are going to a place a bit further out, called Surbiton. We should be safe there, and Daddy can still get to his work fairly quickly by train every day.."

The time passed all too quickly for Finn, and increasingly sadly. With growing despondency he contemplated the loss of his friends, especially Peter Partridge, Old Herbert and Old Findlay. No more rabbiting on Pilsdon Pen. No more going into Broadwindsor with the cart and Winnie. No more walking Winnie round the park. What would they do without him in the football team. Worst of all, no more squash. His lessons in Dorchester were over now, but he still went there whenever he could on the bus to practise, and play in the Junior Section Under 15 matches. He was that good. Where would he play now? On rare occasions, too, he had been into Lyme Regis with the family and been able to see the sea, if not actually to bathe in it. The beach was Out of Bounds. It had been mined and anti-tank traps erected in case of a German invasion. But it was still fun to watch the fishing boats come and go. How would all that ever happen living in this Surbiton place?

All too soon the end of term arrived. Finn tried to put on a brave face. On the last morning he went in as usual – but it was not to be a usual morning. There were no lessons, just desk tidying and sad goodbyes. Finn was handed his last end-of-term Report by Miss Goodbody, the School Principal. "Finn" she said "I am truly sorry to see you leave. In the year you have been with us, you have been a real credit to the school. I so wish you could stay with us. But sadly, life does not stand still for any of us, and I know your parents will be glad to have you with them in your new home. One day, I feel sure, I will hear more of you. Perhaps it will be on the Sports pages, because you have outstanding talent. So good luck Finn. Think about us sometimes. Now off you go" It was too much for Finn. He could not hold back his tears. He ran from the Principal's office and past all his friends. Running.

Running across the playground and out of the main gate. Old Herbert had come to collect him. Not in the Rolls of course, that was laid up, but with Winnie and the cart. Normally he would sit alongside his mother, or Herbert, and take the reins. Today was different. Finn climbed on the back of the cart and hid himself under the old tarpaulin. They were half way home before his sobbing ceased and his eyes dried. When he finally emerged, and climbed alongside Old Herbert, the old man did not speak immediately. Instead he put his hand in his ancient jacket pocket and pulled out a small paper bag. "Here you are Finn, have a humbug. I saved them from my sweets ration last month. Think your need is greater than mine, just now." By the time they reached Rosedown, Finn's eyes had cleared. But his heart was still heavy, and he could not smile.

The last afternoon was a busy one. Finn's three brothers were also back from Beaminster, and they all set-to packing their things and tidying their attic rooms. Claud was down from London. It had been a busy week for him supervising the removal men who were moving all their furniture and belongings from Barnes to Surbiton. Now it was time for him to see his family safely there from Dorset.

Sir Henry and Lady Hester were in a sombre mood that evening. They had got used to the Brownings being there at Rosedown with them. More than that, they had almost become a part of their family, it seemed. Especially Bobby and Finn. Bobby because she was a feminine presence of beauty, elegance and charm. And industrious as well. She had blended into the great house's character. For Lady Hester especially, she had been a practical help and female counterbalance to Sir Henry and Herbert and Findlay, much as she valued them all. Finn was a different kettle of fish. Here was a young boy who had not yet lost his innocence, but nonetheless was spirited and determined. She liked that. Finn had never been disrespectful, nor moody, and he had a rare affinity with the elderly. Old Herbert and Old Findlay would miss him as much as he would miss them. As a farewell gesture their last night dinner was to be held in The Great Hall. Finn had been plucking up courage to ask the Hannahs if Old Findlay and Old Herbert could dine with them, and had sought permission from his parents if he might do so. "I'm afraid not, Finn, they would consider that an impertinence. Staff do not dine with their employers. You will have the opportunity in the morning to say your goodbyes, and I promise you that if Sir Henry and Lady Hester will have us, we will pay them a visit next year, in your summer holidays, perhaps. I am sure your brothers would like to pay a return visit too. In fact, we all would.

But Finn was not to be disappointed. As he entered the Great Hall, he could scarcely believe his eyes. Looking a little uncomfortable, maybe, but standing there none the less, were both Old Herbert and Old Findlay, glasses of beer in hand, and looking remarkably smart.

Not only that. Someone else was there, as well. Peter Partridge, his best friend, and his mother and father Philip Partridge, the Sergeant who had saved the General's life, also stood there. "Thought you might like to see young Partridge, Finn. And it is high time I renewed my friendship with his father. Haven't seen him in a good many years. I hope you like the surprise." The General laughed. "Now let's sit down and have a damned good evening. It does no good being miserable, much as we're sorry to see you all going. And Mrs Hardy will join us shortly. She has brought her own helper, so she doesn't need to worry about clearing up! There's some fine claret to warm us up, and I do declare that even the young lads might be allowed a little, even Finn could have a taste. With parental permission of course. What do you say Browning? And you Partridge? Herbert, would you mind slipping out and ask Mrs H to start dishing up. I do believe she has laid her hands on some venison for the main course. Haven't asked where its come from, but I suspect we might be a beast short in the park! But before that, there is a fellow I know who fishes salmon in the River Test near Romsey, and he has taught himself how to smoke it, so we'll try that to start us off.

It was a great evening, and Finn and all the Brownings managed, if only temporarily, to suppress their sadness at leaving Rosedown. At the end of the evening, Finn and Peter bade their farewells. They both had lumps in their throat, but managed not to shed tears. And they both promised to meet again soon, and to play squash perhaps, on the court at Rosedown, where they had first learned to play. Clive, Douglas and Kenneth were quiet, but they had not been so integral a part of life at Rosedown, and did not have the depth of regret that Finn was feeling. For them, there was another great adventure ahead. A new school called King's College, Wimbledon. New friends to make, new things to do. For Bobby, leaving would be hard. But she had done that before. She had left her family in Norway, and no doubt would have plenty to do in Surbiton. For Claud, there were few regrets, only the warm anticipation of once again having all his family around him, in his own home.

CHAPTER 12

Surbiton lies 15 miles south-west of London. Like Barnes, it borders the Thames, but some eight miles further upstream. Really, it is no more, nor less, than a London dormitory town, a middle class suburb, from which many of its residents commute daily to their work in Central London. There is a fast train service to Waterloo, which takes only eighteen minutes, non-stop – a prime reason for Claud Browning choosing it as a place to live. But, if London were to be bombed by the Luftwaffe, then it was not in that much better a position than Barnes, especially as German bombers would use the Thames as a navigating aid into and out of London.

Also, the town was adjacent to Kingston-upon-Thames, a strategic target for bombing because of its Power Station and Aircraft Factory, the latter frantically producing Hawker Hurricane fighters.

Part of Surbiton lay at river level, and part up the hill. The better properties lay up the hill, and this is where the Brownings chose to live. Their address was 18 St. Mark's Orchard. It was close to St. Mark's Church. a large parish church with a very high, elegant steeple. No. 18 was detached, in a quiet road. It had a nice garden, which was mostly lawn, but in the middle of which was a very old apple tree and an equally old pear tree. The house had been built not many years ago – in the early thirties, and was a great improvement on Nassau road, which had been a semi-detached Victorian villa. No. 18 had four bedrooms. Mr and Mrs Browning had the main bedroom, overlooking the back garden. There was a good-size single room, which was allocated to Clive. Douglas and Kenneth shared the second double bedroom, so Finn was left with a small single room, looking out across the road. It was directly above the garage and would tend to be cold in winter time.

The Brownings arrived from Dorset in early evening on July 24th. The train had been very crowded, and hot. Only Mr And Mrs Browning had been able to find seats, with Finn squeezed tightly between them. The other boys had had to make do with sitting on suitcases in the corridor. Many of the passengers were in uniform, mostly airmen. Douglas seemed keen to chat with one or two of them, and learned that they had been doing flying training in Cornwall, and were now on their way to operational squadrons in East Anglia..

They arrived at the house hungry and tired. Fortunately, all their furniture had been delivered the previous week, and, directed by Claud, installed in its correct place. Well, correct in his view! Bobby and the boys might have different ideas. Bobby had announced before they set out from Rosedown that she had no intention of preparing a meal that night, and everyone would have to make do with a sandwich.

Mrs Hardy had come up trumps, with a packed lunch of home baked bread, lamb from the General's flock, and pickled onions. Washed down with beer for those who wanted it. Followed by raspberries from the Rosedown garden. The last thing Finn remembered that night was Bobby coming to kiss him goodnight and check the blackout. In the months and years that followed, it would seldom be that a night passed uninterrupted - Mr Hitler would see to that - but that first night at No. 18 all the Brownings slept a dreamless sleep. The mixed emotions of sadness at leaving Rosedown, and the enthralment of what lay ahead in this new environment were swamped by sheer physical exhaustion.

Finn awoke late, immediately ready to establish himself in this new environment. Little the room might be, but it was his. There was a small built-in wardrobe, but big enough for his few clothes and shoes and his most treasured possession, his squash racket. Claud had purchased a small second hand kneehole desk and a table lamp, and a miniature chest of drawers. All this only just left room for the bed. The view from the window was across the road, to a row of high Victorian villas, with flights of stone steps rising to the front doors. The house directly opposite was partially obscured by a huge beech tree. It must have been sixty feet tall.

St Mark's Orchard was close to a district of Surbiton known as Berrylands. On their first full day there, Clive, Douglas and Kenneth went off on their bikes to explore, but they were quickly back with some interesting information for their mother and Finn. "Mother, I don't suppose you know, but a few minutes away there is a Tennis Club. It has masses of grass and hard courts. One court is a show court and apparently in peace time they have a big tournament there, with lots of famous players taking part. It even has a grandstand. But that's not all. They have two squash courts! Yes, two! That ought to make you and Finn happy. Well, and us, of course. We went in and asked about being members, and the Secretary said that because so many young men and women have had to join-up, they were very short of Junior Members, and would be delighted if we four boys could join. And you, of course, mother. As well as squash, we could learn to play tennis, which would be nice in summertime, especially as squash is so hot to play then."

Finn, like the other boys, was over the moon when Bobby said that they could, and that she would come round to the Club with them. "However, boys, that will have to wait for a bit. Right now there are more urgent things you've got to help with. We haven't unpacked everything yet. Also, Clive, as you are the eldest, I would like you to sit down and draft out a letter from you and your brothers to Sir Henry and Lady Hester, thanking them for making us so much at home at Rosedown. You other three can write short notes to go with it. So do that please, then get your rooms sorted out. Now, I am going to go and introduce myself to the neighbours, and then go to the shops, wherever they are!"

Bobby knocked on the door of No. 16 first. The door opened and there stood a small but upright old man, with sharp features and a scowl on his face. "Yes? We are not buying anything that you may be selling, and that's flat! We don't approve of door-to-door selling". He began to close the door, but before he could do so fully, a female voice in the hallway behind him called out: "Ebbie, who's there? Are you being rude to someone?" Behind Ebbie there came into view an equally small woman, with grey hair. She wore thick tweeds, even though it was a hot summer's day. She wore no makeup. Her hair was swept into a small bun. Above the bun, she wore a brimless brown hat, held on with an enormous pearl hairpin. Ebbie was elbowed to one side and the woman addressed Bobby: "Well, are you selling something, or not? Ebbie always thinks the worst of everybody, but at least he should find out before he shuts the door in your face. I just cannot get it into his head that there is no need to be abrupt."

"No", Bobby replied. "Actually I am your new neighbour at no.18. I thought it would be courteous to come and introduce myself. My name is Roberta Browning, but I prefer to be called Bobby. Everybody calls me that."

"I see" replied the old woman. "You are not English, are you?" From behind her Ebbie muttered quite audibly "The woman is probably a German Secret Agent. Send her packing.!" "No, actually I am Norwegian by birth. I married a British Army Officer after the Great War and have lived in England ever since." She smiled disarmingly.

"Hmph" was the old woman's response. Behind her, the "hmph" was echoed by the old man. "Well, I suppose that's alright, then. Our name is Boughton. My husband is Ebenezer and I am Minnie. We hope you are not going to be rowdy neighbours. Do you have young children?"

It did not seem a very promising start to life in Surbiton. But at least the introductions had been made. Bobby bade them good morning and returned, past no. 18 and up to the door of no. 20, hoping for better things. She rang the bell, but the door opened almost instantaneously, and there stood a woman as tall as Mrs Boughton had been short. "Well, hallooo there" she beamed. "I saw you coming up the path. You must be our new neighbour! Welcome to St.Mark's Orchard. My name is Belle. Belle Peterson. And you will be Mrs Browning. I heard that was your name when I happened upon Mrs Quick, the estate agent's wife. She said you were coming this week. It is lovely to meet you. Come in and have a cup of tea, I insist." Belle Peterson was, like Bobby, in her mid-Forties. Her eyes just danced with the joy of living. Her cheeks were rosy, her bosom large. Atop her head was a pile of straw coloured hair that reminded Bobby of a beehive. She knew straight away that they would become firm friends.

"Sit down and tell me if you are sorting yourself out. It's good of you to pop round so soon after arriving, and I feel guilty I haven't been round to you first. You've beaten me to it! Still, I've got the excuse that I thought I would give you time to sort yourself out first.. I know what it's like to move home, especially into a strange area. We came here from Dumfries. But then I expect you guessed I was a Scots lassie! Mr husband is a doctor and he bought into a practice in Surbiton a few years ago. Now then, I haven't even enquired what your first name is Mrs Browning. My husband is always complaining that I prattle on too much. How's your tea? And have another of these shortbreads. They are my own patent recipe. I'll let you have it."

Bobby soon learned that Belle Peterson was the mother of two teenage girls, Isabel aged sixteen and Mary aged fourteen. Also a boy called George, who was at a Preparatory School called Branchester House in Surbiton. Belle spoke in glowing terms of Branchester and was sure Finn would enjoy being there, especially if he was good at sports. Belle said she would give Bobby an introduction to the Headmaster. "What other children do you have?" she enquired. "Clive is my eldest. He will be eighteen in November, so it's likely he will be called up soon. I'm terrified at the thought, knowing what my husband went through in the last war."

"Oh, you poor dear" sighed Belle. "Has he a choice of which service he goes into.?"

"Well, I think he can state a preference, but there is no guarantee that is what will happen! He says he would not mind going into tanks, because at least you have some armour plating round you, not like the infantry. But I'm not so sure. Tanks can be as dangerous as anything else. Claud is trying to put him off the idea. He says tanks just get hit with big armour-piercing shells, instead of flesh penetrating little bullets. That sounds a callous way of saying it, but it is true. I'm afraid we will just have to wait and see. Anyway, I hear some lads are being sent down the coal mines. They are calling them

Bevin Boys. That's not a pleasant prospect, but I rather he did that, even."
The conversation turned to schools again.

"Don't blame you, Bobby. Thank God my children wont be involved in
wearing a uniform – well, only Girl Guides and Cubs. You said you had four
sons. What about the other two?" "Oh, Douglas and Kenneth. They are
going to start at King's College School, Wimbledon. It's a day school and
not too far for them to cycle to every day. I think they will be happy there,
and it's got a good record."

Bobby was just about to leave when a small and very excited boy rushed
into the room. He never even glanced at Bobby. "Mummy, mummy, guess
where I've been. I've been next door to see what the new people are like, and
there is a boy there almost exactly my age, called Finn. I told him I thought
that was a pretty queer name, but he said he was called that because his
mother came from Norway. That's a place the Germans invaded isn't it? But
I think it's daft. Surely someone called Finn should come from Finland, not
Norway."

"George, be quiet. This is Finn's mother, Mrs Browning, and yes, she is
Norwegian. Now say hello properly. George flushed with embarrassment,
shook hands with Bobby, and then grinned broadly. "Oh golly, I'm very
sorry Mrs Browning. I didn't realize. I was just excited that I might have
someone to play with next door. It should be super to have a neighbour like
Finn." "I understand perfectly, George, and I'm sure it will be good for Finn
to have someone his own age close by.

His three brothers are a lot older than he." She turned again to Belle
Peterson. "You may know we have been living in Dorset for the past ten
months, and Finn is going to miss the pals he had made at the school down
there, at least until he has made some new ones in Surbiton. Now I really
must get back. I left the boys to sort their things out. Heaven knows what a
mess the house will be in. And George, do come round tomorrow if you
would like to."

The main shopping street in Surbiton is Victoria Road, at the foot of a
steep hill close by Surbiton Railway Station. The walk, down St. Mark's Hill,
would take about ten minutes, but a lot longer trudging up with baskets full of
groceries. Fortunately, there is a small parade of shops in Berrylands itself,
only two minutes down the road, More fortunately, she was lucky that the
butcher there, Mr Grimes, still had some lamb chops. It would do for today.
Tomorrow, or soon after, she could explore Victoria Road, or maybe even
catch the trolley bus into Kingston-on-Thames. And take a son or two, with
her who could carry the bags. Meantime, there was the new home to sort

out, and getting the lay of the land. One day during that lovely early August, Belle arranged an interview with the Headmaster at Branchester House, Mr Felix Carne. He was a balding, ruddy-faced man, who looked as if he had been boiled in a cooking pot, but he was cheerful and seemed to have a sound command of what he was doing. He confirmed his willingness to take Finn this coming September. The boys and Bobby all joined the Tennis Club, and straight away went on the Squash Ladder. In those days, squash tended to be played only in the colder months, but this did not stop Finn and Kenneth in particular from playing whenever they could. Nor did they ignore the main activity at the Club -,Tennis. They also learned that there was a municipal outdoor swimming pool not far away – The Surbiton Lagoon.

Belle and her husband Dr. Dougal Peterson, soon introduced Bobby and Claud to friends and other neighbours. Minnie Boughton's stern manner mellowed to the extent of bringing round a peace offering one day – a large round fruit cake.

England, and indeed most of Western Europe basked that July and early August in magnificent sunny weather. The lull in hostilities on the Home Front at least, beguiled people into a false sense of security. But the war did not stop because it was sunny. Following Dunkirk, and the expulsion of Allied forces from Norway, German armies continued their rapid advance through France. They also occupied a tiny piece of Great Britain. The Channel Isles. Meanwhile Italy, led by their dictator Benito Mussolini, entered the war as allies to Germany. German U-Boats intensified their offensive against British merchant shipping in the Atlantic. Not only that. Five British submarines were sunk in the North Sea.

Buoyed by his seemingly endless string of successes in mainland Europe, Hitler pressed on with planning Operation Sealion – the invasion of Great Britain. But to underwrite success with this plan he needed complete mastery of the sea and the skies.

Especially the skies.

CHAPTER 13

Despite their losses, the Royal Navy was still a formidable force and numerically superior to the German Fleet. whilst Operation Sealion could not be carried out without sea landings along the South Coast, it was Hitler's intention that the major assault would be made by air, as it had been in Norway. By capturing English airfields, German artillery, vehicles and other equipment could be flown in to support the tens of thousands of troops that would be parachuted into Southern England. But this necessitated total control of the skies, and to achieve that, the Luftwaffe must first subdue the squadrons of Hurricanes and Spitfires that opposed them.

Initially, and at just the time the Brownings left Dorset to come to Surbiton, German bombers began raids against targets along the English coast, especially those with important port facilities. Amongst these were Liverpool, Falmouth, Portsmouth, Southampton and Plymouth. Cardiff, Swansea and Aberdeen were also badly hit. Key fighter stations in South East England were also targeted These raids were not made without retaliation. As the Germans pounded Britain, so did Bomber Command make raids over Germany, attacking industrial targets in Bremen, Essen and Hamm, amongst others.

The air war was hotting up, but at first this had little direct impact on London and its outskirts, at least during July. The main visible signs of impending danger were the installation of anti-aircraft batteries on open vantage points, like hills and heathland, and the almost comical appearance in the sky of huge barrage balloons., like herds of enormous silver elephants, floating, tethered by cables, hundreds of feet above towns and cities. They did little to deter the enemy, except that they prevented the use of the terrifying Stuka dive bombers that had screamed like wild banshees over poor Poland, Holland and Belgium as they released their deadly cargo.

Life in Surbiton continued its placid course. By now, people were getting used to limited availability of food, many compensating by growing their own. Most adults smoked, either cigarettes or cigars, and many men or a pipe. But tobacco was a low priority in the holds of the merchant fleet, more concerned with bringing essentials such as food and munitions. Looked at now, in the knowledge of the dangers to health that the world now knows about, it could be said that shortage of tobacco was a good thing. In 1940, that was a hardship for many people. Claud Browning, though he did not smoke himself, due to the effects of mustard gas poisoning in the Great War, began growing tobacco on his allotment, then, when ready, drying the leaves in the garage and later rolling and shredding them. Clive had taken up the habit by now and was seldom parted from his briar pipe. He felt a little more grown up with a pipe, and although he was too young to be called up, he was old enough to join the Local Defence Volunteers.(later their name was changed to Home Guard) This was a body of men assembled all over the country to form a last line of defence in the event of invasion. In the early days, this force had neither uniforms, nor weapons, apart from the odd shotgun or ancient rifle. They did not even have steel helmets, and it was highly questionable if they would have posed any significant opposition to a highly trained and equipped army such as the German Wehrmacht. But, at least it was good for public morale, and by late Summer of 1940, more than a million men had been recruited. Clive was one of them, and there was no doubt that he felt slightly more at home with these veterans of The Great War because he could puff his pipe.

By the end of July, only two or three weeks after the Brownings came to live in Surbiton, vapour trails began to appear high in the skies above Sussex and Essex and Kent. Twisting and weaving and diving as the British fighters engaged the enemy bombers and their protective Messerschmitt fighter cover. By the end of the month, the Luftwaffe had lost over 130 aircraft and the RAF 52. As yet, none of this aerial warfare had been witnessed by the residents of St. Mark's Orchard, or anywhere else in the north of Surrey. This was soon to change.

Hitler had scheduled the invasion of Britain to commence on August 1st, but this was postponed for one month. The interval was to be used to mount the greatest air offensive the world had ever seen. Its objective was the destruction of the Royal Air Force – the only effective barrier to Germany's occupation of this annoying little island, the only thorn in Germany's side. At the beginning of August, the skirmishing continued – small raids here and retaliations there. But in mid-August came the Luftwaffe's mighty thrust.

The fifteenth was a Wednesday, and Bobby and all the boys decided it was a perfect day for tennis. Early on, there had been a ground mist, but this cleared by mid-morning. At first, they noticed nothing unusual, but then Kenneth, who was sitting on a courtside seat while the other four played a doubles match, heard the faintest drone of aero engines in the distance and looking up glimpsed tiny flashes of silver forming great loops of vapour trail high up to the South East.

"Hey look up there" he called to the others, "I think something's happening over there. I think it might be a dogfight. Gosh, how exciting". The game stopped and they all followed his gaze. There was no doubt. Just, only just , they could discern the aircraft. There was no doubting the whine as they dived and twisted in the clear blue sky. Below the fighters, they could make out more dots. These were larger and a little lower, and flying level and straight, in tight formation. The bombers. Heading for London. Their sound was different, a deep, steady drone. Faintly, they could hear the chatter of machine guns; the "Hurries" and "Spits" trying to pick them off. But the Me109s fighter escorts were not giving them an easy time. As the battle gradually moved northwards, nearer to central London, Bobby and the boys watched as one of the bombers detached itself from the main formation and nosedived towards earth, streaming a trail of thick black smoke. It was just near enough for them to see one wing snap off and send the doomed plane into a crazy spin. It disappeared from their view behind the trees, but they heard the deep rumble as it exploded. Oh God! the poor men inside had no chance. They may have been the enemy, but it was still a terrible way to die. For Finn, as for all the others who had been happily playing tennis, the war had suddenly, abruptly, horribly come home to them. This was not war being fought across the seas, in some distant, foreign land. This was now their war, over their country, threatening their lives and homes.

The battle in the sky away drifted away, like some slow thunder cloud, out of their view. This time they had not been directly threatened. They were not the target. That was somewhere else and they wondered where, and hoped the bombs had fallen only on empty docks and factories and not on innocent peoples' homes. But it was only a hope. Somewhere deep in their stomachs they knew this was not the case. Somewhere, not so far away, innocent lives would have been lost, perfect human bodies turned into mere fragments of flesh and bone and blood. For all the Brownings this moment would stay with them for the rest of their lives. And the war would come closer still. Much closer.

They were in no mood to go on playing tennis. They collected their rackets and balls and walked home. No one spoke, not even little Finn.

The raid they had watched had actually been aimed at Croydon, some fifteen miles away. The Germans had been attacking the Airport there. Before the war it had been the principal civil airport for London, but was now being used as a military airfield. That evening on the radio news bulletin it was reported that six enemy aircraft had been shot down, without loss to the RAF. There was no mention of the loss of life on the ground, but later it became known that 62 civilians had died, largely from bombs that had hit homes surrounding the airfield. But that was only one of the raids that fateful day. In all raids on England 76 German planes had been destroyed, for the loss of 50 British fighters.

In the weeks that followed, the air raids were heavier and more frequent and the damage wrought more severe. The Brownings wished they were still in Dorset, in the peace and tranquillity of Rosedown., but those days were gone for ever. This was their real world now, one in which the sights and sounds of conflict and danger were a daily occurrence. It was true that the focus of attacks were against military and industrial installations, but in war bombs do not always fall where they are intended to fall. Everyone, no less Bobby and the boys, tried to lead a normal existence. It would be useless for them, or anyone, to hide in a hole every day. Even under bombardment normal life had to be conducted as best one could. So, as towns and cities everywhere braced themselves for the dreaded moan of the air raid warning sirens, so did men and women, and children too, go about their business. A gas mask had to be carried at all times, and regular practice at putting it on correctly carried out. It had been used in the trenches in the Great War with terrible results and there was no reason to believe that Hitler would not use it against the civilian population twenty-two years later. To many foreign observers, the behaviour of the British people was perplexing. There was an imperturbability about them, amounting almost to indifference, as if the raids were not actually happening. An attitude that whatever they felt inside must not be allowed to show. "Stiff upper lip" was the order of the day. "Damn, the sirens are going. Like another beer old chap?"

Of course, sensible precautions were taken. Windows, especially shop windows, were criss-crossed with sticky tape to minimise the effect of shattering glass. Town halls and office blocks were muffled in sandbags, also as a counter to bomb blast. All vehicles had shuttered headlights, so that they could not be seen from marauding enemy aircraft. Air Raid Wardens, dressed in navy blue battledress and steel helmets with ARP painted on them, began to appear. Their job was to usher people to places of shelter when the sirens sounded, and to be on the scene to help with rescue when the bombs had fallen. In London, the Underground Stations became night time shelters, with thousands vacating their homes to sleep in safety on the platforms far below ground. There developed a strong camaraderie amongst these people, bonds that could only have been forged in times of danger and deprivation. Those who could afford to had thick concrete shelters constructed in their gardens, sometimes completely below ground level. In the strip of land between no. 18 and no.20 the Petersons had had a shelter built. Finn loved to go and hide in it with George – not from bombs, but just to play. It had been well equipped, even to having a small refrigerator and a butane cooker installed, and bunk beds that would accommodate the whole family. Other households could purchase Morrison shelters from the Government. These were made of heavy steel and were designed to be erected indoors, to give protection from falling masonry. They saved many lives in the years to follow. For many, though, the only protection would be the space beneath the stairs. Usually, this was just a storage cupboard, seldom spacious enough to accommodate a whole family. This was the case at no.18. With a squeeze two could stretch out, if they were not too big. The Brownings decided that the fairest way to sleep was in shifts: usually Bobby with Finn, Douglas with Kenneth, Clive on his own, Claud on his own. These two were just too big to share with anyone. It mattered little: Claud spent many nights in London, taking his shift fire watching on the office roof. Clive, too, did Fire Watching duty, and if at home would settle down for the night under the dining room table.

Finn and George Peterson became firm friends. George was shorter than Finn, with red hair and freckles. He wasn't much good at games, but would do his best, and laughed a lot at his own ineptness. George introduced Finn to some other boys who attended Branchester House School. Terence Shaw was one, whose Dad was an Army Doctor. Michael Pegg and Derek Sainsbury were others. They all lived close by, so Finn soon began to feel at home and, although he still missed Dorset, began to think less about it as time went by. It was still the Summer Holidays and for Finn there was much to discover about his new surroundings before he started at his new school. Finn and his new pals spent much of the time at Surbiton Lagoon. As well as improving his swimming, Finn liked to dive off the high diving boards. Much to George's admiration he learned to do somersaults in mid-air. George would amuse himself with great leaps off the topmost board and making as big a splash as possible. That was, until one day he landed too close to an elderly lady and frightened the life out of her. The old dear made a complaint to the Lagoon superintendent who rewarded George with a sharp clip round the ear.

His friends were always telling Finn about the fun to be had in Home Park across the river near Hampton Court Palace, and one day Bobby said he could go there with them, as long as he stayed with them and didn't go wandering off on his own. Four went: George, Terence, Michael and Finn. It was a mile walk down through the main town to the river, where they took Hart's Ferry across to the other side. The park stretched on the Middlesex side all the way from Kingston Bridge to Hampton Court Bridge, a distance of about two miles if you followed the river. It was a great expanse of parkland, studded with great elms and oaks, with the Palace itself at the north end. Sheep were grazing on the rich pasture, alongside herds of deer. To Finn, it was reminiscent of the park at Rosedown, except that this was vastly greater, and in the distance, through the trees, he could see the Palace itself, so truly majestic. George suggested they play Soldiers, and they all agreed, except that no one wanted to be the Germans. In the end Michael and Terence begrudgingly agreed, on the basis that they were only "playing" at being Germans and were not real ones. They were given three minutes to go and hide. The idea was that George and Finn would seek them out and "destroy" them. It was no more, nor less, than Hide And Seek – until that was, the air raid siren sounded from Surbiton Fire Station. At first they could neither hear nor see, the approaching aircraft. The first they knew that the enemy – the real enemy – was close, was when the Ack-Ack Battery near the Palace opened up. The "crack" of guns firing was followed seconds later by the "woof" of shells exploding in the sky above Surbiton half a mile away. Puff balls of black smoke appeared one after another. Then they could see the Dornier 17 bomber. A lone intruder it seemed. It was low enough that they could see the black and white cross on the underside of its wings. Far lower than the Germans usually came over, no more than fifteen hundred feet. As it approached the sky above the park, they were able to see that its starboard engine had stopped, the propeller turning idly in the slipstream. The boys were transfixed. It was struggling and losing height fast. The boys watched its faltering progress, until it banked to the left and began to dive. They knew it was doomed. To their left, upstream towards Hampton Court Palace, the trees gave way and there was an open space, levelled and grassed, and a long lake. The lake must have been three hundred yards long and a hundred wide. Now, no more than five hundred feet up they saw two black dots fall from the dying aircraft and then two grey parachutes billowing open above the lake. A third dot appeared, but this time no parachute opened. The dot plummeted out of their view. And then the stricken aircraft itself. In its death throes it plunged beyond their line of sight, back on the other side of the river, the Surbiton side. Above the distant rooftops, flames shot into the air, then thick, black smoke and lumps of debris, and then, half a second later, the deep "thump" as the plane hit the ground. The "debris" was lumps of people, the boys thought to themselves, though no one said so. Instead, they hurried home. They did not feel like playing soldiers anymore.

Daily now, ten times a day, for the rest of August, wave after wave of enemy bombers droned across the sky. The attacks were mainly targeted at

RAF airfields. But not always. Coastal towns were battered, too. Towns like Dover, and Folkestone and Deal and Ramsgate. Time and time again, exhausted pilots climbed into the skies in their Spitfires and Hurricanes to repel the enemy swarms. For the most part these courageous men were British, but now reinforcements were helping too: Canadians, New Zealanders, Australians and airmen who had managed to escape their invaded homelands, amongst them French, Czech and Poles.

And then, on August 24th, a group of German bombers dropped incendiaries on London itself. They had been intended for an aircraft factory at Rochester, in Kent., but the planes drifted off course. Winston Churchill was infuriated and ordered that British bombers should retaliate by attacking Berlin, the German capital. In turn, this enraged Hitler, who immediately ordered a diversion of German effort from attacking strategic targets, such as ports and airfields, to a campaign of terror bombing on London itself. For eight appalling weeks, by night and by day, the onslaught on the capital continued. The damage and loss of life was catastrophic. Although Surbiton itself was too far from the city to be targeted, it was certainly near enough to receive some stray hits and strike fear into its citizens. Day and night they could hear and see, and even smell the dreadful havoc that was taking place. Great palls of acrid smoke and ash drifted westward on the wind, darkening the sky and depositing a grey carpet on streets and gardens and rooftops. At night, the clouds were lit by an orange glow as the distant fires of London blazed. The beams of countless searchlights roamed the night sky, seeking to trap an enemy bomber in their light, and then the anti-aircraft guns would home in and pound away, dotting the heavens with the flash of exploding shells.

The effect of this bombing was twofold. The people of Britain steeled themselves into a resolve to fight this cowardly enemy. Not for them any submission to terror and bullying. Not for them would there ever be the thought of defeat. Instead of breaking morale, as was Hitler's purpose, morale was given new fibre, and determination redoubled. The second effect was strategic. By diverting effort from the business of destroying England's fighter stations, it gave them a chance to recover; to repair damaged runways and installations, to allow pilots to rest, for new pilots and ground staff to be trained, for more aircraft to come into service. It may well have changed the whole course of the war.

German attacks against Britain continued throughout the remainder of August and September. The third of September, the first anniversary of the outbreak of the war, was marked by another heavy RAF raid on Berlin.

Intensive raids on Britain continued for another ten days. And then there came a strange hush. Still, on every fighter airfield, young pilots waited for the signal to rush to their aircraft, once again to take to the skies. But for a while the calls did not come. In Surbiton, in London, in scores of towns all over Southern England, people glanced upwards , cocked an ear to listen for the sirens. Nothing. An uncanny silence.

By failing to quash the English spirit, by allowing others, most notably the USA, to see that Hitler could be resisted by determined adversaries, Hitler made a fatal mistake. The Battle of Britain had been won. The first of many victories in the years ahead. Not that Finn, or anyone at that moment, could realize this fact. Only history would show that. For Bobby, there was the relief that for the moment at least, her beloved Claud and her four sons, were still alive and safe. For Finn, there was a kind of disappointment that "the fun had ended". The twinges of fear for a nine year old were a kind of thrill. Blood, pain, maiming and death were things his mind could not comprehend.

But that time would come all too soon.

CHAPTER 14

The war in the sky continued, but sporadically, less intensively. People continued to die. Husbands lost wives and children. Children lost parents and grandparents. But most people survived, maybe with tales to tell of their narrow escape, and they carried on with their lives as best they could. For the Brownings it was no different. Claud went to work in London every day and they all prayed he would return each evening – unless he was on night duty, of course. Clive was now killing time until his eighteenth birthday. He had tried several times to see Philippa, but her war duties prevented a meeting. She had been very sweet to him on the phone, but in his heart Clive knew that in all probability it was a lost cause. She was years older, much more street wise and, he felt, would probably have young men queuing at her door. Early in September, he went for his Forces Medical Examination and was passed A1 for Military Service. They asked him to fill in a form stating his preferred service: Army, Navy or Air Force, or the coal mines. He ticked "Air Force", but they told him it meant little really; it would just be down to the Recruiting Officer's whim, or particular needs at any given time.

Douglas and Kenneth started their first term at King's School, Wimbledon. It being the Autumn Term, they were immediately introduced to a new sport, at least new to them. Rugby Football. Everybody referred to it as "rugger". Both instantly warmed to it. The very physical character of the game appealed to them, but of the two Kenneth showed the greater aptitude. He was a faster runner than Douglas, and had a better positional sense. Douglas was more thickset, broad shouldered and best suited to "the engine room", of the scrum and lineout. KCS was mainly a day school, though there were a few boarders, so the boys were drawn from a catchment area that enabled easy access to Wimbledon. The two Browning boys could cycle there from Surbiton, by a back route avoiding main roads, in about thirty minutes. It was tricky after dark, because cycle lights had to be dimmed the same as motor vehicles, but they coped and soon settled in this new environment – air raids or no air raids.

Meantime, Finn began his new life at Branchester House. He liked the uniform: red blazer with yellow piping and a red and yellow quartered cap. On his first day he was apprehensive, but was accompanied by Bobby, on the fifteen minute walk from home. Also Mrs Peterson ,with George. The school was housed in a very large Victorian villa, which had three stories and a basement. Broad stone steps led up to the front door, but this was for staff use only: pupils entered by a side door at basement level. At the rear, what had once been a large garden had been converted into a tarmacked playground, surrounded by high walls. Finn later discovered that the other side of the high wall at the far side of the playground was a girls' school, called Saint Agnes Academy. It sounded a rather grand name, Finn and his pals thought, for a crowd of silly, squealy "Gurlls". They had little to do with them, other than to call them silly names when the teachers were out of earshot.

Finn settled in quickly, perhaps because he had had some practice at starting new schools in Barnes and then Dorset. George warned him to watch out for Mr Carne, the Head. "Most of the time he's not too bad, but just occasionally he blows up for no reason and then watch out, he isn't called Old Carnage for nothing, I can tell you!" But to begin with, all was well and Finn kept his nose clean . He also found that he could cope well with the work. Most of the time he was in Mrs Goose's class. Mrs Goose was very tall and angular, in her forties. She always wore a heavy tweed suit, and heavy rimmed spectacles. Her hair was lank and looked as if it was never washed. She had a mole on her chin with hairs growing out of it. Of course, it was inevitable that small boys would make fun of her name, and Mrs Goose was shrewd enough to know it. When they thought she was couldn't see or hear, they would hiss and flap their elbows and waddle along, imitating the bird. Once George got into terrible trouble doing this and ended up before Old Carnage. It wasn't because she heard him hissing, but because, unbeknownst to him, she could see his antics reflected in the "rear view mirror" of her spectacles. That apart, the other boys giggling loudly would have given the game away. As a punishment, George was made to stand in front of the whole school at assembly, and in front of Mrs Goose and perform his little charade – to his intense embarrassment, and the sight of Mrs Goose laughing her head off. Even Old Carnage managed a quiet smile.

For all that, "Goosey" was not bad as teachers go. She was fair, and outside the classroom quite friendly. She was, in fact, a widow. Her husband had been skipper of a freighter that had been torpedoed in the South Atlantic, in the early months of the war. She seldom mentioned this, but there was once an occasion when it had been Belle Peterson's turn to pick up George and Finn from school, and she had been delayed getting there. Mrs Goose had said she would take them back to her flat and they could pick them up from there. At the flat she had shown the boys photos of her husband and his ship, and some of the exciting places abroad she had visited when accompanying him, before the war. She had also showed them the letter she had received about his being Missing. Later, it had been confirmed that his ship had been sunk by enemy action and that there was no news of any survivors, and that William Gilbert Goose must be Assumed Dead. A month after that Clare Goose had received a letter from the King. It read:

The Queen and I offer you our heartfelt sympathy in your great sorrow. We pray that your country's gratitude for a life, so nobly given in its service, may bring you some measure of consolation.

George R.I.

Finn and George looked upon Mrs Goose in a different light after that. It did not stop the other boys occasionally making fun of her name, but they avoided doing so quite so blatantly, and took great care that she did not see or hear them. As Finn said to Terence, whose father was an Army doctor, "you would not like it if I teased you, if your Dad got killed, would you?"

Apart from kicking a ball about in the playground, there were facilities at the school for only one other sport – boxing. Cricket and football had to be played at the Rec. at the other end of Surbiton, not far from the Lagoon. But Old Carnage was rather keen on boxing and let it be known that he had boxed as a middleweight at University in the early Twenties. It was not difficult to clear a space in the Assembly room and string up ropes to form the ring. One Smart Alec boy asked Mr Carne why it was called a ring when in fact it was a square. "Just wait until your opponent lands you a punch on the ear, sonny. You'll hear the ring in your ears until teatime, so you'd better square up to him first." Smart Alec was not smart enough to see the joke was on him.

"This is to be a knockout competition" announce Mr Carne. "No, that does not mean you have to be knocked unconscious, it means that one contestant wins and stays in the competition and the other loses and is out of the competition.. The winner boxes again in the next round, and so on, until finally there is an overall winner, for whom there will be a prize." Old Carnage declined to say what the prize would be, which left the boys wondering whether the best thing would be to lose in the First Round and avoid some nasty bruising. On the other hand, it might be more painful deliberately to lose, so perhaps after all it would be better to do one's best. There followed a brief practice, wherein Mr Carne and another master demonstrated the Noble Art: right hooks, straight lefts, uppercuts, ducking, weaving, use of the feet and so on. Finn's was the third bout and he had to box against Ganley. Brian Ganley was about two inches taller than Finn, and had a longer reach. But he was gawky, not at all athletic, like Finn. Old

Carnage was the referee and the timekeeper and, indeed, the arbiter of who had won or lost. The bell sounded and Ganley came at Finn like an express train and gave him a hefty cuff round the head before Finn had even raised his guard. With his head ringing from the blow, Finn backed away, but Ganley came lumbering after him, and this time landed a right to Finn's midriff, knocking the wind out of him. Finn doubled up and Old Carnage stepped in to stop the fight. "Finn, you have tens seconds to recover, or I declare Ganley the winner." Finn was close to tears from the pain, but he could not bear the thought of losing so quickly. Straightening up, he took a few deep breaths and said "I'm alright now, sir. I can carry on."

"Righteo, if you're sure. Carry on". And he stepped to one side, which allowed Ganley to make another charge. This time Finn was ready, and deftly sidestepped, catching Ganley a glancing blow on the shoulder as he lurched by. Ganley was unbalanced and stumbled to the floor, amid cheers from the onlookers, but was quickly back on his feet, and infuriated by the embarrassing tumble, charged at Finn again, arms and fists flailing. This time Finn ducked low and landed a haymaker into Ganley's solar plexus. As Ganley staggered, Finn crashed a right on to Ganley's nose. It was a hard punch, and instantly blood spurted from both nostrils. Again Old Carnage stepped in, but this time it was to save Ganley from further damage. "That's it" cried Mr Carne, You can't go on with that, Ganley. I declare Browning the winner. The fight had lasted 44 seconds.

Although pleased to have won, Finn's pleasure was tempered by the thought that he would have to fight again. He was saved from doing so by the wail of the air raid siren, rising and falling to warn of an impending raid. "All right boys, in an orderly line now, and follow Mrs Goose to the basement," announced the Headmaster. "Do not stampede. That is more likely to cause injury than Hitler's miserable bombs." On this occasion it was a false alarm, and twenty minutes later the All Clear sounded. But it was the end of boxing for the day. Mrs Ganley complained angrily to Old Carnage about her son's bloody nose, and threatened to report him to the police if he allowed boxing to continue. There were few pupils at Branchester House who felt disappointed. Apart from Old Carnage of course. He thought the world was going soft.

In London, Claud Browning was feeling the strain. It might be thought that the severe restrictions on newsprint, which had so drastically reduced the size of newspapers, would make the journalist's life an easier one. Not so. In time of war there was more news to report, but less paper on which to report it. This meant tight reporting, that is minimal use of words. It meant a lot of normally newsworthy items had to be excluded. It meant features and advertising had to be reduced. Then there was the problem of censorship. All reports relating to the war itself had to be vetted by HM Censors Office before publication. The Official Secrets Act had to be rigorously observed. Claud was closely involved with such matters, and answerable directly to Gordon Johns, the Editor-in-Chief. On occasions, deliberately untrue statements had to be printed, or news withheld altogether, in the interests of security and maintaining or boosting public morale. Photography was a key tool in this campaign. So a photo of a Dornier or Heinkel plunging to earth, smoke trailing behind it, would appear on every front page. Statistics of German losses were routinely inflated, especially during the Battle of Britain, whilst RAF losses would be minimised. On top of all this, Claud had to take his share of Fire Watching on the office roof, spending long nights watching out for new fires started by incendiary bombs during night raids, and hoping none of them fell on him. Though no stranger to conflicts and danger, Claud still felt fear, as all sane men and women do. Oh, true enough, one hoped it would be some other poor devil that would "cop a bomb", but deep down one knew that it might just as well be you.

Bobby became growingly concerned at her husband's exhausted condition. He was fifty years old now, and had suffered that dreadful heart attack before this war broke out. With some trepidation, she called Gordon Johns. She had met him a number of times, but was still a little in awe of him, and this would be no passing-the-time-of-day call. There was a brief exchange of pleasantries, then Bobby took a deep breath. "Gordon, I am worried about Claud. He is very tired and I think stressed. I am dreadfully concerned that he might have another heart attack if he goes on like this. I hate to do this, but I have to ask you if you can spare him from work for a bit, say a week or ten days. Away from London, in the country somewhere." There was a brief pause before Johns replied. "I have been thinking along the same lines, Bobby. I have seen the strain in his eyes, and if I am honest in his work too. We are all feeling the strain, but most of us are younger than he is. And, if I am to be truthful, we have not had heart attacks either. I will tell him to take ten days leave. I would like to spare him for longer, but we are under tremendous pressure. Is that agreeable? As soon as next Sunday's edition is put to bed I well tell him to pack his bags."

As soon as Bobby replaced the phone she felt a deep relief. She realized how tense she had been before making the call. Now, her shoulders relaxed and she could almost feel the muscles in her neck loosen. Her only doubt was the resentment and anger Claud might feel at her interference in his business life. But when he got home that evening, instantly she knew that he was not angry. As he came through the door, she was standing in the hallway. He read her anxiety, and saying not a word, he smiled gently and took her in his arms and held her. For a long time he just held her, then whispered in her ear. "Thanks." "Boys, I've got a week's leave. I know it's term time, so you can not miss school. But I have a proposition. I want to take your mother away. Just the two of us. We need a little time on our own. Clive is kicking his heels, so he can stay here and keep an eye on you three, and do a bit of cooking. It will do him good to practise a bit. That's if there is anything to cook; the rations seem to be less and less. Then when we get back we can all do something together. Perhaps we can all go to the Odeon or something. Agreed?"

Claud and Bobby did not go very far. They packed a bag and took the Green Line coach to Dorking about twelve miles away. They booked into a small hotel just outside the town, and spent happy, leisurely days walking on Box Hill in the pleasant Autumn sunshine, or taking the bus out to Ranmore and Leith Hill. It was so peaceful there, especially on Leith Hill. There, with its commanding view towards the Sussex downs, it seemed almost that they could see the South Coast and the English Channel. Hard to think that not many miles beyond that lay France and the might of the German Army. They lay on the grass, side by side, gazing at the drifting clouds. Once they saw the tell tale vapour trails far off to the East and knew what that meant: another raid on London, or the Docks in the Thames Estuary. But it was far away, far enough not to think too much about the young men high in the sky, in their deadly machines, trying to destroy each other and hell-bent on delivering sudden, brutal death. For a few precious hours, they could listen to the skylarks and remember the peaceful years. The war, the bombs could recede from their consciousness, and they could watch that little bird hovering above them, an innocent little creature singing a song of pure joy. Their evenings were precious. In the little hotel they dined quietly together. Not the fine luxury of pre-war days, but the Manager could still produce a half-bottle of Claret to help the frugal fare go down. After dinner they would stroll in the hotel gardens. They could see little, except when the moon peeped out between the scurrying clouds, but they could hear the little brook, cheerfully winding its way, and once they spotted an owl, silently gliding between the trees. One evening they skipped dinner and went to the cinema in Dorking and held hands in the back row, just like teenage lovers. They were conscious of their good fortune. They were still together, and their four fine sons were still with them, at least for now. Many families they knew were now divided: sons and fathers had donned uniform, and wives and daughters too in some cases. Even housewives were now doing war work, in fields or factories, or driving trucks. Some women were even ferrying war planes from factory to airfield: Spitfires, Hurricanes and now the new four-engine bombers like the Stirling and Halifax. Amazing! But Claud and Bobby were together and this was their moment, their chance to remember their nearly twenty years as man and wife and parents. A chance to renew their love. For these few days the war seemed a million miles away. Something, almost, that did not involve them.

But the war was still raging, and very close to them – a mere 20,000 feet in the skies above England. The Battle of Britain was not going Hitler's way. The Luftwaffe was suffering heavy losses of planes and men, far worse than the RAF, who were proving their superior skill day after day. Hitler determined to launch one more huge assault. A renewed attack took place on RAF Fighter Stations all over Southern England, and this was backed up by heavy night raids on London, Birmingham, Plymouth and Coventry. In the nights that followed, Liverpool and Merseyside were added to the list and terrible damage was inflicted, with heavy losses of civilian life. Early September saw raids on the aircraft factories in Surrey, at Weybridge and Brooklands. Finally, on September 15th, there were two massive attacks on London. Even Buckingham Palace was not spared, though mercifully the damage was slight. The RAF claimed that on that one single day they shot down 185 enemy planes, for the loss of a mere 53 British aircraft. The next day, and the days that followed, were strangely quiet. The sirens were silent. In fighter stations in Kent and Surrey pilots sat waiting for the summons to "Scramble, scramble", but the call never came. The Battle of Britain had been won. The softening-up of Britain as the prelude to invasion had failed. Like Brian Ganley in the boxing ring, it was the Luftwaffe that had the bloody nose. "Operation Sealion", the invasion of Britain, was postponed. It was the only one of Hitler's planned invasions that never took place, and it meant that he had failed to conquer all of Western Europe. But unlike Ganley, Hitler was not yet defeated, not by a long way. Nor would he leave in peace the cities and homes of England. He would still spill much English blood on English soil. There was a long road ahead for England and its people.

And for the Brownings.

CHAPTER 15

In a speech in the House of Commons the Prime Minister paid the following tribute to the heroes of the Royal Air Force, who had battled so courageously against the odds and won. They had won not only the greatest air battle the world had ever witnessed, but also won Britain precious time. Time to recover strength, time to re-arm, and time to renew its resolve to fight on.

"Never in the field of human conflict was so much owed by so many to so few."

Clive heard those unforgettable words on the radio and prayed that his expressed preference to do his service to his country in the RAF would be granted. For him now, there was no question but that, as gentle and peace-loving a young man as he was, he wanted to be a part of that immortal band of men. He remembered speaking to some of them on the train that had brought the Brownings from Dorset to live in Surbiton. Maybe some of them were already hunters of the sky, or maybe dead, or wounded. It had been only a year ago, but the transition from raw youth to battle-hardened fighter pilot did not take long. If he had to fight this is how he wanted to do it. But his eighteenth birthday was not until November. For the time being he must content himself with the Home Guard parades and training sessions in the Scout Hut. At last they had been issued with uniforms, and a few rifles – old Lee Enfields from the Great War – so he was not wasting his time completely.

Finn was now firmly established at Branchester House. Clearly, Mrs Goose liked this fair, willowy young boy , who so obviously shared his mother's Nordic heritage. He was showing a willingness to learn, and a preparedness to participate, and in particular she admired his growing love of the English language. She showed him no favours of course; that would never do, but she resolved to encourage him in every way she could, in and out of the classroom. And Finn responded positively. She made a point of informing the Head that of all her pupils Finn was the most enthusiastic, and one of the quickest learners. Old Carnage had already spotted that, that day in the boxing ring and was pleased to hear that the lad's zest was not confined just to the physical aspect of school life. At this age, although boys were not expected to take home homework, Finn readily accepted the suggestion that he should do some extra reading, and write brief essays about the books he had read.

As to the physical side, whilst the School did not have its own playing field, it did have an arrangement with the Town Council for the use one afternoon a week of a football pitch at Tolworth Recreation Ground, a mile or so away. Most of this Ground had been turned into Grow Your Own allotments, but two pitches had been retained for schools to use. The older boys, those aged eleven upwards, fielded First and Second XIs and played matches against other Prep Schools in the area. The younger boys were taught the game, but did not play matches. As a new boy, not yet ten, Finn was placed with this younger group. It took only quarter of an hour for Mr Tomelty, the Master in Charge of Sport, to realize that Finn was a "natural", whose ball skills and footwork were exceptional, and he wasted no time in reporting this fact to Old Carnage. "Browning has outstanding natural flair, sir. He may be only nine still, but he would put to shame most, perhaps all, of the boys in the First Eleven. And something else, sir. On the bus back from Tolworth he was telling me that he plays squash. I don't know if what he says is true, but he says, and without any hint of boasting, that he can beat all his older brothers who also play – even the oldest who is going to be joining the forces very soon. I think, sir, if all this is correct, we have a near-genius games pupil on our hands. I know we do not play it here at Branchester House, but if you have no objection, I should like to go and watch him one weekend up at the Tennis Club in Berrylands, where he plays. Maybe we should add squash to our curriculum, if we can get the use of the squash courts there. I just have a feeling that after this cursed war is over, squash may become very popular. In the meantime would you agree we should try the boy in the soccer ten and eleven year old group? He says he will be ten in January anyway, and I am confident he could do more than hold his own with them." Carnage had a healthy respect for Mr Tomelty's knowledge of sports in general – he had been a fine fly-half until injury forced him to retire, and in the process prevented him from doing military service as well. So he had little hesitation in going along with Tomelty's proposal.

It proved to be a smart move. Whilst some of the older boys did not like this upstart being included, others, including the Captain, appreciated that it might well improve their chances of winning inter-school matches. And so it proved. Finn's athleticism was developing rapidly: he had speed, balance and elusive footwork that enabled him to ghost his way past opposing defenders, leaving them open mouthed in frustration. Finn soon became a permanent member of the team, and it showed in their results against other schools. He wished his chums from Broadwindsor could see him playing here in Surrey: they would have enjoyed it. Better still, they would have longed to have him in their side still!

These thoughts were running through Finn's mind late one afternoon after a match against Deanhill School in Claygate. They had won 4-2 and Finn, although on this occasion he himself had not actually scored, had been instrumental in two of the goals. The bus brought them back to Branchester House, where Clive had collected him to walk him home. Of all his brothers it was Clive he liked the best. Although more than eight years his senior, Clive it was who paid him most attention, going with him on bike rides, taking him to the sweet shop and the Surbiton Lagoon and generally showing a warm interest in him.

"Finn, you know it will not be long before my calling-up papers come through. Then I won't see you for ages, probably. I wondered if you would like me to take you down to Dorset for a weekend. I've saved a bit of money and I am sure we could find a cheap hostel to stay in and we could call in at Rosedown and see Old Herbert and Old Findlay, and the General and Lady Hester of course, too. Oh and maybe Peter Partridge and some of your other mates there. Would you like to do that? I'm sure I could swing it with Mum and Dad."

It was still mid-autumn and the weather was pleasant enough, and the leaves still on the trees. Bobby and Claud were happy to let them go, and gave Finn a little extra spending money. They could put their bikes on the train, so they would not need to spend much for buses or taxis. There was a nice surprise for them though when Mr Browning made a phone call to Rosedown, to see if it would be in order for the two boys to call in there. "Call in? Call in?" It was Lady Hester who answered the phone. "Oh, no. They must come and stay with us. We have missed all of you a great deal and I am sure Sir Henry and I would be delighted to put you up. We will arrange a taxi to pick you up. He can strap your bikes on the back."

Finn was given permission to miss school on Friday afternoon and they caught the 2.00 pm train, reaching Rosedown in early evening. The taxi drew to a halt at the great Front Porch and Sir Henry and Lady Hester were there to greet them. So also were Mrs Hardy, Old Herbert and Old Findlay. Finn felt tears welling up; he had imagined he would never be here again, and would never see these wonderful old people again. But here he was, a mere four months after leaving them. Even at his young age, he knew that this place and these people were very, very special, and that he would always love them and remember them. Now he knew something else as well. When he was grown up he would come here under his own steam. Maybe one day he would have children of his own and he would bring them here too.

It always seems to be the same when one is doing something really great – time hurtles by. That first evening, over dinner, the Hannahs plied them with questions about their new life in Surbiton. How was Finn's new school? What was their house like? Had he made new friends? Was he still playing squash? The General wanted to know about Clive's time in the Home Guard, and which Service was he going to join.? Clive wished he knew, but told Sir Henry what his preference was and why. Had they had any air raids on Surbiton? Had any bombs fallen nearby? Finn could not wait to tell them about the German bomber that he had watched crash and two of the crew had parachuted out, but the third's parachute had failed to open. Clive asked after Philippa. Had she been down to Rosedown lately? No, but great news: she had a few days leave and would be down early this Sunday. Clive felt light-headed at the thought of seeing her again. He had tried so often and had never even caught her at home on the phone. It was a shame they had to return to Surbiton on Sunday afternoon, but at least he would see her, could talk to her.

On Saturday morning, Finn and Clive used their bikes together. Finn spent a wonderful hour with his pal Peter, finding out the news of his old School, and telling him about the air raids. He gave Peter a lump of shrapnel he had found in the driveway at home. He wasn't sure if it was a piece of a German bomb, or an English Ack-Ack shell, but it was a real war trophy whichever it was and Peter was thrilled. Afterwards they cycled on to Beaminster. Clive wanted to do a bit of shopping. Especially he wanted to find something to give to Philippa, though he did not tell Finn that. Clive bought his young brother a Ploughman's in the Pig and Whistle and settled into a pint of beer and a pasty. "Want to hear an interesting story , Worm? It involves beer actually. In the old days, water was impure, so people drank beer, because being alcoholic it killed all the bad bugs, so it was safe to drink. But of course youngsters like you could only consume a small quantity, or they would get tiddly. So, at meal times, when the jug of beer on the table got empty, the young lad (like you Worm) would be despatched to the beer cellar to refill it. Now this jug was known as a Pygon. The lad would fill the Pygon and bring it back to the table. But, to ensure he didn't fill his boots whilst he was out of sight of the family, he had to whistle non-stop all the way to the cellar and, most importantly, all the way back. That way, the grown-ups would know he wasn't boozing. This became known as the Pygon Whistle. Through the ages this got corrupted to Pig and Whistle, hence the country is full of pubs called the Pig and Whistle. Not many people know that Worm. That's a tale you can tell your pals when you're older. Pretty useless information, but it might amuse them."

To work off lunch, they cycled on all the way to Seatown where Clive bought a cream tea at the Beach Café. It was dark by the time they eventually got back to Rosedown. Finn was tired out and after a bowl of soup asked if he might go to bed early. But, as so often happens when exhaustion sets in, sleep would not come. He lay there thinking about the great day he had spent with Clive. He had never spent so much time with him on his own before. Ever since he could remember, he had felt a poor kinship with his brothers. They were so much older than him, and their interests different. He was just some sort of irritation to them, he felt, like a fly buzzing round their faces. They had never been really horrible to him, just sort of took no notice. As well as the age difference there was another reason: their father spoilt him, and generally fussed over him, giving him goodies and so on.

Subconsciously, Finn was aware of this favouritism and recoiled against it. But here Clive was being a real pal. After all, he didn't have to have come away with him, there were plenty of things he could do at home. He could have spent the time with Douglas and Kenneth, or down at the Home Guard, or with his friends. It was with these thoughts revolving in his mind that he lay unable to sleep, and he was still awake when Clive joined him in the attic room they were sharing. "Good heavens Worm, still awake? I thought you would have been away with the fairies ages ago. What's the matter?

"I've been lying wondering why you brought me here, and giving up so much of your time."

"Oh, I see. Well, I am not sure myself, really. It just seemed a good idea. You weren't the only one who liked living here, we all did. I loved the peacefulness around here. No one ever in a hurry. No hustle and bustle like there is in the towns and cities. And anyway, I haven't given you much attention, have I? I thought maybe I should for a change. You know I am going away soon. Joining up. We wont see much of each other then, will we? And by the time the war is over, you'll probably be a lot older and off with your pals all the time. You might even have a girl friend. So I just thought it would be nice if we spent a bit of time together while we can. Just hope you are enjoying it, brat!"

The hope fell on deaf ears. Finn was asleep.

Philippa arrived an hour before lunchtime on Sunday. It was difficult for Clive to conceal the thrill he felt at seeing her, but she greeted him warmly, and Finn too. "Gosh, you've grown Finn, I can hardly believe it. In only four months, too! How are you Clive? My father says you've joined the

Home Guard. Well done, but I suppose it isn't long before you put on a proper uniform, is it? Do you know what Branch you are going into?" Clive smiled nervously. "The RAF I hope. I want to be a fighter pilot. I admire so much what they have been doing, and I desperately want to be a part of it. Sod's law says I will probably end up driving a tank, though! That reminds me, I hope you won't mind, but I've got you a little present. It isn't much. Well, the truth is I can't afford much, but I just wanted you to have this."

"Oh Clive, how sweet of you. You really shouldn't. We have only known each other a short while. I wonder what it is!"

Clive produced from his pocket a small package, about three inches by three inches, wrapped in brown paper, and handed it to Philippa. He had made sure no one else was present. In the maroon, velvet-covered box was a brooch. It was the badge of the Royal 'Air Force, a pair of wings, surmounted by a crown and in tiny letters the motto of the RAF: "Per Ardua Ad Astra" (Through Struggle to the Stars).

"I hope you like it. I thought it would be appropriate as you are in the RAF – well the female version of it."

"Clive, I adore it. And I will always treasure it. It was a wonderful thought. Maybe it will bring you luck, too and you will get your wish to become an RAF pilot." She took his hand and gently kissed him on the cheek.

Later that afternoon, Clive and Finn headed off home. They arrived late. On the hall table was an envelope addressed to Clive. It was his calling up papers. He knew that before he even opened it.

CHAPTER 16

Clive took the envelope and walked into the lounge and stood by the mantelpiece. A coal fire glowed brightly in the hearth. It was a chilly autumn. The family were all there: Claud and Bobby sitting in their high-winged armchairs, Douglas and Kenneth standing. All watching Clive expectantly. "Come on, Clive, don't keep us all in suspense - open it man" said his father.

Clive slit the envelope and read it slowly, then looked up and beamed. "It's the RAF. I have to report in two weeks time to RAF Bridgnorth, in Shropshire, wherever that is."

The boys crowded nearer to him. "Does that mean you are going to be a fighter pilot?" Finn asked eagerly. "I hope so, Finn, but one has to be selected for Flight Training first. I think they call them Aptitude Tests. But there will be weeks of basic stuff first. Like square bashing and charging over assault courses and doing cross-country runs and so on. Isn't that so, Dad?" "Yes, that's right. They have to be sure you are in good physical condition and disciplined and then, if they think you have the correct characteristics, such as intelligence, quick reactions, judgment of situations and so on, you may be selected for aircrew. But that does not mean automatically that you would become a pilot". "Well, Dad, for me it's that or nothing. I want to be a pilot." "I'm sorry, Clive. You can't just say that. They'll decide what you are most suited for. For instance, they may think you are the right material to be a Navigator, or Flight Engineer, and you would have to go along with that decision".

Bobby listened, but said nothing. There was anxiety in her eyes. Clive was her first born child, and now at eighteen on the threshold of manhood. In peacetime this would be a time to celebrate: to celebrate the Man, no longer the Boy. But this was war. All over Britain and Europe men and women were dying daily. Britain may have won the Battle of Britain, but many good English and other boys had died in the process. Bobby knew that the war would not end quickly, nor even in an Allied victory necessarily. Win or lose, a lot more people were going to die violent deaths. Now she had to face the departure of Clive, actually enthusing at the prospect of flying a warplane and facing danger, or worse – injury and death. And not only facing it, but actually delivering death. No, this was no time for smiles. Not for Bobby. That night her sleep was shallow, and brief. Next morning, thankfully, she could not remember her dreams, but knew that they had been tormented.

Another torment for her, and for the whole population of Great Britain, was the intensification of Hitler's air attack upon towns and cities everywhere. It was true that his campaign to destroy the country's fighter stations had failed, and it was true that the RAF's fighter force remained a potent one. In fact it was becoming more so, as more pilots and ground crew were trained, and more aircraft poured out of the factories. But Germany was not standing still.. It too, was training men and building an even more formidable bomber fleet. A pattern emerged. It was to be a campaign of terror aimed specifically at the civilian population, especially of London. In one single daylight raid, several hundred German bombers flew up the Thames Estuary and rained down incendiary and high explosive bombs on London Dockland and the communities of East London, Essex and North Kent. The raiders were gone by early evening, but there was to be no respite for the Firemen and Rescue teams. After dark, in the early hours, the raiders returned, wave after wave of them. The night sky became a livid glow of red and orange from burning homes and warehouses and factories and churches. Nothing was spared. Ambulance crews and fire engines could not reach many bombed buildings, because of roads blocked by fallen masonry and wrecked vehicles. The bombers came again the next night, raining death and devastation. They continued to come, week after week. Sleep was difficult at best, impossible for most. Incessant was the rumble of anti-aircraft fire, like deep thunder that never stopped. Sometimes the Brownings, like everyone else in Surbiton, would hear the whistle of bombs raining down nearby, and then the terrible explosion as they hit. Houses would shake, windows rattle, or, if the bomb fell very close, glass would shatter and shower the floor. The "Moaning Minnies" as the sirens were called, would hardly sound the "all-clear" before they would start a new whine, rising and falling in cadence, to warn of another raid approaching.

This grim monotony continued until right through October and into November. The London Area has suffered 56 consecutive nights of air raids, every one claiming more lives, mutilating and burning more bodies. But London was not alone in its suffering. Coventry, in the industrial heartland of England, was pulverised with terrible loss of life. Its beautiful cathedral was gutted, unlike London's St Paul's and Westminster Abbey, which escaped almost unscathed.

The Blitz eased a little at around the time Clive waved goodbye to his family at the gate of No 18, but it did not stop altogether. The people of Surbiton woke up one morning to find incendiaries had hit St Mark's Church and totally destroyed it except for the graceful tall spire. The body of the church was a hollow shell. But that spire somehow embodied the defiant spirit of Britain. Despite all the losses, probably one hundred thousand or more killed and injured, people still managed a joke and a smile. It had brought people together. Common adversity does that. Claud was reminded of that marvellous rallying call in Shakespeare's Henry V:

"But when the blast of war blows in our ears,
Then imitate the action of the tiger
Stiffen the sinews, summon up the blood
Disguise fair nature with hard-favoured rage
Then lend the eye a terrible aspect."

Far from being broken, people were brought even more together. Strangers became good friends. Everyone helped anyone who needed it. Hitler, instead of inducing a whimper of defeatism, generated a roar of defiance. And lost more than two thousand aircraft in the process.

It is the nature of the child, perhaps, but Finn actually enjoyed the Blitz. Well, most of it. The burning skies, which he watched when he crept out at night from his bed under the stairs when Bobby was asleep, thrilled him. The brilliant rods of the searchlight beams sweeping the night sky, the whine and crunch of falling bombs, luckily not nearby for the most part, all this was the thrill of a lifetime. No, he did not like the occasion when an incendiary fell on the Boughton's house next door and the roof was on fire, although even then he giggled to see old Mrs Boughton out in the front garden in her nightie, whilst the firemen put out the blaze. Nor was he overjoyed when his little treehouse in the pear tree was hit by another incendiary and smashed to pieces. That fire bomb failed to ignite and was disarmed by the bomb Disposal Squad. He was overjoyed when they gave him the bomb casing, complete with the tail fin. It was one of his most prized possessions for the rest of the war.

A little before Christmas, Clive phoned from Bridgnorth with two pieces of news. The first was that he had been given leave and would be home for ten days over Christmas and the New Year. The second was that he had been accepted for Aircrew Training, but not as a pilot. He was to become an Air Gunner on bombers, and would be leaving for Southern Rhodesia for training early in January. He was disappointed not to be selected for pilot training, but at least he would have the chance to damage Hitler and his cronies. He might have imparted a third bit of news, but did not do so. Philippa Hannah had been posted from London to an airbase at Upton Magna, only a few miles from Bridgnorth. They had met twice. Clive had never dreamed that the gift of the brooch would have meant much to her, that it might awaken in her a flicker of interest in him as a Man. In his mind not only was she several years older than him, but he was just plain , ordinary Aircraftman Browning, the lowest of the low, whilst she was a Commissioned Officer, albeit a junior one. He was wrong. Very wrong. Philippa Hannah had seen what kind of a man he was way back when they first met at Rosedown. She had seen in him not the macho, muscular hunter, full of courage and determination and drive. She had seen a gentle person, thoughtful, a young man who would do all that he could to promote goodness and godliness. This was so different to the debonair, confident, streetwise, but so often self-interested men whom she had encountered so often in London.

They first time they went out together was in Shrewsbury, to the cinema at the bottom of Mardol, by the river. Clive's pay as a raw recruit was frugal, and he had been embarrassed to ask if she minded going into the cheaper seats, near the front of the theatre. No, she had replied, she did not mind, but had then persuaded him to accept a contribution that allowed them to sit further back. It was not the start that Clive wanted, but at least it would allow him enough change to buy her a drink afterwards. He had seen her onto the bus back to Upton Magna, and had hitched a lift back to Bridgnorth. That night he lay awake for a long time wondering whether he should have taken her hand in the cinema, or perhaps even kissed he on the cheek when they parted. He had done neither.

The second time they met had been at a weekend, when Clive had been given a 36 hour pass. Again they met in Shrewsbury, but at lunchtime. It was December and the morning had been raw and damp, but by the time they met, the clouds had cleared and the winter sun shone brightly and warmed the air a little. "Clive it seems too nice to go to the pictures. I wonder if you would like just to walk in the countryside. We could fine a pub for a sandwich, and then climb the hills at Church Stretton. The views up there are so wonderful, a bit like parts of Dorset, though with a wilder feel. And as you don't have to be back at barracks until Sunday evening, would you think it awful if I suggested we find a guest house somewhere to spend the night and then tomorrow we could roam up on Long Mynd and Stiperstones. Stiperstones are the strangest ridge of rocks I've ever seen, I'm sure you would find them fascinating." Instantly, she realized how stupid she had been. Poor Clive. She had not meant to imply they share a bed, or even a room, but that is what he would think. What else could he think, poor boy. She was pretty sure Clive had never taken a girl out before, and if he had, she doubted he would even have held her hand, let alone kissed her. "Oh, I'm so sorry, Clive. Please forgive me. You must think I am some sort of immoral trollop. Really, I only meant that it seemed a shame not to spend a whole weekend together, especially as the weather is so nice."

Clive had been hopelessly embarrassed and discomforted. Not in his wildest dreams had he ever contemplated that sort of relationship with Philippa. On the other hand, he certainly had no wish to be parted from her. Not now she had shown that she really liked him and wanted to be with him. He collected his thoughts.

"It's alright. Please don't apologize, there's nothing to be sorry about. I would love to be with you all the time. Well, maybe not twenty-four hours a day, that would be very presumptuous. But if you would lend me the money to buy a pair of pyjamas and a tooth brush, and if we could find somewhere with two rooms vacant, then yes, let's stay over" Philippa laughed. Suddenly she felt mischievous, and emboldened said "Well Clive, if the worst came to the worst, and we can only find somewhere with one room, you can always sleep on the floor! It IS wartime and we have to learn to rough it a bit!" Clive smiled and looked into her dancing eyes. It was a magic moment. Later, at a dark moment in his life, he remembered it. Those laughing eyes, her glowing cheeks, her sparkling teeth, her flowing, straw-coloured hair. A December morning in a crowded Shrewsbury street.

Finn finished his first term at Branchester House on the Friday before Christmas, which in 1940 fell on a Tuesday. His Term Report was in a sealed envelope, which was handed to Bobby when she collected him from school. Bobby had promised to take him to Peggy Brown's Tearooms, opposite the Odeon Cinema, to mark the end of term with a cream slice. Of course, as it was wartime, it was not real cream, but it was still sweet and gooey, so near enough. But, she had told him, he could only have it if the Report was favourable. If it was not good, then he would have to make do with a rock cake. They found a table by the window, and were immediately approached by the waitress with pad and pencil poised. "Waitress" said Bobby, "Would you give us five minutes? What we order rather depends what it says in this envelope!" The waitress smiled, and Bobby slit the envelope. Poor Finn!

Bobby started reading, but did not speak. At first, her face was expressionless, but as she read, a frown began to crease her brow. Finn's heart began to sink. The frown deepened and was joined by a deep sigh. At last she laid the Report on the table and looked sternly at Finn. By now Finn knew the worst – it was a bad Report.

"Mummy, I suppose it's only a rock cake for tea, is it?" Bobby managed to keep a straight face. "No Finn, I'm afraid not. Your Report does not merit a rock cake. What it does merit is a cream slice AND a rock cake. It's brilliant. I have never seen such a Report. Your brothers have done well, but never have generated such praise as this!" Bobby burst out laughing and gave Finn a huge hug. People at neighbouring tables looked aghast. Tut, tut, they thought, such affection should be confined to children's bedtime, and even then be more restrained.

"It seems that you are top of your class in English and Mathematics, second in History and Geography and fourth in French, and are the best footballer of any age in the whole school. Perhaps the only disappointment is Religious Studies, which does not actually get marks, just an indication of how attentive and interested you were. Not very, it seems, but at least that shows you are not a total genius."

They walked home up St. Mark's Hill, past the bombed out shell of the Church. Would God let you die if you were in His church praying at the time it was hit: He wondered. And he pondered whether his good Report would be reflected in what was in his sack on Christmas Day. Perhaps, he thought, we should all go to church on Christmas Day. Finn had never thought much about Christianity, or praying, or reading the Bible. The Bible, well it was just all about a load of people from long ago, who lived in the Middle East and....Yes, but why did everyone make such a fuss about this baby born on December 25th? It was odd how his thoughts about a School Report had drifted to what rewards he might get for it in his Christmas sack. There was really no connection, except that..."Mummy, can we go to Church on Christmas Day, please. Now that St Mark's has been destroyed , where would we go? And do you know if they have a Sunday class for people like me? I think I would like to try harder and do better in RE next term."

Bobby was taken aback, but did not show it. As a child she had been brought up in the Lutheran faith, an extreme form of Protestantism, but had turned her back on it, and any form of church going, once she left Norway and came to Ireland and then England. Her husband had never, in adulthood, practised religion, saying only that "I left religion in the sickly mire of the trenches on the Somme." As a result, none of the boys had been encouraged to show an interest in religion, and had not done so. Curious, reflected Bobby, as they reached home, that now the youngest was doing so. "Yes, Finn, of course you can go, and I shall come with you. We can go to the Church down King Charles's Road, I forget what its name is. Perhaps some of the others will come, as well".

If Finn had given Bobby a surprise, then Clive was about to give her an even bigger one.. "Mother, I wondered if I could ask someone to come and stay for a day or two before I go off next week.? "Yes, of course. Is it someone you have met at Bridgnorth?" "Not exactly, Mother. Actually, it is someone you know. It's Philippa Hannah. You met her at Rosedown, remember?"

CHAPTER 17

Bombing continued through December, but with less intensity. Nonetheless, the City of London was badly hit. Once again the orange glow could be seen in Surbiton and once again they awoke to a grey world. At first glance it looked like snow, but it was ash carried on the easterly wind. But for Christmas Eve itself, it was quiet. Perhaps even the Luftwaffe needed a break. But in their case it was more to lick their wounds than to eat Christmas turkey. Finn stayed up late on Christmas Eve to go to the Midnight Service. Besides Finn and Bobby, all three brothers said they would like to come as well, leaving only Claud at home. Of course, as it was wartime, there were no outdoor Christmas lights anywhere, and for the Service itself, the Vicar had illuminated the inside of the church only with candles and oil lamps lent by the parishioners. As with every other building the windows were blacked out, but this did not detract from the beautiful, magical sight, and the church was packed full. All the favourite carols were sung and the service ended with "Silent Night". The very words had a special meaning at this fearful time.

Silent Night equals no air raids this Christmastide. Please God, no air raids. And there were none. There was peace. There was quiet. At least for a day or two.

Although it was nearly one in the morning before Finn got to bed, still under the stairs to be on the safe side, he was awake by 7 am, and sure enough Santa Claus had paid him a visit. The sack was hanging on the knob of the bedroom door, and it was bulging. For Finn, an important part of the fun was to feel the sack on the outside and see if he could detect its contents. Of course, there were the usual shape of things – Board games or model aircraft kits perhaps. But this time there were spherical shapes as well, some small and one much larger. And one in between, about the size of a cricket ball. Finn delved. Out came not one, but four squash balls. He delved again and out came a football. His two favourite sports. How clever Father Christmas was! This left "The Cricket Ball". Once again Finn delved deep into the sack, which actually was a pillow case. What could it be? Not a cricket ball. He had no taste for that game, it was too slow and drawn-out. Whatever it was, was soft. He pulled out an orange. He could not believe his luck. It was more than a year since he had seen, let alone eaten, an orange. No room for such luxuries on the freighters keeping the country supplied. He wondered how on earth Santa had managed to provide one, but then remembered that Santa could fly anywhere in the world with total immunity from the Luftwaffe. He ran to show his parents. This was as good as any toy. Better, in fact. One just does not know the value of things until one is deprived of them. He never knew the true source of that orange.

Christmas Day passed all too quickly in the Browning household, but at least it was a happy one, with all six members there together. From somewhere (one did not ask where in those days) Bobby had managed to conjure a turkey, and Claud had been given two bottles of red wine at the Office. War or no war, wine was consumed by few households at that time. Beer was by far the favourite tipple, or maybe a glass of sherry, but in any case the Brownings rarely drank any kind of alcohol. On this special occasion Claud decreed that Clive and Douglas could have one glass of wine, and Kenneth half a glass. It was agreed by all that Finn was too young, and wine would make him sick. To compensate for his disappointment, Finn received a surprise present at the end of the feast. A tin of Nestlé's Condensed Milk. Especially with confectionery on strict ration, Condensed Milk (it had to be Nestlé's!) was a very welcome and rare treat, which Finn consumed, a teaspoonful at a time, for the rest of the evening.

Philippa's visit was arranged for December 28th, following her Christmas at Rosedown with her parents. Clive met her at Surbiton Station at 3.00pm, and although he now knew that his love for her was, at least in part, reciprocated, he was nervous. He tried to reason with himself that in the course of their meetings in Shropshire they had got to know each other, if not intimately, then very relaxedly. After all, they had shared a bedroom, though not a bed, at the pub in Cardington. By sheer good luck, her carriage pulled in exactly where Clive was waiting on the platform. She saw him immediately, and without a second's hesitation, embraced him. So surprised was Clive that he started to draw back, before realising that she was not about to let him do so. "Don't be a twit Clive, kiss me. Here, on the lips! Don't you know I have been longing to see you ever since we parted after that night in Cardington. Now come ON!

For Clive, the world exploded at that second. Was this really happening to him, here on this draughty station platform on a cold December afternoon? Was he really holding the warm, supple, yielding body of this woman? His youthful dream of those months ago at Rosedown, when he first glimpsed her, was this now a reality? She was not the distant and unattainable goddess he had believed she was. He was holding her tightly and she was saying "Kiss me". He could feel his heart pounding, or was it hers? Or was it both of them? He was not sure, but nor did he really care.

"Come on you two. You can't hang about here all day. The ticket collector is waiting for you at the barrier, and he wants to go for his cuppa." The porter was an elderly fellow, and he was smiling broadly at them. "I daresay you can go on with this encounter in a bit more private a place!" They broke their embrace. Clive reddened, but Philippa laughed. "You rotten old spoilsport, you're just jealous aren't you?" "Dead right, miss" the porter replied, "If it'd been me, I'd of just carried straight on, and sod the spoilsport old porter. But the ticket collector really does want 'is break, so if you wouldn't mind…."

Clive and Philippa walked hand in hand up St Mark's Hill, past the bombed out shell of the Church and over the Iron Railway Bridge. She had a small grip in which was her uniform, but now she wore a camel coloured duffel coat over a turquoise sweater and navy skirt. She wore no makeup, but her face glowed and her eyes shone in the fading December afternoon. Claud was in London, and Douglas and Ken out with friends, but Bobby and Finn greeted the couple at the door of no.18. "Hello" said Finn, "I remember you last Christmas at Rosedown. You're Miss Hannah, aren't you? Why are you holding Clive's hand?" "Finn, how dare you be so rude." As self-possessed as she had always been, Bobby reddened at her son's impertinence. "I am not being rude, Mummy, I just thought it was an odd thing to do when you are not married. It is odd, isn't it?" Philippa laughed and Clive feigned to cuff his little brother's ear. "Get lost, Worm, but apologize to Miss Hannah first."

"You have no need to do any such thing Finn", said Philippa "Let me tell you why we are holding hands. It is because we are very, very fond of each other, and holding hands is a way of letting people know that you are. Do forgive me Mrs Browning, I do hope you don't mind me blurting that out before I'm even inside your door." "No, of course not," replied Bobby, "I am delighted to have you here as our guest. Clive, I've allocated Finn's room to Philippa, if that's all right with you Philippa. Actually, he seldom sleeps there. I prefer him to spend the night under the stairs with me, just in case there is a raid, you know. I realize it's illogical and if we receive a direct hit, it is probable we would all get killed, stairs or no stairs. Meantime, would you care for some tea? After so many years living in England, I have fallen into English ways, such as having tea at 4.00, preferably with cakes and biscuits. Do you like Maids of Honour? I made some this morning."

Until that moment, Philippa had forgotten that Bobby was not English by birth. After all these years in England her accent was perfect, almost too correct in fact. "Yes, I would love some" Philippa retorted, "It was a long journey from Dorset, and I had to call in at my flat in London before coming down to Surbiton, so tea would be very welcome, Mrs Browning." "Oh please, do call me Bobby. It is short for Roberta, which is a name seldom heard in Norway, my home country." "Ah, now I understand where Clive's fair hair comes from" Philippa laughed, "And Finn's too. I visited Norway once before the war, and loved it immediately. Perhaps after the war, Clive, we could both go. I would love to see more of it, especially the North, inside the Arctic Circle. The Aurora Borealis must be a wonderful sight. Oh, but "after the war" may not be for a very long time, and assumes we can get rid of that evil maniac Hitler and his gang first."

Later, after a simple dinner, Clive and Philippa excused themselves and made their way to the "Orleans Arms" in Berrylands Village. It was crowded, and very smoky, but they found a corner table near a slightly open window. Separately, they were both thinking there was so much they wanted to talk about, but the right words were hard to come by. Clive's mind was in a whirl, and had been ever since that close embrace on Surbiton Station. Philippa sensed that Clive was having difficulty, though by contrast, she felt perfectly calm.

"Clive, is something bothering you? You seem a bit quiet. What is it?"

!N-no, there's nothing wrong. I know what I want to say, but I'm not sure how to say it, or even if I should. It sounds so stupid."

"Is it something to do with me grabbing you when I got off the train? Have I offended you? I'm afraid I have always been what my mother calls "forward". I'm truly sorry if you are affronted."

"Affronted! Affronted! No, no, I was just taken aback. I think the best thing is if I just say what's on my mind, and I hope – I desperately hope –that you won't storm out of the pub."

"Oh, I don't think that's very likely, Clive. I love being with you. I've told you that. "Come on, cough it up! What is it you want to say?"

"Oh, God. May I hold you hand? Then you can't rush off." Philippa put her hand gently into his. It was warm and very small.

"The fact is that ever since I first saw you at Rosedown, I felt I wanted you, and only you, and there could only ever be you in my life. I know that sounds slushy, but it is how I feel. When we kissed on the platform it was like receiving an electric shock. Does that sound ridiculous? It's true. If that porter hadn't chipped in, I don't think I could ever have let go."

For a few moments, Philippa did not speak. Her eyes were closed, her hand still in his. Clive felt a total fool. He waited for her to pull her hand away and get up and leave.

"Clive, I think you are the biggest damned fool I have ever met! Why do you think I agreed to meet you that first time, in Shrewsbury? Why do you think I wanted to go walking in the hills? Why do you think I am sitting here with you now? Because I love you, you idiot. Let me say it again. Slowly, and in heavy type. I LOVE YOU, CLIVE. Got it? What is it? Do you think that because I am five years older than you, and you are only eighteen that I can not love you, or you me? There is only one thing that I dread, and that is that you are going to Africa to train, and I will not see you again for goodness knows how long. Now let's go back to the house and with any luck your family will all have gone to bed and we can have a nice cuddle on the lounge sofa."

Luck was with them, and the house was in total darkness. Clive checked the blackout was all in place in the lounge at the rear of the house and switched on the wall light. It was controlled by a dimmer, which he turned to maximum dim. Philippa kicked off her shoes and lay full-length on the sofa. "Come here, Clive. Lie beside me and hold me very tight and don't let me go." Clive did as he was told. There was a tightness in his stomach and throat, a delicious sensation of light headedness. He felt her hand pulling out the tail of his shirt and then its soft warmth as she stroked up and down his spine. "Clive, have you ever made love to a woman? Would you like to make love to me? No, I don't mean here and now, but before you go to Africa. You still have a few more days leave, don't you? Come to London with me tomorrow: there's no one in my flat. We would be totally alone. Will you? Please." Clive could not find romantic words with which to answer her. He kissed her gently. "Yes" was all he could say.

After a late breakfast, shared with Bobby, Douglas, Kenneth and Finn, the couple caught a train to Waterloo, and the bus to the Hannah flat in Bayswater. Clive had told his mother that he would be back late that evening, but he knew that really he would not be returning to Surbiton until the next day. He would not break the enchantment of being alone with Philippa one moment before he had to. That day, they made love for the first time.

CHAPTER 18

The Browning family's New Year celebrations were subdued. They all felt the weight of war; there was no good news for Britain and her Allies. But closer to home they were saddened by Clive's departure for Rhodesia on January 2rd. The whole family saw him off at Surbiton Station. Bobby tried hard to put on a brave face, but as the train drew out, with Clive waving farewell from the open carriage window, the tears welled up. At first it was a single tear that trickled down her cheek, but as the train gathered speed, she turned away and her shoulders shook and she sobbed. Claud took her in his arms, but he also felt a tight lump in his throat. He, better than anyone, understood the dangers that lay ahead for his eldest son. Douglas and Kenneth hurried away to hide their sadness from their parents eyes. Finn, brave little Finn, called out after his unhearing brother as the train rounded the bend and out of sight: "Good luck, Clive. I love you!" Then he, too, could no longer hold back the tears.

The next day, January 3rd, Finn became ten years old. He would never experience a sadder birthday and the whole family were steeped in gloom. Finn habitually failed to do well for birthday presents. – it was too soon after Christmas, but on this occasion a bar of solid gold would have left him unmoved. He wanted Clive to be there, and he had gone. He, the only one of his brothers who had actually taken trouble with him. Douglas and Kenneth had, however, clubbed together to give Finn a new pencil box, filled with colouring pencils. Of course, Finn was past that age, but nevertheless he thanked them as best he could. Clive had left a parcel for him, and its contents were a little more appropriate. It was a balsa wood model kit for a Vickers Wellington Bomber, complete with a modelling knife, brown and dark green camouflage paint, and transfers for the wing, fuselage and tail markings. Clive had written a card that read "Next time you see me, little brother, I may have flown in one of these!" Finn felt the mixture of emotions that only a child could experience: the thrill of the gift Clive had given him, the sadness of having lost his brother.

A few hours after Clive's departure, his father had to leave for the City, not so much to attend to his office duties, as to Fire Watch on the building's roof. Air raids against London still continued, though more spasmodically, and only a single incendiary was enough to set off a fire that could destroy a whole block, if allowed to develop. So he had promised Finn that he would be back next day, Finn's birthday, and would have a special present for him. Before that, however, came another surprise that would be sure to cheer him up. George Peterson came round at teatime, and brought with him a very large parcel wrapped in brown paper. It measured about 24in. by 18in by 12 in. and something was rustling inside it! Finn tore off the wrappings to reveal a wooden box. Well it was wooden on all sides except one. The remaining side was a hinged, wire meshed door and staring inquisitively through the mesh was a minute and very fluffy white kitten. White all over, except for a black patch at the end of its nose.

George grinned from ear to ear and said: "This is a present from all of us at no. 20. Happy birthday Finn, we hope you like it. Well, actually it is a HE." Finn opened the cage and picked the kitten up and held it close to his face and kissed it on the tip of its nose. He had never had a pet. Before the war the Brownings had had a mongrel called Spot. One day it had vanished and never returned. Now he had a pet of his own. "I shall call it Spot" he announced. "And I will love it and look after it always." As if understanding, Spot emitted one tiny, single "mew" and nestled up against Finn's chest.

Bobby smiled to herself and she, also, felt a little less depressed. "Just a moment, Finn, I haven't said you can keep the animal yet, have I?" She looked stern and Finn's face fell. "But you can my little fellow! Oh you can and we will all love him to bits" "Mrs Browning, Mummy told me to tell you that the kitten is potty- trained, but you will need to have a dirt tray, because he is too young to put outdoors all night. We've got a spare one, so I will nip home and fetch it." So saying George shot out the front door.

Whilst he was gone, Claud returned from London, much earlier than usual, and was instantly greeted by Finn holding the fluffy white bundle. "What's this Finn? Taken up knitting? Oh no! It's not a kitten is it? Where did this monster come from?" Claud was entranced by Spot as well as everyone else. "Finn, I've got a good idea. We could play football with him. He could be the ball! However, to do that we would have to take it to the Rec, and you have outgrown your bicycle, so that's going to be a problem. I wonder if you are big enough to manage that rusty old heap that was once Douglas's years ago. Let's go to the garage and find out."

When the garage doors were opened it was not to view an ancient, rusting rattletrap. There, its chrome gleaming, was a brand new bright blue Raleigh, complete with 3-speed gears and front and rear lights, and a neat 6inch flagpole with a Union Jack pennant on the handlebars. "Oh, Dad, that's not for me, is it? Not really!" Finn handed Spot to his father and climbed on the saddle. It fitted him perfectly, just as it was. No need to adjust the saddle height. The lights were operated by a dynamo on the rear wheel. It was a contrivance that looked rather like a stubby metal bottle, with a "top" that revolved against the sidewall of the tyre. It made cycling a little harder, but easy enough for an energetic youngster. "Of course, we will have to fix shutters over the front light, Finn, the same as we have to do on all motor vehicles: we don't want the Luftwaffe seeing the beam and dropping a 500 pounder on you! But the light should still be enough for you to see in the dark, if you go carefully. Anyway, you'll only be cycling after dark on the way home from school and you know that route like the back of your hand" Finn's day was complete. All he wanted now was for morning to arrive and the chance to take out his new machine for a spin.

Sedgmoor Gardens is a cul-de-sac leading off St. Mark's Orchard. It has eight properties along each side and another six ringing the roundabout at the end. The island in the middle was tastefully planted with shrubs and horse chestnut trees. Every September, the children who lived nearby made a beeline for the island to harvest conkers. Finn was up early on the morning of January 4th and after a hurried breakfast, and watched by both parents, rode his new bike for the first time. He soon had the hang of changing gear and quickly disappeared round into Sedgmoor Gardens – out of sight of Claud and Bobby. For any boy of ten, speed is everything, and well before he reached the end of the straight section of the road he was travelling as hard as his legs could pump the pedals. Fast. Too fast. Finn had failed to allow for the sharpness of the bend into the circular section at the top of the cul-de-sac. He shot off the pavement, across the road, head on into the curb of the island and was catapulted over the handlebars. In one sense he was lucky. He could have hit the conker tree head first and crushed his skull. In those days safety helmets had not even been invented, let alone become compulsory. Instead, at enormous velocity, he scraped the tree's bark with his right ear, and crashed in a tangled heap onto the grass at the tree's base. The buckled bicycle landed on top of him.

Blood covered most of his face and soaked his shirt and pullover. The ear was almost detached, just hanging by a shred. Finn was too shocked to move; he just lay there, conscious but quite still. That was how Bobby and Claud found him two minutes later. The ambulance came quickly and Bobby and Claud were allowed to travel in the back with Finn and the attendant. Surbiton Hospital was five minutes from the Browning's home. It was small and airy, with plenty of light, and like all hospitals, smelled of that cocktail of antiseptic and well scrubbed floors. For once, the Operating Theatre was not too busy and Finn was wheeled straight in. Finn was brave. He had experienced the dreaded ether mask once before, when he had had his tonsils out at Putney Hospital. It was horrendous and he gagged. Involuntarily he breathed in the ether and immediately was unconscious.

When he awoke, he was in a small private room. His head felt tight and restricted. It was swathed in a bandage which covered not only his mangled ear, but one eye as well. Bobby and Claud were sitting by the window. "Have they taken it off? Have I only got one ear left?" "No, Finn, you still have it, but only just. What on earth were you thinking of? You are very lucky you did not kill yourself, or at least knock all your brains out, although you could not have been using them. You will have to go very carefully for a few weeks. No games, and no fooling about with your friends. I'm afraid your new bike was wounded even more than you. The front wheel is now egg-shaped and only good for scrap." Surprisingly, Claud was not angry. He was not sure why he had a soft spot for his youngest son, but had to admit to himself that it was so. Perhaps it was because he was the baby of the family, or perhaps it was because he was the only one who had the Nordic look, like his wife. Or was it, he wondered, because the child had this precocious talent for sport, which he himself had never possessed. Kenneth was sporty, but the older two just lacked something when it came to games. Anyway, apart from the annoyance of getting the bicycle repaired, especially after only one brief outing, he secretly admired Finn's enterprise (although you could hardly describe colliding with a large tree as enterprise!).

The hospital let Finn home on the Sunday evening, bandaged, sore and chastened. He got little sympathy from Douglas or Kenneth. They just thought the Worm was getting the limelight again. Nothing unusual in that! By nine a.m. next morning they had cycled off on their own, to meet up with a friend from King's. Claud also left for London to start a new week, and create next Sunday's issue. When the knock on the front door came, Bobby was clearing up breakfast in the kitchen.

Totally without due cause her heart missed a beat. She could feel it thumping all the way to the door. There was no reason for it, and years later when she thought of this moment, she could not explain it. It was just some sixth sense of foreboding. The lad standing there was dressed much like a postman, except that his hat was a little pillbox affair, kept in place by a shiny strap under his chin. A Telegram Boy. He handed Bobby the telegram, saluted and hurried away, saying nothing. Telegrams came in flimsy, bright yellow envelopes. In these days of war, so often they were the harbinger of bad news, the first and usually the only stark notice of the loss of a loved one in combat. The message was short. It came not from the War Office[1], as was usual, but from the NAAFI, the Navy, Army and Air Force Institute, at their HQ in Ruxley Towers in Claygate, Surrey. Claygate was only five miles from where the Brownings lived. It read:

> *"It is with much regret that I have to advise you that the troopship in which your son Aircraftman Clive Harry Browning was sailing, has been sunk by enemy action. An accompanying Royal Navy vessel picked up a number of survivors, but we are sorry to say that your son was not amongst them. With the utmost regret it must therefore be assumed that he did not survive. Should any further news come to hand we will, naturally, notify you immediately. Should you require any assistance, do please contact this office.*
>
> *Yours sincerely,*
> *J. Endicott, Chief Superintendent.*

"Oh God no. Please no. Not my boy. Not Clive. Not Clive"

Upstairs, Finn heard his mother's wail of despair. What had happened? What was wrong? Slowly, Finn rose from his bed and called down to his mother. "What's the matter Mummy? What's happened? Bobby's moans had turned to sobs. Finn found her sitting at the kitchen table, her head buried in her hands, her shoulders shaking. The telegram lay in front of her and Finn picked it up and read it. Finn did not cry, nor did he speak, nor did he rush back to his room. One might have expected any of that. Instead, he went quietly to the sink and filled a glass of water, and took it to Bobby and said very calmly, "Drink this Mum it will help you." Very gently he put his arm around her and she looked up into his eyes, so pale, so calm and steady, and she took the glass and sipped the water. "All of it Mum, all of it. That's what you say to me, isn't it, when you give me the cough mixture?" Bobby stood up and they gently hugged one another. The tears still trickled down her cheek, but she had regained her composure. "Oh Finn, it can't be true. Surely, it is too soon. They've made a mistake. He only left a few days ago. He can't have sailed already, surely? Mistakes are made in wartime. Names can be confused. We must hope, Finn. We must not lose hope, my dear little

---

[1] Message was from NAAFI because Clive was travelling in a Merchantman, not a Warship.

Finn." But Hope was not what she felt in her heart. And yet, what else is there, except despair?

For minutes, the two of them held on to each other, saying nothing, but drawing comfort from each other's closeness and warmth. At last, Bobby drew away.

"I must call your father. He must know what has happened. He must come home." "Mum, shall I do it? I'll do it for you if you like. "No, Finn, you are supposed to be resting. The doctor said you must stay quiet for a few more days, to allow your ear to heal. Go back to bed, my little man." Quietly, her eyes filled with tears again and she turned away from Finn. With her back to him she said: "Leave me alone for a while, Finn, then I will call Daddy." Never before in his brief life had Finn thought about emotions such as fear and sadness, but now he experienced a tenderness, a oneness with his mother that changed him deeply. Spot, the little white bundle, softly mewed and rubbed against his ankle. Finn picked him up and gave him to Bobby and silently left her to her sorrow.

With the war only a year and a half old, already tens of thousands of Britons and their Allies had died, or their bodies had been shattered. The lucky ones died quickly: a bullet, a bomb or a shell and it was all over. No time to feel pain. Others died slowly, limbs blown off, arteries pumping their life stream away, or burned or drowned. Some survived the trauma. They knew pain. They knew the physical pain, and the anguish that followed. All loved ones could do was try and comfort them, and help them rebuild their shattered bodies and minds. But a different kind of victim were people like the Brownings. They had lost a son, a brother who would never come back. Not even a grave to mark his passing. Who would comfort them? For Claud, who had witnessed so much death in Flanders twenty or so years ago, there was a   palliative to help him cope. His work. For most of most days his mind would be focused on his responsibilities in London, and the comradeship of those around him on the Paper. For Bobby there was no such balm. A child in the most literal sense is the flesh and blood of its mother. The loss of that child is almost a physical wound, an amputation. No man, no father can experience this agony and Claud knew this well. For him, comforting Bobby was in itself a balm, a healing emollient, and he applied himself to this task with all his strength and tenderness. The boys, too, looked to him for support and he knew that he must stand tall and firm for them, especially Finn, who was so young and had looked up so proudly at his eldest brother. But children are resilient and as the weeks passed, the heartache began to ease, and the boys once again became absorbed with their schooling and their friends.

Bobby's grieving turned inwards and ate at her very spirit. She spoke little and rarely smiled, and she went through the motions of everyday life in a mechanical trance. Hard as Claud, and the boys, tried, nothing seemed to help. Friends, especially Dr and Mrs Peterson next door, tried their best. She was asked out to tea, or to play bridge, but always refused. When the chores were done she would turn to her diary, but would let no one see what she had written. Occasionally, if the weather was kind, she would leave a note for the family to say she had gone for a walk, always alone, usually in Home Park across the river. Claud persevered. He took her to the cinema, and once up to Town to a play. The bombing had not closed the West End theatre circuit. Sir Donald Wolfit in King Lear, superbly staged and acted, was not sufficient to rouse Bobby from her listlessness. One bright Sunday he hired a skiff at Hart's Ferry and rowed her and Finn up stream to Hampton Court, and a stroll in the gardens there. In the privacy of the bedroom he would stroke her hair, which she had always enjoyed, but now with no response. She let him make love to her, but for her it was a joyless act. Secretly, she felt that it was almost shameful to the memory of their lost son. She felt so alone. Even darling little Finn and the other two boys were getting back to normal. Only she, it seemed to her, still mourned for Clive.

CHAPTER 19

The United States of America had watched events unfold in Europe with concern, even a degree of sympathy, but with a firm policy of non-intervention. Why should it act any differently? There was no perceived threat to American territory, citizens or property. On the contrary (though it was not widely known until after the war was over) numbers of American corporations were quietly supplying the German Axis with goods and materials that directly or indirectly aided their conduct of the war. However, their President, Franklin Roosevelt, became increasingly minded to help Britain, who alone and courageously, was resisting the Nazi ambitions. Roosevelt struck a deal whereby the USA supplied warships to Britain (mostly of World War I vintage) in exchange for 99 year leases on British bases on the Atlantic seaboard, from Canada south to South America. American factories tooled up to produce armaments, much of which were sold to Britain (in addition to what they were already selling to Germany) at a crippling cost to Britain's currency reserves. By early 1941 American public opinion also began to shift in favour of supporting Britain. To them it was Good fighting Evil – St George and his funny old Dragon. RAF pilots were sent to America for training, and American warships took up escort duty for trans-Atlantic convoys, ostensibly to protect American merchant shipping.

Meanwhile, Italy, under its Dictator Benito Mussolini, had entered the war by linking arms with Hitler in mid-1940. His ambitions lay largely in the conquest of Egypt and Libya, which would give him unfettered access to the Red Sea, and then on to the East African territories he coveted. His army was confronted by a small, but well-trained British force, lead by General Wavell and they soon showed they were a match for the Italians. By the beginning of December Wavell had driven them out of Egypt all together, and back deep into Libya. Virtually overnight, the Italians lost forty thousand men, mostly as prisoners, for these men had little stomach for the fight. Only a few hundred British and Allied troops were lost. But worse was to follow for Il Duce Mussolini, for by the end of December a further forty five thousand prisoners had been taken and the wrath of Hitler incurred for the Italian Army's incompetence and cowardice. At this point, Hitler decided to intervene, and it was an ill omen for General Wavell when a German force of troops, artillery, tanks and aircraft was despatched, under the command of General Erwin Rommel. There could be no doubt that Hitler now saw Mussolini as a buffoon, of little value to the furtherance of his ambitions.

By early in 1941 other events were taking place, too, and all were to raise fresh fears and to deepen gloom in the Allied camp. Europe had been plunged into war initially because of Hitler's greed to conquer Poland and Czechoslovakia. A few countries apart, such as Spain and Portugal, Sweden and Switzerland, Western Europe was in Hitler's control. The major exception was Britain.

Too late at this juncture, Hitler failed in his attempt to prevent Mussolini from invading Greece. As in North Africa, the Italians bit off more than they could chew and met fierce resistance from the Greeks. Once again, Germany stepped in and they, also, invaded Greece and then followed this with the occupation of Yugoslavia. There followed in the Spring of 1941 a fierce battle for control of the strategically vital island of Crete. Outgunned and outnumbered, the Allied forces were compelled to withdraw. With or without the Italians, Germany seemed unstoppable, and now had control of virtually of almost all European shores of the Mediterranean Sea.

By February 1941, General Rommel had taken up command of the Afrika Korps and by late March had launched his first testing offensive against the British Eighth Army. Success soon came. The Germans (supported to some extent by the remnants of the Italian Army) rapidly advance eastward some five hundred miles, and soon large elements of the British Force were surrounded and besieged at the key port of Tobruk, less than one hundred miles from the Egyptian frontier. If all that was not to lower morale back in Britain, then the battles of the Atlantic and Mediterranean Sea were also proving disastrous. Hundreds of ships, both warships and merchantmen were being pursued and sunk, some by aerial attack, some by U-Boats and some by the powerful German surface fleet of battleships and cruisers.

One of the most feared of these craft was the battleship "Bismarck", a fast, modern ship of 41, 000 tons, armed with eight 15in. guns. In May she was detected steaming north-west off the coast of Norway, clearly heading out to hunt in the North Atlantic. She was accompanied by the powerful cruiser "Prinz Eugen". A British fleet headed out from Scapa Flow to intercept. It was led by the battleships HMS "Hood" and HMS "Prince of Wales", plus six destroyers. On the second morning "Bismarck" was sighted and engaged by the British squadron. There was a dreadful outcome: a single shell from "Bismarck" hit HMS "Hood" and penetrated to her magazine. The largest explosions of the Second World War were the two atom bombs that destroyed Hiroshima and Nagasaki in 1945. The next largest was the eruption of the Hood. In the space of a few seconds she ceased to exist. Of her crew of one thousand, four hundred men, only three survived.

"Bismarck" then attacked HMS "Prince of Wales", causing extensive damage, but fortunately failing to sink her. However, "Bismarck" did not go unscathed and her Captain was forced to head for a French port in Northern France, to effect repairs to her fuel system. Her progress was tracked from the air, until a second contingent of British warships, accompanied by "Swordfish" torpedo bombers, finally sunk her. Whilst this was a successful conclusion to the episode, it had to be viewed against the terrible losses "Bismarck" inflicted on the Royal Navy's capability and prestige.

CHAPTER 20

The British public were kept informed of how the war was progressing in several different ways. First, there were the daily radio news bulletins, keenly listened to by virtually every household in the land, and also in every pub. Second, there were the daily and Sunday newspapers, thinner than in pre-war days, for paper was in short supply. Then there were the cinema newsreels; not so immediate , but with the great advantage that they showed moving pictures, not just still photographs. In those far off days there was no TV service, nor in fact was there until some eight years after the war had ended. Throughout the war, people flocked to the cinema every week, sometimes several times a week, to lose themselves for a few hours in the fantasy world of the Big Screen. There were the delights of the Hollywood Musicals, or a melodrama about The Wild West, as cowboy confronted Red Indian – and always won. These were the days when Fred Astaire danced like a dream with Ginger Rogers. When James Stewart, or Gary Cooper, or John Wayne all brave and imperturbable, bestrode the screen like gods. Of course, the newsreels were censored. So were the newspapers and the radio. It was vital to maintain the public's morale, and if success on land and sea could not be achieved, then at least failure should be played down or suppressed.

There was one other medium of communication. Word of mouth. Often enough this manifested itself as rumour, conjecture or just plain gossip. This could never be censored. People still had freedom of speech. But it was important that this freedom was not abused, and it was especially necessary that care was taken about imparting information, or even opinion, in public that might be useful to the enemy. Posters bearing the slogan "Walls Have Ears" and "Careless Talk Costs Lives" appeared everywhere in public places, even public toilets, and most especially in pubs and restaurants.

Thus it was that one evening in March 1941 Claud Browning stood at the bar of "The Turk's Head" just off Fleet Street, passing an hour with Gordon Johns before catching the train back to Surbiton. To an extent Claud had come to terms with the loss of his son Clive. He was finding it more difficult to come to terms with the continuing, unrelenting gloom that had enveloped his wife, and so was more ready than once he had been, not to catch the earliest train available. An extra pint was a small, but real, comfort.

"Claud, I don't know where this damned war is going. It isn't going well, that's for sure. It's all very well for Winnie to make defiant speeches, but there's damned little to show on the credit side of the balance sheet. We need some real, solid advances somewhere. But where? We've been thrown out of France, Rommel has got us on the run in North Africa, our convoys are being decimated in the Atlantic and Med., and here at home the public has taken a pasting from the Luftwaffe. It would certainly help if the Yanks would come off the fence, but I can't say I blame them for sitting firmly on it.

The irony Claud, is that I don't really think Adolf wants to add us to his conquests; he would much rather have us on his side. It's Russia he really fears. Communism. That's his real enemy. That and the Jews. Rumours are that the most appalling things are happening to those poor bastards all over Occupied Europe. Word is that Hitler has set-up what are being called Concentration Camps and is shipping trainloads of Jews into them. God knows what happens to them once they get there."

"I feel much as you do, Gordon. It's not looking good. But it's no good talking ourselves into a depression. And I'm sorry to say this, Gordon, because you are my boss, but I don't think we should be talking like this in a public place. We don't know who is listening to this conversation, and we don' t want to spread despondency."

"No, you are right Claud. My fault. I should know better. Let's have another half and then I'm off home. So had you better be. Has Bobby chirped up a bit yet?" But he knew she hadn't.

It was past eleven pm when Claud got to Surbiton Station and he took a taxi up St. Mark's Hill. Usually, he walked – the only daily exercise he took since his heart attack all those years ago. Tonight he was weary, too weary to have had more than a quick sandwich at Waterloo before he caught his train. The house was silent and in complete darkness. Bobby and the boys were long asleep. With the easing off of air raids, Bobby and Finn had reverted to sleeping in their usual beds, a welcome relief for Finn, and Bobby from being squashed together in their cramped quarters under the stairs. Claud crept quietly upstairs and was about to settle in bed beside Bobby when he saw a glimmer of torchlight under the door. Someone was moving about. Claud watched as the figure holding the torch moved from the foot of the stairs towards the kitchen, and he saw the kitchen light come on. It was Finn.

"Finn, what are you doing awake, son? It's getting on for midnight"

"I was thirsty Dad. I was just going to get a glass of water. I'm sorry if I woke you up."

"It's alright son, you didn't. I've only been home a few minutes and was just getting to bed."

"I'm hungry as well as thirsty. Is there something in the larder I could eat?"

"Let's have a look, You're growing so fast these days, Finn, that's your problem." They both laughed. They sat at the kitchen table.

"Dad, I wish you were home more of the time. I hardly ever see you. None of us does. Can't you come home earlier some evenings? Or at least have Saturday off sometimes? Mummy's so sad all the time. We try to cheer her up, but it never seems to work. She needs you, Dad. And another thing, you never get to see me play football. I scored a goal last Saturday."

"I'm sorry, son. I only wish I could. But I have to put work first, otherwise what would we live on? Then on top of that I have to take my turn Fire Watching on the office room some nights, so I never get home. I tell you what, though. Do you ever play mid-week matches? I could try to get a Wednesday afternoon off and come and see you play. But Saturdays are hopeless I'm afraid. Sunday papers have to go to press on Saturday nights, so it is the busiest day of the week."

"Yes we do play mid-week sometimes, and it would be great if you could come. There's a match on Wednesday fortnight. By the way, what's happening in the war? I ask Mummy sometimes, but she hardly replies. I think she's sad about Clive, but I think she's worried about Granny and Grandpa in Norway as well. Are we winning yet? I ask Douglas and Kenneth, but they can't be bothered to tell me anything, and I would really like to know what's going on. It's not as if I'm a baby Dad."

"No of course not Finn. I tell you what might be a good idea. I could bring home the newspapers every day and you could read them and cut out the bits you think are especially interesting or important and put them in a scrapbook. It would be really worth doing that and keeping them until after the war. They would be a marvellous record of events. Would you like to do that? Good. Now it's high time you were asleep, and me too. Make sure you're quiet and don't wake the others."

A few days later, Claud gave his youngest son a large scrapbook, a pot of paste and the previous day's papers. The first cutting in the book was the report of the naval action in the Eastern Mediterranean , off Cape Matapan, when the Royal Navy engaged the Italian fleet and sank three cruisers and two destroyers. But it was a hollow victory when set against the chain of calamities on land and sea that followed in seemingly endless succession.

CHAPTER 21

Claud Browning did manage to see Finn play a soccer match before the end of the Spring Term. He could see that his youngest son had the lithe athleticism of his mother. Although only ten, he was tall, already close to five foot in height, with broadening shoulders, rod-straight back, narrow hips and long legs. His hair was as blond as Bobby's, his eyes were her eyes – ice blue as only the Nordic race seem to be. "My God" Claud thought to himself, "I've spawned a true Viking!" Clive had had fairish hair, but that apart he, like Douglas and Kenneth took after him: stocky, broad-chested with wavy brown hair, and brown eyes.

Finn had already shown his skill on the football field and, before that, on the squash court. At only ten he was already in the Under-14 squash team at the Berrylands Tennis club, and the Club Captain had predicted that he would be in their First Team by the time he was fourteen, and playing for Surrey before he left School. Now, as the Easter Holidays approached, Claud wondered how he would get on at Cricket. Though no star performer, Claud had played club cricket before the Great War, and had thoroughly enjoyed it. The game intrigued him, and secretly he was sad that neither Clive, Douglas or Kenneth had shown interest nor aptitude for it. He determined to try to involve Finn, and scrounged around for second hand stumps, bat and ball. That Easter of 1941, Claud took Finn to the Rec. to teach him the rudiments. First, Finn with the bat and Claud with the ball, and then the reverse. The Rec. was usually busy, and at one end a quarter-mile cinder running track had been laid. After a few visits, it become noticeable that although Finn had a good eye and could strike the ball well enough, the enthusiasm was lacking. His gaze kept wandering to the running track. In the end Claud lost patience.

"Look Finn, you wont get far with cricket, if you don't concentrate. Nor with any other game, come to that. Have your brothers put you off? I know they think it's too slow. Perhaps you do too. Is that it?"

"No Dad. I quite like it actually. It's just that I keep seeing what those boys and girls are doing on that running track over there. I don't know if they are trying their best, but I think I could run a lot faster than almost all of them. That's what I would really like to do: I'd like to have a race with some of them. Do you know if we do athletics at Branchester House?"

"No, Finn, I'm not sure. But I will give Mr Carne a call and find out if you like."

"Yes, please Dad. But do you think we could just go over and watch for a bit?"

"Come on, then. P'haps there is a coach there we could go and talk to"

There was. Her name was Shirley Black, She was in her late thirties, Claud guessed, and she lived in Tolworth with her husband Edmond, except that Edmond was serving overseas in the Tank Regiment. She did not know where, of course, but was fairly certain it must be in the Western Desert. They had no children. Before the war, back in the early '30s, Shirley had been a quarter- miler, and had made the National Team. She told them that she had just missed out on selection for the 1932 Olympics in Los Angeles. When Claud introduced himself and Finn, she seemed really pleased. "It's always nice to see a new recruit, and they're never too young to start. How old are you Finn?" "I was ten in January Miss". "And you really like the idea of doing some serious running?" "Yes, miss. I've been watching these boys practising and I think I could do better than some of them, at least." Claud chipped in, laughing, "the truth is Mrs Black, that he thinks he could do better than any of them. I'm afraid Modesty is not his middle name!" "Well" smiled Shirley, "there is only one way to find out. What do you think your best distance is Finn? 100 yards, 220 or 440?" "I don't mind miss. I'll try anything you say. But I think it would be a good idea if you showed me how to start properly. I've noticed they don't stand up to start; they all seem to crouch down somehow. Why do they do that?" "Well, there is no better place to begin learning anything in life than the start, is there? But before we do, it would be a good idea if you wore more suitable clothes and shoes. Do you have any proper running shoes? I mean spiked shoes? It makes a huge difference, especially on the bends. What size are you. We've got some spares in the bag, perhaps we could fit you up."

By the time Finn had been shown how to position himself on the blocks for a flying start, and had practised for a while, the other children had called it a day and gone home. That left just Finn, his father and Shirley Black. "Right, Finn, I think for starters we will time you over one hundred yards. Now don't expect to break records straight away - you won't do it. You are very young still. You just have to practise – it really is the key. It is not easy to train the body to perform at its very best, it takes time. I would be delighted if you could run the hundred yards in fifteen seconds at your age. But I'm thinking anyway that you may be a bit too "leggy" for the hundred, two-twenty might be a better distance for you. Anyway let's just see how you get on over a hundred yards first."

Finn's time was good, but a little over fifteen seconds. The start let him down – he had hardly had time to master it. "Right, take a few minutes to recover and then we'll try you over the 220. While you're getting your breath back, let's adjust your starting blocks a little." Out of earshot, Shirley turned to Claud. "I am very surprised he did so well Mr Browning. If he's never done a proper sprint before, his time was excellent. He'll crack fourteen seconds in no time if he perseveres. Quite remarkable. But I am pretty certain he will do even better at the furlong, or even the quarter mile, but he's too young for that just now, and it would be silly to overstretch him. Let's see him over the 220.

Finn had never run 220 yards before, but he had no difficulty with it, and did a time that pleased Mrs Black. "I think that's a very good start Finn. I would be delighted to give you coaching on a regular basis, if you would like to, and can spare the time." She turned to Claud. "He really has talent. It's perfectly clear that he could do well. Does he do any other sports?" "Oh yes" laughed Claud. "He does little else given the chance. He is in his school soccer team, and he began to learn squash rackets when he was still nine. He can beat all his three older brothers at that, and one of those is in the...." Claud's voice faltered. For a millisecond he had forgotten that Clive had been lost at sea. "I. I'm sorry Mrs Black. We have lost one of his brothers. His ship was torpedoed on the way to South Africa. He was eighteen." "Oh. Oh I'm so sorry. How dreadful for you. I don't know what to say. I live in dread of news that like about my husband." There was a pause and neither spoke. Then Shirley Black brightened: "I don't know much about squash, but it is a growing sport. It just needs more courts to be built, but of course there is not much chance of that while the war is on. Anyway, Finn should keep it up. Now, back to the track. I think the best thing would be to come when the other youngsters are not here. They're all older than Finn, and, if I'm honest, I think they are less talented, though I should not say so. Could Finn come down on Sunday afternoons? I can give him an undiluted hour then? How would that be?"

Finn and Claud hurried back home to tell the others. Bobby was delighted, the boys displayed indifference. Could there have been a touch of jealousy, Claud wondered to himself. There shouldn't be, of course, they should have expressed delight. Especially Kenneth, who was showing solid ability at rugger and was already in the Colts XV at KCS. And Douglas had made the School Second XV after all.

Bobby, with all the children at school much of the time, had joined the WVS, the Womens' Voluntary Service. Her grief at losing Clive had ebbed only slightly. Belle Peterson was perhaps her closest friend now and had tried tirelessly to raise Bobby's spirits. Persuading her to join the WVS was a master stroke, and Bobby was throwing herself into the work, tackling anything that she was asked to: manning canteens, tending the elderly at home, queuing for the aged at the shops, helping the injured after air raids and even driving ambulances on occasion. But it was her own exposure to grief that most helped her, in comforting the bereaved and the inconsolable. She wore her uniform proudly and at last felt she was really contributing to the War Effort. This work left little time for anything else, other than meeting the needs of her own family, especially the voracious appetites of her three sons. However, she did find time to manage the half dozen hens that the family had acquired and which pecked and clucked happily in the sturdy henhouse and run that Douglas had constructed, down the end of the garden. Finn had wanted a cockerel as well, "well, he could help us have more hens, and then more eggs Mummy". But the line had been drawn – "the neighbours would ostracise us if we had a cock crowing away at four in the morning Finn."

The Home Guard was now better organised and equipped than when Clive joined it and now Douglas decided that he was old enough, and high time, for him to "do a bit for his country." The trouble was, though, that he would not be seventeen until September, so technically too young to join. Douglas was undeterred, and a school friend told him that the recruiting people never asked to see a birth certificate, and if he looked old enough, and let his stubble grow for a few days they would grab him with open arms. They did, and one weekend in early Summer he walked out of the house to go for weekly training in "civvies" and returned proudly wearing a khaki uniform, with his white shirt and grey flannels tucked under his arm. "It's great Mum, I really feel I'm doing something now, and next weekend we are going to learn how to handle a rifle."

Air raids continued, though rarely in daylight, and even the night raids seemed to be carried out on a smaller scale. The RAF now had night-fighters, one of the most successful being the Bristol Beaufighter, a twin-engined aircraft, heavily armed with 20mm cannons in the nose, and six .303in machine guns in the wings. But the real Secret Weapon was RADAR, then in its infancy, but a deadly aid in tracking Germans at night. The story was put about, deliberately intended to mislead the gullible, that Group Captain John "Cats Eyes" Cunningham, the most successful of all night-fighter pilots, had extraordinary eyesight because he ate large quantities of carrots. This piece of propaganda served two purposes: it confused the German secret agents in Britain who reported it back to Berlin, and it encouraged the British population to grow, and eat, this very nutritious vegetable.

However, there was another reason for the decline in bombing raids on the UK. In June of 1941 Germany invaded the USSR. Hitler had never made any secret of his loathing of Communism, a credo totally at odds with Fascism. Despite this, Hitler and Stalin, the tyrannical dictator of the USSR, had in 1939 signed a Non-Aggression Pact. Privately, Hitler had every intention of setting out to eradicate the Communist threat to Germany's total domination of Europe and the Pact was useful in buying him time, while he subdued and subjugated Europe's western countries and the Balkans. It is possible in addition, that he harboured the delusion that he could enrol Great Britain as an ally in his campaign against the Communists. History has revealed that Winston Churchill tried to warn Stalin of the impending invasion of his country by Germany, only for Stalin to accuse Britain of trying to spread ugly rumours and appease Hitler. Just how wrong he was, he was soon to discover.

The Summer of 1941 bloomed. Hitler was at the height of his powers. The world, or at least a very large part of it, was at his feet, or rather under his heel. The Jews throughout Europe and Russia were being eliminated. And it would not be long before the British Empire was put to the sword from another direction, as Japan entered the war. What had been no more than a War in Europe and North Africa, terrible as that was, was soon to become a truly global conflict – The Second WORLD War.

CHAPTER 22

Clive's troopship was called "The Spirit of Sansom". Samson is best known for having his head served up on a platter at the request of Delilah. But it is also the name of a very beautiful, uninhabited island in the Isles of Scilly, off the Cornish peninsula.

When the torpedo struck, she was sailing some 250 miles west of the Canary Islands. The sun was about to dip below the horizon, a glowing orange ball that seemed to grow larger as it sank into the haze. Clive was on the uppermost deck watching the beautiful spectacle with his new friend Paul Ringer, a young airman from Lincolnshire. "It reminds me of marigolds" Paul said, "but even more beautiful." They were leaning on the starboard rail, the Western glow fading.

So great was the shudder of the explosion, on the port side, that Clive and Paul were thrown violently onto the deck. Instantly, the ship lurched steeply to port as the sea flooded into the massive gash below the water line. Clive could not stop himself sliding across the polished teak planking, until stopped by a protruding air vent. All over the great ship men were shouting and scurrying in all directions, like a giant disturbed ants' nest. Crew members appeared, calling to passengers to don life jackets and make for the lifeboats. The Captain's voice boomed from the P.A system: "Abandon Ship, Abandon Ship" Everyone had gone through the lifeboat drill several times, and were supposed to be wearing life jackets whenever they left their quarters, but many were not doing so and these included Clive and Paul. Quickly, crew members were struggling to release life boats on the stricken port side. At least these were overhanging the water. On the starboard side, rapidly rising as the shop listed more to port, the boats could not be lowered normally, as they were now not above the water, but the hull itself. Clive saw Paul trying and failing to struggle to his feet, bleeding badly from a head wound and clearly in great pain. "I hit that damned hatchway one hell of a thump. I think I've busted a leg and cracked a collar bone. You go over to the other side and see if you can get into a boat. I don't think I can manage it." "No, Paul. They'll be jam packed. Maybe I can release that raft. No one seems to have noticed it. If we can somehow get it over the rail, we can slide it down the side of the ship on this side, and follow it down. We'll have to be quick though, before this old bucket turns turtle."

Paul shook his head. "Clive for God's sake get real. I can't even stand and I can't help you with the raft. You must leave me and look after yourself. Go on. Go on man, you can't hang about. Do it!" Clive did not know he had such strength, but somehow he heaved Paul over his shoulder and struggled up the sloping deck to the rail. "I'll have to heave you over, Paul. It will hurt like hell, but at least you'll have a chance. I'll try to follow with the raft, if I can get it free. Here goes." Paul screamed in agony as he slid helplessly down the ship's side and with a huge splash into the sea. It was getting dark. Everywhere men were struggling in the water. It was obvious that many had never learned to swim, and many others were injured. Some wore life jackets, but most did not. A few had managed to release rafts and had clambered aboard and were trying to haul others out of the water. One lifeboat was floating upside down, with men desperately clinging to it.

Clive and two other men had managed to release a raft, but now the ship was listing so severely that they had no chance of lifting it clear of the starboard rail. Their only chance was to go "downhill" to the port side, where the sea was now lapping the deck of the sinking vessel. The raft was just a flat wooden platform, with four paddles strapped to it, and secured to steel buoyancy drums. Desperately, Clive and his new companions paddled to get away from "Samson". They knew she was doomed. In a few minutes she would take her final plunge and suck anyone near by down with her. Their task was made harder by other, desperate survivors clinging to the rope holds lashed all round the raft. One poor soul was clinging with the only good arm he had left, the other was just a mangled stump. All around them men cried out for help. For others it was too late – they were just floating corpses, already white and bloated. Many wore RAF uniforms. Others were naked. Debris was everywhere and the water stained with blood and thick slicks of oil. In the fading light it was hard to tell oil from blood, man from wreckage. Some of the men emitted ghastly choking and coughing sounds, their lungs full of water and oil. Probably, they had little chance of surviving. But still they were luckier than their mates who were trapped inside the ship and were destined soon to be taken to the ocean floor.

The man with an arm stump could hold on no longer, too weakened by loss of blood, and he slipped away into the darkness. Soon, another took his place and was strong enough to scramble on to the raft. He was unhurt and could take his turn with a paddle. Two other clingers-on tried to climb on board, but even with a helping hand, could not manage it. Soon, they too just drifted away. The cries and screams grew weaker, then faded. The four with the paddles continued their frantic paddling. Thank God the sea was calm. Clive wondered if Paul had made it, been picked up somehow by a boat or raft. "Samson" gave a final lurch. Then, with a huge hissing sound and grinding of metal, she made her final plunge and vanished. Very soon, the quiet became silence, but for the lapping of the water against the raft. There were no more shouts, nor cries, nor moans. Just the water lapping and the rhythmical swooshing of the paddles. In the end, the paddlers tired. Anyway, in the darkness they were unsure even if they were going in a straight line, let alone which direction. One by one, they laid down their paddles, and then their tired bodies. And they slept.

The first, faintest streak of light rose in the eastern sky. Shock had brought exhaustion, and then sleep, and temporary release from the terrible trauma of a few hours ago. Clive was roused by a cry from one of the other three. Turning wearily in his sleep, the man had fallen overboard. Quickly, Clive and one of the others, also roused, hauled the man back on to the raft. "I suppose you thought you were going to find a mermaid, you berk!" The light grew and the sun began its daily ascent. The sky had cleared overnight and now there was not the tiniest cloud. The four men searched the horizon, but there was nothing except the endless sea. No ship, no lifeboats, not even any wreckage. Not even a corpse. "We've got to watch out for the sun" said Freddy, the oldest of the quartet. He was a regular RAF man, a mechanic on his way to carry out maintenance on the training aircraft in Rhodesia.. "We must keep our heads covered, and cool too. Use a wet handkerchief if you've got one. Otherwise you'll get sunstroke and go barmy. That's if we don't roast to death first."

For three days they drifted. There were no iron rations on the raft, but that mattered little. Worse, far worse, was the thirst, a growing, insidious, all enveloping thirst. They all knew they must not drink sea water. Not a single drop. That way lead to madness. They agreed there was no point in paddling, it would just drain their strength and inflame their desperate need for water. On the second night Clive remembered something he had read in a novel, about stretching a cloth over an empty tin, putting a weight in the middle to make it dip a bit, and the drop in temperature overnight would induce condensation on the cloth. The moisture would collect in the centre of the fabric and pure water could be wrung out of the cloth. When the "Samson" was struck, Freddy had been on his way to the canteen for some tea, and had his mess tin clipped to his belt. It was still there. The experiment worked. The condensation was not much, but just enough for each man to have a few drops, enough to live a little longer. During the day, they kept cool by taking it in turns to take a dip in the sea, making sure to hold on to the raft with one hand.

They did not know it, but they were on a regular sea route between Spain and South America. Spain had not long emerged from a brutal and bloody

Civil War, which had only ended in 1939, when General Franco, with German and Italian assistance, had defeated the Communist Republicans. Though neutral during the Second World War, Franco's sympathies clearly were towards Hitler, and Germany took great care not to interfere with Spanish trading with South America, especially Argentina. On the fourth day of their ordeal, and now suffering dreadfully from malnutrition and thirst, Clive and his comrades were spotted by the SS "Francesca", making her regular supply run to Buenos Aires. It was a miracle they were still alive. Their raft was not designed to withstand rough seas. Had a storm blown up, and in their desperately weak condition, they would have been tossed into the sea like corks. But their gods were with them. The "Francesca" hove to and one of her lifeboats was lowered.

It is a rule of the sea that lives should be saved, whether friend or foe. But the "Francesca's" Captain was indifferent towards Great Britain, and certainly had no interest in ensuring Clive and the others got back there, Once recovered from their ordeal, they were brought to his Cabin. "Gentlemen, I hope you are feeling a little better than when we picked you up. You are extremely fortunate. Very few merchantmen are sailing these waters even in peace time, but in time of war the main inhabitants of this ocean are the German Navy! So far, they have been kind to Spanish shipping – I am sure you can understand why – so I can say to you with some assurance that we should be able to set you ashore at our next port of call. This will be Buenos Aires in Argentina. Until we reach there, you will be fed, but apart from one hour per day for exercise, I must request that you stay in your quarters. That is all."

They reached Buenos Aires ten days later, and were handed over to the Port Police. In those days Argentina, as well as Spain, was no friend of the British and its sympathies lay- thinly concealed, with Germany. It was not difficult then, to grasp the reaction of the Port Police to having four Englishmen dumped on their dockside.

The function of the Docks Prison was to save the City Authorities the irksome nuisance of trying and accommodating drunken seamen, illegal immigrants and stowaways, and any other ne'er- do- wells from visiting shipping. It was crowded and very hot. It was infested with vermin. Decent sanitation was thought to be a superfluous luxury. Clive could scarcely believe the filth and stench, and the degradation of the place. Genteel, middle-class Surbiton it certainly was not.

At least the four airmen were allowed to be together in one cell, even though it was intended for only two inmates. It contained nothing but a double-bunk and a slop bucket. Once a day the men were taken to a minute exercise yard and allowed to pace up and down for half an hour. They were not allowed to mix with the other inmates. Why, they were not told, but saw it as a relief, rather than an injustice. Time went by. They had no access to books, newspapers or radio, and they had no idea what was happening in the outside world. Their requests to see British Embassy representatives were ignored. None of the four spoke Spanish, nor their jailers any English. For eight weeks the world forgot them, and then the routine abruptly changed. They were given work. Freddy and Clive in the prison kitchen, the other two in the laundry. At last, they had someone else to rub shoulders with, and it was clear that the prisoners working in these places were regarded as a little less ant-social than the hard cases confined to their cells all day. They began to pick up a few words of Spanish. Only the odd few words at first, but enough to discover that none of the inmates had ever been given a trial or a fixed sentence. They had just been thrown into this hell-hole and would stay there until "the Guv, nor got pissed off with feeding them" and then they would be returned whence they came on the next available merchant ship from their own, or a friendly country.

By now, it was well into Springtime in England, eleven weeks since they sailed out of the port of Liverpool bound for South Africa.

Alvarez was a warder detailed to guard prisoners working in the kitchen. He was fairly new to the Prison and was only twenty years of age. He had spent his entire life living in B.A. and had little knowledge of his own country, let alone Europe, or Europeans. To him, Clive and Freddy were curiosities, lighter of hair and skin, and speaking a tongue of which he knew not a single word. But he was bright enough to grasp that these two foreigners were not as repugnant as the rest of the ragbag of humanity that passed through his hands This intrigued him, and he wondered why they were here. It is astonishing how two people can communicate when they do not have a common language. Signs, gestures, a smile or a frown or a quizzical look, maybe a sketch on a piece of paper, this is all that is needed. So it was that Alvarez got to know how Clive and Freddy and the other two in the Laundry came to be in the Port Prison.

Off duty one night, Alvarez mentioned to his father how he had come to meet two Englishmen at his workplace, and that there were two others there. Also that they had been dumped there off a Spanish freighter, that had picked them up in mid-Atlantic after their ship had been torpedoed. Alvarez Senior, in his turn, mentioned this story to his friend Giuseppe Sanchez, who worked as a gardener at the British Legation in B.A., and Sanchez in his turn, passed on this information to a clerk in the Diplomatic Minister's Office.

CHAPTER 23

It was Douglas who answered the phone. The line was crackly with static, the voice distant:

"Hello, am I speaking to Mr Browning? Mr Claud Browning?"

"No, this is his son Douglas. Who is this speaking , please?"

"My name is Fredericks. I am the British Diplomatic Minister in Buenos Aires in Argentina. I have some very good news for you. It is about your brother Clive, Mr Browning. He is alive and safe here in Buenos Aires, and in good health. I am hoping to arrange his return to England very soon, but meanwhile I am sure he would like to speak to you himself."

Douglas screamed. It was the loudest sound he could make, a yell of total, indescribable joy:

MUM! DAD! EVERYONE! IT'S CLIVE. HE'S ALIVE. HE'S ALIVE. HE'S ON THE PHONE. HE'S COMING HOME!

CHAPTER 24

During his incarceration, Clive had agonised every day at his inability to contact his family. He could well imagine the agonised emotions they must be suffering at the loss of a son and brother. Clive had always been sensitive to the feelings of others, and especially his mother's. He knew she would be inconsolable.

Each of us is born of woman, and is of her flesh and blood, and spirit. To any mother, the death of a child at any age, is like the severing of part of that woman. An amputation of her flesh, the tearing out of her heart. But now there was in Clive's life another woman and she, too, was heartbroken when she heard he had been lost at sea. Philippa Hannah was the one person outside his own family whom he loved, and would always love, and that love had been unforgettably consumated before he left for Africa.

The Minister allowed him a second phone call to England. When the phone rang, Philippa was languishing in a hot bath. Soon after Clive had set sail, she had been seconded back to the Air Ministry in London, the stint at High Ercall having been only a temporary posting. It had been a long day in Whitehall. In wartime Britain, the entreaty was "Save fuel – only fill your bath to five inches." Of course, it was a plea that could not be enforced, and on this evening Philippa was ignoring it wilfully. She was exhausted, and anyway, she had said to herself, I haven't had a soak for days.

The phone rang. Hurriedly, she wrapped a towel around her dripping body and ran to the bedroom.

"Hello, this is Bayswater 2219. Who is speaking please?"

"Guess who." Two short words only, and the line was stiff with static.

"Please don't play games. It's late. Who is this?" Her voice was angry and water was dripping on to the carpet.

"It's Clive. Clive, Philippa."

"Whoever you are, please stop fooling around. This is not funny, it's just cruel. I'm putting down the receiver."

"NO!! Philippa, it is me. It's Clive. I'm alive. Don't put down the phone. I survived the sinking. I was rescued and taken to Buenos Aires in South America. I'm coming home, darling. I don't know how long it will take, but I am coming home, and I want to see you. Oh God, I so want to be with you. I want to....oh, hell, I want to, you know. Like the night before I left. Oh, to hell with it, I'm sorry Mr Fredericks, Philippa I want to make love to you! I'm sorry sir, I just had to say it." Another voice came on the line. "Miss Hannah, this is Anthony Fredericks, I am the Senior Minister here. Perhaps I should not say this to someone I have never met, but for god's sake tell Mr Browning that you will, er, see him in the way he, er, means, otherwise I think he may do himself some harm!"

"Thank you Mr Fredericks. I know that this call may be monitored, so I will be brief with Clive. Please put him back on the line."

"Hello, darling."

"Clive, I understand. I want you, too, and I love you too. Just hurry home. Oh, dear Jesus, this is the happiest day in my life."

The phone went dead. The bath was still hot. Philippa jumped into it again wildly, not caring about the water splashing on the floor. She splashed and she laughed and she cried for joy. And then she splashed again, and again, just like a child…

CHAPTER 25

Clive's journey home took 13 days. It was circuitous: first, the US acceded to a request from London to fly him out of Argentina. He landed at Miami, in Florida ,and there switched planes to New York. The Americans were still outside the conflict in Europe and so it was safe for their freighters to ply their trade across the Atlantic. The four airmen returned thankfully to English soil at Liverpool, after a smooth voyage. An RAF transport aircraft flew them to Brize Norton in Oxfordshire.

The medical examination and de-briefing took two days. "You're in pretty good shape, Aircraftman. I am very surprised just how good" the M.O. announced. "Have you spoken to your family? No. a damned silly question, of course you will have, and I am sure you are anxious to see them. I recommended that you be granted three weeks leave, but I'm sorry, it has been cut back. I'm afraid the heat is on: we have lost a lot of aircraft and crew, and so you'll have to make do with only 14 days. Make the best of it. It could be your last leave for a long time, especially if you're packed off to Rhodesia again! Off you go!"

Clive phoned Philippa to ask her if she would meet him at Waterloo and travel down to Surbiton with him. "Oh darling, I am desperate to see you, but you must put your family first. It's only fair. Then you can come up to the flat and we can be together, just the two of us. How about you spend an hour with the family and then thirteen days and twenty-three hours with me! I hope you won't be too hungry, because I want to keep you in bed the whole time. Every minute. And I just hope you are not too weak, because the demands I shall make upon your poor body will be very exhausting."

Waterloo to Surbiton takes eighteen minutes non-stop. To Clive it seemed like eighteen hours. To his family, it seemed like eighteen days. But what was that, compared with the dark weeks and months of despair they had endured. The train passed through all the familiar stations at speed: Clapham Junction, Wimbledon, Raynes Park, New Malden. Soon after Berrylands, the last station before Surbiton, it slowed. Approaching Surbiton there are two road bridges crossing the railway line. First, the Iron Bridge, where the road it carries runs from Tolworth to Kingston-on-Thames. How many times had he cycled or walked over that bridge? Hundreds it must have been, and hundreds of times over the last dark months had he wondered if he would ever cross it again. The family would have walked over it to reach the Station where they would greet him. Only two hundred yards now. Sickeningly, the signals turned red and the train came to a halt. Craning out of the window, he could see the Station, and he knew they would all be there on the platform, seeing the train waiting, and wondering if he would really be on it. Slowly, agonisingly slowly, the train edged forward.

Finn was the first to spot him. He broke away from the others and ran down the platform towards the approaching train. Waving, shouting. "Clive. Clive. Cliiivvve!

Clive swept his little brother into his arms and hugged him and ran his hand through the little boy's blond hair. Little boy? In just three months he cold see he had grown. "Hello, Worm. How are you? Have you missed your big brother?" Clive could not choke back his emotions. He felt the dampness in his eyes, the lump in his throat, as he embraced his mother, and then his Dad and then, in turn, Douglas and Kenneth. There weren't any words. The moment did not need words. Words were for later. To see, to touch was all that was needed.

The Brownings were whole again. One family. One love. Re-united.

Kenneth was a very practical boy. He was also a sweet tooth. He was sometimes called "Billy Bunter" after the fictional schoolboy character renowned for his gluttony. With rationing so strict, it was difficult for him to indulge as he would wish, but he was sufficiently disciplined to save his sugar ration, and also to trade with school friends: their sugar, for his collection of shrapnel. He was also an eager learner, and by reference to cookery books in the Public Library, had become a competent baker of cakes. As soon as he heard of his brother's "Return from the Dead" , a tale he related with imaginative embellishments to his school chums, he cajoled even more ingredients out of them, including a dollop of Icing Sugar. It was natural enough that Bobby had prepared as fine a Coming Home dinner as she could manage, and friends and neighbours, even including the redoubtable Mrs Boughton next door, had rallied round to contribute to the celebration. Mr Boughton, yes gruff Mr B., was a connoisseur of wine and had carefully accumulated before the war some excellent Burgundy. Terrorised by dire threats from his wife if he did not do so, he presented Claud with a bottle of 1932 Vintage, even managing a thin smile as he did so. The Petersons chipped in as well. Dr Peterson had indulged in game shooting in Scotland, before moving south to Surbiton, and used his contacts on Deeside to despatch not one, but two brace of finest pheasants - frozen, of course, as it was out of season, but none the less palatable for that. But the Piece de Resistance was Kenneth's cake. It was square and iced in blue icing, to represent the Atlantic Ocean. At one side, in bright yellow, was an outline of the Moroccan Coast and Sahara Desert, and on the other side, in green, was an outline of the East coast of South America. Not far from the African Coast was a blob shaped like a ship, in red, and from that point a line had been drawn to a point in South America, marked B,A. for Buenos Aires. Further lines had been traced from there to "NY" for New York (actually down the side of the cake, and then a final line round the cake's remaining perimeter to "S" for Surbiton. Next to the "S" was the message: "Welcome Home Clive". It was a work of great accomplishment and Kenneth had devoted all his skill and many painstaking hours to produce it. Clive smiled as it was brought to the dinner table. "Well done, Ken, it's wonderful and I am very grateful. It must have taken you days and days to do. I will treasure this moment. But his smile was short-lived. It just died and his face became set and distant. It was the red blob. The "Samson". But I'm sorry Ken, all of you, it raises terrible memories that I shall never forget. That evening when it happened was so peaceful, so beautiful. The sea was utterly tranquil, like burnished gold. I was on the rail with my friend Paul. We were happy and excited at being where we were and what we were going to do. To be flyers in the RAF. We were going to learn how to fight, and defend our country. WE had become men, it seemed. Then, in a moment, it all changed. A huge explosion. The ship shuddered and then began to list. Everyone shouting and rushing about. Pandemonium. We could hear the screams from down below decks. Paul was injured. I had to help him over the side. I never saw him again. Men were floundering, covered in oil, begging for help. It was so terrible. Oh, I am so lucky. I'm here with you. But for hundreds of others that sunset was the last thing they ever saw. I'm sorry, I don't want to spoil this wonderful occasion. But seeing that red blob on your marvellous cake, Ken, just brought it all back. And I am especially sorry for you, Finn, you're far too young to be hearing about men dying. I apologize. Now. Let's get on with the party!"

For a couple of days, Clive relaxed at home with his family. Friends called to see him. He went to the pub and was greeted as a hero by those who knew him. Not so many survive being torpedoed. But two days were enough. As much as he loved being back home, he was desperate to see Philippa as well. Of course, he wanted her physically and knew that she wanted him in the same way. But it was more than that. He was certain beyond any possible doubt that he loved her and wanted to share the rest of his life with her. He knew, too, that "the rest of his life" might not be very long. He had escaped death once, but flying bombers over Germany was infinitely more dangerous. The chances were small of surviving a tour of 30 missions. A few weeks only, that was all. The Luftwaffe was now developing sophisticated Radar systems that enabled their night fighters, like their British counterparts, to detect attacking bombers before they ever reached their targets. And if one evaded them, there was still the danger of German flak. Clive had been told that he would learn the trade of rear gunner in Lancaster bombers. The rear gunner was enclosed in a swivelling glass turret, a bubble, in the tail of the aircraft. His only access to the rest of the aircraft and crew was via two small twin doors that opened outwards from the bubble. So it was only when this bubble was aligned correctly that entrance or exit could be made. If the turret was trained laterally, then the doors opened into space, not the rear of the fuselage. But – oh there was a big "but" – the gunner's parachute was stowed in the fuselage: there was insufficient room for it in the turret. So if the turret jammed, or was damaged when it was misaligned, then its occupant was trapped. Doomed to go down with the aircraft, or free fall through space. Clive did not disclose this information to his family, nor to Philippa, though as a WAAF Officer she probably knew anyway.

In Victoria Road, Surbiton's main shopping street, there was a jeweller's called Tyrrell's. On RAF Aircraftman's pay, Clive could not afford anything expensive, but Mr Tyrrell understood this well enough and produced a tray of second-hand rings for Clive to inspect. "There is one rather unusual one here you might like Mr Browning. It's called a Crossover design: two diamonds appearing to intertwine. It reminds me a bit of a handclasp. Two people shaking hands, or dare I say, kissing." Clive loved it immediately "Yes, that's the one alright, but I need to know the price before committing to it." "No. Mr Browning, just tell me what you can afford. I am sure we can make a satisfactory agreement. I served in the Great War, and I know a little about Service pay, so don't worry, please."

Philippa was late getting back to the flat, but Clive was not yet due from Surbiton. All day the thought of seeing him had distracted her from her work. She just could not concentrate. Papers had been mislaid, even misfiled, telephone messages forgotten. Her boss had noticed and asked if everything was alright. "Oh, yes, sir. I'm very sorry. It's just that I am seeing my boyfriend this evening. We haven't met since he was torpedoed in January. He was on the "Sansom" when she went down, if you remember, sir." "Oh, of course. I had forgotten. That was a terrible business. We lost so many young airmen. I would let you go early, but I'm afraid there is just too much at the moment."

Philippa stripped off her uniform and ran the bath. A day in the office and then the crowded Tube had left her in no state to greet Clive as she was. The warm water enveloped her. She closed her eyes and dreamed of the moment when she would see him again. In only one hour. Or less. And then she could hold him. Feel it was real. Caress him. Her mind began to slip into that strange void between consciousness and sleep, where it knows it is sliding away…

The bathroom door opened silently. Clive stood looking at her, stretched naked before him, her eyes closed, oblivious to his presence. Silently, he tiptoed to the bath and knelt beside it. Still she dreamed in her own private world, unaware. He could not resist her. His hand stretched out and gently covered her breast. She did not open her eyes, but she knew it was him. "Kiss it", she whispered. The nipple stood erect and he kissed it, first with his tongue and then completely with his lips. "Now undress and get in with me. There's room enough for both of us, and I need to feel all of you. Every inch." She opened her eyes then, and saw him for the first time as he stood looking down at her. "Do you like what you see? Do I have a nice enough body for you Mr Browning?" She asked. "I hope so. I want to give it to you. Now hurry up and get in before the water gets cold!"

Hours later, exhausted from their passion, they heard the air raid sirens wailing their dire warning to all of London. Philippa rose from the bed and drew back the blackout curtains. Searchlights swept the sky. It was a clear night. A quarter moon. In the distance she heard the thump-thump of ack-ack fire and the crump of exploding bombs. Clive lay still, looking at Philippa's naked body silhouetted against the window, back-lit by the flashes of shell and bomb and roving , searchlight beams.

It was then, only then, that he remembered the ring. She still had her back to him, and he went over to her and wrapped his arms around her, feeling the warmth of her against his chest and groin. "That's nice" she sighed. "Hold me tight and don't let go. Not ever, please."

"I have something I want to give you, darling" he replied.

"Oh sweetheart, I don't need presents. You are enough. You must know that."

"You don't understand. Turn round and look at me." Philippa turned. There was no embarrassment any more at their nakedness.

"What is it you want to give me, darling. It must be very small, I can't see anything in this moonlight. Well, I can see one thing", her eyes lowered to his groin and she laughed "And it is a bit small I suppose."

"You are disgusting Philippa. Be serious. I want this to be a special moment that we will always remember." Clive knelt on one knee in front of her.

"Philippa Hannah, will you marry me?

"Of course I will, darling. It's almost as if we already are, and well, after tonight, we really should be. Yes, Clive. I will marry you. And I will love you, and I will bear you children. Now get off your knees and let's go back to bed. Oh, what was it you wanted to give me?"

Clive unclutched his hand and taking her left hand, slipped the ring on her fourth finger. "For you. For life. I hope you like it."

"Oh, Clive. It's beautiful. It's sparkling even in this dim light. I love it, and I will never take it off. By the way, though, what would you have done with it if I had said No?

"Oh, I knew you couldn't resist me!

And they went back to bed.

CHAPTER 26

Clive and Philippa were married in Kensington Registry Office, two days before the end of his leave. It was hurried, as Clive was due to leave for Rhodesia for the second time, and it would be several months before they could be together again. Both families, the Hannahs and the Brownings, attended. In these times of war,, marriages were often a low key ceremony, with little or no Reception afterwards. Both the bride and groom wore their RAF uniforms, she a Flying Officer, he a mere Aircraftman. Douglas was Best Man and, to her immense surprise, Bobby was asked to be the Matron of Honour - a highly unusual invitation for a Mother-in-Law to be! Finn was a natural to be a page, and in these austere times there was no question of a special outfit, just his school uniform. Bobby did persuade him to have a haircut for the occasion.

Though long retired from the Army, Sir Henry, with the help of a local seamstress to let out his trousers, was able to get into his General's uniform. Lady Hester wore a long, burgundy coloured dress, probably not worn for ten years judging by the smell of mothballs. It was a joyful day. It helped that all involved already knew each other. From Rosedown, Finn's dear old friends Herbert and Findlay attended. "My, my" said Old Herbert "How you'm grown, young Finn, and it seems no time at all since we last saw you." "Ay" chimed in Old Findlay, "Hardly knew it was you, and looking so smart, too. How does living in the Smoke suit you, young'un?" "Well, its alright I suppose, but all that bombing's a bit scary when it gets too close. And once I saw a German plane coming down and the crew baling out. But I think on the whole I'd rather be at Rosedown, going after rabbits with you Mr Findlay."

The General and Lady Hester were staying at Claridge's, widely regarded as the best hotel in London. They had taken a suite and (after a little persuasion of the Manager) been allowed to bring into the hotel a case of champagne, brought up for the occasion from Rosedown. "Well" Lady Hester had pointed out, "The hotel can't let us have any, so they could hardly refuse us bringing our own, could they ?" After the ceremony, all the guests, and happy couple, gathered in the suite. Even in the austere days of war, the hotel was able to produce a fine table of sandwiches and patisserie. It was a long time since Claud and Bobby had tasted fizz, and for the boys, it was a new experience. In Finn's case, the ration was severe, just half a glass.

Douglas was a bag of nerves at the thought of proposing a toast to the bridesmaids, especially as the only "bridesmaid" was his own mother. In the event he did well, and ended by saying that if Philippa came to love her as much as he did, then it was no more than she deserved. And it would be quite nice to have a sister at last, even if she was only one "In Law".

It had been Clive and Philippa's plan to spend their wedding night in her flat. There was no way on an Aircraftsman's pay that he could afford an hotel. It was as the evening was drawing to a close, that the General dropped his bombshell.

"Clive, Philippa, I know that it is the custom for the bridegroom to whisk his bride away in a fine car and for all of us to wave goodbye and make unseemly comments about the night ahead. Well, I propose to reverse the process. It is all of us that will wave goodbye, whilst you stay right here. I have arranged for your mother's and my effects to be removed from this suite, and for you to take up residence here, not only for tonight, but for tomorrow as well. Your and Clive's clothes and toiletries have been spirited here by Herbert. Ladies and gentlemen, I have the feeling that we should all head for the door! Oh, and don't worry, Clive, you don't have to foot the bill. Anything else you need just ask the management. Oh yes, I nearly forgot, I have also arranged a change of clothes for each of you, courtesy of Harrods. Cost me damned near a year's Clothing Coupons, so I couldn't afford pyjamas. I doubt you'll need them, anyway!"

"Henry! How outrageous" bellowed Lady Hester.

Three days later, Clive left England for the second time. Leaving his bride, and no less his family, was a sickening experience, exacerbated by the memory of what had happened to him the first time. This time, however, he flew in a Sunderland flying boat , escorted part of the wayby a flight of Hurricane fighters from the squadron based on the Isles of Scilly, to Gibraltar. There, he switched to a convoy of freighters with Royal Navy destroyer escorts and sailed safely to Alexandria in Egypt. Two further flights, the first to Nairobi and the final leg to Salisbury, completed his passage.

Months later he returned to England, as a Flight Sergeant and as a fully trained Air Gunner.

He would soon come to use his new skills.

CHAPTER 27

War or no war, Finn was a happy boy. Overjoyed at the safe return of his favourite brother – even if he had gone off again – and doing well at school, there was not even a tiny cloud to blight Finn's joy at life's course. His mangled ear had long since healed completely and he had persevered with his track training with Shirley Black. In the warmer months of late Spring and early Summer, squash tended to take a back seat, though he kept his hand in once or twice a week. George Peterson had by now become quite proficient at the game, at least to a level to exercise Finn a little, though he had been careful not to demoralize him by playing all-out. So athletics was the real focus for his Summer sport activity.

Shirley Black was more than ever convinced that Finn could reach very high levels of attainment as a sprinter, but should better concentrate on the 220 yards and quarter mile distances. Mr Carne at Branchester House regarded athletics as only a minor sport – there was just the Sports Day itself in the Summer Term, and no practise sessions. However, after discussion with Mrs Black, it was agreed that Finn could miss out on the school's cricket afternoon and use the time instead to work with her at the track, or just train on his own when she could not be there with him.

On one such afternoon, as Bobby sat reading at the track side and Finn practised starts and short sprints, a tall, fair haired man approached and sat on a bench nearby. He was quite young, perhaps in his early or mid-thirties, she guessed. He wore a check sports jacket over an open-necked shirt and grey flannel trousers.

"Good afternoon, madam." Bobby was a little startled, but nodded her head politely. "Is that your son?" In those long gone days it was rare for gentlemen to approach strange women and even rarer for a woman to respond unguardedly. Society was far more formal then, and women in England did not welcome uninvited approaches. "Why do you ask? I do not think we know each other, do we?" "Oh, please, excuse me, madam. I do not mean to be discourteous, nor to intrude." "That is exactly what you are doing, sir, as you must realize" Bobby's response was stiff. "Madam, I apologize. It has been unforgivable." The man reddened , then rose and hurried away.

Bobby tried to resume her reading, but her concentration was broken. She felt unsettled and knew she had been ungracious in her rebuff. The man had made no attempt at over familiarisation, and had clearly been embarrassed at her reaction to him. A few minutes later, Shirley Black arrived back from the track and came and sat with her. "Finn is doing marvellously well, Bobby. I am really thrilled with him." Finn ambled across from the track. "Finn, well done. Those starts are definitely sharper. Keep it up." "Thanks Mrs Black, but I think I can still do better. By the way, Mum," Finn turned to Bobby "Who was that man you were talking to? You're always telling me not to talk to strangers, and you didn't know him, did you?"

Shirley Black interposed: "Oh Bobby, does he mean that tall fair-haired chap watching the athletes? I know him. His is a terrible story. Like you, he is Norwegian. When the Nazis invaded Norway he became a partisan, fighting them from mountain hideouts. A group of them would come down at night and sabotage German installations, and blow up trucks and so on. One night things went terribly wrong and the group were ambushed. Lars was shot in the shoulder, but managed to escape. Most of the others were either killed or captured. The dead ones were the lucky ones. Those captured were brutally tortured, and forced to give information about their comrades. Once they knew who they were, they went to their homes and took their wives and children, and anyone else living in the house, and shot them – even the tiny babies. It was barbaric. They were utterly merciless. Amongst those they shot were Lars's wife and son. When Lars discovered what had happened, he determined to escape from Norway and take his revenge by fighting with the British. He was lucky – many Norwegians were being secretly spirited out by crossing into neutral Sweden. His shoulder wound was treated there, but still has not fully healed. So now he is here in the military convalescent home just down the road in Tolworth. I met him much as you did. He came to watch the children on the track. He is broken-hearted at losing his wife, and his young son Kjell. But he has this deep, blazing anger to go back to Norway to help his country, rather than join the British army. He has sworn to kill as many Germans as he can lay his hands on. He says – excuse me Finn – he wants to kill each one very slowly, with a knife. You may wonder why he is watching my little cubs on the track. The answer is that he was a fine athlete in the pre-war days, in fact he represented Norway in the 1936 Olympics in Berlin. He was a high jumper. Watching these kids helps him put the horrors out of his mind for a little while."

Bobby's remorse at the cold way she had repelled the man's innocent approach was now ten times worse, and there was salt in the wound in the knowledge that he was one of her own countrymen, and she had never realized it. Both his, and her English accents were faultless, as is the way with many Scandinavians. She resolved to make amends.

Finn had been totally enthralled by Shirley Black's account of this tall, blond Norwegian's exploits. Here, at least until a few minutes ago, was a real, live killer of Germans, watching him running and speaking with his mother. He was awe struck. To Finn, to any young boy, the man was a hero, a godlike figure. "Mum, do you think we will meet him again? I would like to listen to his stories about fighting the Germans". "Yes, Finn, I would like to see him again also. I want to apologize to him for being so rude. Now Mrs Black has told us where he is staying, I will ask him if he would like to come to tea and meet your father and brothers. He must be dreadfully lonely. It would be a kindness, the least we could do."

A few days later, Bobby phoned the Convalescent Home and asked to speak to Lars Hansen. A short pause. Then a muffled voice calling "Hansen, it's for you. Some lady!"

"This is Lars Hansen, who is speaking please?" Bobby's reply was in Norwegian:

"Mr Hansen, my name is Roberta Browning. You do not know me, but last week you spoke to me at the athletic track. I was discourteous towards you, and I am very sorry. I'm afraid I am unaccustomed to such approaches from strangers, but Mrs Black has since explained your background, and I would like to apologize. Also, I understand that you are a Norwegian, as I am, so we have a common link, but I have lived in England so long that I imagine that you did not detect I was not English. The same is so with you - your English is utterly perfect." "Mrs Browning, it is very kind of you. Of course I should be happy to meet you, and, perhaps, your young son. He is a promising athlete. That is clear from watching him. However, I should perhaps tell you that I do not expect to be here at this Home for much longer. The war is not going well, and I wish to serve the Allied cause in some way. And the sooner, the better."

Lars and Bobby agreed to meet at Peggy Brown's Tearooms in Surbiton. There would be no time to arrange a visit to the family at St. Mark's Orchard. She had, of course, told Claud of the encounter with Lars, and he was quite happy for her to meet him. In any case, Finn would join them as soon as he came out of school. Finn was dying to meet his new hero in the flesh, and his presence would forestall any tittle-tattle by Bobby's friends who might see her with this male stranger.

Lars entered Peggy Brown's a short while after Bobby, who had selected a table looking out onto Victoria Road. As Lars approached her and shook hands, Bobby noticed the faintest wince flash across his face. "Excuse me, Mrs Browning, my shoulder still troubles me a little. Yet another reason for my hatred of the Nazis, though certainly not the chief one. They managed to put a bullet through it. Would you prefer tea or coffee?" Lars smiled, a smile that entranced Bobby. She loved the creases at the corner of his eyes. They were kind eyes, his gaze steady. Not the eyes one would expect of a merciless killer. "I hope I may make amends for my importunity at our first encounter, and I also hope you will call me Lars." Bobby laughed. Already she felt totally at ease with this magnetic man. "Of course, and please call me Bobby. I know it does not sound Norwegian, but my husband thought Roberta sounded a little too formal, so "Bobby" I became. The English are very odd in some ways, they even turn a female name into a male derivative.!" Lars grinned. Again those laugh-lines creased his cheeks. He poured the tea and as he passed the cup, their hands touched momentarily. It was as if his hand was a live electric wire. A tremor shot up her arm. Their eyes met for a second, but the second seemed an eternity to her. Something had passed between them. Indefinable, but real. There was something basic, animal about it. It alarmed her and yet thrilled her simultaneously. "You are very beautiful, Roberta. You are not a "Bobby", I think. No , to me you are a Roberta – it is a beautiful name." Lars passed her the plate of biscuits. As she put out her hand to take one, Lars took it gently into his and this time held it. She did not resist and again their eyes met. "You remind me very much of my late wife Else. I have not held a woman's hand since she died." Bobby drew her hand away. "I am so sorry Lars, but this is not right. I may be compromised. We are in full view of everyone in the tearoom and people passing by. And this is not to mention that we have only just met.

I understand your loss, and your need, but I am happily married. And Finn will be here at any minute." For a moment Lars' eyes closed, his face saddened, but then a faint smile reappeared. "It's alright Roberta, please don't worry. It was just a memory…" Quietly, Bobby said "Do you wish to tell me what happened to you and to your family? Please do, if it will ease your pain, and I do not mean the pain in your shoulder, I mean the pain in your heart."

As she spoke, an Army Staff Car pulled up outside, easy enough to spot with its brown and green camouflage livery. A young girl in ATS uniform emerged from the driver's seat, and waved as she saw Lars seated at the window table. "I am sorry, sir, to interrupt your meeting, but there has been a call for you. You must come immediately. Excuse me , madam." Lars rose. "I think this young lady will not take No for an answer, Roberta. I will have to do as she says." Turning to the ATS girl he said "I will be out in a minute; just wait for me."

"I'm so sorry, Roberta. We have had such a brief time together. You have given me a moment of happiness that I thought I would never feel again. Thank you for that. Maybe I will come back one day. I should like to know you better, and also to have time with Finn and the rest of your family." He bent and kissed her hand. "Thank you." He turned and left. As the Staff Car drew away, he waved.

Bobby sipped her tea and waited for Finn. He arrived two minutes later. "Hello, Mum, where is Mr Larsen. Hasn't he got here yet?" "Yes, he came, Finn, but unfortunately he got called away unexpectedly. I don't know when we will see him again. People come and go so much in wartime, my darling. But when he comes back, I will make sure he comes to see you running." In her heart she did not think he would ever return. There had been something final, fatal almost about his parting words: "Maybe I will come back one day."

A week later an envelope arrived addressed to Finn. The postmark was Fort William in Scotland. It was from Lars and it read;

Dear Finn,

I have had to leave Tolworth and I am working here in Scotland for a time. Although it is summer, the weather is not kind. Many days it is raining and fog as well. Just like my home in Norway!

I am sorry we did not meet for tea. I would have liked that. There are two things I would like to say to you. The first is that I truly believe you have the potential to be an outstanding athlete. I know one when I see one, because before the war I WAS one myself. But even with your natural talent, it is essential that you practise, practise, practise. Then, when you are tired and want to stop, go on practising a while longer! It is the only way to be really successful.

The second thing is that I think, if we had met, that you would have wanted to ask me about the things that happened, and the things that I had to do, before I came to England. They were terrible things, and in my heart I hated doing them. But for the sake of defeating the evil of Nazism, I had to kill men. Even though they were my enemies, they were still human beings – husbands, fathers, sons. It was not something to be proud of – it was just part of war. It is just Man's folly. It is born of Man's greed, envy, hatred of fellow men. Hopefully, before you are old

enough to fight, the war will be over and the world will be free
again and at peace.

You are a fine boy, just like my son was a fine boy. I hope one
day we will meet again.

Run hard!
Your friend,

Lars Hansen

A second letter arrived in the same post, also from Fort William, this one addressed to Bobby. It read:

I can say little, because if it has not already been said, then it cannot be
Said....I think you will understand. Thank you for our so brief
Acquaintanceship. It may surprise you, but twenty minutes in a teashop
Has given me strength to go on and do what has to be done to rid Norway
Of these evil people.
Very much, I hope that one day we will meet again, and that I may then
Meet your husband and all your sons. Take care of them all, and take care
Of yourself.
Lars

Bobby showed the letter to Claud. "An interesting man" Claud said "I wish I could have met him too. Whatever did you say to him to rouse him so much? Incidentally I notice that the letters are postmarked Fort William. That's interesting, the Royal Marine Commandos train up there, though I am not supposed to say so.- the Official Secrets Act, you know. I wonder if Hansen is up there with them!" Bobby felt a tremor of fear. She hoped that her husband was wrong. Probably, they would never know.

CHAPTER 28

In the summer of 1941 an event took place that changed the course of the war. Apart from the Axis's strategic need to control both shores of the Mediterranean Sea, the war had, until this moment, been an essentially European affair. This event was spawned by one of Hitler's twin obsessions. The first was the eradication of the entire Jewish population of Europe and by mid-1941 this was well under way. Many had been gassed or shot to death in Concentration Camps. Most of those still surviving would have been exterminated by the war's end in 1945. This left his second obsession: his hatred of Communism. In 1939 Hitler had signed a Non-Aggression Pact with Josef Stalin, the USSR's dictator. In retrospect it can be seen that this was no more than a stalling device, to hold the USSR at bay, whilst Western Europe was crushed. And by mid-1941 this also had been largely achieved. Only offshore Britain remained undefeated and in Hitler's estimation she was a spent force. How wrong he was!

For months, there had been warning signs that Hitler was soon going to look East. Indeed, Winston Churchill sent a message to Stalin warning him of Hitler's intentions, but this was rejected on the grounds that Britain was just spreading ugly rumours. The assault on Russia was known by the codename "Barbarossa". It was launched in the early hours of June 22nd. The scale of the attack was massive, taking place along a front of nearly two thousand miles, stretching from the Black Sea in the South to the Baltic Sea in the North. It involved over three million Germans, opposing an even greater number of Russian troops. The sheer scale of the offensive, its appalling brutality and the massive loss of life both military and civilian personnel, has no equal in the whole history of mankind. Numerically, the Soviet forces outnumbered their attackers, but in the early stages they were no match for the leadership, training and equipment of the Germans. The speed of the German advance was mesmerising and by the end of the very first day they had advance eighty or more kilometres in some places. Their progress deep into Russian territory continued throughout the summer, but with unremitting losses of men and equipment. By the end of August, German casualties had exceeded the whole of the previous two years of the war. Approaching half a million lost, of whom probably more than a quarter were dead. The Russians lost over a quarter million men, three thousand guns and a similar number of tanks and armoured vehicles. At the onset of the campaign the Russian Air Force, far inferior to the Luftwaffe, had largely been eliminated.

But, as Summer turned to Autumn, the situation began to change. The temperature plummeted, as it always does, and the dry plains became seas of mud. The speed of the German advance slowed in consequence. Troops were ill equipped for these conditions, as were their vehicles. Worse, Hitler personally took a hand in the direction the operation should follow. Moscow, he decreed, should be taken at virtually any cost, but more than that he ordered that Leningrad (now St Petersburg) in the North, should also be overcome, and no German ground should be relinquished in any circumstances. But The Little Corporal failed to appreciate two factors that would weigh catastrophically against him. First, the Russian weather. Inadequate account was taken of the sub-zero conditions of bitter cold and driving snow. Many Germans literally froze to death due to lack of insulating clothing. Their vehicles became bogged down in the mud, or their engines simply froze-up. Second, the Russians were pouring huge resources into the training of men and the production of guns and equipment. German triumph was turning into hideous disaster and ultimate defeat, but not before horrific, suicidal attempts to overcome the Russian Bear had been made.

At almost the end of 1941, on December 7th, a second event took place that further determined the eventual outcome of World War II. The Japanese attacked the American Fleet at Pearl Harbour, in Hawaii, which finally brought America into the war, and turned it into a fully global conflict. The background to this assault was the spectacle of the war in Europe, that opened Japan's eyes to the possibility of a parallel conquest of South-East Asia, and the vast wealth that would bring. It looked easy, with only the USA standing in its way. It was a catastrophic misjudgement of the strength and determination of the American people and their military capability. The plan was to blitzkreig the American Pacific fleet, which was concentrated in Pearl Harbour, and swiftly to follow this by overrunning such countries as Korea, Thailand, New Guinea, Malaya, the Phillipines, Borneo and the South Pacific Island States such as Fiji, Samoa and the Aleutians. All this , Japan determined, could be achieved with small losses, before the USA could recover to foil its ambitions. As for the Allies, well Britain and her Empire's military resources were already fully stretched against Germany and Italy.

The attack on Pearl Harbour was carried out by carrier-based squadrons of Japanese bombers and fighters, and began at 8 am on Sunday 7th December. It is incredible, but true, that some ten days earlier, the American military and naval commanders on Hawaii were warned of an imminent attack. Complacently, they ignored the warning and did nothing, either to disperse the fleet, or to protect the hundreds of planes on their air bases.

Even forty-five minutes before the first Japanese aircraft appeared, a radar sighting of them by a young American officer was interpreted as a squadron of American bombers that were expected that morning from mainland America. That warning, also, was not acted upon.

In the space of two hours terrible damage was wrought on the Americans. The USS Arizona, a great battleship, was hit by a bomb that blew up her ammunition magazine. In minutes, she went to the bottom with her eleven hundred crew. She remains there today as a permanent memorial of that terrible day. Another battleship, the "Nevada" was hit by torpedoes and capsized and sank in less than a minute, taking her complement of four hundred sailors with her. At the time nearly all were below decks, many still in their bunks. They were alive, but trapped, with no chance of escape. Some were still alive seventeen days later on Christmas Eve, but doomed to die on the ocean bed in their impenetrable steel tomb. By 10 am, only two hours after the first bomb was dropped, the attack was over. Besides the two battleships, six other warships were destroyed or disabled. Scores of aircraft were disabled on the ground. Two and a half thousand American military and civilians died and a further thousand or more were wounded. But what the Japanese failed to realize was that none of the American aircraft carriers were in harbour and eighty or more other warships were undamaged and ready to fight. The next day,, December 8th, the USA declared war on Japan, and were joined immediately by Great Britain.

Rashly, oh so rashly, Germany and Italy declared war on the USA. Had they but realized it, they were signing their own death warrant. The tide began to turn. Whilst Pearl Harbour had been a success for Japan in military terms, in the context of the coming years it was akin to poking one's head into a hornet's nest. Mighty as was Japan's military might, the forces that would confront it were mightier still.

CHAPTER 29

Day by day, Finn's scrapbook was becoming thicker. Although the events of 1939 and 1940 had all taken place before he was given the book, Finn's father had access to his newspaper's archives and had dug out copies of most of the major events. Thus there were cuttings and photographs of the Battle of the River Plate (almost the only item on the credit side), Germany's invasion of Denmark and Norway, the fall of France and the British withdrawal at Dunkirk, the terrible losses of merchant ships (much watered down by the Censors), and more than anything, the Blitz – the Luftwaffe's aerial assault on London and Britain's other great cities. In more recent times there was the sinking of the Bismarck, but even this notable event had to be seen in the light of the appalling loss of HMS Hood.

In that Summer of 1941, Finn began pasting in cuttings showing events on the Russian Front. As the year wore on these scenes would become ever more terrible, as the Russians' resistance grew stronger, and the weather more bitter. There began to appear pictures of German transport, much of it horse-drawn, becoming bogged down in the mud and snow and slush, of massive fires in the cities, raging under the bombardment of German artillery, of frostbitten German soldiers, literally frozen into clothing designed for the milder climates of Western Europe, even to the point of being unable to relieve themselves in the sub-zero temperatures.

To this, as the year drew towards a close, Finn pasted in the scenes of devastation at Pearl Harbour: crippled and sinking warships, their crews leaping into the water to save themselves from a watery death; great palls of oily, black smoke rising into the bright blue morning sky, smashed aircraft and hangars at the US airbases.

But before these cataclysmic milestones in the war's progression, in Finn's young life there were other events taking place. Towards the end of the Summer Term at Branchester House, Mr Carne arranged the hire of the sports field at the Old Paulines Rugby club in Thames Ditton, for Thursday July 23rd.. The annual School Sports would take place, commencing at 2.00pm. Sports being of minor importance, there would be no field events such as throwing the discus or javelin. Apart from running there would be the Long Jump and the High Jump, but without the benefit of a sandpit. Such sophistication was unheard of at junior and primary schools. With the help of the Groundsman, Fred Grimmett, a 440 yard circuit was marked out on one of the rugby pitches. It being summer, the grass was lush and not particularly short, because for the coming rugger season, played predominantly under muddy conditions, it was felt wise to keep it fairly long.

Finn, being 10 1/2 years old, had entered for the under 11 races at 100, 220 and 440 yard distances. Mr Carne had advised Mr and Mrs Browning that in his view this was likely to be too exhausting for the lad, but Bobby knew his capabilities. She knew the coaching and fitness training that he had undergone with Shirley Black. Mr Carne had no such insight.; he had been fully occupied with teaching the boys Cricket. Buses had been hired to take both children and parents to Thames Ditton. Disappointingly, Finn's father had to remain at work in London, but Bobby was there, and so was Shirley Black. She had high hopes for her protégé. It was a fine, sunny afternoon. Rows of fold-up wooden chairs lined the finishing straight and behind them, tables were set out in a marquee. Some of the mothers had managed to produce cakes, tartlets and biscuits. A separate table was set out for the prizegiving. Apart from the usual book prizes for race winners, there were two Victor Ludorum cups, one for the seniors and one for the eleven and unders.

The first races were for the tiny tots, the young brothers and sisters of the boys at Branchester House. This was followed by a Mother's Race, which Bobby entered. Although now in her mid-forties, Bobby was still fit and lithe. It was the Start that was her downfall. Some of the younger mothers, many still in their thirties, or even twenties, shot ahead of her at the word "Go", and left her trailing. But Bobby had long legs and soon began to make up lost ground. She overtook four of the other runners, but by the finishing tape was still only fourth. Nevertheless Finn was proud that she had even entered, and finishing so high in the field was certainly no disgrace for the oldest competitor.

Next was the Eleven and Unders 100 yards – Finn's first race. Really, it was unfair: Finn had had all the coaching and practice from Shirley Black. From "Go" he shot into a two yard lead and by the finishing tape was a full five yards clear of the field. Results in the 220 yards followed a similar pattern, except that he won by seven yards, easing up. Old Carnage could not believe it and was torn between pleasure at having such an outstanding young pupil, and concern that all the other boys were left trailing. There was still the 440 yards event. Tall as he was for his age, there was one boy, Vincent Cole, who was even taller, and sturdier, and for the 440 stamina was a key factor, not just sheer speed. Finn's fast starting in the shorter distances would have less value in the full circuit of the track, so Mr Carne calculated that with "a bit of luck and a following wind behind Master Cole" he would be saved the embarrassment of virtually every Junior event prize going to one pupil – Finn.

As expected, Finn was off to a flying start.. At 50 yards he was six yards ahead of Cole, who in turn was three yards ahead of the third runner. Finn felt good. The two previous races had not really taxed him: after all, he had only been sprinting for less than a minute and under Shirley's tutelage that was nothing out of the ordinary. But Cole was no slouch and in the full-lap distance long legs count for a lot. He began to close on Finn. By the halfway mark, on the far side of the track from the spectators, Finn could hear Vincent closing up on him. The six yard gap was down to three. Finn dug deep, every sinew straining. He remembered Shirley Black's insistence about keeping his rhythm, using his arms as well as his legs, and above all not allowing his breathing to become shallow and hurried.. They reached the final bend and now Finn became conscious of the shouts and screams of the spectators. They reached the final straight and then he could see Vincent Cole almost level with his shoulder, ready to pass him. Now Finn could see the finishing tape. 30 yards to go. His head throbbed; the sunlight became dazzling. Everything seemed white. Both boys flung themselves at the tape, but as Vincent did so, one knee buckled and he collapsed in a heap. Finn had won. It was only by a hand's breadth, but he had won. Finn was totally spent. For a few moments he lay prostrate on the grass. Then what he had achieved dawned on him – he had won all three races he had entered, and apart from the jumping events, he had won everything in his age group.

The first to congratulate him was Vincent Cole. Vincent was dreadfully disappointed, but he was man enough not to show it, and sportsman enough to compliment his victor. Bobby could hardly believe it and as she walked over to Finn, she suddenly remembered Lars Hansen. How he would have enjoyed this afternoon, though, in different circumstances, he would have been able to watch his own son, perhaps. But little Kjell was dead, an innocent victim of this appalling war. As she congratulated her son, she wondered where Lars was now. What was he doing? Was he even alive? Probably, she would never know. Surreptitiously, Bobby shed a tear. It was a tear of joy for her son's achievements, but it was also a tear of sadness for Lars.

Finn Browning won the Junior Victor Ludorum . Perhaps, he thought to himself, he would win it as a Senior next summer. Shirley Black had no doubts about that whatsoever.

After the prizegiving, Shirley took the opportunity to buttonhole Mr Carne. "Hello, we spoke on the phone. I am the lady who has been training

Finn Browning. I am really grateful to you for releasing him from cricket and other activities, and I do not think you will regret it. On today's showing, he is an outstanding prospect. If we can ever manage to win this wretched war there is no doubt in my mind that he will develop into an athlete of international calibre, possibly Olympic standard, provided he sticks at it. I do hope you will give him every encouragement."

"Yes, madam. I can see that he is outstanding. Are there, perhaps, other Athletic Meetings he could enter? I mean competing against other schools"

"Oh, yes." Shirley smiled. "There is a Surrey Schools Athletic Championships. Perhaps you should enter Branchester House for it. It is too late for this year, but if you are keen I will get the details for the 1942 event. I would be happy to help you out, if you want to upgrade Athletics in your Summer games programme. One other point, though, the Surrey Championships is only open to children of twelve or over, so I am afraid Finn would have to wait until 1944. But there must be other boys who would be good enough to take part."

And so it was agreed. In 1944, Finn would take part. But that is another story. A tragic story.

CHAPTER 30

The terrible events on the Russian front, and the attack on Pearl Harbour, had not yet occurred when Finn started his Autumn Term at Branchester House. For Finn it had already been a memorable year. He had had great success in the school Summer Sports. He had had the thrill of meeting Lars Hansen, a real hero who had actually killed Germans. Best of all, his cherished brother Clive had returned from the dead, and had married Philippa. Now, a new term, and football and squash would be the highlights on Finn's agenda.

Claud and Bobby had slightly different ideas. They made it abundantly clear to him that, whilst sport had its place, there was still the matter of classroom studies. Squash and Athletics were amateur sports which could not provide a living in adult life. "Once this war has been won, Finn, and once your school days are over, you need to go to University, if possible Oxford or Cambridge. Whatever career or profession you decide on, that is the key to making it good. And that means hard work in the classroom now. There are no short cuts."

Finn took the message to heart. Still short of being eleven, he was too young fully to understand the demands of adult life, but he did understand that his parents were deadly serious and he had better take notice. So, for the next few months, although maintaining his sporting involvement, he focussed on his lessons. At least, from Monday to Friday. Weekends, with full parental approval, he trained with Shirley black and played in Junior Squash matches at Berrylands. And he kept his scrapbook up to date too.

Douglas turned seventeen in September, and the realisation grew in the minds of Bobby and Claud that in a year's time their second son would be donning uniform. In summer 1942 he would sit his Higher Schools Certificate and scarcely before he had the results, his Call-Up papers would be arriving through the letter box, and he would be off. Kenneth would miss him; they were very close. Perhaps then Ken would pay a little more attention to Finn, his younger brother. It had been apparent for years that to a large extent Finn had been virtually ignored by his elder brothers, excepting Clive. Bobby and Claud had not intervened, believing that to do so would only exacerbate the situation.

With Clive away in the RAF, and Claud away in Fleet Street nearly all week, and the other three boys at school except for the holidays, Bobby had time to herself. The onset of Autumn was no sadness for her, as it was for many, with the vivid summer colours fading, and the leaves falling. For Bobby Autumn had a special magic. There was a peace about it, a feeling of mellowness and calm. Autumn was Nature catching its breath after the excitement and whirling dance of Summer. Bobby adored to see the green of the trees turn to gold, a last hurrah before they fell. There was still some colour, but more subdued: the chrysanthemums echoed the burnished hues of the trees, and there was still the delicate pinks of the belladonna lilies. Autumn had its special smells: camomile, damp grass, the musk of mushrooms. When she had time she took a Greenline bus into the countryside and walked in the hills and valleys to the west of Dorking. Her favourite place was White Downs, on the north face of the valley that stretched west to Clandon and Shere and on towards Guildford. At the top of the Downs was woodland, largely beech trees, but also elm and oak. But lower down the trees gave way to bare downland and there she would sit, perhaps with a Thermos and a bag of sandwiches, and gaze across to the far side of the valley to another beech wood, a carpet of gold. There was a small cluster of cottages there, with a wisp of white smoke curling up from their chimneys. Perhaps the distant bark of a dog barking for its master. Was that master off at the war, she wondered. Sometimes her mind would drift back to her home in Moss, and she would wonder how her family and friends were surviving under the Nazi occupation. Occasionally, her thoughts would be interrupted by the chuff, chuff of a little steam train far below, labouring its way from Guildford to Dorking and on to Reigate and Redhill to the East. She promised herself that when Finn was a year or two older she would cycle out here with him; he would love it here. They could bring a picnic, and lie listening to the music of the skylark hovering far above.

But the war could not be put aside for long, and not all of it was happening far away. Hitler's focus may have shifted to the East, to the Russian Front, but the Luftwaffe had not totally abandoned attacking London. The prudent citizens of the Capital, and all the other industrial centres, still made their way nightly to the public air raid shelters, and Underground Stations, bundles of blankets and flasks of hot drinks under their arms. The wail of sirens, rising and falling, would begin at about 11pm, sometimes later if you were lucky. Then, if it was a clear night, the searchlights would begin their restless sweep, back and forth, until, with luck, one of them would fix on a tiny silver speck two miles or so above the city. All the other searchlights would join in, and then the "woof, woof" of the anti-aircraft guns would begin. Like exploding stars, the shells would burst and pepper the night sky. Only once did Finn see an enemy bomber hit. The silver speck turned suddenly into an orange ball, falling so slowly it seemed, trailing flames like some comet out in space, until it disappeared from view beyond the rooftops. That night a mother in Dusseldorf, or Pforzheim, or some pretty Bavarian village, lost a son. A child lost its father, a sister her brother, a wife her husband. But that was far, far preferable to a whole family being wiped out in Brixton or Barking. War had no mercy.

It was nearly dark one October day when Finn cycled home from school to find a barrier had been placed across the entrance to St.Mark's Orchard, guarded by a helmeted soldier, his rifle at the ready.

"Hold on a minute, young lad. I'm afraid you can't go on that way. They've found an unexploded bomb in the back garden at no 26, and they're busy trying to defuse it."

"But I live here, at no.18"

"Ah, that's a bit different then. You go straight home then, son. No dawdling about – there's nothing to see. And you'll be a lot safer indoors.. Off you go."

Finn found his mother busy criss-crossing windows with broad strips of brown paper tape. "Are you doing that because of the bomb down the road, Mum?" "Yes, Finn. A bomb disposal Officer called and said this tape might help prevent flying glass if the horrible thing goes off. You can help me if you like. Douglas and Kenneth are not home yet."

The Bomb Disposal team were at no. 26 for more than a week. They knew where the bomb had fallen alright, and it was a big one – 500lbs, they thought. The problem was that it was sinking in the soft earth, and sinking faster than they could safely dig after it. Foot by foot, the hole had to be shored up with stout planking. There must be no risk of a collapse which might detonate the bomb. That week it had rained hard every day, which made the excavating even more difficult, and also helped the bomb sink even faster. At last, after 12 days, the bomb was visible, about fifteen feet down. It had encountered a firmer layer of soil, in fact clay.

A young Lieutenant gingerly descended into the shaft and after what seemed an age, but was only half an hour, the detonator was safely removed.

To everyone's amazement, the Commanding Officer of the operation said that the neighbours could come and inspect the bomb as it was raised out of its tomb. Amongst the first was Finn. A cradle had been secured round the monster and it was slowly winched to the surface. It was a dark green cylinder about four feet long and eighteen inches in diameter. "There is enough explosive in there" announced the CO, "to blow everyone here to smithereens, and flatten every house in a fifty yard radius. But worry not; without its detonator it is as a harmless as a hen's egg" The officer noticed Finn staring wide-eyed at the lethal object. "What's your name, son?" "Finn, sir" "Finn! How appropriate. Would you like a souvenir? I think a tail fin would be appropriate, don't you?"

Finn could not believe his luck. He had always hoped to find an anti-aircraft shell nose cap, but had never done so. This would be worth a hundred nose caps. But he would never part with it. Never.

CHAPTER 31

During Clive's absence training in Rhodesia, the Brownings had seen little of Philippa. Her Air Ministry duties kept her busy enough in London, and additionally she had to visit airfields all over Britain. She regularly kept touch with Bobby by phone, but, at last, in late September, she asked if she could visit the family in Surbiton. She intrigued Bobby by saying she had some news, but that she would rather impart it face to face. They were a little surprised when she arrived at the door in a taxi. She was young and energetic and would normally think nothing of walking up the hill from the Station.

There was no need for an explanation. The reason for the taxi was immediately apparent to the naked eye. Philippa Browning was pregnant. Before a word had been exchanged she burst out laughing. She had seen the astonished look on Claud and Bobby's faces. "Oh, I'm so sorry" she giggled, "I should have told you before, but I wanted to be absolutely certain that I WAS expecting, and that there were not going to be any complications in the early stages. I do hope you are not going to mind being a Granny and Grandpa!"

"My darling girl how could we be anything but thrilled. It's wonderful news. We are absolutely delighted, But does Clive know?" "He ought to know by now. I wrote to him nine days ago. But I have not heard back from him yet. The post these days a bit iffy, especially to the darkest depths of Africa.. Of course, I have told my parents in Dorset, and I am hoping to go down there in a week or two's time. Oh, by the way, the baby is due in February, so that makes it a honeymoon affair, I suppose. Well, it could hardly have been anything else; Clive sailed three days after we were married!"

Wisely, Philippa omitted to mention Clive's first visit to her flat on his return from South America….! Nor did she mention that they had made love before that. Thank heavens she had not got pregnant then! That would have raised some eyebrows, not least at Rosedown!

Finn had mixed feelings about this news. He adored his sister-in-law, and she had always been fun to be with, and he could see how happy she was now. But her having a baby would make him an UNCLE. He was none too sure about that.

Uncles were old men, not that he had any himself, but his friends all had, and they were invariably fat and bald, with puffy purple noses. Or so it seemed. He decided it would be best not to tell his chums. Well, not until the baby had actually arrived, anyway.

Early in November, Clive returned from Rhodesia. His flying course had gone according to plan and he was now a fully-fledged Flight Sergeant Air gunner. Training had been in old Avro Ansons, firing at drogues, a funnel-shaped device a bit like a wind-sock, towed behind American Harvard Trainers. He was given one week's leave before taking up his posting with a Lancaster bomber squadron based in Lincolnshire. From then on he would be on Ops., flying bombing missions over Germany and Occupied Europe. He well knew the dangers. On average, bomber crews survived fewer than thirty missions.

Clive well knew that from her work in the Air Ministry, and her visits to Bomber Command Stations, Philippa was already fully conscious of what could happen to him. Twice, she had been present when bombers came limping home from raids. She had seen the dead, the dying and the wounded, often terribly burned bodies being lifted out. She had seen, too, the haunted eyes of those who had survived. They knew that next time they might be the ones gently lifted down, if they were lucky enough not to be shot down first.

But for the week of his leave, the order of the day was "Smiles All Round". Clive was in heaven at the thought of becoming a father. He could hardly bring himself to let Philippa out of his arms, or even out of his sight. She looked radiant. She had been fortunate not to experience any morning sickness, nor pain. By the time of Clive's return to England, the baby was making its presence known in no uncertain manner. Philippa was still working, but had been given a special dispensation to wear civilian clothes. With her bulge, uniform was just not on, her boss told her. Clive spent most of his leave with Philippa in the flat, but his family loyalty was strong and he did not neglect them. All three brothers were intrigued with his flying kit, but Finn was especially awe struck. Clive let him try on his leather flying helmet and goggles, and Douglas donned his all-in-one-piece padded and insulated flying suit, and calf-length fur-lined boots. The suit was made of a new, synthetic material called Nylon. Clive informed him that one day, he had been told, men's shirts and underwear would be made of this material, and in America, ladies' stockings in Nylon were all the rage – far cheaper than silk, apparently, and longer lasting too.

The week passed all to quickly and Clive left to join his squadron. There would be a period of conversion-training on Lancasters, and then in the New Year, he expected to commence operations in earnest. Clive could not distinguish in his mind between the triple emotions of Excitement, raw Fear, and the Sadness of knowing that he and his comrades would be killing innocent German men, women and children. There was nothing mixed about the emotions of Clive's parents. They sensed only Fear – the cold, numbing fear that they might soon be losing their first-born child. Of course, they conveyed none of this to Clive, nor to his brothers. Douglas and Kenneth in particular were callow enough to perceive their elder brother as a hero in the making, who was going to knock hell out of Hitler and his stinking cronies. To Finn, Clive was now a God, a shining knight riding to the defence of his country. The thought that he might be wounded or killed never occurred to him. That fate would be reserved for the Germans.

Christmas came and went and soon after, Finn celebrated his eleventh birthday.

CHAPTER 32

Pearl Harbour was attacked in the early hours of December 7th 1941, and declaration of Japanese hostilities against Britain followed later the same day. Simultaneously with a bombing raid on Singapore, Japanese forces were landed at Kota Bharu in Malaya. Meanwhile, other landings took place in Thailand to the East. On December 8th Japanese forces attacked the British Garrison in Hong Kong. Other landings took place at Bataan, south of Taiwan, and in the Philippines, both American Territories. In the first six months of 1942 a series of appalling defeats were inflicted upon both Britain and America. That was not surprising when it is realized that Japan had under arms no fewer than one and a half million men. Her fleet constituted 11 Aircraft Carriers, 40 Cruisers, 120 Destroyers and more than 60 Submarines. Her Air Force numbered more than two and a half thousand aircraft.

An early disaster for the Allies was the loss of the two battleships HMS "Repulse" and HMS "Prince of Wales". They had sailed with an escort of three Destroyers to surprise the Japanese Army landing troops and equipment at Kota Bharu, Unfortunately, they had not been provided with any air cover, and consequently were attacked from the air, as well as by enemy submarines. Although over two thousand crew were later rescued from the sea, eight hundred and forty officers and men went down with their ships. This devastating loss was not only an humiliation for Britain's naval might in the Far East theatre, but rendered Japan's invasion of Malaya, Singapore and the Philippines a great deal easier than might otherwise have been the case.

Defeat followed defeat: Malaya, Singapore and Hong Kong were quickly overrun. In the Philippines, the American General Douglas MacArthur defended strongly and the battle raged for several months. But eventually, the Philippines, too, were wrested by the Japanese. The largest surrender in American history resulted in the capture of twelve thousand American troops. Although their battle was over, their suffering was not. Having taken their prisoners, the Japanese forced them, already ravaged by hunger and exhaustion, to march 55 miles from Mariveles to the railhead at San Fernando. Over two thousand Americans and seven thousand Filipinos died on that terrible journey. After the war was over the Japanese commander, General Homma, was tried and executed for this crime against humanity.

Meanwhile, Japanese successes continued throughout South-East Asia. Next to fall was Sumatra, then Borneo, then Java. Celebes and the Moluccas fell in January and February 1942. Wake Island and Guam followed after the fiercest resistance by the Americans. The Japanese seemed unstoppable.

Thailand, then known as Siam, fell with virtually no resistance, and so the Japanese Armies moved on to the border with Burma. Burma was strategically important to the Japanese because of its oil and other resources. But here they did meet fierce resistance from the British Army. Sadly, though, this force had little air support, and through January and February they were forced to retreat northwards, until the capital, and the vitally important oilfields fell into Japanese hands. By early April the whole of Burma had fallen into enemy hands and the British forced to withdraw back into India. They were indeed dark days for the British Empire and for those thousands of our men who fell into Japanese hands.

Finn was now eleven years old. Like any normal boy of that age his thoughts for the most part were on matters close to home: events and activities at school, and within the circles of his family and friends. Until now, the war had encroached on his consciousness only in terms of its direct impact on his life: first, the evacuation to Dorset and the year with the Hannahs, then the air raids and bombs, seeing the German bomber crashing over Home Park, then his brother Clive joining the RAF and being torpedoed and believed dead. At eleven, though, his horizon was broadening. In no small measure this was the result of his father's involvement in Journalism and his own dedication to compiling his scrapbook. By now it was filling up with cuttings and photos showing the palls of smoke and flame rising from England's shattered cities, to the stalking of the Graf Spee and sinking of the Bismarck, to battles raging in North Africa, to the terrible events at Pearl Harbour, and now the new, demoralising string of unremitting defeats at the hands of the "Little Yellow Men" of Japan.

Now, at last, it began to dawn on Finn that maybe England and her Allies were not quickly, nor easily going to defeat their enemies. Oh, he knew that Hitler had not so far crossed the Channel, but, that apart, all the conversation everywhere was of Allied retreats on land and shipping losses in the Atlantic, and now the Pacific as well. From Russia the news was grim and there was even talk of Germany from the West linking up with Japan in the Far East. Would the banner of the Rising Sun be flying in Delhi alongside the German Swastika? Would the free world be vanquished and subjugated into slavery? This was the kind of talk that Finn began to hear and absorb. Of course, such gossip was stamped upon, and hard, and certainly was never voiced in the Press or on the Radio. Nor could it be said that the morale of the British population was low. Had we not survived the Blitz and Dunkirk? We may have suffered grievous losses at sea, but we still had probably the largest battle fleet in the world, we thought. Actually, both the USA and Japan had larger fleets, but that was not general knowledge at the time. And were not our Armies still formidable both in numbers, equipment and professionalism, to say nothing of courage and determination?

The entry into the war of the United States also lifted the morale of the British people, and increasing heart was taken from the bond formed between Winston Churchill and the President of the USA, Franklin D. Roosevelt. Seldom, if ever, was there such a consistent and unanimous sense of purpose as these two great men established, and which inspired the peoples that they led, both at home and on the battlefield. Thus in early 1942 there were these currents and counter currents of viewpoint, rumour, doubt and inspiration. Darkness now, but maybe chinks of light.

Maybe, soon, the tide would turn.....

CHAPTER 33

Charlotte Annabelle Lee was born on February 12th 1942 and weighed 7lb11oz. Her first view of the world was in the Maternity Wing of Chelsea Hospital for Women, and she bawled lustily from the word go. Philippa had little difficulty with her confinement, but wished Clive could have been present to see his new daughter arrive. (The presence of husbands at the actual birth was unheard of in those days and it would be another 20 years or more before it became a common and accepted practice.) But Clive was near to going on his first bombing mission over enemy territory and could not obtain leave to go to London. He and Philippa had discussed whether she should perhaps go to Dorset to give birth, to be near her parents. There were excellent facilities in Dorchester, or maybe the child could be born at Rosedown itself. Either alternative would have delighted Sir Henry and Lady Hester. In the end they plumped for London, as it would be more easily accessible for Clive to get to from Lincolnshire. Also, his family could easily visit from Surbiton and if Philippa ever needed practical support bringing up the child, then Bobby would be happy to oblige, and was more readily to hand. Besides the Hannahs were getting a bit long in the tooth for that!

As to the infant's names the parents had decided at the outset that if he was a boy, then Clive would choose and if it was a girl, then Philippa would decide, with the proviso that if either of them intensely disliked the other's choice, then a veto could be exercised, and a discussion take place until a consensus was reached. There was no conflict when Philippa made her choice and spoke to Clive on the phone: "I want to call my baby Charlotte Annabel Lee." "What!" exclaimed Clive. "Where on earth did those names come from?" he laughed.

Philippa was an avid reader of classical fiction and especially was fond of the Bronte sisters. Her favourite book of all was Charlotte's "Jane Eyre". But she also adored the works of William Makepeace Thackeray. "Vanity Fair" was his best known novel, but there was a quotation from a lesser known work, "The Sorrows of Werther" that had always tickled her sense of humour:

"Werther had a love for Charlotte
Such as words could never utter
Would you know how first he met her?
She was cutting bread and butter.

So Charlotte it would be. And Annabelle Lee? "Oh" she told Clive, "it was a poem by Edgar Allan Poe that I loved, called "Annabel Lee".

"This maiden she lived with no other thought
Than to love and be loved by thee
I was a child and she was a child
In this kingdom by the sea
 But we loved with a love that was more than a love
I and my Annabel Lee."

And so it was. There was no need for debate Clive was over the moon, not only at being a father, but that this child should have such enchanting names And although she would be known as Charlotte, he loved the Annabel Lee association It encapsulated perfectly his adoration for his wife and, he knew, her love for him. All that was missing was his inability to see his newborn child.

"But we loved with a love that was more than a love......."

Philippa was in the Hospital for ten days and during that time joyfully received her parents. Lady Hester, so austere for much of the time, rediscovered all her maternal instincts and cuddled the baby as if it was her own. The route from Dorset to Chelsea somehow passed by Harrods and although clothes rationing severely restricted the availability of baby clothing, nevertheless the store was able to provide a fine pink Moses Basket made from raffia, a shiny, black pram, and a play pen, the latter two items to be delivered to Philippa's flat. There was also a very large Teddy Bear, dressed in the dark greeny/grey dungarees of a Land Army girl, and holding in its paw an imitation bunch of carrots "Well" announced Lady Hester, "If this bloody war goes on long enough, Charlotte may have to be a real Land Army Girl one day!" Sir Henry had been brought up to keep a firm rein on his emotions, or better still, not to have any. Success as a soldier would not be achieved by "being soppy" his father had insisted. But Sir Henry, too, beamed at his first sight of his new grand daughter and even gave the infant a gentle pat on the head. "Looks fine, Philippa. Well done. A bit quick off the mark though, you two, you've scarcely been married nine months. Oh well, with a war on I suppose there was no point in hanging about."

Bobby and Claud had their first view of Charlotte when she was two days old. For several months Bobby had been busy with her knitting needles, and presented her first grandchild with two complete outfits of leggings, jacket and bonnet. For Philippa, Claud brought a massive bunch of Narcissi. "An early crop from the Scilly Isles" the florist said, "We're lucky to get them with this war on; they fly them across to the mainland, but they never know but that the old Rapide biplanes might not get shot at by a stray Messerschmitt".

Douglas and Kenneth came to see the new arrival together. When out of school they were seldom apart, especially now that Douglas had only a few months left before his call-up. Philippa invited them to hold their new niece, but both declined: they were clearly ill at ease with the whole business of babies.

Finn came with Bobby on her second visit to Chelsea and was delighted to arrive just as Philippa was breast feeding her daughter. Bobby beamed "Oh, I am so glad she's having a good guzzle, my dear. I'm sure it makes all the difference to their healthy growth. Finn here just would not have anything to do with my milk, I've no idea why. At one stage we thought we might lose him, but the medical people finally found some vile mixture called New Zealand Cream and Carillac. I never discovered what constituted it and it smelled awful, but Finn liked it!" Finn's face reddened at the sight of Philippa's naked breast, having never seen one before, not even his mother's, but he soon got over the shock and asked if he could hold his new relative.

"Gosh, it's a shame Clive can't be here. It seems funny that we will all have seen it before her father gets a chance.!"

""It" is not It, young Finn. She is a she and her name is Charlotte" scalded Philippa, smiling, "and I shall expect you to take an active interest in her upbringing and wellbeing – that's what uncles are for and don't you try telling me you are too young to be one just because you are "only eleven!" You are a fine boy and will be a fine uncle – even if I have to cuff your ears!" they all laughed and even Charlotte gurgled happily.

A week later Clive completed his Lancaster conversion course. He and the rest of his crew were now ready and eager to take the war to the enemy. It was payback time for the Blitz., for the destruction of Britain's cities and the death of thousands of innocent citizens. Of course, there was the nagging knowledge in Clive's and the others' minds that they might die, or worse be maimed or burnt or both. Although Clive was conscious of these risks, like most young men his fears were subordinated to the elation he felt at the thought that he would be in action. And anyway, they only had to get through thirty missions before being transferred to a "Cushy number", maybe "flying a desk" for a while. Until the next round. Another thirty. Young men like Clive did not, dare not, think of that.

Before their first op. aircrew were usually given a 48 hour pass. In view of the special circumstances, Clive was given 72 hours. As his train rumbled through the frost-laden fields of Cambridgeshire these thoughts were thrust to the back of his mind. He was a father now. Could it be real? Was he really a Dad? For heaven's sake, he was not yet twenty, not until later in the year.

But he was, and now he was going to see his child, his daughter, for the very first time. He could touch her, hold her, smell her sweetness. She was made of his flesh. Together with Philippa, she was HIS. A new life and part of his life. Oh God, let me survive the inferno ahead.

Two hours later he walked into the Chelsea Hospital for Women. There was no prouder, nor happier a man on God's earth.

CHAPTER 34

Until now, the enemy campaign in North Africa, against Britain and her Allies had been conducted by Italian forces under the command of General Graziani. During the latter half of 1941, the smaller Allied army had humiliated the Italians and had pushed them back westwards deep into the Libyan desert, and in the process had captured an astounding 130,000 men, including 22 Generals, and even one Admiral! Hitler had been infuriated by this defeat and ordered Graziani's replacement by a young German General, Erwin Rommel. Additionally a strong force of German troops, plus armour and air support had been sent to reinforce the pathetic Italians. It was an odd coincidence that Rommel took up his appointment in Africa on the very same day that Charlotte Annabel Lee was born – February 12th 1942.

One new English life, but, though it could not be known, the signal for the end of many other English lives in the African desert, for Gen. Rommel was to show himself to be a resolute, cunning and fearless adversary. He fully earned the title "The Desert Fox". In the space of six months he lead the Axis armies from major defeat to almost total victory. By September 1942 he had regained all the 500 miles the Italians had relinquished, and cast his shadow over the great port of Alexandria and the Egyptian capital Cairo. He had done this largely by persuading Hitler to provide him with men, tanks , guns and aircraft desperately needed on the Eastern front, to the intense annoyance of his fellow German Generals battling the massive Russian armies. But their loss was Rommel's gain. The British, who had so successively outfought Graziani, were now on the receiving end again, faced now, not with Italians who traditionally had little stomach for a fight, but with a disciplined, highly trained, well-equipped and implacable Afrika Korps, brilliantly led by Erwin Rommel.

It was not easy for Rommel. The British defended every yard and the fighting was brutal and intense, made worse by the conditions both armies had to face: searing heat, sand and sand storms, lack of water, and sickness. For several months some 36,000 British and Commonwealth troops defended the strategic port of Tobruk, completely surrounded by the Germans, shelled and bombed day and night, but still vitally preventing Rommel bringing in fresh supplies to sustain his advance. Instead, Rommel had to rely on Tripoli, 500 miles to the East, as his lifeline. But this meant that the Royal Navy, from their base in Malta, could attack the German supply ships crossing the Mediterranean from Sicily, thus rendering supplies even more difficult and spasmodic. It was this that forced Rommel in September 1942 to pause in his advance eastwards. But it was this pause that also enabled the Allies to re-group. The fact is that both sides were bruised and exhausted. The Allies, like their enemy, needed more armour, guns and air support. By this time Tobruk had finally fallen to incessant and concentrated attacks from land and the air, and more than thirty thousand Allied troops were taken prisoner.

Churchill was losing patience, as well as precious resources. The Commander of the British forces, General Claud Auchinleck, had delayed any attempt at a counter attack, on the grounds of inadequate resources being available. But now Churchill became more insistent. There must be action. It was his good fortune that at this stage Roosevelt heard of the fall of Tobruk to Rommel. Almost without asking, the Americans arranged the supply to the Allied Forces of the powerful M4 Sherman tank, with its superior speed and lethal 75mm gun. It was fully a match for the German armour. This, plus the supply of one hundred self-propelled howitzers, did much to redress the balance of power between the two armies. Another potent weapon was Churchill himself. He was an inspiration to the British people in their darkest hours, and now he became an inspiration to the Allied forces in North Africa, by paying them a personal visit. Auchinleck was replaced by General Harold Alexander, and to become Field Commander 8th Army under him, there was appointed General Bernard Montgomery.

The scene was set for the Battle of El Alamein, without question a major turning point in the whole war. Later, Churchill was to say that the victory at El Alamein was "Maybe not the beginning of the end, but it was certainly the end of the beginning."

CHAPTER 35

The telephone rang at 1030am on a dull Monday morning. Bobby was alone in the house, doing the Monday wash. Being early March the three boys were all at School. Bobby answered:

"Elmbridge 3308, who is it calling please?"

"Is that Mrs Roberta Browning:" The caller was male and his voice was deep, cultured and a little formal, Bobby thought. Bobby noticed that his English accent was a little too perfect. Not an Englishman's English.

"I asked you who is this calling." Bobby repeated.

"Mr name is Greig, Mrs Browning. Thor Greig. It is Mrs Browning, isn't it? I am calling from the Norwegian Embassy in London."

"I see". Bobby was on her guard. "Yes, I am Mrs Browning. Why are you calling me?"

"Mrs Browning, I believe that you are acquainted with a Mr Lars Hansen. Is that correct?"

"Yes, we met briefly. Why are you enquiring?"

"Mrs Browning, I am afraid in these days of war, it is inadvisable to say too much on the telephone. Especially on calls to and from the Embassy of a country that has been overrun by Nazi Germany. Calls can be, and are, tapped. Or in plain English, they are listened to by the enemy. There is a matter of some importance that I wish to discuss with you, and I am wondering if you would be kind enough to visit me here in London. We will, of course, send a car for you. Would you be agreeable to doing this for us? I can promise you this is a genuine and important matter, and one that could, if you go along with a proposal that we wish to make to you, help the war effort. Will you come, please?"

Bobby was perplexed and disconcerted. What should she have to do with the Norwegian Embassy? And how on earth should this stranger know of her encounter with Lars Hansen? And what on earth could be in his mind that she could, or would do to help the war effort, beyond her service with the WVS, and the contributions of her eldest son?

"I am not at all sure that I can help you Mr Greig. I am a middle aged woman bringing up a family in a Surrey suburb. It seems more than a little far fetched. In any case, I would not agree to meet you unless my husband was also agreeable, and present at the meeting. I think also that I should have some verification of who you are."

"You are quite right. May I please call you Roberta? "Mrs Browning" is terribly formal. Yes, in these dangerous times it would be foolish of you to go into anything blindly. I suggest that you speak to your husband, whom I understand works in Fleet Street, and then call me back. The number of the Norwegian Embassy is in the London Telephone Directory. When you get through, ask for the Department of Communications, and then me by name. I will await your call, Roberta, but please get back to me as soon as possible- today if you can. By the way, you might like to know that Lars Hansen sends his warmest regards. I can tell you that he is in good health and his wound has fully healed – if not forgotten. But that is all I can say, as you may understand."

Bobby's mind was in a whirl. It was hard for her to grasp what had just occurred – some total stranger ringing out of the blue and asking her to go to the Norwegian Embassy in London, and suggesting that she might be able to help in the war effort, in some totally unspecified way. More than that he clearly knew of her brief encounter with Lars Hansen. But how? Who was this man? What did he want?

She picked up the phone and called her husband in London. Usually he would have been at home on a Monday, but some panic had required him to go to the office.

Claud listened to her story. "Well, Bobby, it doesn't sound like some sort of hoax. This man Greig did not give you any old phone number to ring, he said the Norwegian Embassy, and that number is certainly in the book, so if they have a Thor Greig he must be genuine. We can soon check that out. No, I think you should go along with the man and see what he wants. We can always say "no" if we don't like the sound of his proposition. And I'll tell you one thing, darling – YOU'RE NOT GOING TO GET PARACHUTED BACK INTO NORWAY. Who'd cook my dinner every night?!" Claud laughed and rang off.

A few days later Claud and Bobby were ushered into the Embassy in Belgrave Square, and shown into a waiting room on the ground floor. It was simply, but tastefully furnished, and on one wall there hung a portrait of King Haakon of Norway, a tall, gaunt but aristocratic figure. After the German invasion of his country, the King had stayed in Norway in support of his defending forces, but when defeat was inevitable and only at the last possible moment, he had fled to England.

The man who entered the room wore a dark blue double-breasted suit. He was probably thirty five or thirty six years old, slim but with broad shoulders, and his blond hair cut short. His eyes were ice blue. He smiled and held out his hand. Good morning! I am Thor Greig. Thank you so much for agreeing to come. I am, or was, a fighter pilot in the Norwegian Airforce. It is a pleasure to meet you both. As I am sure you are very busy, I will not waste time on pleasantries. Would you please follow me to my office. It is on the first floor, and we will not be disturbed there."

The office was small and sparsely furnished, but here too hung a portrait of King Haakon. There was also a photo of Greig sitting in the cockpit of an old biplane, and waving happily at the camera.

Greig began: "You are, naturally, mystified as to why we have contacted you. It must seem like some episode from a Hollywood spy movie. But maybe the mystery will be lessened when I point out that we know, Roberta, that you were born and brought up in Norway, in the town of Moss. I also know that your family are still there. Although for many years you have lived in England, you will not have forgotten your mother tongue, I feel sure. Am I correct so far?" Bobby nodded. "It is a little rusty, but basically yes, of course my Norwegian is as it always was. But what use is that to you here in England?"

"I will explain. You know that I work in the Communications Department of this Embassy. Although our country is occupied, we maintain links with it. These take various forms, and I will leave it to your imagination what some of them are. They are highly secret, of course. Suffice to say that they enable us to be a considerable nuisance to the Nazis. In addition, we have recently launched a Free Norway radio channel on short wave, with the object of underpinning the morale of our oppressed countrymen and women. Most Norwegian homes still have radio sets, and although people are only permitted to listen to German operated stations, we know how dearly they would like to listen to broadcasts by Free Norwegians, and are quite prepared to risk doing so. Now the fact is that here in Britain there is no shortage of Norwegian men who can make a fist of talking to men about those things that will appeal to men. It is not so easy, though, to buoy up the morale of women.

You do not need me to tell you that life there is anything but normal. There are severe shortages of food and warm clothing. In fact virtually everything. Although Norway is heavily forested, movement is restricted, so people can not even go to the woods to gather fuel to keep warm. Well, we can not change that, but what we can do is make broadcasts about everyday matters that may boost spirits, and provide hope. There is no register of Norwegian women living in Britain. We have located a few, but only a few, and even fewer, if you will forgive me, of mature years, with a wide knowledge of life both here and in Norway. Also, we think it would be preferable if the ones we choose were mothers. We want our appeal to be to the broad spectrum of the population at home. So what we are saying, in short, is that with a little coaching we think you, Mrs Browning, could make such broadcasts from Britain to the people back home. WE are confident you could successfully do the job for us. That is it really. We want you to be one of maybe only two or three "Mrs Norways", making regular weekly broadcasts. Oh! I should add that we obtained information about you from Lars. Lars Hansen. He is an important link for us with the Resistance Movement. He spoke very warmly about you."

Bobby was stunned. She had scarcely known him and never expected to hear of him again, much as she secretly admitted to herself that she would have liked to. And as for becoming some kind of folksy radio hostess......

"Roberta!" Thor Greig interrupted her thoughts, "I am sure all this is a bit of a shock, and you may well want to think about it for a while, and discuss it with you husband." Claud interposed. "You are dead right, Greig. It needs a lot of thought and I think it would be quite wrong to make any commitments here and now, either in favour of doing it, or the opposite. Don't you agree, Bobby?"

Bobby did not know how to answer. The proposal was so outlandish, so beyond her world's normal orbit. Ridiculous almost. And yet....and yet....She said nothing for a few moments. Then, instead of answering Claud, Bobby turned to Greig: "I have English citizenship and have lived here for many years. My husband and my four children are totally English. Apart from an occasional visit to see my parents and family before the war, my whole life has been lived as an Englishwoman. But there is part of me that can never be English and can only ever be Norwegian. If you really believe that in some small way I can help my mother country, then I must do it. I have that obligation." She heard herself saying these words, but it was as if someone else was saying them. She felt disembodied almost. But there was the image. No, there were two images. One was of her parents home in Moss. Of her little room, of the garden, and of the sea nearby. Of a childhood full of light and sparkle, and innocence. The other image was of that tall man who had approached her at the Recreation Ground and whom she had at first rebuffed, and whom she had thereafter had only the briefest meeting with, before he was whisked away. Lars.

"Mrs Browning. Roberta, I am very grateful. More important than that, your country will be very grateful. I am sure you have made the right decision. Thank you."

Claud took her hand: "Bobby, are you sure? It wont be easy. It may take a lot of your time. But if you are really sure, then go for it, and I will support you all the way. And so will the children. I'm afraid that in war we all have to make sacrifices and if doing this will help the Norwegian people, then it is right you should do it. But, there is one thing I think we should clear up with Mr Greig here and now. Tell me, sir, will it be necessary for my wife to spend much time away from home? I spend much of the week overnight in London, and Finn . our youngest son, is only eleven. We must not put his welfare at risk. Nor for that matter, the other two, even if they are older."

"That will be no problem. We anticipated this might be the case" Greig interjected. "Our proposal is that Roberta's broadcasts will be scripted and recorded, here in the Embassy. Ideally, she should spend about two or three days a month working and living in the Embassy. She should be able in that time to prepare four one-hour broadcasts, to go out one a week. During that period we would finance a kind of surrogate "mum", who would act as housekeeper in Roberta's absence. Of course, it would be someone of your choice, someone who would do all the cooking, cleaning, shopping and general housekeeping. You may already know such a person – perhaps a relative or friend. Would that be acceptable?"

Bobby laughed loudly and took the two men by surprise. "Acceptable? Acceptable? I should be delighted. And I think I do know just the person." She turned to Claud. "You know the Greenards in Ewell Road? Wendy Greenard does a lot in the WVS. She has a daughter Ethel, who is just seventeen. Nice girl, but too young yet to put on a uniform. She would be happy to earn a few pounds. She's just kicking her heels at the moment. I just wish we could afford her full time!"

"Well", said Greig, "If this project goes well, that might become possible. Ideally, we would like to make this a daily broadcast, not weekly. How would you like that?"

"Oh heavens! I don't think so. I am nervous about doing it at all. I have had no experience of public speaking, let alone broadcasting on the radio."

"Fine", said Greig. "When is the first few days you can let us have you? It would probably be only for coaching, rather than making an actual programme. And we have not yet discussed what we want you to talk about. The idea is to give the potential audience – all of whom will be risking a severe punishment even to listen-in – talks on a wide range of non-political subjects, such as bringing up children, education, domestic science, health tips, how English women are managing in wartime, art and literature and so on. It would be a sort-of Norwegian version of the BBC's "Woman's Hour" I suppose. Now that's enough of business. Not far from here there is a pleasant little restaurant that we in the Embassy often use. May I treat you to lunch? And oh yes, then I could tell you a little about your friend Lars' activities. He is causing the Huns no end of bother!"

Later, Claud returned to his office and Bobby caught the train home from Waterloo, to be home in time for Finn's return from school. Maybe he was only eleven, but he did not fail to notice his mother's elation. There was an unusual sparkle. "What's up, Mum, you look really excited about something?"

"I will tell you Finn, but I would prefer to wait until Douglas and Kenneth are back. They should be here quite soon."

"Well, it must be something good. Are we going to be surprised?"

"Yes, I think so, Finn. I certainly was. But you will have to be patient for a bit."

As soon as the front door opened, Finn rushed to greet his elder brothers. "Doug, Ken, Mum's got a big surprise for us. She's been to London this morning and something really big has happened, and whatever it is, it's something GOOD. Come on. Hurry up! They all went into the lounge, where Bobby was sitting in her favourite high-back, winged armchair looking relaxed, but still with a knowing smile on her face, a smile which said "I've got a secret and I'll let you into it."

"Sit down boys. Right. You know, of course, that I was born and brought up in Norway, and your grandparents, my mother and father, are still there, but now under Nazi occupation. You also know, and Finn in particular knows, that when he was doing athletics training at the Tolworth Rec. that I met, we both met, a Norwegian gentleman who had had a narrow escape soon after Norway was invaded. He had been shot in the shoulder and was recuperating in a military convalescent home in Tolworth. Well, now he is back in Norway fighting with the Norwegian Resistance Movement. It seems he has been able to maintain contact with the Free Norwegian organisation here in England, and these people have been in touch with me. I have been to see them today in London, with your father, because they think I can help them."

"You Mum? How on earth can you help them?" Doug cut in.

"Be patient, Doug, and I will explain. And before your imagination runs away with you, no, I do NOT have to parachute into my homeland spraying the whole Wehrmacht with a sub-machine gun as I float down. I am not going to be some heroic middle-aged lady saving my country from the German jackboot."

When Bobby had finished recounting Thor Greig's proposition, the three boys all in turn hugged and congratulated their mother.

"It's terrific" cried Finn

"Unbelievable" grinned Douglas.

"Mum, it's absolutely fantastic, beamed Kenneth.

"What does Dad think? Did he meet this Greig fellow?"

"Will you get paid?"

"Will you have to be away much?"

Question followed question, but there was no doubting the boys' delight at this extraordinary development. They all knew someone whose Dad, or brother, or cousin was fighting the war. But , apart from the odd friend who had a sister who was a Land Girl, or a WAAF, or an ATS girl, or A WRNS, none of them had a Mother who was doing anything half as glamorous as this would be. And thankfully, the boys did not seem to mind the prospect that Bobby would be away for several nights at a time. Doug in particular liked the idea of Ethel Greenard coming to stay. He did not know her well, but had seen her around and liked what he had seen!

It was not long before Bobby was summoned to London, to the Norwegian Embassy, for her first coaching session and a week later, the first broadcast was beamed to Norway. No direct propaganda or reference to the war was included. The thrust was purely domestic: how British householders were turning their gardens from flowers to fruit and vegetable growing; how some women were putting on uniform and joining the Women's Land Army, working in the fields and on the farms: a pleasant change for many of them, having lived dreary lives in the cities. Another slot was entitled "How to…" instructions in carpentry and furniture making.

Another was to read a serialisation in Norwegian of famous English classics, such as Dickens and Thomas Hardy. There was a religious section too, but this was covered by one of the other two "Mrs Norways". But Bobby's favourite in that first broadcast was how to turn fruit into wine. She was sure that would be popular! Bobby was allocated a Nom de Plume: "Bobby Borg". Greig said this was to help ensure that German Secret Agents in Britain did not trace her, as they would certainly want to do, especially if the broadcasts took a less folksy turn.

Some six weeks after the broadcast began, Greig handed Bobby two letters. The envelopes were marked simply: "Bobby Borg". "Do not ask me how these came to us, " Greig entreated.

Bobby opened the first envelope. It was from her father. The handwriting was a little shaky, she thought.

171

"Dear Roberta, it is hard to believe that we heard your voice when we
tuned in a few days ago to Free Norway Radio. Of course, we knew
immediately that "Bobby Borg" was out darling daughter. There was
no mistaking your voice. It gave us great heart to know that you are
alive and well. What a miracle the wireless can be! We want you to
know that we are both well, but getting a bit ancient these days.
Your mother's eyesight is not too good, and my knees are playing up
a bit, but otherwise we are surviving. We do not venture out much.
 The Germans are everywhere and they do not treat anyone very kindly.
They have no respect for our advanced age, so it is best we stay
Indoors as much as possible. We wonder how our grandsons are
faring. Clive must be old enough to be in the Forces now. We do
hope he is safe and well. And the other three. How are they? And
Claud of course. Is he well? We know you can not reply to these
questions. We just hope that one day we will all see each other
again. Until then, take care, my angel. Keep broadcasting. They
really are good, and more and more people are taking the risk and
listening in. they really help; our people's morale. I only hope you
get this letter. We were very surprised when this young man came
to the house asking for us. At first we thought he might be a Gestapo
agent. But he said how he had met you and that he had ways of
getting a letter to you. So we only hope he succeeds. His name you
will know. Lars Hansen. All our love. Mum and Dad"

Bobby fought back her tears, but Greig could see her distress. "Don't
mind shedding a tear, Roberta. It is very understandable. Of course, I knew
who the letter was from, and Lars told me he had contacted them, but I
promise it has not been opened. Perhaps you should read the other letter."
 It was short:

"Dear Roberta,
I hope this reaches you safely, as I hope too that the one from your
Parents does, also. It was good to meet them. They are frail, but in good
spirits. You remember you told me where they lived, so it was not hard
To find them. They thought at first that I was one of those Gestapo
bastards!
I am fully fit. My shoulder is fine, as good as new. The Nazis are,
I am glad to report, paying a price for what they did to my darling wife
And son. As long as I draw breath, they will continue to do so. We

Met so briefly, but I have not forgotten, nor ever will forget your kindness
To me. Well, apart that is from your frosty first reaction to me!! I think
Of you often, and the memory will not dim. It is now sustained by the
Broadcasts you are making. Well done! You are a "natural". More and
More people have heard about these broadcasts and are secretly listening
In.
God willing, we will both survive this terrible war, and I hope that we
May then meet again.
Your Friend, Lars.

Bobby did not weep at this second letter, but there was a lump in her
throat. She knew that she also would not forget this brave man, and prayed
that, as he did, they would meet again when the war was over.

CHAPTER 36

Clive had been posted to No. 431 Squadron, flying Lancasters, based at Slingsbury in Lincolnshire. Like much of that county, the airfield was as flat as a pancake, swept by chilly winds blowing off the North Sea. "God" thought Clive when he first set eyes on it, "This must be the bleakest place in the whole of England". Bleak maybe, but ideally suited to its purpose, for Lincolnshire was just about the nearest point to the land mass of Northern Germany and the industrial Ruhr. All the main targets were within range: Cologne, Frankfurt, Essen, Dusseldorf. The shipyards of Hamburg, the largest port in Germany. Bremen, the heartland of the iron and steel industry and oil refining. Berlin, too, could be reached. Hitler's capital was bound to be a prime target.

The airfield lay one mile to the east of the village of Slingsbury and had been farmland until the war. The main runway had deliberately been laid East-West. With the wind largely blowing in off the North Sea the aircraft would take off into it, and straight onto their course, without circling over mid-England away from their target areas. This would save precious time and more important, fuel   Clive and his fellow crew members were not all billeted together. Of the crew of seven who would fly F Fandango, the Skipper, David Easton, the Co-pilot cum Wireless Operator, Peter Philpott and the Flight Engineer, Jimmy Hicks, were all commissioned officers and had their own quarters and Officers Mess. Clive and the other crew members were all either Sergeants or, like Clive, Flight Sergeants. There were Julian Ould the mid-upper Gunner, Digby Fox, the Bomb Aimer cum Nose gunner, and Simon Prevost, the Navigator. Only David Easton and Hicks had been in the RAF before the war. David was 24 and Jimmy 25. Jimmy was a flight Lieutenant and David a Flying Officer, one rank lower, but in the aircraft David had command, just like the skipper of a boat. Rank became immaterial. In any case, on F Fandango they all got on well and drank together in the village local, The Seven Smugglers.

By the beginning of March they were ready for Ops. For nearly two months they had trained as a crew, practising various procedures, becoming familiar with every switch and knob, every nut and bolt of the Lancaster. They attacked dummy targets over Scotland and Wales, rehearsing evasion tactics, simulating engine failures and fires on board, learning each others skills in case of emergencies. The Lancaster was the very latest bomber to come into service. Prior to the "Lanc" there had been the Short Stirling and the Handley Page Halifax. Neither had proved a great success. The Stirling was too slow and the Halifax insufficient range but the Halifax was still in service. The Lancaster was faster than both of them and could fly over two thousand miles with a full bomb load. And by the end of the war, it had been so developed and modified that it could carry a bomb load of 22,000lbs – nearly 10 tons.

F Fandango was new off the production line. It gleamed. Not a scratch on its green and brown camouflage paint work. Inside it even smelled new – a mixture of leather, metal and lubricant. To Clive, it seemed almost a shame that they would have to soil its pristine newness by loading it with bombs, and risking damage or worse, destruction, over Germany.

Their first briefing was detailed, and to the point. Their target was to be Wilhelmshaven, a strategic North Sea naval base on the west side of Jadebusen. "Jadebusen" the meeting was informed, translated as Jade Bay, but the water would not be very green by the time they had pounded Wilhelmshaven. The weather, they were told, would be fine and clear, with a quarter moon. Good for seeing the target, but equally good for being seen themselves by the enemy nightfighters and searchlights that would certainly greet their arrival. The only small consolation was that it was a coastal target. At least they would not have to penetrate deep into Germany's heartland, so would have a better chance of survival back to Slingsbury. Four other squadrons, one of Halifaxes, were to take part in addition to 431 Squadron. 431 would be the third wave making their bombing run, so there should be plenty of fires burning by the time they got there to illuminate the docks and oil storage tanks. Hopefully, the civilian population would largely be spared. (Not now, but later in the war, the RAF would specifically pound civilian urban conurbations, with the objective of killing and demoralising as many Germans as possible. For example, in a single night of bombing of Dresden, fifty thousand civilians would be killed.)

The briefing took place at 1000am. Lunch that day was the last meal they would have before they returned in the early hours of the 5th. For some of Clive's comrades in the squadron, it would be their last meal ever. Clive ate lightly. The mixture of excitement and anxiety was no recipe for eating a heavy meal. However, he made sure that he had a supply of Mars Bars to sustain him during the assignment – it would be a long time before he touched down again.

The crew assembled at 1700 hrs, all kitted up and checks completed. Last minute update on weather both at take-off and over Wilhelmshaven, and a brief Good Luck and God Speed address from the Station Commander and finally a word from their Squadron Leader. Into the trucks and off to their aircraft. Then flight checks: fuel, oil, hydraulics, controls, instruments, guns, and power. For Clive a thorough check that his four Browning machine cannons were fully operative, and ammunition belts fully loaded. Finally, check the power to the rear turret, where he would be closeted for the next seven or eight hours. Leave nothing to chance. This was no time to find the turret would not swivel, least of all if he needed to retreat into the main body of the plane! Too late, he remembered that he had not posted the two letters he had written that afternoon: one to Philippa and one to his parents. He had left them in his bedside locker. Perhaps, he reflected, it was as well, for both of them had spoken of his love for them all, and although he was speaking from his heart, nevertheless it might be embarrassing if he returned safe and sound after all! Increasingly, lately, he had found himself turning to God. Perhaps it was the war, and the dangers that now faced him, perhaps it was because he now had a partner and a child to share his life with and whom he yearned to be with more and more. Now, encased in his goldfish bowl, cut off even from his fellow crew members, he prayed. His prayer was simple:

Deliver Me O God, And Forgive Me For What I Am About To Do To Innocent People.

One by one, the four great Merlin engines sprang to life and shattered his prayer. There was something reassuring about that roar, that deep; growl that he had first heard in 1940 as The Few, as they had now become known, rose in their Spitfires to take on and eventually repel the Luftwaffe armada. The great plane vibrated and gently rolled forward. It was dark. Clive could not see the ground beneath him, nor light of any kind except the small glow of the exhausts of the Lancs on the apron behind, queuing up to turn on to the runway. This was it. There is no turning back now Clive. No saying I wish I had not volunteered for aircrew. You did. And now you are it. Off to war.

Please God, guard over us all in F Fandango. Bring us home safely.

PLEASE GOD.

F Fandango rose into the night sky.

CHAPTER 37

Deliberately, Clive had notified neither Philippa nor his family that he was about to fly his first mission. He knew the apprehension it was bound to engender. Philippa had given birth only a few weeks ago and Charlotte was putting on weight nicely. Clearly, the infant was happy with her mother's milk and he had no wish to put that at risk by precipitating Philippa into drying-up from anxiety. Equally, he was mindful that it was not that long ago that his father had suffered a serious heart attack. He did not wish stress to precipitate another one, another that might be fatal. Of course, he realized that some time soon – assuming he successfully dodged the German flak and night fighters – he would have to come clean and tell them all that his war had started in earnest.

So, as F Fandango headed out over the North Sea that night of March 4th, the Browning family pursued their normal routine. Bobby prepared an evening meal for the boys. Douglas and Kenneth cycled home from Wimbledon a little the worse for wear. They had spent the afternoon playing in the inter-house Rugger competition, Douglas with his head buried in the Second Row and Kenneth performing heroically at Full Back, the last line of defence. For Douglas this would be the last time he took part in the competition. He would be leaving at the end of the next term, the Summer Term. So he was especially happy that he had scored a try. Admittedly it was a break-out from a melee near the opposition's line: he had hardly done more than flop over their try-line, but it was his try, and he was thrilled. Ken, being only fifteen still, had been playing for the Colts. He liked playing full-back. There was nothing more satisfying than stopping some fancy speed merchant on the opposing wing from scoring in the corner, or worse, under the posts. He had also gone a long way to perfecting his goal-kicking skill and was usually given the task in the School Colts XV as well as the House Colts.

As for Finn the day had been pretty uneventful: classes all morning and afternoon. He had been saddened to learn that two of his pals were leaving at the end of term to go to another Prep School. Shawbury House School was at Long Ditton, about two miles away. Too far to walk to every day, but not too far to get to by bicycle. Apparently, one of them had a chum who raved about the School, saying that they had the most marvellous playing fields, and a swimming pool. "The pool is great" they were told "It's outdoors of course, so not much use in winter, but come the Summer Term, we can use it every day. It even has frogs swimming about in it, so you have to keep your mouth shut, in case you swallow one!"

Finn tackled Bobby on the matter. "Mum, two of my best friends, Simon and Philip, are leaving Branchester and they're going to Shawbury House next term. They say it is miles better for sports, and some of the boys weekly board, too. I wouldn't mind doing that, and think of the meals it would save you getting." Bobby smiled "I think you are forgetting something, Finn. I have to get meals for your brothers, and oh! have you forgotten I need to eat from time to time as well."

"Well, yes, I suppose so, but the main thing is that Shawbury House has huge playing fields and they have a full size running track marked out in Summer. Mummy, will you please think about it, and talk to Dad about it. Branchester is not bad, but I really think Shawbury would be better, and I promise I would work really hard there."

"Alright, I will talk to your father about it, but I don't know about weekly boarding; we would have to consider if we could afford it, and also how you would get there. It's a long way from here, and I do not like the idea of you cycling all that way on your own, especially after dark Now get on with your supper and you've got some homework to do." Claud was staying overnight in London. Even though the air raids on London had dwindled in recent months, they had not stopped all together, and it was his stint to be on the roof of the office building, "tin titfer" and all. That was the bit he liked least. The steel helmets were identical to those used in the Great War and it always reminded him of those ghastly times in the trenches in Flanders. He hoped Douglas would never have to go through that kind of experience. A shiver went through him: Douglas only had a few more months before he would be called up too. It was bad enough thinking about Clive flying in Bomber Command. He would very soon be risking his life over enemy territory. There were few easy options in wartime. Which service would Douglas end up in? Whichever it was, with luck he might avoid a combat situation. The Air Force was not ALL about flying. The fliers needed ground support in all sorts of ways: Engineering, Transport, Ground Defence (there was even an RAF Regiment now for that very purpose.) Or the Royal Navy? The same applied. It did not automatically mean going to sea.. And for that matter, there were more Army personnel out of front line situations than in them. So really it was no good worrying. Hopefully, this bloody conflict would be over one way or another before young Ken had to join up, and God help us if it was not still going on when Finn was old enough to serve! Silently, he prayed to the God beyond those stars twinkling in the clear night sky above him that they would all come through safely. And on the winning side.

Two hundred miles to the East, 15,000 feet above the dark ocean, F Fandango droned towards Germany. The intercom crackled: "OK fellers, stop your day dreaming, we are about forty minutes out from the target zone. Time to keep your eyes peeled for the bogeymen; we're in their patrolling range." Clive shifted his cramped position, as much as the turret would allow, then checked his guns yet again, swinging them up and down, through their full vertical arc. This done he swivelled the turret itself, first left then right. Fat lot of good it would be, he thought, if a bloody Messerschmitt turned up and I couldn't have a go at it!

The Intercom crackled again: "Skipper here. Any sightings anyone? We'll be crossing the Dutch coast in about twelve minutes. We are attacking from the south, repeat south, so we should be over land just north of Emden. Their night birds will be looking for us, so Julian and Clive keep searching for them. With this moon, they'll see us clearly enough, but we should be able to spot them too. Out"

Ahead, and slightly to port, but still far off, David Easton and Digby saw the distant glow. The Pathfinders and the first squadron to go in had found the target. Well, hopefully they have, David said silently to himself. I don't want to dump this load into the sodding fields. Just then they saw the first flashes. Brilliant bursts of white light, above them and to their right. "OK, guys, the fireworks have started. That's their ack-ack, probably at Emden. At least their night fighters are leaving us alone, hopefully." In the moonlight Clive saw two or three other Lancasters trailing behind them. Other Lancs from 431 Squadron. I wonder who they are". The shell bursts were closer now, close enough to be audible even above the engines' roar, and close enough, for the plane to shake momentarily. Clive felt tense, hyper alert, but not truly terrified. Strange, he thought to himself, why aren't I shit-scared? Searchlights swept the sky, one momentarily catching them in its glare, before it lost them as they entered a small cloud. In seconds they were out the other side. David held his course, no deviation allowed. Dangerous to take evasive action with other aircraft close around.

God, how awful it would be to die by colliding with another Lanc. Julian, the dorsal gunner, came on the Intercom: "someone's been hit poor bugger. Looks like his outer starboard engine, but I can't be sure. He's holding up. He's slightly above us at 110 degrees. The searchlights spotted the burning plane and homed in on it. The glare must have completely blinded the Lancaster's crew, already struggling to keep it on an even keel and get to the target. Without warning the Lancaster exploded. Just one massive ball of fire plummeting to earth. No one in that inferno would have known anything about it. That was a mercy at least.

David Easton came on the Intercom: "All right lads. There's nothing we can do. Just concentrate, and pray to your God and thank Him that it wasn't us." The fireglow at Wilhelmshaven was brighter now, much closer, and spreading over a wider area. David began his turn – from almost due East to almost due North. Shell bursts became more frequent, and more accurate. With a great metallic "clang" something hit the underbelly of the great plane and it shook like some wounded animal. David checked his controls and instruments. Everything seemed to be working still. "Everyone OK? Report in, please. Jimmy? Digby? Simon? Clive?" In turn, each crew member reported they were undamaged.

"Right, we are nearly there fellas. Bomb doors opening! Digby, it's your show now. Take us in nice and steady, and drop your eggs. Then we can get the hell out of here and home for a nice cup of tea."

From his vantage point in the tail, Clive saw the burning city far beneath him. Huge areas were aflame. He could pick out the docks and sheds, and what looked like a railway marshalling yard. He could see the water in the bay, the fires turning it into a vast, shimmering sheet of gold. He recoiled as some missile struck the glass of his turret with a resounding "ping". He was lucky, the shrapnel must just have glanced it, without penetrating it. Clive heard Digby giving David his instructions: "OK Skip, you are bang on line. Keep her steady. Steady. Right two degrees. Steady. Steadeee! Bombs away. Eggs all gone!" The Lancaster gave a slight shudder. Suddenly it was four tons lighter.

At last, to his huge relief, Wilhelmshaven began to recede. The ack-ack was left behind. He kept alert. Now was when the night fighters liked to have a final fling, when the bomber crews had relaxed a fraction, after the holocaust. He saw nothing. F Fandango headed out across the dark North Sea.. "Home James, and don't spare the horses!" It was Jimmy on the Intercom. "I want that cup of tea, skipper, so step on the gas please. Actually I need a pee before the tea!"

Their first mission was over. They had all survived. They would fight another day. But how many more "other days"? Clive knew the chances of surviving the regulation thirty missions were only one in four. He could only hope that he was the One and not the other Three.

Over London, the night had been quiet.. Up on the roof of the building in Fleet Street, Claud Browning looked to the East and saw the dome of St. Paul's Cathedral silhouetted in the first glimmer of morning light.

At No.18 St.Mark's Orchard, Surbiton, Bobby, Douglas, Kenneth and Finn slept peacefully.

CHAPTER 38

The phone rang just as Philippa, with baby Charlotte, was walking out of the flat door. It was Clive.

"Hi, darling, how is life in Baby Land? How is my little offspring? And how are you, my angel?"

"Fine, Clive. I'm just going out shopping. Well, if you can call it shopping, just standing in queues and hoping there are still a few scraps left when you get to the head of it. It's all very well having Ration Books, but that's no guarantee there will be any food to use the coupons on. What have you been doing? Still dreary training I suppose?"

"Well actually no, Philippa. We did our first trip yesterday. For real. The whole squadron went and blitzed Wilhelmshaven. I didn't like to tell you ahead of going, in case you got worried, but actually it was a piece of cake. And we made a hell of a mess of the docks there" Clive made no mention of the losses they had suffered. The Lanc they saw explode was not the only aircraft not to return. P for Popeye had failed to get back and no one knew what had happened to it. Another Lancaster had taken a hit on the port wing, which had knocked out both port engines. Somehow it had managed to stagger home on the two starboard motors. A bloody miracle. A massive lump of shrapnel had penetrated yet another plane and had almost cut the Wireless Operator in two, poor bastard. He died instantly. None of this did Clive mention to Philippa.

Momentarily, Philippa felt faint. She had known all along that Clive would not be sitting on his backside in Lincolnshire for the rest of the war. But the sudden knowledge that he had actually been raiding Germany, and had probably – no certainly – been facing enemy night fighters and flak from the ground, was an enormous shock.

"Are you still there? Hello! Hello! Clive's voice jolted her back from these thoughts.

"Yes, I'm here, darling. It just came as a bit of a surprise to realize you had actually been flying in anger, that's all. You ARE alright, aren't you?"

"Yes, I'm fine. It really was just like falling off a log. We never saw a bogeyman the whole trip, so I didn't even get to have a pop at them. There was a bit of a dent in our lovely new baby, though. We got a bit too close to one of Fritz's fireworks I expect. They'll soon have her back as good as new, though"

"Do you know when your next trip is going to be? No, that's a silly question; I should know better than to ask. I'm sorry, darling. Have you called your mother and father?"

"No, Philly, you come first now. But I will phone them straight after this. But the other thing I wanted to tell you is that after another four ops. we get a spot of leave.

Only a few days, worst luck, but I wondered if we could go down to Rosedown? I'm sure they would like to see Charlotte. What do you think?"

"I think it's a great idea. I had been thinking of going anyway. Just let me know the dates they give you. And for pity's sake be careful. I hate to think of you flying over Germany, and I know the risks. Don't forget I was a working girl 'til not long ago."

"I'll be all right. I'll take my Teddy Bear for company. He should keep me out of trouble.!"

Finn was so proud when Bobby told him that his eldest brother had actually bombed the Germans. At aged eleven he could not fully understand the risks and dangers that Clive was facing. Nor could he conceive of the stress and fear that his brother had to endure. His imagination did not stretch to men plummeting thousands of feet to certain death, to being roasted alive, or having limbs blown off. These horrors, mercifully, he was spared. For Finn, it was simply the case that his brother was bashing the Germans, giving them back a bit of their own medicine.

Finn could not contain his excitement at school next day, telling friends and teachers alike what his brother had been doing. One of his pastimes recently had been assembling the balsa wood kits of the different types of fighter planes. Mostly, it had been Hurricanes and Spitfires, and the American Mustang, and occasionally an enemy plane, such as the Messerschmitt 109. Now, he set about saving his pocket money for an Avro Lancaster, and when the assembly work was done he had made up his mind that he would get some transfers and put Clive's aircraft's name on it. F Fandango. And it would have pride of place in his bedroom, hanging from the middle of the ceiling.

Finn's scrapbook, so long full of Allied retreats, losses and disasters both on land and sea, now began to record a few chinks of light in the dark curtain. Notable among these were the incursions by Allied bombers into Germany and Occupied Europe. From America, squadron after squadron of B.17 Flying Fortress bombers began to arrive at airfields all over Britain, but mainly in East Anglia and the Eastern Counties. The B.17 was very heavily armed, so much so that it was sometimes called the Flying Porcupine, after the proliferation of cannons protruding from gun turrets front and rear, above and below the fuselage, and on either side. Its primary role was daylight bombing, the belief being that it was so heavily armed that it could defend itself from enemy fighter attacks, and would not need its own fighter escort. In the early stages this was not available anyway, not until Mustangs with extra fuel tanks under either wing, which could be jettisoned, became available for escort duty. The cost of all this extra armament, and the personnel to man it, meant that the Flying Fortress's bomb-carrying capability was only a fraction of its British counterparts. Nevertheless, it struck hard at Germany's industrial targets, through sheer force of numbers, though with terrible losses, far higher than were suffered by the British .

Finn's ears were glued to the radio news bulletins, and he diligently scoured every newspaper that Claud brought home for him, just to get news of the latest British and American bombing raids. He was not to know that such reports did not always tell the unvarnished truth. It was important that public morale should be maintained and that the German High Command's should be depressed as far as possible. If this meant inflating enemy losses and exaggerating Allied success, then that was acceptable. So seldom a day passed when Finn and the rest of the Browning family did not tune in to the news. But better than that was to go to the cinema.

During the dark days of war no one thing better relieved worry, fear and stress, than a family saying "Let's go to the Odeon, there's a really good flick on". It did not really matter if the film was a good one, whatever was showing was an escape from the grim realities and austerities, if only a fleeting one. For children, in addition to the regular feature films, there was a Saturday Morning showing of films especially made for them, and the Regal, Granada or Odeon would all be packed out. Finn seldom attended these sessions, he was too busy at athletics practice with Shirley Black, or playing squash. But whenever he could, he did go with his mother or brothers to see the latest Walt Disney production. "Snow White and the Seven Dwarfs" first appeared in 1937, two years before the war began, and enchanted both adult and child alike. It was screened time and time again, and still is to this day. By 1940 Disney was at his peak. First, there was "Pinocchio", screened just as the bombs began to rain down on London. Then there was "Dumbo" about a baby elephant, and in 1942 "Bambi" the story of a little deer in the forest. All these films captivated , charmed and uplifted people of all ages. Perhaps more than any other film, "The Wizard of Oz" lifted peoples' spirits. Who all those years ago, and who right up to this day, is not entranced when they hear

Judy Garland singing "I'm off to see the Wizard, the Wonderful Wizard of Oz" or "Some Day Over the Rainbow"?

No visit to the cinema was complete, though, without the Newsreel. Here, in stark black and white, were depicted the actual events of the war: war in the air, on land and at sea.. War in Africa and war in the Far East, and on all the Oceans. War in the factories and in the fields. "Dig for Victory" was the exhortation. "Save your old saucepans", along with pictures of Spitfires coming off the production line. And, most popular, film of Heinkels and Stukas being shot out of the sky, or the rare depictions of U-Boats being sent to the ocean bed. Finn relished above even these the shots taken from the air of German cities and installations being plastered. To him this WAS the war. This was Clive's war. And so it was FINN'S war. He promised himself that when he was old enough, if the war was still being waged, that he also would fly in Lancaster bombers.

It was on Clive's fifth mission that things went badly wrong. F Fandango reached its target – Hamburg – and its bombs found their target in the Dock area. The Lancaster was following the Elbe downstream to the coast, heading out into the North Sea, when the German gunners got lucky. The shell exploded directly behind Fandango and fragments struck Clive's turret. To begin with, he felt nothing, except the blast of freezing air enveloping him. Then he saw the blood pumping from the wound in his right thigh. Still no pain, just numbness. It is hard to think of Good Fortune at such a moment, but he was lucky in two respects. First, his Intercom still worked and second, his turret was so aligned that its exit doors would open into the fuselage, and not into space.

"I've been hit, Skipper. Can you get someone down here, I'm losing blood by the bucketful."

Peter Philpott reached Clive before he lost consciousness and managed to drag him back out of the gun turret and in to the fuselage. There was only the dimmest bulkhead light, but Peter could see a large, jagged fragment of metal protruding from the wound, and blood oozing out and soaking what was left of Clive's flying suit trouser leg. Helped by Jimmy, who had also made his way to the tail, Peter unzipped his own suit, pulled off his shirt, ripped off one of its sleeves, and wound it in a tight tourniquet above the gaping wound. The blood flow slowed, but could not be stopped completely. "God, I hope he can last out 'til we get him home. I think it's going to be touch and go, skipper. Any chance you can crank up our speed?"

David Easton already had the great plane on maximum revs., but by dumping some fuel and putting the craft into a shallow decline he was able to gain precious m.p.h and time. Almost certainly it saved Clive's life. The surgeons reckoned that another twenty minutes loss of blood would have been more than the human frame could sustain.

F Fandango touched down at Slingsbury just before 2.00am. Clive was still unconscious, but later, he vaguely remembered the cold spreading through his body and a faint ringing in his head as gently he was lifted out of the aircraft. Everything, but especially Peter's voice trying to reassure him, seemed distant and faint. He likened it to being in a cathedral, empty except for someone's muffled murmuring from the crypt. The ambulance was beside the aircraft even before the engines fell silent, and Clive, his flying suit a torn and blood-sodden mess, was eased gently into it. By 2.30am he was in the operating theatre. The shrapnel had ripped through the powerful quadriceps muscle that flexes the leg, had fractured the femur, fortunately in a clean break, and protruded through to the inside of Clive's thigh.

"Hello, young man. I suppose you weren't told that you got me out of bed at 2.00 in the morning!" Clive was scarcely conscious, his eyes still closed. The friendly voice came from above. Ridiculous, but Clive wondered if he was at the gates of Heaven. Or Hell. He opened his eyes to see a pair of the palest blue eyes he had ever seen twinkling kindlily at him. The man was about fifty, balding and a little portly. He was wearing the uniform of a Group Captain. "I am your surgeon, Browning, name of Blenkinsop. Had one hell of a job sorting out your thigh. However, you will be pleased to learn that no permanent damage has been done. At least not by that lump of steel that got stuck in it. Of course, my surgery may have buggered it up. Ha, ha. No, I think you will be just fine, but it will be a few months before you will be fit for flying duties again, and I cannot guarantee you will be given the go-ahead for combat duties. We'll keep an eye on you here for a while, and then we'll get you off to a convalescent home. There is an excellent RAF Convalescent Home at Headley in Surrey. Oh, by the way, we have informed your wife that you are here and in reasonable shape, and there is no reason at all why she can't get up here to see you. In fact, I daresay she is on the way now. I believe she was a WAAF until recently, so I daresay she has wangled a free ride in a staff car!"

Philippa arrived at the Hospital that evening soon after six. The Matron had spoken to her and advised not to visit until Clive had full got over the effects of the anaesthetics. In any case, he had hardly had any sustenance since taking off for the joyride to Hamburg the night before. She was warned that the effects of the morphine injections for his pain might make him drift off from time to time. Philippa felt in an emotional entropy – a chaos of conflicting emotions. Joy versus anger. Relief versus dread. Uncertainty versus determination. At such times, clarity, steadiness comes from an unexpected quarter.. In Philippa's case it was the small bundle that nestled in her lap as the staff car sped up the Great North Road to Lincolnshire. Charlotte Annabel Lee. Apart from one breast feed, the baby slept all the way from London and only stirred momentarily when Philippa alighted at the hospital.

Clive had been allocated a room on his own. He was lucky – the hospital was a civilian establishment where patients were accommodated in wards of eight or ten beds. But at this moment it was overcrowded, mostly with casualties like Clive – wounded and sick airmen. So it had been necessary to convert some of the staff rooms to sick bays accommodating just one patient, and Clive had been allocated one.

No moment in the whole of Clive's life had been so precious, so totally unforgettable as this. The door opened and Philippa stood there, her face a mixture of anguish and love. But it was not this that, in later life, Clive would recall. No, it was something far more elemental. Charlotte Annabel Lee began to cry. Clive held out his arms, unsure whether it was Philippa or the babe he wanted more to hold. But women have an instinct that never fails, and gently, oh so gently, Philippa held out the infant, and Clive took her in his arms and held her to his chest, and not really knowing why, he silently cried.

CHAPTER 39

Knowing that their son was going to be transferred, when well enough, to the RAF Convalescent Home at Headley, the Brownings did not visit Clive in hospital in Lincolnshire. Headley is not far from Epsom, a comparatively easy journey from Surbiton. They were savvy enough to understand that much as they would have loved to see him sooner, all the visitors he really needed, were Philippa and Charlotte, and his pals from the base, and Fandango in particular.

The Hospital Almoner was a kind woman and found local accommodation for Philippa and the baby, so they were able to visit Clive daily. It was ironic that only his dreadful wound enabled Clive to spend so much time with Charlotte, but he took full advantage of the opportunity. It was ten days before Blenkinsop allowed him out of bed and onto crutches, and then only to take a few tentative steps, with the injured leg well off the ground. But the few steps soon lengthened to going to the loo along the passage. David Easton and the rest of the crew came in a bunch one evening. Hospital rules in those days were strict: No More than Two Visitors May See A Patient At Any One Time. The Duty Sister was duly bribed with the promise of two pairs of silk stockings (almost impossible to find in those war days, and kindly donated by US Army Airforce personnel from the neighbouring American base at nearby Crimpton. These guys seemed to have unfettered access to stockings, cigarettes, chocolate and all manner of luxuries.)

"Hi, Clive, good to see you sitting up.. We were afraid we'd lost you for a minute or two. We never realized a body could spill so much blood. Made a fucking mess of the old crate, you did." Clive smiled. He was so happy to see that all his friends were still alive and well. "Have they fixed Fandango yet?" he asked. "Yes, Clive. You've got a completely new greenhouse to grow your tomatoes in, and lovely new guns to go with it. Jerry just can't wait for you to come and have a good pot at him." They all laughed. David said "Actually, we've done two more missions while you've been wallowing in luxury. We borrowed a rear gunner from the Yanks would you believe. Nice guy, but he can't shoot straight for toffee. We hit Hamburg again, and Kiel. 'fraid we lost two of our squadron though, although we think we saw some of them bale out from B Banana. What's the prognosis on your leg? It'll be good to have you back on board."

Clive felt the warmth of comradeship that only comes to men, and men grouped together in the face of danger. They stayed an hour, and he was saddened to see them depart, even though he had the consolation that he would see Philippa and Charlotte next day.

He did not - could not – know that as they turned and left his bedside, he would never see them again. Two nights later, over Cologne, F Fandango received a direct hit from the German ack-ack. The shell exploded just beneath the bomb-bay doors. If it had hit a minute later, after their bomb load had been released, they might have survived. David, Peter, Jimmy, Julian, Digby and Simon never felt pain. They were vapourised in a milli-second.

CHAPTER 40

If the Lancaster was the most famous and most successful British bomber of the war, it was not the only one to target the Third Reich. There was also the Stirling and the Halifax. On April 11th a Halifax became the first bomber to drop a single bomb weighing 8,000 pounds, or nearly four tons. Raids over Germany grew in number, size and ferocity. But the war was also being prosecuted in many other regions of the world, and Finn took growing satisfaction in scouring the newspapers his father brought home, and in filling his scrapbook. Just in April of 1942, there were stories and pictures of the campaign in North Africa, the Pacific and South-East Asia. In the Atlantic a US destroyer for the first time sank a German U-Boat. In the Mediterranean an Italian Torpedo Boat sank a British Submarine, HMS Upholder. On the 18[th,] to the world's, but more especially Japan's, surprise, a force of US bombers took off from an aircraft carrier and raided Tokyo, and having done so flew on to China without losing a single aircraft. The raid was planned as a psychological shock to the complacent Japanese, and equally a psychological boost to the Allies. The fact that little damage was dealt to Japan's capital was of little consequence.

By this time, Finn had double the pride in his family. Now, not only was his mother "fighting the cause of freedom" with her broadcasts to the oppressed people of Norway, and incidentally Denmark as well, but his eldest brother was bombing hell out of the enemy's factories and shipyards, and had been seriously wounded in the process. There was no doubting the awe in which Finn was held by his friends and school chums. Of course, many of them also had family members in uniform, but none has so far achieved the heroic status of Bobby and Clive. Finn's own activities merely enhanced this veneration. No one could touch him on the squash court – not even much older boys – and no one could catch him on the running track. Life was good, even if there was a war. In fact, it was the war that was, in a perverse way, a key element in making him feel happy.

Whenever he could, he would accompany his family to Headley. He loved Clive even more now that he was a true warrior. Clive was healing well and looking forward to a return to flying duty. Not so his parents, nor Philippa. They knew all to well that next time he might suffer something worse than an injured leg. They silently prayed that he would be found a non-combatant assignment of some kind. Philippa had similar aspirations, but although she retained "connections" in the Air Ministry, she knew Clive would never forgive her if she used them to influence his postings. Nor did she forget that she came from a military family. What on earth would her father, a Great War General have thought? She shuddered to think about it, had she tried to curry a favour. Sir Henry and Lady Hester travelled up from Dorset to see Clive and wish him well. It was a great opportunity for them to see their granddaughter at the same time. When the time came for them to leave the Convalescent Home, Sir Henry surreptitiously handed Clive a package, wrapped in brown paper Quietly, the old man whispered to Clive "Don't open it now man. If you do, you will get me and yourself into deep bother with the Matron. But it might come in handy once you are out of here." It turned out to be a bottle of finest single-malt Scotch whisky.

That April marked other events in the war, eagerly absorbed by Finn. The first Arctic convoy arrived in Murmansk, in Northern Russia, bringing desperately needed tanks and munitions. Nineteen merchant ships had set sail, but five were sunk by German submarines or surface warships, despite Royal Navy escorts sinking one German destroyer. In the Mediterranean, Malta – that tiny outpost of the British Empire – was seen b y the Axis as the one barrier to their control of the Western Mediterranean. Virtually defenceless, except for a small flight of RAF fighters, some of which were slow pre-war Gladiator biplanes, Malta was pounded by more than one thousand separate Luftwaffe attacks. An average of seven raids every day. The population went underground, burrowing shelters, first aid posts and communication centres deep into the soft limestone, and emerging only when it was absolutely necessary. Valetta, the capital, was devastated beyond recognition. The Grand Harbour, home to the British Mediterranean fleet, was under such constant bombardment, that submarines were forced to stay submerged until after dark. In an unprecedented gesture, King George awarded the island the George Cross, the civilian equivalent of the Victoria Cross. The citation read:

"To honour her brave people I award the George Cross to the Island Fortress of Malta, to bear witness to a heroism and devotion that will long be famous in history"

On 25th of April, Princess Elizabeth registered for war service, four days after her 16th birthday. She was one of about 200,000 girls of sixteen who did the same thing, though few actually did wartime labour until they became eighteen.

And so Spring came to its full bloom, including 18 St Mark's Orchard. Claud and Bobby had long since dug up the lawn in both the front and back gardens and planted vegetables. Though Bobby had a deep love of flowers, this simple pleasure had to be shelved in favour of growing food. The front garden was given over to root crops, mostly potatoes and carrots, but also swedes and onions. The back garden was devoted to fruit: tomatoes, raspberries, strawberries, gooseberries and blackcurrants. Soon after the family moved to Surbiton, Claud had planted some young apple and pear trees which by the summer of 1942 were beginning to bear their first few fruits. But in one corner of the back garden, Claud grew tobacco. Like every other commodity from overseas, tobacco was scarce, and whilst none of the Browning household smoked, many friends and colleagues did, so Claud's little production line was very welcome. When ready for picking, the leaves were dried for about ten weeks in the garage, then rolled into "sausages", soaked for curing in a mixture of sugar and honey for a further six weeks or so, and then finely chopped and packed into old tins. Claud's friends at the office said it tasted like old boots, but was better to smoke than nothing at all!

With the help of Shirley Black's coaching, and with the strength and speed of being a year older, Finn's exploits on the track were even more startling than in the summer of 1941. Once again, in is school sports, no one could get near him over any distance below the half-mile. But Finn was still only eleven and a half, and so still could not enter the Surrey Schools Championships. He felt a boyish impatience at what, to him at least, seemed unfairness. He knew he could beat older boys: after all, he was doing it at Branchester House year after year. So why should he not challenge boys from other schools? Bobby had promised to discuss with Claud a switch of schools for Finn, but nothing had been concluded. Claud was uneasy about the boy cycling 2 miles through busy streets, especially after dark, when motor vehicles had to proceed with masked headlamps. So the matter had been shelved. Now, Finn raised it again. He was smart enough to realize that his new successes at the sprint distances was a matter of pride to his father, so maybe he would relent, and agree to the switch to Shawbury House.

"Dad, I know you were anxious about me going to Shawbury House last autumn, but I wonder if you and Mum would think about it again. After all, I am going to be twelve next January, and the great thing is that they take Athletics a lot more seriously than they do at Branchester House, and they have their own playing fields, so I could practise even more. Please Dad. Oh, and did you know that George next door, and Terence Shaw are there now, and they say it is much better in every way, and the Headmaster is great, and they have a Maths master who was a pilot in the Royal Flying Corps in the Great War, and they have their own swimming pool. I really do want to go there. Oh, and one other thing: they play Rugger there in the Spring Term. I'd really like to try that, instead of football. What do you say, Dad?"

"I would say that that is quite an impassioned speech for an 11 year old. I'll tell you what I'll do. Mummy and I will make an appointment to go and see the School and meet the Headmaster. But I am not promising anything. Is that understood?"

The Headmaster at Shawbury House was always referred to, by pupils and staff alike, as "H.M." The assumption that this referred to his position of Headmaster was only partially correct, for his name was Dudley John Vincent Hamilton-Maxwell. H.M. was a tall man, whose great height – 6ft 4in., stemmed from the length of his back, rather than the length of his legs. He was about fifty years old, slim and balding. His eyes were unusually large, and sad looking, which utterly belied his jocular manner. He always wore faded blue rugger shorts that came down below his knees. It was abnormal to see him without a pipe in his mouth, and even more abnormal to see it actually alight. It seemed it was just an accoutrement, some sort of comfort object. Bobby and Claud were shown into H.M.'s Study by the Housekeeper, who said that HM would be along in a minute, but added that "a minute" might stretch to five or even ten, as he was often delayed by something or other.

H.M.'s Study was a study in itself. His desk was enormous and Claud imagined that once it may have belonged to some Indian Rajah. It was ebony, and covered in faded green leather. Very untidily, it was littered with papers, magazines and books.. In a silver picture frame was a photo of a much younger H.M., wearing a striped blazer and, surprisingly, white flannel trousers, and holding a croquet mallet. Beside the frame stood a heavy, cut glass double ink well, containing red and blue ink. Three badly worn leather armchairs stood round a generous brick fireplace. The stuffing was bulging through the arms of one of the chairs. The carpet in front of the fire was pockmarked where burning wood had shot out of the log fire. In one corner stood a glass display cabinet containing a handsome display of silver cups and shields. The French windows behind the desk let out on to a gravelled terrace from which steps led down to a pair of grass tennis courts.

H.M. strode in and introduced himself. His handshake was unexpectedly light for such a large man. "I am terribly sorry to have kept you waiting, Mr and Mrs Browning. Our French teacher is absent unwell, so I had to step in myself. Before we go any further, I should tell you that one of my boys has already spoken to me about your son – his name is Finn I believe. An unusual name. I hear he has unusual talents, according to Terence Shaw at least.   Just the sort of lad we want here – we play a lot of inter-school matches, but sadly at the moment we are at a low ebb, so he could be a great asset. Of course, he would need to pass the Common Entrance Exam. Now, that's enough from me. You must have questions you would like to ask, before I show you round the school."

There was no doubting the facilities Shawbury House could offer, and the mere size of the grounds alone was impressive: three full size   football pitches, an outdoor 25 metre shooting range and the two tennis courts, plus the famous swimming pool. Bobby and Claud failed to spot any frogs, but that was probably because the water was an   inpenetrable cloudy green colour. It reminded Claud of the green leather on H,M.'s desk. It seemed the Head was unaware of, or indifferent to any Health Regulations, but in 1942 these were low on anyone's list.   And, in any case, none of the boys had suffered illness from it. Because perhaps they took good care not to ingest the pool's contents. Also in the grounds was a Fives Court, a game neither Claud nor Bobby had ever heard of, plus a well equipped gymnasium. Another plus was that the School accommodated boarders on a week day basis. H.M. liked the idea of boys, at least partially, breaking the parental apron strings. It was all hard to resist. A week later, Finn was interviewed by H.M. and there and then sat, and passed the Entrance Paper. It was agreed he would start his new school in the September term.

CHAPTER 41

Finn left Branchester House with many regrets. Although one or two of his best friends had earlier left to go to Shawbury, nevertheless a good number remained, and he was sad to think he might see little of them in the future. He was sad, also, to be saying goodbye to Mrs Goose, who had been so kind to him throughout his two years there. And Mr Carne, "Old Carnage" was not such a bad old stick when he was not foaming at the mouth! The gloom was more than countered by the exciting prospect of life at Shawbury House. H.M. might be a bit of an oddity in his baggy old rugger shorts, but he had not seemed in the least awesome or intimidating. On the contrary, at his interview with Finn he had spent most of the time talking about all sorts of different sports. It emerged that he had been a fine cricketer in his younger days who had even played the occasional game for Surrey County, and had captained their Second Team for two years between the wars. But now his main interest was Croquet. At this he had excelled to the extent that he had captained the England Team to tour New Zealand in 1938, and furthermore made plain his intention to continue doing so, if asked, after the war was over. Obviously, it never crossed his mind that England might not win it, and even if they lost, then he would set about teaching the Germans the game!

During the Summer holidays Finn spent much of his time with George next door. It was a fine summer and it seemed the sun shone every day. Sometimes they cycled to Surbiton Lagoon for a swim, not returning until the first chill of the evening and the pangs of hunger intervened. They enjoyed going further afield. Oxshott Woods was fun, cycling at breakneck speed along the sandy paths to the Black Pond. There were fish there in its murky depths, but they rarely caught one. They did wade in over the slimy bottom and splash about sometimes. Then they would dry off and race each other back home. George's company was good for Finn, for he saw little of Douglas and Kenneth. The age gap was just too much for them to share their time with him. They had other interests, amongst which, for Douglas at any rate, was Girls. Douglas had taken at least three different girls to the cinema to Finn's certain knowledge. He left King's Wimbledon that summer, his last before being called up for military service, and he intended to make the best of these precious weeks. For Douglas that meant girls. His interest had first been aroused one evening when he had blundered into the bathroom just as Ethel Greenard emerged from the bath stark naked. Ethel had settled in well to her occasional duties when Bobby was in London, and she got on well with all the Browning boys and their father and mother. But it was certainly not part of the contract to appear in the buff to anybody. It was her fault of course for forgetting to lock the bathroom door. Douglas hastily retreated, but not before he had had his first glorious vision of a well-endowed young female. He never forgot it, and only wished it could have been for longer than five seconds.

As for Kenneth, well he had his own friends and devoted a lot of his time to playing tennis at the Berrylands LTC, so Finn was left much to his own devices.

It came as a major surprise to all the family however, when Claud returned from the office one Sunday morning to announce that he had arranged a holiday for them in Cornwall. "Look" he announced, "We have not had a holiday together since the war began. I know that I need a break and your mother could do with a rest as well. She's trying to run a home as well as making all these radio broadcasts. And it will be Douglas's last chance before he joins up. Now it is not anything fantastic. The beaches are all out of bounds, either mined or tank-trapped or both, but I have an ex-colleague who runs a pub in a quiet village in East Cornwall, and he has guest rooms enough to accommodate us all. So I've said we'll go in two weeks time. I hope everyone is agreeable? Oh, and one other thing. I've spoken to Clive and Philippa and they can join us too. Clive is almost fully recovered, but he does not have to start his new posting until mid-September."

To the huge relief of his family, if not to him, Clive was not posted back to his squadron. He had pleaded with his C.O. to go back on combat service. Gently, but firmly, the plea was declined: "No. Browning. You've done your bit for now. You might not be so lucky next time, if you can call that dreadful wound "lucky". However, I do have quite a nice consolation for you. We are putting you forward for a commission, and I have no doubt you will get it. But the icing on the cake is you are going to return to Rhodesia to train new gunner recruits for a spell. I know it means being away from you family, but that's war I'm afraid. Hopefully, the tide will turn a little more in our favour in this damnable war and you needn't be away too long. This does not mean, Browning, you will never go back to flying missions again. There may well come a time when this will be necessary. And remember one other thing, Clive: if you hadn't got your leg smashed up, we wouldn't be having this conversation! You would have gone the way of your good chums in F Fandango." This last remark brought Clive up short. Clive remembered his pals and was suddenly grateful to his God that he had been spared.

CHAPTER 42

The journey to Cornwall involved taking two trains. The first, to Plymouth, and than a change to the local line from Plymouth to Callington, and then taxis to Pithiock   Clive, Philippa   and Charlotte had made separate arrangements: they were going to stop off at Rosedown for a few days to see the General and Lady Hester. The journey was tedious. The train seemed to stop at nearly every station, and was packed out with not a seat spare. Even the corridors were crowded and the majority of passengers were servicemen in uniform, either going on, or returning from, leave. On the whole they were a good-natured bunch , especially those going to reunite with families. Understandably, those returning to their units were more subdued. Some, no doubt, were due for postings overseas. Some would not return to Britain until the war was over. Some would never return.

The connection to Callington was a different story. The rolling stock must have dated from the Great War, or before; it was bumpy, uncomfortable and dirty. The train was hauled by a very tired and grimy steam engine. Even the brass nameplate was scarcely decipherable: "Royal Princess". Anything less regal could hardly be imagined. Slowly, it wheezed out of the war-torn city. Plymouth had taken a terrible battering from the Luftwaffe the year before and the evidence was sickening, even to the Brownings who had not been spared the terror of bombing. Acres and acres were just rubble. The docks had been badly hit and sunken vessels were still visible in the Tamar and the harbour mouth. Eventually, the city gave way to fields and hills and woodland. It was a relief to see the peace and tranquillity of the countryside, with little farmsteads, grazing cattle and sheep, and golden corn ripe for harvesting. The war, it seemed, had not touched rural Cornwall. "Royal Princess" puffed bravely round the winding track, but the inclines were another matter. The poor old darling hissed and wheezed, steam and smoke clouding the sky. And then, with almost a sigh of relief, it reached the crest of the incline and eased into a quiet descent. So it came as a surprise when, on a flat and straight stretch through a cutting, the train slowed to a gentle halt. And then – silence.

Windows already half open on this warm August day, were lowered as far as they would go and heads appeared to see what had caused the stoppage. After a time, the guard marched by from his van at the rear, and from the engine the overalled driver walked back to meet him. A brief conference took place. At first, those in earshot, could tell that the interchange between the two men was earnest, but calm, but very soon voices were raised and it was clear that tempers were rising. Abruptly, the driver broke off the discussion and stumped back towards the front of the train. Embarrassedly, coach by coach, the guard announced what had happened: "Royal Princess" had run out of water. It would be at least an hour before the journey to Callington could resume, pending a tanker being brought down the line from Callington. Since it was a pleasant, sunny late afternoon, and as there were no toilets on this old relic, passengers would be permitted to climb down off the train to stretch their legs and (ahem, ahem!) "admire the view from the top of the embankment". No danger from oncoming trains this was a single-track line. Some passengers took the opportunity to pick some early wild blackberries growing on the banks. Others had a snooze on the warm grass. They arrived at Callington just after 7 pm. The one hour journey from Plymouth had taken three and a half.

It was past 8 pm by the time the Brownings reached Pithiock and the "Vyvyan Arms".

CHAPTER 43

Pithiock is little more than a small hamlet, accessible only by one of those narrow, high-banked lanes that twist and turn and meander throughout much of rural Cornwall. Sometimes, there are passing places, but seldom when they are needed. Very occasionally, they are penetrated by American visitors, who are totally mystified by them.

"Hey, man, what's wrong with a straight line, and why so goddam narrow? How the hell do cars get past each other? You're all crazy!" Well, of course, the British understand these things, and more than that, we treasure the social history that brought about such deep; and narrow furrows. We KNOW that once they were muddy tracks winding and skirting round each peasant's tiny plot of land. And what's the hurry anyway. There is always another day!

The "Vyvyan Arms" was thatched and whitewashed and stood beside the church. A great yew tree in the churchyard stood sentinel over the pub. Across the way was the village pond, and in the middle of the pond was a tiny island, umbrella'd by a weeping willow. As all village ponds should be, this one was host to a family of ducks and another of water hens. It was a peaceful scene. A million miles from Surbiton, London and War. The bright summer's day was fading into dusk when the Brownings arrived, tired and hungry and distinctly frayed at the edges. There seemed to be no one there to meet them. Indeed, not a single soul could be seen anywhere. But, as they unloaded their cases and paid the two taxis that had brought them, a very tall, very fat man emerged from the pub and lumbered towards them holding out his hand. It was Frank Avondale, the landlord, and Claud's erstwhile friend.

"Long time no see, Claud. Welcome to Pithiock and my humble hideout. You are very late: I was expecting you hours ago. What happened? This must be the gorgeous Roberta. How do you do, my dear." Bobby took an instant aversion to the man. He was gross. His breath smelled of whisky. His nose was bloated and purplish. His tweed jacket bore clear evidence of spilled food. He had not been to a barber for a considerable time and he had not shaved for days. He turned away from them and addressed the pub. "Georrrrge, come and help with these bags. Come on.

Where the hell are you, you old fool?" Presently, a wizened little man, bent and distinctly ancient, shuffled out of the pub door. "Oh, there's no need for that" protested Claud "These boys can manage all that. By the way, you haven't been introduced to them, Frank." Tentatively, Douglas, Kenneth and finally Finn took their host's hand. Their expressions were blank, but it was not hard to guess what they were thinking about this repulsive individual.

The "Vyvyan Arms" was large by village pub standards, and doubled as the local hostelry for whoever needed accommodation in the district. The Brownings had been allocated four rooms. All were sparse in size, furniture and fittings. One bathroom served all four rooms. The occupants of the bar below were not especially rowdy, but were certainly audible – no great aid to a peaceful night, at least not until after Last Orders was called at 10.00pm. There were two further bedrooms: one for Frank Avondale and one for his Housekeeper, Mrs Dilys Trevena. There did not appear to be either a Mr Trevena, nor, for that matter a Mrs. Avondale. There was a second bathroom serving these two rooms. Claud and Bobby's room, if cramped, at least had the merit of a double bed and a fine view over the pond to the cluster of dwellings nestling around it. It also faced West, so they were able to enjoy the sunsets, always assuming the weather stayed fine. Unsurprisingly, Douglas and Kenneth shared a twin-bedded room, and the room with another double bed, plus a cot, was reserved for Clive and Philippa and their baby, now six months old. The fourth room was minute, but suited Finn well enough, except that it looked out over the rear of the building, directly onto a row of galvanised dustbins, into one of which a grubby looking youth was emptying scraps.

Back along the corridor, Bobby and Claud were unpacking. "Where on earth did you meet that awful man, Claud. He is dreadful. Surely you never worked with him, did you?"

"Well, the truth is, my dear, that I used to work with him in the mid-thirties. He was a good reporter. Crime mostly. Ten years ago he was very highly thought of in Fleet Street. He frequently had front page credits and covered stories on the Continent as well as here in Britain. Then his marriage broke up. It's a common enough story. People think of news reporting as glamorous: you know, travelling to exotic places, meeting famous and notorious people, staying in fine hotels. The fact is that much of the time you are stuck in a dismal Guest House in some god-forsaken provincial town with nothing to do, except wait for some Court hearing to take place. And what happens? I'll tell you. One of two things happen. Or both. You start propping up the Bar, or you find consolation with some wretched woman, hopefully not a prostitute. Of course, this does not happen to every reporter. Some, like me, just give up reporting and go into Editing – sitting at a desk all day. But Frank, I'm afraid, started hitting the bottle. In particular, Scotch Whisky. Also, he was a victim of his own success; he was away too much and his wife got sick of it. They had no children, fortunately. The marriage just disintegrated. She met someone else and that was more or less that. Frank drank even more heavily and started to miss deadlines. Gordon Johns read him the riot act and for a time things got better. Then the war started and Scotch became hard to get. But by then, he just could not do without it. He found the solution here. By buying a Pub he not only had a ready and virtually limitless source for his "habit", but he didn't have to worry about travelling all over the place to cover stories. He solved two problems at a stroke. Neat really. Now, I know he did not make a very good impression when we arrived, but he is not nearly as awful as you think. Give him a bit of time to get used to having us here. Most of the time, he's just dealing with the locals, or the occasional travelling salesman or suchlike. Come on, let's round up the boys and see if Frank can find us some supper. I'm famished, and I daresay so are they.

Douglas and Kenneth were already in the Public Bar. Douglas, near enough eighteen as didn't matter, had bought himself a pint of bitter, but Kenneth had to content himself with Ginger Beer. The Bar area was split into two, one known as the Saloon Bar and the other as the Public Bar. The Public Bar was very austere, with just a couple of tables and plain wooden chairs, poorly lit with the exception of the light above the darts board. There was an unlit wood burner in the hearth. It's main merit was that it was cheaper than the Saloon Bar. The Saloon Bar was more spacious, with a log fire burning merrily at one end, even though it was Summertime. Frank had pushed two tables together for the family and had even stretched to a cheap glass vase of chrysanthemums. "I'm sorry I can't offer you a menu, Claud. It's getting late, and the Chef is grumbling at being kept from going home. Anyway, I hope you will settle for a bowl of vegetable soup and a lamb stew. Drinks, anyone?"

They were all too tired to care. They would happily have tackled horse meat if they had had to. Frank had the sense to leave them to themselves and as soon as the meal was over they all retired to bed. All except Douglas who asked his father to stay behind and have a nightcap.

"I don't want to linger for long, Douglas. Is there something on your mind? I have a funny feeling there may be."

"Well, yes Dad, there is. I want some advice. It's difficult though. Maybe I'm not very articulate or something and I don't want to sound soft or emotional. The fact is that I'm a bit scared about joining the Navy. I put Navy as first choice, because Clive had opted for the RAF and got a bust leg for his trouble, and was lucky he did not get blown to bits like his mates. I thought that I might have a better chance of surviving in the Navy, but now I am not so sure. And if I'm going to get killed, maybe it would be better the way those bomber boys went. At least they knew nothing about it. My prospect is to be trapped in some ship's engine room or somewhere and get taken to the bottom trapped like a rat. We've taken terrible losses at sea. What do you think I should do? Is there anything I can do?"

"Son, I do know how you feel. How do you think we felt in the trenches in Flanders? Nothing could be worse than that. For God's sake, we lost sixty thousand men in one day on the Somme, but I and thousands like me are here today to tell the tale. You probably have a better chance in the Navy than either the RAF or the Army. Especially as you may never even go to sea. I am not being critical. We all know fear. Every winner of the Victoria Cross felt fear, but they are still rightly called heroes. There is one thing I can suggest, and you may think it odd coming from me, because I have never been a churchgoer and I have never pushed the Christian faith at any of you. But it is true, I think, that the House of Christ, whether you are Christian or not, is a good place to go with a troubled mind. Church. Any church, is a place of peace, calmness and tranquillity, and it really can sometimes help; clear the mind and rationalise things. Anyway, it's worth a try, isn't it? In fact why not pop in there now while it's on your mind? We are all going to bed, so no one will know that's where you have gone, if you don't want them to. I'll tell Kenneth you've just gone for a stroll. And we can talk some more tomorrow if you want to. OK? See you in the morning".

Claud left the bar and joined Bobby upstairs. In the bar there were still a few lingering locals. Douglas bought another half pint of beer , downed it quickly and walked out of the door. Outside, there was still a glimmer of light, a single fading streak of pink in the West. In the church, it was just enough to illuminate the West window. Douglas could see that it was a representation of The Last Supper. It occurred to him that Jesus must have felt a thousand times more afraid than he did, for He KNEW he was going to die – and soon. Douglas walked towards the altar and sat in a pew near the transept. He closed his eyes: it may have been the tedium of the long journey from Surbiton, or the stew, or the beer, but in seconds he was asleep.

Douglas awoke with a start. Somewhere very close by he could hear a small scratching sound. It was now almost pitch dark, but he could just see, scuttling along the back of the pew in front of him, the shape of a mouse. It was only a baby, and it paused only a foot or so from him. Douglas froze, fascinated. The mouse looked at Douglas and Douglas stared at the mouse. It did not move. If he was quick he could have grabbed it and squeezed the life out of the little creature. He was thousands of times its size, and yet it showed no fear of him. It just sat and eyeballed him. His own fear of a painful, elongated death was natural, but not based on any certainties. Had not his own father witnessed the most appalling slaughter in the trenches twenty-five years ago, along with tens of thousands of other men? But survived? Had not his own brother been inches from death? If that lump of red hot metal had struck Clive not on his thigh, but a foot or so higher, he would be dead now. But it had not, and he was alive and active again. Death is a certainty. It is only a matter of when and how. Living in fear of it gets you nowhere, except to debase the years that precede it.

So, come on Doug! Spare the mouse and God might spare you. At least for a while. A long while hopefully. As the French would say: "Courage Mon Ami!"

Later, when Douglas thought back to those moments in Pithiock Church, he smiled wryly. Wasn't it odd that his mind had been straightened out, not by God, but by a baby mouse. Or was God somehow involved too?

The next morning was bright and warm. Eggs and bacon were on offer – a rarity at home in these days of strict rationing. But here, deep in the Cornish countryside, pigs and chickens were reared by almost everyone, so life was a little easier at least in one respect. The whole family tucked in voraciously. Even the demure Bobby, so tall and slender, devoured two eggs and three rashers of bacon. "After that little snack I think we had better get some exercise to settle it down. Who's in favour of exploring the neighbourhood? We've got most of the day, though Mother will want to be back to meet Clive and Philippa at teatime." Everyone agreed. Bobby had remembered to pack everyone's Ration Book, so she was keen to seek out the village store. Pithiock General Store and Post Office was larger than they expected. It was no more than one hundred yards from the "Vyvyan Arms", set back off the road, from which it was separated by a pretty garden. It was really a thatched cottage. What had once been two front rooms had been knocked into one, and the stairs to the upper floor were still in place. To the left of the stairs was the Post Office section, set behind a wire grill. This took up only part of the space, the remainder being shelved, with stationery, a few toys, post cards, cigarettes and tobacco and "fancy goods" To the right of the stairs was the food and groceries, including confectionery, plus a modest range of dry goods. At first, the Brownings could see no sign of an Assistant, until a squeaky voice from a gloomy back corner of the food section piped up. Behind the counter, and only just visible, was a tiny and distinctly elderly woman. She could not have been more than five feet tall. Her face was the colour and texture of a walnut, and her hair was concealed under a bright red knitted woollen cap. However, her smile and the sparkle in her rheumaticky eyes were a clear sign of a lively nature.

"We'm not used to many strangers in here" she stated uncompromisingly, You don't be German Spies, do you? But even if you are I'll serve you, I need the money, so help yourselves. And if you want to know, my name is Sybil. You can call me Syb for short." She cackled and subsided totally out of sight on to her stool. "An' if you be wantin' the other side for stamps, well I'm down for that too." Finn warmed to her. There was something about old people that appealed to him. Whilst he had no wish at his young age to become one, he quite liked the idea of getting old – he was perceptive enough to appreciate that Old People said what they thought straight out.

More than that, they were able to talk about times past, and they generally had time to pass the time of day and show a genuine interest in people of his age. They were a bit like museum exhibits in some ways, he thought.

"We are staying with Mr Avondale at the Vyvyan Arms for a short holiday. He is an old colleague of mine," Claud volunteered. "Our name is Browning and we live in Surrey. Do you mind if we just browse around, Syb?" Bobby interjected: "Well, actually, Syb we thought since it's a warm and sunny day we'd make up a picnic and explore the countryside a little. We would be glad of any suggestions for a nice place to walk to." Sybil bobbed up off her stool: "Just a minute. Are you SURE you baint be Germans? You sound a bit foreign, if you'll forgive me saying so."

"No" Bobby laughed. "No, actually I am Norwegian, so I have no love for the Germans. And my eldest son is in the Royal Air Force. Douglas here is joining the Royal Navy next month, and my husband served in France and Belgium in the Great War. I hope that reassures you, Syb." Syb's face creased into a smile. "Well, p'raps I were bein' a tiddy bit hasty. You can never tell in these dreadful times. And I lost my ol' man and both my boys in the last lot. Dan was blown up early on. Should never 'ave been there at his age, him havin' turned forty-one. Then Phil and Fred both went to Wipers as they called it, in 1917. I bin runnin' this store ever since, and not a soul to 'and it on to. Anyways, I 'as got to live on summat – the lads never 'ad nowt." Syb slumped back on to her stool, and her smile faded into gloom.

I thought we might escape this damnable war for a few days" Claud thought to himself. "The Twentieth Century is not yet half over, and war, and death and misery are everywhere. What sort of world are we living in Even here in sleepy old Cornwall." He looked at Bobby and the boys. He loved them all so very much, and that bastard Adolf Hitler was doing his best to deprive me of them. He turned to Sybil. "I am so sorry. We all are. I was in France and know how lucky I was to survive. We can only hope we all get through it this time and destroy Hitler before he destroys us. Now, come on, you lot – it's time we got out and scouted round this village. Sybil, it is nice to meet you and I am sure we'll be back in here before we go home."

CHAPTER 44

It was a happy, memorable week for the Browning family. They were all together, a rare event nowadays. The late summer weather was perfect, the days still long and warm. Clive and Philippa ,with little Charlotte – now six months old – had joined them on Day Two and during the succeeding days all eight of them walked and picnicked in the woods and meadows, and beside the River Tiddy that bubbled along a valley just west of the village. Kenneth helped Finn make a rod and line, and a feather lure, and the whole family were astonished when, after several patient hours, he landed a small trout. Small maybe, but big enough that Finn was able to persuade the kitchen staff at the inn to grill it for his evening meal. Once a day a bus ran into Callington and then on to Tavistock, on the western edge of Dartmoor. On the last day of their stay at Pithiock, they all caught it and spent happy hours shopping and having lunch in Tavistock. Douglas and Kenneth were more enterprising. They found a cycle-hire shop and headed out of town on to the Moor itself, and reached Princetown and a view of Dartmoor Jail, before it was time to head back. The war seemed so far away in this peaceful setting. No sounds of war here: no screaming bombs, no thunder of artillery, no roar of aircraft, no chatter of machine guns, no screams of the wounded and dying. But the war did sometimes intrude, it was inescapable. For Claud, it was the thought of doctoring news of the war's progress, knowingly going along with manipulating the truth, of minimising the defeats and disasters and deaths, of exaggerating the victories, all for the sake of Britain's morale. It was called Propaganda, and Claud did not like its deceitfulness. He worried about something else. Clive would soon set off for the second time to Rhodesia. Could lightning strike twice? German U-Boats were still very active and successful in the Western Approaches and the Atlantic. Bobby shared this fear, and was anxious about her second son going sea, in the Royal Navy. She tried to dispel the thought of Douglas being torpedoed, of him floundering in a burning oil-strewn ocean, or worse still, trapped in the bowels of his ship as she plummeted to the ocean bed. For Philippa, the joy of motherhood was tempered by the loneliness she knew she would suffer once Clive had gone to Africa. Clive, himself, wished he could stay in England, but that would probably mean combat duty and he knew he should be grateful to be spared that. Douglas appeared on the surface at least to have calmed his troubled mind. And wondered if the incident with the little mouse had helped him. He just prayed that if push came to shove he would find the courage and calmness to face danger and death if he had to. Only Kenneth and Finn seemed totally free of care and apprehension.

Far from these idyllic valleys and woodlands and bubbling trout streams, the war raged on. In Russia, the German advance seemed unstoppable, despite all the ferocious resistance of Stalin's forces. On August 3rd German Panzers crossed the River Don and on the 4th Stavropol fell as the Panzers headed south towards the oilfields of Maikop.

Unknown to the free world, on August 4th also, the first trainload of Jews was shipped from Belgium to Auschwitz Concentration Camp, to be followed there three days later by the shipment of a thousand Jews from Holland.

In the Pacific, off Guadalcanal in the Solomon Islands, the Japanese sank three American and one Australian cruisers in a night attack, with the loss of over one thousand Allied sailors. In the Mediterranean there was one small glimmer of good news – one tiny star in a very dark sky. The oil tanker "Ohio", together with four other ships, reached Malta on August 15th, but as she approached the island, "Ohio" was hit five times by enemy aircraft. She had to be towed at only two knots for the last forty miles of her voyage. No convoy had been so powerfully escorted, by no fewer than four aircraft carriers, two battleships and several cruisers. The aircraft carrier "Furious" carried desperately needed Spitfire fighters to reinforce the pitifully small air defence of the island. The convoy was under attack repeatedly. Soon after passing through the Straits of Gibraltar, on its way to Malta, the aircraft carrier "Eagle" was sunk by four torpedoes.

And before August was over, another ghastly episode took place. An Allied Commando force attempted an ill-fated assault on the French port of Dieppe, in a futile endeavour to seize it and destroy the German defences. Of the 6,000 strong force of British, American, Canadian and Free French troops that took part, 4,100 were reported killed, wounded, taken prisoner or merely missing. The force went ashore on an eleven mile stretch of coast, with the port in the centre, hoping to destroy a series of German shore batteries and radio location (nowadays called radar) stations.

The statistics were horrifying:

One destroyer sunk	33 landing craft destroyed
106 aircraft shot down	27 out of 27 tanks destroyed

On the 25th August, the battle for the great Russian city of Stalingrad began. German troops reached the banks of the Volga, whilst artillery and the Luftwaffe pounded the city itself. But the Russians vowed that they would never surrender, and would defend and fight on every street and house and factory floor. Stalin's order was "Not a step backwards", and so the siege and the battle raged into September.

In the Far East, a terrible report came through concerning the Japanese treatment of prisoners of war. In Hong Kong hundreds of prisoners were roped together, and systematically bayoneted to death. In Changi Jail in Singapore, a new form of torture was devised: unless each prisoner, in direct conflict of his duties as a POW, signed an agreement that he would not try to escape, all 15,400 prisoners would be confined to the sweltering heat of a barrack square measuring 270 yds by 135 yds – roughly the size of two football pitches – with only two water taps, until they changed their minds. Any show of disrespect to their captors would result in immediate decapitation.

In Lwow, Poland, 75,000 Jews were rounded up and deported to Concentration Camps between August 11th and 31st.

Deliberately, Claud had insisted that during their break at Pithiock, none of the family would listen to the radio, or read any newspapers. Thus, they knew little of these terrible events until they returned to Surbiton. Frank Avondale was seen seldom, largely because he was seldom sober, and seldom up-and-about before lunchtime. Apart from Sybil, contact with the villagers was confined to polite greetings and Syb herself was not one to impart news about the war's progress. She had had enough of war and its horrors twenty-five years ago.. On the last day, Clive and Philippa left early, to make their way back to Rosedown for a day or two with the General and his wife. The rest of the family bade their farewell to Sybil in the General Store and to their host, Frank Avondale. It had been as much as he could do to emerge from his drunken slumber and stagger downstairs to see them off. They arrived home late and tired and in no frame of mind to catch up on news of the war, or anything else. Tomorrow's problems could wait for a few hours. They went to bed.

A few hours later they were brought back to the realities of everyday life. It was the first of September 1942. Almost to the day, three years ago, the then Prime Minister had made his fateful radio broadcast to the nation, telling them that Great Britain was at war with Germany. So much had changed in that brief span, both in their personal lives, and in the survival of the nation. There was no sign of the war ending, or even of it being won. They had lost friends, and colleagues, and in Clive's case, comrades in arms. And yet, and yet, Hope had not diminished. It occurred to no one, neither the Brownings, nor anyone else in the country, that eventually it would not be won. Spirits had not been broken, not by the terrible pounding of its cities, nor by the seemingly endless succession of defeats and setbacks to its Forces overseas.

The Brownings themselves had survived thus far, if only just in Clive's case. And more than merely survive, they had contributed; it may have been small, but enough to entitle them to stand unashamed.

By now, Finn was old enough, and aware enough of the world's turmoil to wish he too could contribute to Britain's war effort in some way. He said as much one day to his father. "Dad, can you think of something I could do to help us win the war? I know I can't join up like Clive and Douglas, but there must be something I can do." Claud smiled and put an arm round the lad's shoulder. "I am proud that you should ask, but you are still very young and at school. I admire you, but at your age I think the best thing is for you just to concentrate on learning as much as you can, and enjoy these precious years of your childhood and youth." Finn saw this retort as him being fobbed off. There must be something he could do. Something more than just collecting old metal to be turned into Spitfires. The answer came soon after, when he happened to speak to Clive when he phoned in one day, shortly before he left for Rhodesia to take up his new assignment. Finn told Clive how he would like to do something, however small, for the war effort, but that their Dad had said he was really too young and should concentrate on his schooling. "He's right in one way, but I think he is wrong in another, brother. Yes, of course you should work hard and do your best at school, but I think there is one thing you really could do that would help, and it need not interfere with anything else. Do you remember visiting me at Headley, at the Convalescent Home? Well, I was lucky. By chance my family lived not far away and could visit every weekend practically. But a lot of those guys there, who incidentally were in far worse shape than me, never had visitors. In many cases they were New Zealanders, or Canadians, or from other parts of the Empire. Oh, the staff did their best, but they were hard pressed and could afford little time just sitting at bedsides. What was wanted was voluntary visitors: ordinary people who could do just that, just sit and chat, and listen, and maybe read poor blinded souls a book or newspaper. Or run errands perhaps. Or even just help the staff a bit. Anyone willing could do that, and you as well as grown-ups. Would you be interested? If so, I'll ring the Matron there and see what she says."

The Matron was Daisy Goodfellow and she was delighted when the proposal was put to her by Clive. She was more than ready to accept any help she could get – even from an eleven year old if he was sensible. "Let's give it a try and see how it goes. Of course, he would only be able to come at weekends, but that's better then nothing." Claud and Bobby were happy to fall in with the idea. Finn could easily get to Leatherhead by bus, where a staff car from the Convalescent Home could pick him up.

On the 3rd September Finn started his first term at Shawbury House. It was the third anniversary of the outbreak of war, but there were no dark thoughts as he walked through the gate on his first morning. Claud had offered to take him, to ease him in a little, but Finn declined. He did not want his peers there to think him "soft". In any case (though he did not know it) he was coming with a bit of a reputation: his prowess at Athletics and Squash had preceded him and circulated right through the school. H- M greeted all the new boys at Assembly in the Gymnasium. Finn was the oldest by a distance; the other new boys were just starting Prep School and had no idea what to expect. Each new pupil was introduced to the rest of the school by H-M, and informed which would be his classroom. Finn was left until last.

"Last new boy in is Finn Browning. He is unlikely to be last at anything else. Some of you may already know that he has above average ability at some sports, notably athletics and squash rackets. So I am sure he will be an asset to us on the playing fields. I only hope he does as well in the classroom. May we assume that, Browning?"

Finn reddened. "I will try my best, sir." "I am sure you will. Oh, and I address this to all of you, please do not address me as "Sir". I prefer "H-M". Please remember that.

In my view, use of the word Sir should be confined to military circles, and when addressing titled and senior figures in public life. Now, as some of you know, and all of you should know, today is the third anniversary of the outbreak of this dreadful war. Thus far, the forces of evil arraigned against us have had the upper hand. If God is on our side, as I am sure He is, in the end we will prevail. But it will be a long road. So we will say a prayer, but before we do so I should like to remind you of a statement made by our Prime Minister Winston Churchill, back in the Spring of 1940. This is what he said:

"What is our aim? Victory. Victory at all costs, victory in spite of

All terror, victory however long and hard the road may be. For Without victory, there is no survival."

We are fortunate that we have a great leader, boys, and we must pray that he will remain our strong leader until the conflict is finished and the victory attained. Now join me in prayer."

Dear Lord, preserve us from the evil of the Axis, that seeks to deprive us, and all who are oppressed, of their freedom and dignity. Help our soldiers, sailors and airmen, to fight the enemy and destroy him, so that we may once again live in peace. Amen.

Assembly dispersed and Finn joined his new class. The Class Master was a slight, elderly gentleman, with a soft voice and a kind smile. His name was Keith Lyle, whose wife Denise taught French. He had fought in France in the Great War, flying Sopwith Camel fighter planes, which is where and when he had met Denise. Finn liked him immediately.

That first afternoon there was a Soccer practice and Finn was put straight into Game One. That evening he went home a very happy boy. He was going to like Shawbury House.

CHAPTER 45

Douglas reported for duty in Rosyth at the end of September. Induction into any Armed Service at that time filled young men with trepidation. There was the normal anxiety of the unknown, of being pitchforked into a strange new, all male society and environment. Of putting on a uniform for the first time. Of being barked at by seemingly psychotic Little Hitlers, besotted with their petty power. All that was normal. But overriding all that was the knowledge that this was a prelude to something far worse. Going to sea to fight for one's country. Putting one's life on the line and coming to a sickening, agonising death in icy waters, or an inferno of flames. Brother Clive had only just survived being torpedoed, and he wasn't even in the bloody Navy! It was a small consolation to Douglas that he was just one of many facing the same emotions, though some seemed to be taking it in their stride and showed no qualms about what they were committing themselves to. No, he told himself, I've got to cope on my own; no one is here is going to hold my hand. This is what becoming a man was all about.

Douglas was about five weeks into his basic training when one morning he was ordered to report to his OC's Office at 1000hrs. No indication was given as to why his attendance was required. He was not aware of having fallen behind, or having committed any heinous crime. Lieutenant Commander MacLeish was a stocky man with a weathered face, probably about 45 years old. Douglas guessed he had risen through the ranks.

"Sit down Browning. And don't look so bloody nervous: you are not being carpeted!" the hint of a smile creased MacLeish's leathery features. "Your records show that you went to Public School and I am aware that many private schools have Combined Cadet Force detachments. But very few have Air Training Corps sections. I am wondering, was there any Cadet flying at your school?"

"No, sir. King's did not. There was an ATC squadron for the Surbiton area, where I live, but I did not join it, because my brother was – is – in the RAF. He was a Rear Gunner on Lancasters until he was seriously wounded, so I felt I might be a bit safer in the Royal Navy, sir. I am joking of course, sir!"

"Hmph. Well I have no reason to grumble at your decision. I have been informed that you have been well up to the mark with your Basic Training thus far. However, you will no doubt be aware that the Royal Navy has an air wing, the Fleet Air Arm. Currently, there is a shortage of aircrew, largely due, I will be frank, to heavy losses of aircraft and crews. and I have been requested to put forward the names of potential candidates for aircrew training. This is on a voluntary basis. If you are interested say so now. And if not interested, also say so now. You will not be thought the worse of, if you say No. I will give you the rest of the day to think about it, lad, if you like."

"No, sir, I do not need time." Douglas remembered the dread he had developed of being torpedoed, and the tiny mouse in Pithiock Church who had been so fearless of him. "I would be happy to volunteer". "Good man. That was a quick decision. I'll forward your name and we will see what happens. Carry on, Browning." Douglas figured that many FAA squadrons were shore based, and he might just be that lucky, and even if he were attached to a carrier that went down, well there was always the chance he'd be airborne when it happened!

Douglas heard no more of the matter until mid-November, when he was summoned again to MacLeish's Office.

"Browning, wheels turn slowly sometimes in the Royal Navy. However I have received a posting for you. You are to report to the Fleet Air Arm Establishment at Yeovilton, in Somerset. There you will be assessed and if you pass your aptitude and technical capability tests you will proceed to Initial Flying Training School. Well done, young man. I hope you will be successful. Dismiss. No, wait! You qualify for a 7 day pass before you report to Yeovilton. Enjoy your leave. You never know, it might be your last if you don't point your aircraft in the right direction!" For a moment, there was a mischievous sparkle in the old officer's eyes.

CHAPTER 46

Finn knew on Day One that he was going to enjoy Shawbury House more
than his old school. For a start, he already had pals here. He liked his new
Class Master, Mr Lyle, and, of course H-M. the facilities were great, but then
he was approached by a tall, stooping master, with thinning red hair, and a
forbidding air about him. His name was Henry Hanbury. He taught Maths.
"You're Browning, aren't you?" "Yes, sir." "And you play squash?" "Yes,
sir, I learned several years ago, at the beginning of the war, when I was eight,
sir."   It was a brief exchange. Finn did not know it at this moment, but
Hanbury had spotted him playing at Berrylands, and was secretly excited that
he had now come to Shawbury House. He would certainly make the School
Team. As well as being Finn's Class Master, Mr Lyle also taught English
and History. He had a very relaxed manner and never seemed to get cross
with his pupils. His was a slight figure, though very erect. His wife was very
different. She sported pince nez, held on by a black cord to stop them falling
off . she was very temperamental and excitable, and kept breaking off into
rapid, unintelligible, under-her-breath French which no one could understand.
But she could laugh, too; great gales of laughter, often for some quite
unintelligible reason.

    Finn had been at the School for only one week before he was selected to
play for the First XI Soccer team. He felt a huge glow of pride when, for the
first time, he pulled on the Black and Scarlet shirt. His glow was warmer still
an hour or so later, when the final whistle blew at the end of their first School
Match against Dean's Court. Finn had scored the only goal in the game.

    Bobby's work in broadcasting to Norway was demanding, but gratifying.
Apart from the satisfaction she felt at the benefit she might be doing for the
morale of her compatriots in Norway, she enjoyed speaking her native
tongue which, after so many years of disuse in England, had become a little
rusty. Also, she had formed warm relationships at the Embassy in London.
Though the hours were long, there were breaks, and she was able to relax in
the Staff Dining Room, or even on rare occasions, she would be taken out to
lunch by Thor Greig.. Not long after her return from Pithiock, he called her
into his office and handed her an envelope. Instantly, she recognised the
handwriting: "Roberta Browning".

    "I think, Bobby, that you would prefer to read it in private. Yes?" Thor
smiled, and Bobby felt herself reddening. She felt, too, a frisson of
excitement, even expectation, a tightening in her throat. "Our backdoor
postal delivery service through Sweden seems to be working quite well

Bobby. Of course, I know whom the letter is from. Your friend Lars Hansen. There was other material in the package from him, dare I say of a less personal nature, but none the less vital to our interests. I can tell you that he is well, and also that he says your broadcasts are a great comfort to many of our people at home —not least your own family. Naturally, we do not give your real name in these broadcasts, that would be fatal. The Germans would certainly take reprisals against them. But your family know your voice: how could they not? Now, I will leave you in peace. I am sure you are anxious to read what Hansen has to say. I will see you a little later.

The letter read:

"Dear Roberta,

I have to be brief. We are going on an operation in an hour's time. It will be dangerous, as they all are. I want so badly to put some thoughts on paper to you. I do not want to sound dramatic, but this may be the last chance – one never knows in this damnable war. I know that you are a happily married woman, and I would never wish to change that. But when we met that last time, in the teashop in Surbiton, there was a moment, so brief, so instantaneous, but unmistakable to me, when our eyes spoke to each other and our hands touched. For me at least that moment left an indelible mark on my heart. Maybe it is because in my heart there is an emptiness where once there was darling Else All I can say is that if this war ever ends I would so dearly like to see you again, and maybe, if you allow it, just to touch your hand once more. Nothing more than that, I promise. Will you grant me that? I will have to wonder and hope I suppose.. For now at least I can listen to your voice on the radio, if only occasionally. It is so strange to hear you talking about simple, mundane subjects, but it is this very ordinariness that gives a strength to our people, the strength to continue the struggle. The Germans are brutal, and care nothing for the sanctity of life. That is why I am fighting them, on behalf of all decent, peace loving Norwegians, but especially Else and my dear son I know that you will be unable to reply, but perhaps you will think of me sometimes. Be sure of this: when the war has been won I will return to England, and I will see you again. Take care dear Roberta.

Lars.

Roberta sat quietly for a while. She knew that although she loved Claud and would never hurt him, or leave him, she also would like to see Lars again. Then she uttered a word that she had never, ever, spoken before, and which disgusted her.

"Fuck. Fuck this fucking war!"

CHAPTER 47
SEPTEMBER 1942

1st. Germany claims to have captured Kalach, 40 km west of Stalingrad. The British Eighth Army in Egypt repels a German attack on the Alam Halfa Ridge

3rd. The third anniversary of the outbreak of war. German troops penetrate the outskirts of Stalingrad.

5th. German troops lay siege to the Black Sea naval base of Novorossisk. Next day the Soviet base falls into German hands.

10th. RAF bombers raid Dusseldorf and cause heavy damage to factories and storage depots.

14th. In the North Atlantic, attacks by a wolfpack of U-Boats on a Murmansk bound convoy resulting in the loss of 12 freighters and one Canadian destroyer. One U-Boat is hit, but does not sink.

17th. Vidkun Quisling, the German's puppet Premier of Norway, reintroduces the death penalty in Norway. One wonders why he bothers, since the Occupying Force has no compunction in executing innocent citizens already!

18th. In Paris, 116 people are executed in retaliation for recent attacks on German soldiers.

On the same day in Berlin, it is decreed that all social misfits are to wear badges proclaiming their "crimes". They are triangles of different colours, depending on which "crime" they are guilty of.

Pink = Homosexuals

Green = Petty criminals

Purple = Pacifists

Dark Blue = Anti-Social

Red = Political Activists

Brown = Gipsys

Yellow Star of David = Jews

All such "asocials" should be handed over to forced labour without proper sustenance, or medical help. In effect, this is a death sentence. In the first two years of the war 80,000 German citizens identified as "useless elements" were exterminated.

21st. Figures released in London claim that in addition to the untold number of Jews, 207,373 non-Jews have been executed by the Germans in Occupied Europe. This is almost certainly an under-estimate.

27th The Liberty ship Stuart Hopkins, armed only with a single four-inch gun, sinks and is sunk by the German raider Stier.

30th In a speech Adolf Hitler ridicules the Allied leadership as "military idiots…mentally sick or perpetually drunk."

During this month of September, 14,000 Jews from France, 6,000 from Holland and 5,000 from Belgium are deported to Auschwitz. Also, 20,000 Polish Jews perish at Belzec Concentration Camp.

Some of these stories Finn noted in his Scrapbook. Others are kept from the public domain.

October 1942. All war is a tragedy, but smaller tragedies occur within the whole ghastly sequence of folly that is the History of Mankind. On October 1st., in the China Sea, a Japanese ship carrying Allied Prisoners of War, became a sealed coffin when she was torpedoed by a US submarine. Before abandoning ship, the Japanese guards battened down the hatches on the 1,816 prisoners. Of these 843 went to the bottom. The remainder managed to open the hatches in time and dived overboard, only to be machine-gunned by Japanese escort vessels. On October 2nd, the great pre-war TransAtlantic liner "Queen Mary", now used as a troop carrier, mistakenly rams one of her naval escorts, the cruiser HMS "Curacao", sinking her with the loss of 338 lives.

On October 8th Josef Terboven, the German Commissioner for Norway, today arrived in the port of Trondheim. By mid-afternoon, 10 people had been shot for sabotage and a further 700 arrested. The port is used as a German naval base from which attacks on British convoys to Russia are mounted. Norwegian resistance fighters are believed to have sabotaged military communications in the area.

"Oh God, may Lars not be one of them."

CHAPTER 48

Finn felt no nervousness when he arrived at Headley Court for his first visit as a Helper, largely because he had been there before to visit brother Clive. And, of course, he had met the Matron. Daisy was not in the least like the cartoon version of a Matron -   a large full-chested spinster of stern demeanour and commanding speech. Daisy was petite, and still in her thirties and the convalescing airmen worshipped the ground she stood upon. She was kind and gentle, but firm, as she needed to be with young, full blooded males. "You may be heroes, and commanders of men, but here, lads, I am the commander of men and you will do as you are told" she would frown. And then her eyes would dance and her pretty face crease into a smile, and she would add: "But if you are good boys, and off medication, you might – only might – be allowed down to the "Carpenters Arms" for a beer on Sunday evenings. And I might come with you to make sure you don't over do it. I will not have you rolling back half-pissed!"

Daisy herself met Finn and drove him to Headley. "Finn, you know I really should not be having you here helping, you are far too young.. But your brother spoke very highly of you and we really do need every help we can get. And it is not often that civilian adults volunteer. Not because they don't want to, but because in these days of war, everyone is working so hard already for the war effort. You know, even the elderly are doing something, such as the Home Guard or the WVS, and not everyone is at ease dealing with terribly injured and disfigured young men. You must not imagine Finn, that this is going to be nice work, but we will spare you the difficult and nasty side. To begin with, I thought you could take round the tea trolley to the lads who are well on the recovery road. It's not too demanding and I'm sure some of them would just like a bit of company. You know, when you have been badly wounded and are far from home, it is nice to have someone to chat to. And you might find them very interesting. Is that alright?"

Later that evening, when Finn got home, he told the family about his day at Headley. "Matron did not let me go into the worst wards, you know, the ones who had been disfigured by burns, but it was bad enough being amongst some of the others, especially two who were blind and would never see again. One of them asked if I would just sit on his bed and hold his hand and talk about what I was doing at school. It was very difficult for me not to cry, but at least I was helping a little bit, and I definitely want to go again. It's funny, I felt they really needed me.

Daisy Goodfellow phoned soon after Finn had gone to bed to check that he had got home alright. She said to Bobby that "her boys had really cheered up after meeting him and hoped he would come again. So did she."

Claud assured her that he would.

CHAPTER 49

Finn's first term was passing quickly. It was more usual for boys to begin at Prep. School at age seven or eight, not eleven as he was. But this was no handicap as far as he was concerned. On the contrary, he fitted in to his new school's society very quickly, in no small measure because of his success on the football field and the squash court. H-M warmed to him from the word go and went to great pains to encourage him at all sports. His classroom performance was well up to scratch as well and he seemed to be making friends with some ease. All in all, there was little to criticise in the lad. But Finn was no Goody-Goody. There were boys he did not like. Symons for instance. Symons picked his nose, and broke wind frequently. He thought Finn was H-M's pet and told him so to his face and stuck out his tongue at him. Finn was not one to take such insults lightly, and when the opportunity came one day, pushed Symons into the swimming pool fully clothed. For that HM kept him in after school for two hours to help clean up the classrooms. Secretly, though, he approved of Finn's retaliation. It showed the right spirit, and he too thought Symons was an unpleasant and talentless individual.

At home Finn had little time to be idle. Homework took far longer than it had under Old Carnage. This was partly because he was that much older, and Common Entrance was looming in a year's time. Then at weekends, if he was not involved in school soccer matches, he was round at Berrylands playing squash, and on Sunday afternoons doing his stint at Headley Court. He was more accustomed now to the sad and sometimes gruesome sights of some of the injured airmen, and felt little revulsion at the sight of raw leg and arm stumps, and terrible burns. He was relieved that brother Clive was well out of danger in Rhodesia, but missed him deeply. Douglas he missed little. Douglas had never taken much interest in The Worm, but Finn was none the less proud that there was going to be another flyer in the family. Douglas had taken to the air like a duck to water, and in a few months should receive his Wings, all being well. As for Kenneth, well he had his own circle of friends from KCS, and if not with them, then he was at Berrylands, though tennis, not squash was his preference. Finn sometimes wondered if this was because all that time ago at Rosedown, Ken had been vanquished by this little squirt of a brother, but he never had the temerity to suggest it to him.

The Luftwaffe's raids on England were now much more sporadic; they were too busy on the Eastern Front battling with the Russian Bear. Finn had now reverted to sleeping in his bedroom above the garage It would have been an awful squash sleeping under the stairs as he had a year or more ago. George Peterson and Finn had found a way of producing lead soldiers, by making moulds out of Plaster of Paris, so between the two of them they spent happy hours having " battles" on Finn's bedroom floor. Douglas had done one thing for Finn: he had passed on to him all his own toy soldiers, artillery pieces, forts and model tanks.

Another leisure pastime was Monopoly, but with a difference. The two boys had become "bored with the board", and invented their own version. Gone were Park Lane, Marlborough Street and Fenchurch Station and the rest. Their board was lined with Pine Walk, Loveday Gardens and Berrylands Station. And instead of St. Pancras and all the other utilities, they substituted the likes of Surbiton Lagoon, Kingston Power Station and the Water Works. Also they added a nought to all the bank notes, so £10 became £100, with comparable inflation on all the properties. They were ingenious with the Chance Cards. "Give £500 towards the War Effort" and "Receive "£1,000 for shooting down a Dornier bomber." A hot favourite was "Fall in a bomb crater and go back to GO".

Claud Browning still did night time fire-watching on the roof of the Office in Fleet Street, in addition to his normal day time job. These days he seemed quieter and looked older. The strain was telling, Bobby thought to herself. The break in Pithiock was not enough. He needed a longer and total rest, maybe just pottering on his allotment, or in the garden. When he was at home he seemed not to want to do anything, or say anything much. When she enquired what was the matter, he just replied "Oh, it's the war. It seems to be nearly all bad news, and some of it I am not even allowed to divulge, not even to you. The War Office just slap D Notices on it. It's getting to me I suppose. I'll be alright when things start to get better", and then he would slump into his favourite armchair and fall asleep. Bobby was not convinced. There was something more that Claud was not saying. She did not press him. Whatever was troubling him would emerge sooner or later. It always did.

As she sat on the train between Surbiton and Waterloo her mind drifted to thoughts of Lars. It would be so much easier if she could talk to him. Writing was impossible, she knew. As the train rounded the curve at Clapham Junction the idea hit her. It was so obvious. Why on earth had she not thought of it before? And why had not Lars, either? She was speaking to Lars every week. She was speaking to anyone in Norway who dared to listen to her broadcasts. Provided Thor Greig, her minder agreed, she could send a message to him. Of course, it could not be direct, like "Lars Hansen, I think about you every day", but it could be couched in such a way that there would be no mistaking the intent and meaning, or whom it was from. Had she but realized it, her excitement betrayed her true feelings for Lars. Like it or not, her regard for him was way beyond platonic friendship, or even fear for his well being. Greig agreed with her idea. He went further, and informed her, in strictest confidence, that Lars like all the other active members of the Norwegian Resistance, had a codename. Simply by addressing her message to that codename, there was no risk, either to Lars, or to anyone else. It was simply a matter of carefully wording the message. He told her that Lars's codename was Tall Larches, "larches" being his forename with "che" inserted before the "s". The message she broadcast a few days later was:

"A pigeon has flown in from the tall larches and has landed safely in Bobby's hands. The pigeon can not fly back whence it came. Not now. But it will be treasured and one day Bobby will come to tall larches and return it by hand. Yes, hand to hand."

This could easily be explained to any friends or family who happened to hear her broadcast as a coded message from Free Norway Intelligence to an agent in Norway. In a sense, that is what it was.

CHAPTER 50

The years of defeat, disaster and humiliation for Britain and her Allies had been long, and hard to bear, but late in October 1942 the tide began to turn. And it began in North Africa, in the desert west of Alexandria, on the border between Egypt and Libya. This place was called El Alamein.

Late in the evening of the 23rd, 195,000 troops of the Allied Eighth Army prepared for an assault upon Rommel's Afrika Korps. There had been many months of careful planning for this offensive, and a long accumulation of men and machines until now, at last, they were numerically superior to their enemy. Shortly before 10.00pm the silence of the desert was shattered as a thousand heavy guns opened fire on the German lines. The Allies' engineers advanced into the mile-deep German minefield, clearing lanes, marked with white tapes, for the troops and tanks to advance. The artillery barrage lasted for fifteen minutes and then the silence was broken by the skirl of bagpipes, the cue for the infantry to move forward, with bayonets fixed. The Allied Commander was Lt. Gen. Bernard Montgomery, who later became Field Marshal The Viscount Montgomery of Alamein. He was a sharp-faced, humourless man whom, years later, Finn met when The Great Man inspected the Army Cadet Force at Finn's school, St. Luke's College at Dorking. "Monty" had no option but to make a direct frontal assault, the terrain not allowing for any encircling movement to the South and the sea preventing it to the North. The infantry were supported by Sherman and Grant tanks, and much depended upon them. In the initial assault, the German Panzers lost ninety of their tanks, but the Allies more than two hundred.

Rommel should not even have been in command of the German forces. He had been replaced by General Stumme, but Stumme died of a heart attack, and Rommel was forced to return from his sick bed in Germany to take over again. Luck plus the weight of the Allied attacking force, was against him. 195,000 confronting 104,000; 1,000 tanks against less than 500; 2,000 guns against 1,200. Even in the sky, Rommel was outnumbered; 750 aircraft against 675. Soon, the Desert Fox was in retreat. The Afrika Korps could not contain the brutal assault by Monty's 8th Army. As October gave way to November, so Rommel gave way to Montgomery. It was a definitive turning-point in the war, and an added twist took place on November 10th, when a large Allied Expeditionary force landed in Algeria, far to the West of Rommel's forces, to attack him in the rear.

In a speech at the Mansion House in the City of London, Winston Churchill uttered these words:

"Now this is not the end. It is not even the beginning of the end. But it is perhaps, the end of the beginning".

CHAPTER 51

Finn was now on his second scrapbook. From the beginning it had recorded an almost unremitting series of defeats and disasters. Now, at long last, there were clear signs of change. The Battle of El Alamein had a dramatic effect on everyone. Claud seemed a little less depressed and wearied, thank heavens, and that had cheered up Bobby. People seemed to be smiling again. Now, Finn was pasting in accounts and photos of the North African campaign. One in particular he liked: of a German soldier standing in a tank turret with his hands up, as British infantrymen with bayonets fixed, advanced towards him. Others showed the night sky lit up as the British artillery opened fire on a concentration of enemy tanks. Another showed Monty as he was universally nicknamed by now, talking to officers of the Highland Division. There were pictures of the combined British and American force wading ashore near Oran, with a background of an armada of landing craft and escort warships. This force were now progressing eastwards towards the retreating German Army in Libya. At Shawbury House, H-M addressed the boys at Assembly:

Boys, I am sure you all know what has been happening in the war in North Africa. It is good news. The Germans are on the run. At long last, something has happened to give Adolf Hitler a bloody nose. But do not think the war has been won, there is a long, long way to go. Europe is still under Nazi domination and we here are still under threat from the Luftwaffe. Also, we are still suffering terrible losses at sea and in the Far East. But when good news does come, let us savour it, and remember it, and remember to thank our fathers and brothers and uncles, who are making it happen. We must pray for their and our safe deliverance.

Please stand. Let us pray.

Oh God, we give thanks to you for the victory in North Africa

And the greater victory that will come one day, with your help.

Preserve and protect the men and women of our armed forces.

Deliver the oppressed in Europe and elsewhere from their evil

Oppressors and give our leaders the wisdom, courage and

Determination to fight the good cause to the end.

Now boys, get to your classes before I become your oppressor with this cane."

It was clear by mid-term that Finn was the star of the school soccer team. They had played six matches and won five, drawing the sixth. Goals for and against in the six matches were: For=14, Against=6. Of the 14 goals, Finn had scored 7. On November 14th at Assembly, H-M announced that Finn was being awarded his 1st X1 Colours. An hour later, he was still glowing with pride and pleasure, and dying for the day to end when he could go home and tell his family, when the Housekeeper entered the French classroom and whispered something to Mrs Lyle, glancing towards Finn as she did so. Mrs Lyle beckoned Finn to come forward. "Finn, will you please go with Mrs Bannister, the Headmaster wishes to see you immediately."

Finn was puzzled. H-M had awarded him his colours and been very complimentary. So why this summons? What had he done wrong? The walk from the classroom to the main building was only 70 yards or so, so Finn wasted no time quizzing Mrs Bannister as they crossed the playground. But Mrs B. would say nothing, except "You'll have to see the Headmaster, Finn." Her tone was flat, her expression set.

When he entered the study, he immediately noticed the serious expression on H-M's face. "Sit down, Finn. I am afraid I have some bad news for you. I think you are old enough for me not to beat about the bush. I have had a call from your mother and must tell you that your father has been taken ill at his office. He is now in the intensive care unit at St.Mary's Hospital in London. I have arranged for a taxi to pick you up and run you home. I am so sorry, especially on a day when you must have been feeling very pleased with life. You are excused school until such time as your Mother tells me you are ready to return. However, perhaps I should add that although your father is clearly gravely ill, this does not mean that he can not recover, so do not get dejected. Now, off you go and pass my best wishes to your mother and my hopes that your father will soon be well again."

When Finn got home, Ken was already back from King's and sitting with their mother. She looked pale and had been crying, but was now re-composed. Finn went to her and hugged her. "What's happened to Dad? Is he very ill? Tell me. Please Mum." It was Ken who replied. "Finn, our Dad has had another heart attack. He had one before the war. I think you were too young to remember, but it was a serious one, and this one is serious too. We aren't exactly sure just how bad it is. We are all going up to London to see him now. It probably means staying overnight, so you'd better pack a few things. We can stay at Philippa's flat. We've told her, but until we are sure of the situation, we are not telling Douglas and Clive. There is no point in worrying them unnecessarily, especially as they are on flying duties."

Bobby managed a wan smile: "It's all right Finn. I'm sure he will get over it, just like he did last time." But she did not sound very convinced.

At St.Mary's Hospital in Paddington, Bobby and the boys wee met by a senior consultant, who ushered them into a small, poorly lit room in the Intensive Care Ward. His expression told them nothing. His features were set. He neither smiled, nor frowned. "Mrs Browning, your husband is very ill, and weak. It seems he was at his desk and had appeared perfectly normal during the morning until about eleven. It was then seen that he had apparently fallen asleep, his head on the desk. Colleagues tried to rouse him, but quickly realised it was something more serious, and called an ambulance. We have done various tests, including an electrocardiogram and an angiogram. This is an X-ray technique for measuring the blood flow through the heart. We have found that there is some constriction in a coronary artery, which is one of the two arteries which supply blood to the muscular tissue of the heart. We are not sure what has caused this constriction, but research is going on into something called cholesterol, which is an accumulation of fatty substance in the arteries that causes a thrombosis or blockage, partial or complete. In your husband's case, we can tell you, the blood flow from the heart to the brain is not affected, thankfully. He is going to need complete rest, here, for several weeks. During this time we are going to put him on a low-fat, no meat diet, and if this works he will need to remain on it permanently. Actually, Mrs Browning, it is no bad thing. All of us would feel a lot healthier, with less weight and more energy, if we followed this regime. Not that that is so difficult in these days of rationing, of course." For the first time, the doctor's face showed the hint of a smile. "Now, I am sure you would like to see him, although when I last looked in on him, he was still unconscious. For now, I must limit you to five minutes. After you have seen him, your sons can spend a few minutes with him as well."

Philippa and Charlotte arrived as Bobby returned to the Waiting room. "How is he?" she asked anxiously." Claud, no less than all the Browning family, had become an integral part of her life since her marriage to Clive, and he had often been in her thoughts, especially when the Blitz on London had been at its most intensive. She knew how he had stuck it out in Fleet Street, when many a younger man would have found some pretext to get out of the cauldron and back to the comparative safety of suburban Surrey. Also, she knew how fond her husband was of his father. Now that he was thousands of miles away in Rhodesia, she had to represent him at this anxious time and hopefully be able to write and reassure him that Claud would recover.

"Bobby, will he be alright?" she repeated.

"We don't know yet. He is still unconscious. One thing we have been told, though, is that he will have to change his lifestyle. A much more careful diet. Less work and less stress. Those are the doctor's word, not mine, but I have been worried about him for some time - he just has not been himself. You know, withdrawn, morose almost.

I've tried to get him to open up to me, but he just rebuffs me. Is that the right English word, "rebuff"? I think he must have sensed something was wrong, but wouldn't or couldn't say what. You can go and see him as soon as the boys come out, darling, but only five minutes, mind."

Their father opened his eyes just as the two boys entered the room. His eyes were blank, as though sightless. Claud Browning's eyes had always been a bit pale and watery, but this blankness was new. Then, very slowly, he raised his hand. Ken and Finn stood a few paces from the bed, not quite knowing how to respond. Limply, Claud beckoned and the boys drew closer. He spoke in a weak whisper: "It's good to see you both, but I feel so tired. Where is your mother Ken, is she anywhere near?" "Yes, father, she is just outside. I'll fetch her."

"Ken, don't alarm her. I'm all right. I'm going to be all right. It's another heart attack, I know that. but I don't think I'm going to peter out just yet. Just get her in, Ken. Finn, I don't suppose you know I had one of these attacks before the war. That didn't finish me, and this one won't, so don't be frightened. I'm very tired, so come back tomorrow, will you. I just want to have a few moments alone with Mummy." Claud's eyes closed and he slept, snoring faintly, but evenly. He was still snoring when Bobby re-entered. She was unsure whether to touch him, or leave him to sleep, but the decision was taken from her when a nurse walked in and took Claud's wrist to check his pulse. Claud awoke and very faintly, smiled and whispered: "Bobby, perhaps you should leave me alone with Sister here, I rather like the treatment she's giving me." The nurse laughed: "your pulse is far too weak Mr Browning to be left with any females other than your wife, but it is a little steadier than it was, so that's good. Mrs Browning can stay for five minutes and no more. Then you must rest." She nodded to Bobby and smiled: "I'll be back in a few minutes. Please do nothing to excite him. Oh, and I'm sorry but your daughter-in-law will have to come back another time, I'm afraid."

When they were alone, Bobby sat on a chair beside the bed and took Claud's hand. "Darling, I am so relieved you are a scrap better. You must take great care. We can not afford to lose you. Not for a long time. Not ever." Her face was pale, but her eyes spoke of her concern and her love for him, too. She was appalled that at such a tense moment a sudden vision of

Lars flashed through her mind. What a strange beast minds are, she said to herself. Why now, when my husband is so ill? Go away, Lars. Not for ever, just for now, until I get Claud strong and well again. Then I will think of you, and speak to you, too. The nurse returned. "I am afraid you must leave him now. Shall we see you tomorrow? I am sure he will be better able to appreciate you after another peaceful night."

Bobby rejoined the others in the Waiting room. "Philippa, I am terribly sorry that you have not seen him. Can you come back tomorrow? He'll be brighter then, I think, and he would certainly like to see Charlotte, as well as you. Now we're all in Town perhaps we can find somewhere to have something to eat. Even better, I will call the Embassy – they have quite a nice Staff Dining Room, and I don't think they will mind me bringing you all in. that's provided you don't mind eating raw fish. It's very popular in Scandinavia!" It was not easy for Bobby to sound so cheerful, but she knew it was important to appear so, especially in front of the boys. They were at no age to betray to them her real worry about their father.

The news next morning was encouraging. Claud's consultant phoned Bobby at breakfast time and told her that Claud had rallied, that his pulse was strong and regular and that he had taken a little soup for sustenance. He was sitting up and asking to see a morning paper, and his family. Yesterday, there had been no moment for Finn to tell his father about winning his Colours. In truth, it had gone right out of his mind; he was too scared at seeing his father in such a poor condition and possibly close to death. Today he would give him the good news and it might even help his father's recovery a little.

But there was another event on that morning of November 15th that would bring good cheer to Claud Browning. Since June 1940, all church bells throughout Great Britain had been silent: only to be rung in the event of a German invasion. Today, this Sunday, the ban was lifted for the one single occasion. From Westminster Abbey to Truro Cathedral, from York Minster to the tiniest chapel in John O'Groats the bells rang out to celebrate the great Allied victory at El Alamein. Even in England's most remote church, on the tiny island of St Agnes in the Isles of Scilly, old Osbert Hinks rang the single bell until his arms ached, and then his nephew Jeremiah took over and kept on ringing until it was time for lunch and a large jug of good Cornish cider. At St. Mary's Hospital, the Matron had the good sense to warn Claud and all the patients that the bells would be ringing, not as an Invasion Warning, but for a great victory. The Victory at El Alamein.

It was a turning point for Claud in his fight for life, and for the Allies in their fight for freedom from tyranny.

CHAPTER 52

November 1942 was a time of mixed fortunes for Britain and her Allies, and indeed for the Free World as a whole.

In Papua New Guinea, the Australian Army advanced steadily over the Owen Stanley Mountains from Port Moresby. They found evidence that the retreating Japanese had been reduced to eating not only grass, but the flesh of dead Australian soldiers.

Many thousand miles away that brave outpost of Malta, so long under siege from Germany's Luftwaffe, at long last gained further relief by the arrival of a heavily escorted convoy of freighters from Port Said. It was known as Operation Stone Age. Sadly, the cruiser HMS "Arethusa" was hit by an aerial torpedo and arrived under tow in the Grand Harbour at Valetta burning fiercely. One hundred and fifty-five members of her crew were lost.

The Russians threw a ring of steel around the German Sixth Army, trapped in Stalingrad, so recently doomed to be captured by the Germans "before the end of summer". Now it is the Germans who are doomed; more than a quarter million men. General Paulus, the German Commander, pleads with Hitler that he be allowed to break out of the net, but Hitler refuses. Hermann Goering gives an assurance that the Luftwaffe will be able to airlift adequate supplies and reinforcements to the encircled Germans. This is a terrible miscalculation.

In Poland, the deportation of Jews to Concentration Camps nears completion. 600,000 have been murdered at Belzec, 360,000 at Chelmno and 840,000 at Treblinka, a total of 1.8 million.

On the 20th November, Lancaster bombers drop the new 8,000lb bomb on Turin. In eleven raids the RAF hit the City with 100,000 incendiaries, and high explosive bombs.

The 8th Army pushing westward, recaptured the Libyan port of Benghazi, but elsewhere in North Africa Allied armies met tough resistance from German forces who are now receiving reinforcements from the air.

Far away, in the United States, a decision is reached to take over a fifty thousand acre site in the New Mexico desert. Its purpose is to house a secret laboratory, to research the feasibility of constructing an atomic bomb.

The world is about to change for ever.

CHAPTER 53

Claud Browning was glad to get home, and Bobby was greatly relieved to get him there. They had kept him in hospital for two weeks, during which he lost a stone in weight. This was mostly due to the rigid diet that was imposed upon him and which he was advised to adhere to for the rest of his life. Allied to that, he was told that he must change his lifestyle, and take a lot more exercise. The Consultant, Godfrey Field, made things very clear: "Get yourself a bicycle and work up gradually to regular rides of not less than five miles. In addition, you should do plenty of walking. Do you play golf? It's a great game and makes walking a pleasure, instead of a chore. Unless, of course, you keep hitting the ball out of bounds, that can be tedious! One thing you need not give up is alcohol. In moderation it will do you good, especially red wine if you can get it. Of course, most of it comes from France, Germany and Italy, which makes it difficult at the moment, but do what you can." Claud had played a little golf between the wars, but with neither skill nor regularity. Being unavailable on Saturdays had not helped. As to wine, in was virtually unheard of in most homes, and the Browning household was no exception. But there were formal occasions, or journalistic dinners and the like, where Claud had imbibed. He determined to do as he was advised if he could find a supply. Perhaps the appalling Avondale at Pithiock could help.

Gordon Johns, his Editor-in-Chief, came down to Surbiton to see him. "Claud, I partly blame myself for this damned heart attack of yours. This bloody war has been dragging on for three years now, and we have all been working our socks off. But you are not as young as some of us, and you have done far more than many much younger people . Especially that damned night time firewatching in all weathers. That will have to stop when you get back to Fleet Street. I shall insist on it. And don't be in a rush to get back either. Get yourself really fit and well, man. That brings me to another matter I had meant to raise with you before all this business. How would you like to get back to writing? No, I don't mean reporting. I mean writing a regular weekly column. I don't know if it is up your street, but I think a lighthearted or humorous column would go down well. The public needs something to brighten their lives, and it would help our circulation. Have a think about it Claud. I think you might actually enjoy it, rather than spending your time sub-editing."

Claud did think about it – a great deal, since he had little else to do. Being at home all day, and in a house which for much of the time was empty, was a strange and unnerving experience which he did not enjoy. Gordon Johns was giving him a great opportunity to see if he could write creatively. It would not be easy, but it could be extremely satisfying if he could hit upon the right formula, and he would actually be doing a worthwhile service for millions of readers. A laugh or smile was the best medicine of all – for himself, and everyone else. Over the years, both as a journalist and as a soldier in the Great War, Claud Browning had come closely to observe his fellow man, both in terms of their character, their fads and foibles, and in their reactions to the variety of situations in which they had found themselves. He had quite a collection of "characters", and these were just the ones he had known. Over the centuries there had been countless numbers of colourful and eccentric people, some good and some wicked, but all interesting. It should be possible, he thought, to produce interesting and amusing profiles of these people, providing he could access records of them. For instance, there was Charles Wells, a swindler who duped people into financing his "inventions", such as the Musical Skipping Rope. It had been successful enough to enable him to buy a yacht and sail into Monte Carlo, where he actually won £16,000 at the Casino, a huge sum in 1892, which earned him the title of "The Man Who Broke The Bank Of Monte Carlo". Unfortunately, news got around and enabled enraged investors to trace him and have him convicted of fraud and he was sentenced to eight years imprisonment. Wells was not deterred and on release continued his wicked ways until his death in 1920.

Claud began to convince himself that this could be the formula he wanted, and as his recovery progressed he devoted long hours at the Public Library on the Ewell Road to compiling his List of Loveable Rogues. The other attractive aspect about this idea was that it could appeal to all ages, and he decided to put this to the test with his own family. Their reaction was beyond his hopes, they all loved it, and not least young Finn. Finn said that at least two of the Staff at Shawbury House would be candidates. Keith Lyle and H-M himself. It had been some while before Finn learned about Keith Lyle's exploits in the Great War. He was a quiet, mild mannered man, nothing flamboyant, nothing heroic, but beneath the skin extraordinary never the less. It had all begun as an infantryman in the trenches around Ypres – "Wipers" as the lads called it. Like so many, he had witnessed terrible things, unspeakable some of them, and certainly not to be repeated to young school boys. In the end he had been shot in the leg, his shin shattered, which "did for me doing all that charging over the top at the enemy, thank goodness." Back in England recovering from his wound he got to hear of the latest new tool of war, the Aeroplane, which was just being deployed on the Western Front. It had two different roles to play: as an aerial attack craft, and as an artillery OP (Observation Post). It was amazing how soon one of man's greatest scientific advances – the conquest of air – had been put to the cause of killing Man. The Wright brothers had only made the first tentative flight ten years before the Great War broke out.

Keith Lyle had had an elder brother who worked in the War Office, who in turn got Keith an introduction to a Senior Officer in the Royal Flying Corps – in those days a branch of the Army. The upshot had been that in the space of a few weeks he had been trained as an Observer. In those early days of air warfare, the Observer had multiple roles: as a spotter for his side's artillery on the ground, as a bomber to drop bombs (by hand) on enemy ground forces, or directly onto enemy aircraft flying below, and finally as a gunner to repel attacks from enemy aircraft. Now, 25 years on, it was hard to imagine that these craft had been small biplanes and triplanes, built from wood and canvas, with a swivel-mounted Lewis machine gun as its sole defence, and that flew at little more than double the speed of a motor car. Keith Lyle had done well to survive, Twice he had been shot down and lived to tell the tale   He had dropped bombs over the German lines at Passchaendale and he had downed three of the infamous Baron Richthofen's famed and feared Flying circus.   This slight, self-effacing little man, decorated by the King for his gallantry, was now an anonymous master in a boys' Preparatory School in Surrey. Could not he be an ideal candidate for Claud Browning's new feature? Well, maybe. Claud promised his son that once the new Feature was established, he would certainly consider him as a possible candidate, but, as a living person Keith Lyle would have to give his permission. Privately, Claud felt that he would not do so. The country was full of unsung heroes, whose dearest wish was to remain totally anonymous. No, what Claud wanted was "Loveable Characters".

H-M, the eccentric bachelor who always wore rugger shorts, summer or winter, who had captained England at croquet, whose hobbies beyond running this marvellous boys school, included collecting Chinese ivory carvings and the study and cultivation of rare orchids in the conservatory that was attached to the end of the school's main building (and into which no pupil might enter, on pain of a Slow and Grisly Death), and who now, in time of war, had sacrificed his precious croquet lawn for the production of vegetables to feed the live-in staff and the boarding pupils, HM might possibly be another.

Finn, no longer quite so worried about his father's health, continued his busy young life. School came first of course, especially football and squash, though he did not neglect his classroom studies, nor his Sunday morning athletics training with Shirley Black. He still found time to visit the Convalescent Home and was now "part of the furniture" as Daisy used to say. December brought fresh war news and fresh cuttings for his scrapbook. On the 3rd, for instance, it was reported that Allied troops advancing East towards Tunis had come face to face with a gigantic new German tank, the 56 ton Tiger. Not only that, they were subjected to terrible attack by German dive bombers, the dreaded Stuka. In the Mediterranean, a British destroyer, HMS Quentin was sunk by aerial torpedo. In Rome, the Italian leader Benito Mussolini revealed that since entering the war, Italy had lost 40,000 men killed, 86,000 wounded and 231, 000 taken prisoner. To what purpose he made this admission no one knew.

Not all Italians lacked the stomach for a fight. Italian frogmen on underwater "Chariots" entered Algiers Harbour undetected and sank two Allied merchantmen severely damaging two others. And U-Boats in the South Atlantic sank one troop carrier with a thousand South African troops on board. In the North Atlantic, U-Boat U515 sank the British troopship "Ceramic". Only one man, a Royal Engineer, survived.

The war in the air had by this time reached a point where German bombers rarely ventured into British airspace, so depleted were they by demands to deploy more aircraft on the Russian Front. Conversely, USAAF and Bomber Command pounded targets in Germany and Occupied Europe every night. However, there was great concern at their losses: 1,400 shot down and double that number damaged.

The "Purification" of Europe continued unabated and on the 16th December Himmler ordered the deportation of all Gypsies, or persons of mixed Gypsy blood to Auschwitrz. Many would not live until Christmas Day the following week, and none would survive far into the New Year. On New Year's Eve Himmler informed Hitler that "363,211 Jews were executed in Occupied Europe during the past twelve months."

And so a New Year began. 1943.

CHAPTER 54

On 3rd January Finn reached the age of twelve. By now brother Clive was on the way to being twenty-one, Douglas was eighteen and Kenneth would be seventeen later in the month. Though he resented being called it, Finn was the only "child" left. Some days, Bobby's thoughts drifted to the appalling possibility that if the war dragged on for a further two years Kenneth would be called up, and if it continued for another five years even Finn would have to bear arms. Oh God! Let it be over soon. Let us have an end to this dreadful loss of life on all sides. Yes, it was clear how brutal the enemy was being, but they were still human beings, with mothers and fathers who loved them, who probably had no idea that they were not "their little angels", forced to kill their enemy. It was all so pointless, so unnecessary, so barbaric.

News from Clive in Rhodesia was infrequent, and usually via Philippa. He was safe; that was the main thing. More than that he was quite enjoying his work.

Training "these callow youths" as he jokingly called them, was rewarding, in the sense in that he knew they would go back to Blighty and join squadrons to bomb hell out of the Huns. Occasionally he wished he could go back with them, but then he would pause, and reflect on what had happened to him. He had been lucky! Many of these men would die, and in horrible circumstances. If they were lucky they would end up in some ghastly POW camp. If they were VERY lucky they might end up like him, or pushing a desk, or something equally frustrating. As he trained these young men he came to realize how little they understood the full reality of what they were training for: long, freezing hours in a glass bubble, 25,000 feet above Germany, shitting themselves at the realisation that death was a whisker away, a mere microsecond. No, they just saw the glamour of firing their guns at the enemy Messerschmitts and Focke-Wolfs, and pasting hell out of Hitler's munitions factories, and then home James and a few hours at "The Rose and Crown", and if things worked out right, meeting a WAAF with a wasp waist, blonde hair and big tits. Perhaps it was as well they could not see the truth, and Clive took care never to disillusion them. Anyway, if he had, they would have gone to every length to fail the course!

Clive desperately missed being at home with Philippa and his child. She was crawling now and very soon she would be toddling about. He was missing out and it hurt. Increasingly, and he knew not why, he found himself going to the little Christian Chapel on the Station. It was a comfort. He was unsure if he believed the Gospel story. There seemed to be too many contradictions. But one thing shone through for him, and that was the unconditional and all-consuming love that Jesus felt for his fellow men and women. Did He really, knowingly, give up his life to save mankind?

Was the Almighty so cruel as to let this man who said He was The Son Of God, go to a prolonged and agonising death, nailed to a tree? Was THAT how God saw Love? Clive was training men to kill. Clive had submitted himself to be so trained. How could he do this, when his heart told him that he should love his enemy, even as he loved his own child? Increasingly, Clive became confused. The Chapel was shared by all denominations, and it was really pure happenstance that Clive was approached by Fr Padraig McCarthy, the Roman Catholic Chaplain to the Base. "Hello son, I've noticed you here a number of times recently, though not at my services, unfortunately! Can I help you in any way? Is something troubling you? You know, even you pagan, barbarian Protestants have a right to my time if they need it!

Anyway, I don't see many other customers in this forsaken country, so I might as well indulge myself with you, if you wish it." The priest's smile was broad and his eyes twinkled. Over the ensuing weeks Fr McCarthy encouraged Clive to study the Gospels and to discuss them with him. Clive was drawn increasingly to seek McCarthy's company, and not just for religious guidance. They became firm friends and found they had common interests. They began to explore the magnificent scenery and wildlife surrounding their base near Gwelo. There was an abundance of wildlife to watch and more than anything, they sought the chance to meet and mingle with some of the Matabele bushmen in their settlements. Mc Carthy used his influence (was it God given?) to persuade the pilot of one of the training aircraft, an Avro Anson, to fly them west over Bechuanaland to view the famed Okavango Delta. And on another occasion to fly North West and swoop low over Victoria Falls Clive turned to Padraig and smiled: "It was no run-of-the-mill God who created all this!"

"No, my son, and He is no mere journeyman who enabled Man to fly over it to see it in all its glory!" they both laughed.

It was a great shock to Philippa early in January 1943, to receive a letter from Clive to say that he had converted to Catholicism, and that he hoped when he eventually came home, that she would listen to him and follow his example. Clive sent a similar letter to his parents, though he refrained from suggesting that they might also switch to Rome.

Meanwhile, Douglas at Yeovilton was dubbed "a natural". Not his words, but the words of his C.O. Douglas had always thought that he would fail his aptitude tests as a pilot, but might scrape through as the second crew member, who carried out the Navigation and Gunnery roles in the Fleet Air Arm's Fairey Fulmar, and later on the Firefly. The Fulmar had been in service since 1940 and did sterling work protecting the Malta convoys. But whilst it was heavily armed, it was slow by 1943 standards, with a maximum speed of only 250 mph, and was being superceded. To his surprise, however, he was appointed to Pilot Training. The course was intense: crew losses had been heavy, especially in the Mediterranean theatre, but also in the Far East, and the need to recruit and train replacements was acute. All pilot training followed similar routines: the principles of flight, handling of an aircraft's controls, mechanics, navigation, and meteorology. Classroom stuff. The real fun started when a trainee took to the air and actually flew a machine. First of all it was in Tiger Moth biplanes, then a graduation to Harvard Trainers. Take-offs and landings were the trickiest procedures, especially the simulated landings and take-offs from Aircraft Carriers that were constantly moving and not just in a smooth, forward direction, but pitching and rolling as well. This was a nightmare for Douglas, and worse still was knowing at what speed the ship was travelling, and the speed and direction of the wind. The thought of doing it for real, at sea, was a terrifying prospect. Advance Training was at Lossiemouth on the Moray Firth. "Full circle, Dad" he told his father. "I started up here at Rosyth and now I'm even further North than that. It's a bleak place, especially at this time of year, but there's no time to worry about that. I'm worried stiff at the thought of really flying an aircraft on to a carrier's deck, but at least I can swim if I miss it! Except that I would freeze to death in these waters." Privately,, Douglas recalled his enduring fear of going down with his ship. He still shuddered to think of the hell of being trapped as the steel monster sank to the ocean floor. And at such moments he recalled the baby mouse staring up at him in the Church at Pithiock. Fear existed to be overcome, he kept telling himself.

*****

The new term at Shawbury House started soon after Finn's twelfth birthday, and for Finn there was a new experience on the playing field. Rugby Football. Finn had heard of the game, but had never seen it played. To start with, Finn was at a disadvantage: his contemporaries had all learned the rudiments of the game the year before. But his natural talents at football and athletics were enough for H-M to believe that he could rapidly adapt to Rugger. It proved to be the case, and H-M himself gave him extra coaching, showing him how to tackle, swerve and sidestep, pass the ball, place kick and kick from hand. Finn loved it. He knew instinctively that this was the game for him, more than soccer and more, even, than athletics. Two aspects of the game particularly enthralled him: tackling opponents in full flight, and scoring tries. Every player likes to score tries. But not every player relishes tackling.

It can be a painful activity; not just for the victim but also the perpetrator. Finn carried it out with maximum legal ferocity, and the bigger the opponent, the better, and the harder they fall. It was never an issue that Finn should play amongst the forwards, the Heavy Mob as H-M called them. Their job was to provide the ball for the Gazelles (sometimes referred to as "Girls"), the fast, graceful and elusive creatures who operated in the wide open spaces where their speed cold best be exploited. But neither did Finn mind when, as often happens, he found himself at the bottom of a heap of players with face buried in the mud, or when he himself was the target for a determined tackler.

The 1st XV had played three and lost three matches before Finn was given his chance to play in the fourth match, against Rowney School. He was selected to play Centre Threequarter. The problem with this was that Shawbury House fielded a lightweight scrum, and worse, lacked a really tall boy for the lineouts. The result was that Shawbury House had virtually no attacking opportunities during the entire first half and Finn never had a touch of the ball other than to field the opposition's high "Up and Unders" which he did with aplomb, but usually simultaneously with the arrival of two or three of the Rowney Heavy Mob.

Somewhat fortuitously, Shawbury House was only down 3-0 at half time. "We've got to try to take the initiative in the second half, any ideas anyone?" It was H-M who asked. "Sir" Finn had the temerity to speak first. "I know I'm new at this game, sir, but it seems to me that the Rowney tactic of high Up and Unders in these muddy conditions is working well for them.

Why don't we copy them? Give them some of their own medicine. We are quite fast in our threequarter line, and we are not afraid of thumping them. They might make a mess of fielding the high kicks and give us a chance of scoring." "Fair enough" H-M replied, "Unless anyone's got a better idea."

The tactic worked well. The second half was scarcely under way, before, for once, the ball emerged from a loose scrum on Shawbury's side.

Henry Taylor, Shawbury's scrum-half, lofted the ball high and deep into the Rowney 25 yard area. Only their full-back was anywhere near it and, unnerved by the sight of Finn bearing down on him, he misjudged the catch. A lucky bounce and Finn was over the tryline under the posts. A try and an easy conversion. 5-3 to Shawbury House. It was the only score in the entire second half . From that moment on the only team sport Finn wanted to play was Rugby. He had excelled at Soccer, but there was a thrill in Rugby that was lacking in the round-ball game. In many ways soccer was more skilful, but it lacked the contact element. It was the unmatchable satisfaction of Man against Man, muscle against muscle, of extreme physical endeavour that left the player drained by exhilarated. Rugby was not without skill: the hand-off and swerve or sidestep had to be practised diligently. Likewise passing, especially the quick inter-passing between players. And tackling was a precise art. It was easy to tackle too high and fail to bring the opponent down, or to tackle too low and catch his boot in your face. No better way to lose a tooth or two!

Whilst Finn enjoyed his new sport, and his recent birthday cake, the German Sixth Army found no joy in their terrible entrapment in the ruins of Stalingrad, and their Commander's refusal to accept the Russian offer of honourable surrender.

Gen. Paulus felt obliged to carry out the Fuhrer's order of No Surrender Under Any Circumstances. How the hearts of those men sank. Starving, short of armour, guns and ammunition, with totally inadequate clothing to withstand the bitter winter, they saw their last hope recede.

On the 14th January, in Casablanca, President Roosevelt and Prime Minister Churchill met with their military advisers to plan future strategy, for defeating the German and Japanese enemy. Josef Stalin should also have attended this summit, but declined, on the grounds that he was unable to leave Russia at this tense and difficult time. "My Army needs me near them" he stated, but pointed out the urgency of a Third Front, to take pressure off the Eastern Front. Churchill and Roosevelt could see an early and victorious end to the campaign in North Africa. The German forces were being squeezed and would soon be forced to withdraw across the Mediterranean, back to Italy and Greece. The two Western leaders felt that they were now capable of launching an assault into Western Europe, and regarded Sicily, then Italy, as the route forward. This in itself should help Stalin, by diverting German forces from the Russian Front to defend Italy.

From Stalingrad, a German soldier wrote home: "Hitler has left us in the lurch. We are alone and doomed. When Stalingrad falls you will hear about it. Then you will know that I shall not return" It is not recorded how such a letter found its way back to Germany, nor why it was not censored by the Gestapo.

January 23rd and good news from North Africa. Monty's Eighth Army heading west takes Tripoli. As tanks of the 7th Armoured Division roll into the city, there is no sign of enemy forces and Monty takes the surrender from the Italian Mayor. Virtually the whole of Libya is now in Allied hands.

January 31st and the German Gen. Paulus in Stalingrad surrenders to the surrounding Russians. The losses to the German Army are almost beyond belief: 90,000 killed and a further 120,000 taken prisoner. Several thousand tanks and self-propelled guns are destroyed or captured. During this terrible campaign, German forces also lose 500 transport aircraft shot down trying to maintain supplies to the troops below, plus 700 bombers and fighters. Whilst the War is a very long way from being won by the Allies – in fact more than two years away - Germany will never fully recover from this defeat. Although Churchill did not repeat his immortal words of the previous November after the victory at El Alamein, it is at last true that "this is the beginning of the end" of Hitler's dream of world domination.

CHAPTER 55

"We are the master race – the lowest German worker is, racially and biologically, a thousand times more valuable than any of the population here." So spoke Erich Koch, the Nazi Commissioner for the Ukraine on March 5th 1943. A strange, deluded statement in the light of the virtual massacre of Germany's much-vaunted Wehrmacht and Luftwaffe at Stalingrad. Nevertheless, Germany was far from defeated on the Eastern Front and nor would Adolf Hitler recognize defeat for two more winters to come. But for the ordinary, foot-slogging German soldier, there was no greater fear than that of being posted to the Russian theatre of war. Not only would he face the Russian Army. Increasingly, Russian partisans were becoming better organised and trained to wage war behind the German lines. One German officer wrote in his diary: "We entered a gloomy wilderness in our tanks. There was not a single man anywhere. Everywhere the forests and marshes are haunted by the ghosts of the avengers. They would attack us unexpectedly, as if rising from under the earth. They cut us up, and then disappear like devils into the nether regions. Night is setting in and I feel them approaching from out of the darkness. They are the ghosts and I am frozen with fear." Were these the words of The Master Race?

Nearer to home, and given much prominence in English newspapers, was the Allies growing aerial offensive against targets deep in Germany. As both the US and Britain's air strength grew, so did the intensity of their attacks against targets in Germany's industrial heartland. In one such night raid, in early March, 400 British bombers dropped over one thousand tons of bombs. This followed a raid a few days earlier on the German capital, Berlin, during which the RAF dropped thousands of incendiaries and 8,000lb high explosive bombs.

By this time Claud was beginning to feel a new man. His idea for a weekly column had been accepted enthusiastically by Gordon Johns; even though the diet of gloomy war news had been lightened a little in recent months, still the public were war weary. Rationing and austerity had been gnawing away at morale, but even worse was the continuing loss of loved ones, either killed or prisoner of the enemy. All this had taken its toll, and it had taken its toll on newspaper circulation as well. Advertising revenue had diminished as the war wore on, and so had profitability. But Claud's new column began to find the paper new readership; small to begin with, but gradually increasing.. Claud was delighted, but his real pleasure lay in how he felt in himself. He had lost weight and was positively enjoying exercise.

Every weekend now, instead of being incarcerated in a cramped and dismal office in Fleet Street, he was able to walk in the countryside, or watch Ken and Finn playing their various sports. He loved to cycle and would go all the way to Epsom Downs, where he would walk over the Racecourse and then cycle home again. Finn, being a year older, could cycle all the way to the Convalescent Home at Headley, and Claud would sometimes accompany him and help out there too. He had a first-hand understanding of the wounds of war, and not just the physical wounds, but what it did to the minds of men who had suffered total fear as well as appalling pain. He had been there twenty five years earlier, after all. Strange as it might seem, Claud seemed a happier man after his second heart attack. He realized that maybe they need not have happened if he had led a different lifestyle. Well, he could not turn back the clock, but he could, and had learned from the experience. Bobby noticed the difference in him. She could see a new bounce about him. His eyes had lost that dull, weary look. He smiled more, was slower to anger and depression, had more patience and was more attentive towards her and the children. Best of all, he was able to spend more time with them all and they even began to ask friends and neighbours round for coffee, or a light supper when rationing allowed. And Spring was around the corner. Bobby always liked the month of March. Though it could sometimes be bitter, with driving rain and piercing gales, it could also smile upon the earth and the first signs appeared of new life – little bright green leafbuds on the trees, the first celandines and violets and primroses, the sparrows chattering and hunting nesting materials. Life seemed good again. Not perfect, far from it, but "on the up". It lifted her spirits.

Finn had lost none of his friends from his old school and had made many new ones at Shawbury House. His days were full, if not in the classroom, then on the squash court or the rugger pitch. He was diligent about his attendance at Headley, rarely missing a Sunday afternoon with the convalescents. Eventually though, the term ended and there was time to do things with his pals. Of course, George next door was never far away. On rainy days they used to ask a couple of friends round to play Monopoly or L'Attaque or Tri-tactics, a board game involving Army, Navy and Air Force pieces. But all of them were happier to be out and about, and venturing farther afield on their bikes. Finn had two favourite places: White Downs, so loved by his mother, where once he watched a Spitfire flying fast above the railway line below him. Below him! He could actually look <u>down</u> on the pilot and could swear that the pilot looked <u>up</u> at him, and waved. The Army had constructed pillboxes along this slope years back to defend against a

German push north from the Sussex coast. Finn and friends would creep into these gloomy concrete tombs and play "soldiers" firing on the enemy advancing up the slope. No one actually wanted to be the enemy, but it was fun to see if you could actually get right up to a pillbox without being "shot" by its occupants.

The other favourite enterprise was to cycle to Wisley. Not far off the Portsmouth Road, half way between Esher and Guildford, screened by a thick ribbon of woodland, a thousand acres of farmland had been annexed and converted into a military airfield. There was no greater thrill than to pretend to be a German Spy, and creep through the trees to the very perimeter of the field to spot through the barbed wire fencing the comings and goings of aircraft, vehicles and personnel. The field was used by the Vickers Company for the construction and testing of Wellington Bombers. The Wellington was a twin-engined medium bomber that saw action throughout the war. It lacked the glamorous image of the Lancaster, Stirling and Halifax heavy bombers, but was more versatile, being used for attacking German convoys in the Mediterranean, bombing military and industrial installations in Germany itself, and as a torpedo bomber in the Atlantic and Far East theatres of war. For Finn, the Wellington was a sort of icon for all British aircraft. It was "his" bomber, even though his brother Clive had flown in, and nearly died in, Lancasters. He wished he could fly one, and in a dreadful distortion of his young mind, he hoped the war would go on long enough that he might do so. At the same time he still liked to pretend that he was spying for the Germans and would get caught and shot by a firing squad. Mature for his age he might be, but not all childish things had evaporated from his mind, and, anyway, he knew he wasn't really a spy and if necessary his father would intercede on his behalf.

All this came to an abrupt end one day when, after watching activity on the airfield for an hour, he was stealthily retreating back to the Portsmouth road, when out of the bushes there appeared a very large, uniformed airman with a terrifyingly malevolent looking Alsatian, straining at the leash and growling malevolently. Finn recognized the man's Flight Sergeant insignia.

"What do you think you're up to , sonny? Don't you know this is Air Ministry land. You have no business here. You's be well advised to hop it, before I set the dog on yer."

Though frightened, Finn did not see why the man had to be belligerent, and stood his ground. "I know the airfield is forbidden, but I did not think these woods were part of it as well. I was only watching the Wellingtons.

My brother was in Lancasters until he got wounded. He's training air gunners in Rhodesia now."

The airman's stern expression softened a little. "Oh, I see, son. Well I can understand why you are so interested in Wellies then. 'spect you'd like to get close to one then, wouldn't you. Now I don't have a whole lot of clout on the Station, but I'm sorry if I and old Snarlichops here gave you a fright, so I'll tell you what I'll do, but no promises, mind. I'll have a word with the Station Adjutant and see if I can swing you a visit. Would you like that? Yes? Well, give us your name and where you live, and I'll see if it can be organised. Have you got a telephone at home and do you know the number? How would that be, eh?" Finn could scarcely believe what was happening. An actual inspection of the Base? Was this real? Well, no. The man had only said he would see what he could do. No promises. But that was better than being sent packing! The Flight Sergeant smiled. "By the way, I know old Snarlichops looks a bit vicious, and he would take your arm off if I told him to. But he can be nice as pie. If I tell him to lick your hand, then that's what he would do. And if I say "pat, pat", he'll let you stroke him. Want to try?"

Finn was unsure. This was no gentle Spot with appealing brown eyes, like they had before the war in Barnes. And another thing: Alsatians were also known as German Shepherd dogs, and the Germans definitely were not at all friendly! "Go on, son. I promise he wont hurt you, or even growl. It don't do to be afraid of animals, they always seem to know and they react badly sometimes. By the by, what's your name lad?" "Finn. Finn Browning, and I live in Surbiton. We all hate the Germans. My Dad was in the trenches in the Great War and as well as my brother being an Air Gunner, I've got another brother who is training to be a pilot in the Fleet Air Arm. My Mother was born Norwegian and her family, my Gran and Grandpa are still in Norway, worst luck." "Is that right? Well I never! OK Finn, off you go and I promise I'll call you, whether I can swing you a visit or not. Fair enough? But before you go, go on, give Snarlichops a pat!" Hesitantly, Finn went down to the prone animal and gave it a light pat on its back. The dog twitched one ear and gave a contented "woof". "There", said the man, "Told you it was all right. He's your friend for life now. By the way, you ought to know my name. It's Bill. Bill Owen. Now, off you go."

Finn cycled home. Wisley was about 45 minutes hard cycling from Surbiton by the main roads, but Finn knew a few short cuts, and was home in half an hour. He was about to tell Claud and Bobby what had happened, before his father cut in and said "Finn, we have had a phone call from the

RAF Station at Wisley about you. It seems you have been spying on them and they have it in mind to have you arrested, tortured and then put in front of a firing squad. What do you have to say for yourself?" Claud smiled, as he saw Finn's face freeze with anxiety. "Don't worry lad, it was the Station Adjutant,, and he said that if you like to present yourself at the Guardhouse at the entrance, and say who you are, they will give you a tour of the hangars. Furthermore, they will let you sit in the pilot's seat of a Wellington. They are sorry, but they have to draw the line at letting you go up in one. The Adjutant said that he was giving you this opportunity only because the patrolling officer, someone called Owen, had told him that you had stood firm when challenged, and had actually stroked the guard dog. Apparently you are the first person, adult or minor, who has dared to stroke the animal. That impressed them. It seems Saturday would be a good day, because they do not test the aircraft on that day: the test pilots have a day off!

That night, Finn hardly slept, and when he did, he dreamed he was bombing Berlin.

CHAPTER 56

When Douglas sat in the gloom of Pithiock Church, consumed with fear that he might die at sea, and watched the fearless baby mouse staring up at him, never could he have imagined that months later he would pass out of RN Flying Training School as a qualified pilot ready for operational duty. Not all his colleagues were so lucky. Only about 55% lasted the full course. Sadly, a few were killed, more often than not when they attempted deck landings and either hit the deck too hard, or plunged over the side of the carrier. It was a dreadful sight once to see a mate land too far for'ard on the carrier's deck and shoot straight over the bows to be crushed as the ship passed over the stricken plane. The poor bastard and his plane were never seen again. Douglas had the embarrassment of overshooting once and aborting his attempt to land and having to circle to make a fresh approach. Another time he landed too heavily and collapsed his plane's undercarriage. But these mishaps were par for the course, and it was a rare event if a trainee pilot passed out without something going wrong somewhere. In retrospect, he enjoyed the course, and the sense of achievement was enormous when finally he was handed his Wings and had them sewn on his tunic. Nor did he object that it meant a sizeable increase in his pay packet

Of all Claud and Bobby's four sons, Douglas was the one who outwardly was the most manly. He was a handsome young man, with broad shoulders, hazel eyes, wavy brown hair, and a winning smile. He was a little on the stocky side, but muscular. At school he had not excelled either in the classroom or on the playing field, but neither had he been a failure; just middle-of-the-road satisfactory. Where he DID excel was in his ability to attract the opposite sex and over the last year or two he had had an enviable string of girl friends - but none for very long. Unlike Clive, whose love for Philippa had been his only and unwavering love, Douglas's "love" usually lasted no more than a few weeks. He met Celia on the London-bound train soon after completing his flying training. The joy of becoming an operational pilot was enhanced by news of his first posting. Malta. His dread had been to be carrier-based, but a shore station was just fine, even if life there was likely to be hairy. Malta had taken a terrible pasting at the hands of the Luftwaffe. Attacks upon it continued incessantly, until eventually the Germans were driven out of North Africa and back into Sicily and Italy. That day was yet to come, and fighting in the region was savage and unrelenting. But for now, there was two weeks leave to enjoy, back in Surbiton with his family.

Celia was a member of the Womens Royal Naval Service, universally referred to as Wrens. On many women the dark blue serge jacket and straight, below-the-knee skirt were unflattering, but Douglas thought Celia would look elegant in old sacking. When he entered the compartment, two Ordinary Seamen and three Wrens were already there. None of the Wrens were officers, so Douglas was the only occupant of Commissioned rank. The two seamen clearly already knew two of the Wrens and were engrossed in light-hearted banter with them. Douglas took a window seat opposite the third, who gave him the faintest of smiles. She had long auburn hair, swept into a bun, but with a pretty fringe at the front. He noticed that her hands were long and slender and Douglas thought they must match her figure. When standing, he thought, she must be nearly six feet tall – taller than him for certain. The arrival of an Officer in the compartment was clearly an inhibiting factor upon the two seamen, and it was not long before they, and the two Wrens with them, departed. Douglas was alone with the remaining redhead Wren, and it was Douglas who took the plunge and broke the ice: "It seems they did not like our company, or perhaps I should say my company. I hope you don't plan to leave as well!" Celia smiled: "No. of course not. But you <u>are</u> an officer and I am just an ordinary Jenny, sir, so you should not have been surprised had I done so." "No, I suppose not. By the way my name is Douglas Browning. May I ask yours?" "Of course, I'm Celia. Celia Simpson and I am very glad to be heading south from chilly old Scotland. Back to Wimbledon for a week's leave." "Wimbledon! We don't live far apart. I/m a few stops down the line. Surbiton. Do you live with your parents?" "Yes. And you?" "The same. We lived in Barnes before the war, but Dad thought it was a bit too close to London when the war started, so he moved us out a bit, but really I don't think it made much difference. I was at King's School in Wimbledon" "Really? So was my brother. His name was Philip. He was lost at sea in 1941. He was on Motor Torpedo Boats." "Oh, I am so sorry. It must have been devastating for you and your parents. Is that what prompted you to joining the WRNS?" "Yes, before Phil went down I had intended to join the Women's Land Army. I rather liked the idea of living on a farm and milking cows!

Though I don't think my Dad was too keen. He thought I'd get seduced by a country yokel, I think. Also there was the small matter to contend with of him having been a Rear Admiral. How about you?" "Well, my older brother went into the RAF, so I thought I'd try the Navy. God knows why, because I have a horror of my ship going down with me trapped down below. Oh! Oh God, I'm so sorry. How dreadfully insensitive of me. I should have thought before I opened my stupid mouth, knowing what happened to your brother. Do forgive me please. Anyway, I've got a shore posting. Malta. And as no doubt you have noticed, I'm Fleet Air Arm, so at least I won't be seasick all the time."

Long before the train reached London, Douglas and Celia had agreed to meet during their leave. They crossed London together to Waterloo and boarded the same train. He waved goodbye from the train window at Wimbledon Station. He did not expect the blown kiss in reply.

CHAPTER 57

March 23. Himmler's chief statistician, Dr Korherr, reports that since the outbreak of war, the number of Jews exterminated has reached 1,419,467.

In the first three weeks of March at least fifty Allied merchant ships have been sunk in the North Atlantic. The U-Boats usually strike in mid-Atlantic, where only very long-range Allied aircraft can reach them. They are virtually immune to attack.

March 29. Hitler orders the construction of a missile launching site on the French side of the English Channel to bombard England.

March 30. It is reported from Moscow that Stalin is furious at the suspension of Allied convoys to Murmansk, because of heavy losses. He suspects political rather than military motives for the decision.

April 2. Russia claims that 850,000 German troops have died in the winter campaign.

April 5. Tunisia. As Allied troops prepare for the final push against Tunis and Bizerta, British and American aircraft launch the biggest ever air assault against Axis targets in the Mediterranean, flying more than one thousand sorties. Fourteen Junkers

Ju52 bombers, loaded with petrol, were shot down off the Tunisian coast. Allied bombers set fire to three supply ships and sink an escort destroyer.

April 10. American Liberator bombers raid La Maddalena at the northern tip of Sardinia and sink the Italian cruiser "Trieste"

The war in the Mediterranean theatre is not yet over, but there is now no doubting the Allies growing supremacy and eventual victory there.

CHAPTER 58

Claud and Bobby were immensely proud of Douglas's achievement in becoming a Fleet Air Arm pilot, but were, perhaps, better able to mask their pride than was their youngest son. Finn wanted to follow him everywhere he went – at least when he was in uniform. Finn wanted all his friends and school mates to see the gold wings on Douglas's chest, and though mature for his age, lost no opportunity to let them know that he was soon going to be shooting Nazi aircraft out of the sky. Douglas had different ideas. He wanted to make the best use of his leave, well knowing that it might be his last for a long time, or even ever. And Celia was not far away, and he longed to see her again. A mere four stops by train. On the third day of his leave, he could restrain himself no longer, and he phoned her.

The voice that answered his call was deep and gravelly. "Who is this and what do you want?" "Good morning sir, may I speak to Celia please.?" "You may or you may not. Depends who you are." "My name is Browning sir, Douglas Browning. Are you Celia's father?" "I am. Would you by any chance be the young man my daughter met on the train from Scotland?" "Yes, sir. It was a long journey and it seemed, well, almost discourteous to ignore each other." "Am I correct in thinking you have just qualified as a Fleet Air Arm pilot?" "Yes, sir, I am due to be posted to the Mediterranean theatre at the end of this leave. I shall be joining a land-based Seafire Squadron in Malta." "Uum. Interesting. I should like to meet you. I was in the Navy myself and wish I still was, now there is a war on. They say I'm too old. Old!! I'm still short of sixty and all the damned Ministry will say is that I could serve my nation in the Home Guard. Bloody ridiculous. It's ships I understand, not marching about with broom handles."

A voice in the background called out: "Daddy, is that call for me? Is that Douglas? For Heaven's sake, let me speak to him!" there was a grunt at the other end , and the phone was passed over.

" Oh Douglas, I'm so sorry, where are you?"

"Well, at the moment I am at home, but I was wondering if you would care to meet up? Perhaps for a drink somewhere. I could easily get the train back to Wimbledon."

"Douglas, just hold on a minute. Daddy's saying something in my other ear."

Douglas heard the gravelly voice of Admiral Simpson in the background. "If you are planning on seeing that young man, I'd like to meet him first, and I do NOT mean to vet him. I have no doubt that if he had the good sense to join the Royal Navy and get commissioned, then he must be suitable company. I just want to meet him and chat about Navy matters for a while. Ask him to come to the house, will you."

Douglas sensed that there was going to be no avoiding meeting the old man, and in any event, it would do him and his career no harm to do so.

Celia met Douglas at Wimbledon Station. Yesterday's clouds and rain had cleared and the sun shone warmly. Celia was dressed in a dark green tweed skirt and a pale yellow, roll neck sweater. "Hello, Douglas. Good to see you again. Seems odd to see you in a sports jacket and flannels, though. Still, you've not seen me out of uniform, either. God, I get fed up with that navy blue serge. It's a joy to put on decent clothes again. By the way this is Shovell, spelled with two Ls. The Black Labrador wagged enthusiastically and jumped up at Douglas.

"Why two Ls"

"Ah, well maybe you ought to know that before you meet my father. Shovell with two Ls refers to Admiral Sir Cloudsley Shovell. He was the poor man who put himself and his squadron of English men o' wars onto the rocks in The Isles of Scilly, back in 1707. It was the biggest peacetime disaster the Royal Navy has ever suffered.

More than 1500 sailors died that night. A black night. A black Labrador. Hence the name Shovell. It's a shame really, since he's such a jolly animal. Still, you don't argue with Daddy about a thing like that."

"I doubt if I will be arguing with him about anything, Celia. I am too wet behind the ears to take issue with Admirals."

"Oh, he's all right actually. He barks right enough, but very rarely does he bite. And I've got him wrapped round my little finger, so have no fear."

They strode up the hill from the Station, and without thinking, Douglas took Celia's hand. She responded firmly to the gesture and Douglas felt a clear signal had passed between them. As Celia fumbled to insert her key into the front door, it swing open and Douglas caught his first sight of the Admiral. He was tall – well over six foot, with a slight stoop. His grey hair was receding, and his green eyes sparkled from a leathery, weather beaten, somewhat gaunt face. That sparkle betrayed a strong sense of humour, and Douglas thought to himself "I'm going to get on with this man."

"Come in, Lieutenant. I'm sorry you are not in uniform. I would have liked to see those shiny new wings you've just won. Well done, well done. Never got the chance to be airborne myself: too busy driving destroyers."

Douglas was shown into the rear sitting room, which bore all the signs of the owner's past life. On every wall there were photos of Royal Navy vessels at sea, some with guns blazing. One photo portrayed the Admiral on the bridge, peering through binoculars. On the mantelpiece were three framed photos: one was of Celia in WRNS uniform, another of the Admiral with, presumably, Mrs Simpson. The third portrayed a young naval officer. Douglas guessed it must be Philip, the Simpsons' son.. Above the mantelpiece was a large reproduction of Turner's "The Fighting Temeraire".

"Take some tea Lieutenant, or coffee? 'fraid it is pretty awful stuff, but you can't get anything else these days. Bloody U-boats are seeing to that, damn them. Hilda, are you in the kitchen? Put the kettle on darling will you, and then come and meet this young flyer. He's going to take care of the Nazi buggers in the Med, so we'd better look after him."'' Douglas stayed for lunch. He warmed to both the Admiral and Celia's mother, a slight woman who, like so many wives, on the surface was subservient to her daunting husband, but in reality was at least as assertive as he was when the need arose. In a way it reminded Douglas of Lady Hester – only she was half that woman's daunting bulk. With their menfolk so often away at sea for long periods, Navy wives became pretty independent and well-organised. But beneath her composure, Douglas sensed she was still grieving for her lost son, and noticed her gaze often veering to the photo on the mantelpiece. He prayed silently that his mother would never be in that situation.

Later, Celia and Douglas walked on Wimbledon Common. There seemed little need to talk much, and once again each of them sensed that a bond was growing. The simple act of holding hands created some kind of connection, beyond mere physical contact. It was a feeling Douglas had never experienced before. It was as if some warm current was passing from him to her and from her to him. He felt that he must care for her, now and for always, that that was his desire, his duty and his destiny. He could not explain it, not even to himself.

Their leave passed all to quickly. They met every day. Douglas took Celia home to meet his family. The weather remained kind and they walked in Richmond Park, sitting by the ponds, watching the deer, and the sheep that had been introduced to help the national food chain. One day they walked along the Thames from Kingston to Hampton Court. Twice they went to the cinema and once to London to the National Gallery, then lunch at a Lyons Corner House. They did not speak about the passing of these precious days, until the day they would have to say goodbye, but the thoughts were there. The heaviness. For each of them there was a growing heaviness in their heart. They had not spoken of love. They did not even realize that they did love one another. They were too young for that, perhaps. But they knew that they wanted to stay together – not just now, but beyond now, beyond, beyond, beyond. Together there would be Safety. Without each other, Uncertainty and Loneliness. It was the curse of war.

On April 18th, Douglas reported to Lee-on-Solent. A Sunderland flying boat would fly him to Gibraltar, and then on to Malta. Celia returned to duty in Scotland.

CHAPTER 59

By early May the Allied offensive in North Africa was reaching its climax. Early on the morning of the 7th armoured cars of the 11th Hussars entered the city of Tunis to be met by cheering women blowing kisses and throwing bouquets of flowers. Tanks of the Derbyshire Yeomanry rumbled in behind them. German resistance was isolated; a few snipers in rooftops and high in the minarets and mosques. A day earlier, Allied forces had demolished the German 15th Panzer Division. Simultaneously, the US II Corps began its final assault towards Bizerta, entering it in late afternoon after heavy fighting on the outskirts. Now, the 8th Army from the East, that had fought all the way from El Alamein in Egypt, met up with the 1st Army advancing from the west. Finally, the Germans were about to be squeezed out of the whole of North Africa.

A delicious irony occurred ten days later when Monty, back in England, won more applause than the cast, when he attended a West End performance of the play "Arsenic and Old Lace".

On May 19th, Goebbels announced that Berlin was "Free of Jews".

On May 22nd, elsewhere in Germany, the Luftwaffe ace Adolf Galland test flew the Messerschmitt Me262 at 520 mph. It was the first jet warplane on either side, and he claimed that it would regain air superiority for Germany. It never did.

It was around this time that SS Major-General Stroop reported to Himmler that the Warsaw Ghetto "was no more". Fourteen thousand Jews had been killed in the fighting, or transported to Treblinka Death Camp. Another forty two thousand had been deported to labour camps. Although Stroop said the ghetto had been destroyed, groups of Jews were still in hiding, or had escaped through the sewers to seek refuge in Christian districts of the city.

On May 24th Dr Josef Mengele took up the post of Camp Doctor at Auschwitz.

On May 28th the award was announced of the Victoria Cross to Wing Commander Guy Gibson, the "Dam Buster" who planned and led the raid on the Ruhr Dams.

On May 30th German raiders bombed a church in Torquay, killing 25 worshippers, of whom 20 were children.

CHAPTER 60

The Summer Term at Shawbury House was a quiet time for Finn, at least on the Sports Field. Finn had never really taken to cricket, and participated no more than he had to, which meant batting in the middle order in the Second Eleven, and in the Inter-House Competition. For Finn, this summer meant only one thing. This was that he had to sit and pass his Common Entrance Examination. Being "TheWorm", the baby of the family, had made Finn very conscious that a) his brothers were people apart, not really interested in him and his activities and b) that he had been thoroughly spoiled, in particular by his father. He felt, rightly or wrongly really did not matter, that his brothers' disinterest stemmed largely from the simple fact that they knew he was being favoured and so, unconsciously maybe, he became in their eyes a semi-irrelevance. This was especially true of Douglas and Kenneth. Finn loved his father dearly, but dearly wished he would desist from showing such favour. His mother was not totally guiltless either. It was an open secret that she had been hoping for a daughter.

Finn made up his mind that if he were to escape his parents' over indulgence, the best course would be to go to boarding school. He realized this would not cure the problem entirely, but it would help for a large part of the year. His friends at Shawbury House were all destined to go to boarding schools, and just because his brothers had all gone to day schools was no reason for him to follow suit. Many of his contemporaries at Shawbury House were going to Malvern ,some to Sherborne in Dorset and one or two to Christ's Hospital near Horsham – the famous Mustard Stocking school, where the boys all wore clerical black, with black knee breeches and long yellow stockings.

But plead as Finn repeatedly did, Claud was loath to let him go. It was not just a question of cost. Two of his sons were already away in the Forces, both overseas and soon enough Kenneth too would have to join up. He wanted Finn at home, not away for months at a time. Bobby felt the same way, but deep down admitted to herself that Finn would not be happy unless he could emulate his peers. Finally a compromise was reached. Finn could weekly board at a school not too far away from home. There was a number of choices: KCS Wimbledon was one, though most of the boys were daily students. Epsom College, with its strong association with the Medical Profession; Charterhouse, Cranleigh and Whitgift were other possibilities. It was H-M who in the end advised them to visit St. Luke's College, Dorking. Four of the Houses were Boarding and one was for Day Boys. It was not a huge school, about 350 boys. Originally St.Luke's had been sited in London, but had moved out to Dorking in 1872. H-M told the Brownings that not long before the War, a new Headmaster had been appointed, called Jack Doncaster. "Donny" as he was known, was a little eccentric, but had won the hearts and respect of both Staff and pupils. It might be relevant, bearing in mind Finn's sporting prowess, to mention that Donny had captained Cambridge at Rugby back in the early 1920s! An appointment was made to meet him.

Claud, Bobby and Finn were ushered into Jack Doncaster's study by his secretary. She apologised that Donny had been detained by a problem on the Playing Fields, but would be along in a few minutes. The Study was rather dark, the only window facing North and looking out onto a tall, Victorian red brick edifice which stole most of the light. It was light enough, though, that Finn could see a large, glass fronted display case full of silver cups and shields. Soon Donny entered, wearing a shabby, blue pin-striped suit, with the jacket elbows reinforced with leather patches. Strips of leather had also been sewn on the cuffs. Well, it was wartime, so no great surprise. Donny himself was stocky, about 5ft 9in., with thinning hair. Claud guessed he was about forty-five. Around his neck was a length of coarse string to which were attached a referee's silver whistle, and a large brass key. He was a little breathless, and beads of sweat shone on his forehead.

"Sorry to keep you waiting Mr and Mrs Browning. This is Finn, I take it. I've run up from the 1st XV pitch. Some stupid boy has had his head kicked in. He'll survive though. Solid bone from the neck upwards! An hour in the Infirmary should sort him out." Without any further preamble, he turned to Finn and asked "Do you enjoy rugger , lad? Are you keen? Looking at you, I'd say you were either a centre three quarter, or a scything fly half. Right?" Before Finn could reply, Donny turned to Mr and Mrs Browning: "He doesn't look stupid, and H-M at Shawbury House gave a good account of him. I'll take him if you wish, and stick him in North House – their House Rugby teams need some fresh blood. Would that suit you?"

Claud and Bobby looked at each other and then at Mr Doncaster. " Don't you want to know a little more about our son, Mr Doncaster? You haven't asked him, or us, anything yet, other than if he plays rugby football. And he hasn't had the chance to say yes or no yet." "Not necessary " was Donny's instant response. "I know a good prospect when I see one, and I have already had a long chat with H-M about him. Finn will do well here, and we will do well for him. It would be a partnership that would prosper. I know it. But of course, there may be matters you wish to discuss with me. Please do not think I am jumping the gun. By all means ask away. Oh, but first I should tell you the acronym to which I work and expect the boys t follow. It is MARKS, which might seem odd to you when the School's name is Lukes. "M" is for Multi-Activities. I think a boy should not be single-track minded. Yes, he should like games, but also music, or debating, or nature study. The wider his range of interests the better. We want to turn out a rounded individual. "A" is for Application. Boys should never be half-hearted about any aspect of school activity, or indeed life itself. For better, or sadly, worse on occasions, but hopefully for better, they should apply maximum effort to whatever they do. "R" is for Religion. We follow Christian principles vigorously. Boys are expected to worship regularly, and to study for Confirmation into the Church of England. "K" is for Kindliness. It is my conviction, and experience, and practice that better results are achieved by persuasion and reason, rather than force. I will not tolerate any form of bullying – and there are many, I assure you. And although we allow Senior Prefects to apply the cane in certain specified circumstances, it must only be done with prior permission from the House Master. Far too often, and I include my own experience as a boy, anger and intimidation can have dire results on the whole life of a young man. Oh. sorry! I'm going on a bit. Oh yes. Finally, there is "S". S is for Sports. I like boys who are good at sport. Invariably they fit in quicker. Of course, not all do, or can, and they will not be militated against, or disadvantaged because they do not like, or can not excel, at sport. But it is good if they do enjoy some form of sport." Donny sat back in his chair and formed his hands into a church spire. "When will Finn be 13? January 44? Right. He had better start that September. Will that suit you? Must rush now. Got a meeting with the Bursar. The Matron says she needs more bed linen. Heaven knows where that's coming from, it's bad enough just feeding the boys. But perhaps the Bursar can scrounge something from somewhere. Otherwise we will have to get parents to provide their own sheets and pillow cases, though I would have to draw the line at that frilly stuff that ladies like so much! Let me know what you decide as soon as you've discussed it. Been nice meeting you Finn. Oh! If you would like a tour of the School I will ask my Secretary to organize it. Cheerio. Trust we will meet again next year." With that, Donny Doncaster rose, waved a cheery hand, and strode from the room. They heard him call out to his Secretary. "Jean, take these lovely people on a quick tour will you. There's a dear".

Finn glanced anxiously at his parents. They looked bewildered. Finally, Claud said "Well, I did at least think he would have time for us to ask him a few questions about the School. He may have liked the look of you Finn, but what about us liking him, and the School?" Finn was quick to reply. "Well, I liked him Dad. I think he's great. I wonder what he uses that key round his neck for?" Sixteen months later, Finn found out. On his very first day at St. Luke's.

CHAPTER 61

By May 1943, the Second World War had been raging for three and a half years, and for most of that time it was the Axis of Germany and Japan who had been recording victory after victory against the Allies, there had been occasional successes, such as Stalingrad and El Alamein, but these were the exceptions, and terrible losses were still occurring in the Atlantic and in the Far East and Pacific.

On May 13th this changed. At that time Winston Churchill was in Washington meeting President Roosevelt. That afternoon he was handed a teleprinter message. It was from the Allied C- in- C in North Africa, General Alexander. It read: "Sir, it is my duty to report that the Tunisian campaign is over. All enemy resistance has ceased. We are masters of the North African shores."

All these years later, it is hard to describe the elation that was felt, not only amongst the British Commonwealth and American Forces, but throughout the free world. Finally, there was something really important to celebrate. It was a momentous day. The newspapers were plastered with photographs of General Montgomery receiving the formal surrender from the German and Italian commanders, and of disconsolate enemy forces being herded into captivity. On a beach near Bizerta, a squadron of Royal Hussars found 9,000 Germans awaiting rescue, some trying to build boats to take them across the Mediterranean to Sicily or Italy. Another 8th Army unit found itself with 10,000 exhausted Afrika Korps troops. A few escaped in small boats, only to be rounded up by the Royal Navy. In all, about 125,000 German and a similar number of Italian forces were now prisoners of war. This was a dreadful blow for "Old Adolf", who had anticipated that these men would have been available for the defence of mainland Europe. "Mainland Europe" – The Allies could now plan to re-enter the Continent, secure in the knowledge that it was they, not the Axis, who now held the initiative.

There was, too, a little icing on this cake. In the Atlantic, the British Navy sank 3 out of 7 German U-Boats hunting convoy HX-237. And British Intelligence was able to confirm the success of Operation Mincemeat, in which a corpse was deliberately floated ashore in Spain carrying papers designed to convince the Germans into thinking that the Allies planned to invade Greece. A delicious deception!

Finn was over the moon pasting into his scrapbook accounts of these events (though not Operation Mincemeat which would not become public knowledge until after the war). At Shawbury House, H-M declared a half-holiday; boys could go home at lunchtime. The boarders too, had the afternoon off lessons, and were given a shilling to spend at the tuck shop – not that there was a great deal of tuck to be had that was not on Sweet Ration coupons. That evening at Staff Dinner H-M remarked that in his entire life there had been only one occasion that had given him greater joy, that being Armistice Day in 1918, the end of the Great War. "Ladies and Gentlemen" he said "I wish to mark this day, this dinner, in a special way. Cook has made a Union Jack cake. Come in, Cook, and join us please to devour it." It was a marvellous replica of the Union Jack, topped with a statuette of Adolf Hitler lying prostrate, with St. George's right foot planted squarely on his chest. "As you know, Ladies and Gentlemen, the boys receive a daily half-pint of milk. Today I have deprived them of the cream off the top and this has secretly been converted into a large bowl of clotted cream for us to eat with this splendid gateau. I hope the boys don't notice, but if they do, I hope they don't mind.

It was with a light heart that next day Bobby travelled to London to the Norwegian Embassy to make a special unscripted broadcast to the people of Norway to tell them of this Nazi defeat and to exhort them to stand fast for the day that they also would be freed. She felt honoured that she, of all the broadcasters on Free Norway, had been chosen to break this momentous news. Back home that evening, Claud produced a quart bottle of Watney's India Pale Ale and announced that not only Kenneth, but Finn too, might drink a toast to Monty, his men, the Americans and to further great victories. It was a memorable day.

Through June, the war waged on , on all fronts: the Pacific, in the Soviet Union and increasingly, by air over mainland Europe. The Allied bombing of targets in Germany intensified. But so did aircraft losses as the Luftwaffe improved its fighter tactics. The American daylight bombers were now accompanied by increased numbers of support fighter planes, but the fighters' range was more limited and they could not give this support for the more distant targets. The British adopted a new tactic, known as "Shuttle" raids. Lancasters undertook a remarkable mission which took them to the shores of Lake Constance to bomb the former airship factory at Freiedrichshaven. Then, instead of returning home, they flew on to a base in Algeria, where they rested and re-armed before attacking the Italian Naval Base of La Spezia, and thence back to England. Other bombing raids were carried out against targets in Sicily and Italy, by aircraft based in North Africa, clearly a signal of the forthcoming re-entry of Allied forces into mainland Europe, for the first time since 1940.

On the last day of June, at a ceremony in the Guildhall, Winston Churchill was awarded the Freedom of the City of London. His speech of thanks included the words:

"We bear the sword of Justice and we resolve to use that sword with the utmost severity, to the end."

CHAPTER 62

As Finn grew, so did his muscles muscles strengthen and his sprinting speed increase. H-M was more than happy for him to concentrate his Game Periods on Athletics, at the expense of Cricket, Tennis or Swimming. In the summer of 1943 there were not many Shawbury pupils who had any chance of success at Burns Court, and Finn was by any standard the outstanding prospect for honours. So keen was H-M that he was happy to recruit Shirley Black to visit the school in mid-week to give Finn extra coaching. She did not spare him: in one session he would have to practise as many as thirty starts, and trot/sprint/walk the circuit a dozen times. This consisted of 100 yards gentle trot, then 100 yards all-out sprinting, then 100 yards walk. To wind down he would have to jog the 440 yard circuit three or four times, and finish up with static exercises to strengthen legs and lungs. Finn needed no cajoling to complete this punishing routine, but it did leave him physically drained. On such days H-M excused him homework and told him to go home and have a quiet evening and early to bed. Perhaps not conducive to success in his Common Entrance exam, but H-M was confident he would pass, and anyway had met with Donny Doncaster to discuss the boy's capabilities on and off the playing field. Getting him into St. Luke's would not be a problem!

On the last Saturday in July, the South-East Inter-Prep Schools Athletic Championships took place at Burns Court, Esher. The temptation had been to enter Finn in four events, from 100 yards through to 880 yards. Undoubtedly, Shirley thought, he would have had a chance of a place in all four events, and Finn was eager to have a go, but Shirley Black advised H-M against it. "There is no question that he would have a chance, but his best distances are 100, 220 and 440. I suggest that he goes for these three races, and does not attempt the 880, which precedes the 440. It would tax him too much and he might then fail in the 440, where he has an excellent chance of winning." H-M acquiesced. There was another good middle-distance boy, Henry Simons, who could represent the School at the half mile and might do very well.

Competitors from twenty-two Schools were taking part. Most were Schools in Surrey, but some were from Sussex and Kent, and one or two from Hampshire. Each individual competitor had to attain qualifying standards before the Big Day, and no more than one competitor from a school could take part in one particular event. It was a warm, sunny summer's day, with a light breeze. The grandstand, in peacetime more often used to watch rugby matches, was packed with parents and staff from the competing schools. Shirley Black sat with Bobby and Claud, so happy that he did not have to toil until midnight every Saturday finalising the next day's issue, and also happy in the knowledge that his Column was enjoying increasing popularity.

Heats for the sprints began early, at noon. First the 100 yards. Shirley had advised Finn to explode out of the blocks, but if he was certain at 80 yards that he was going to finish no lower than second, to ease up fractionally – he was in for a testing afternoon. This he did, coming second some three yards ahead of the third placed runner. The first three qualified for the semi-final. It was a similar story in the 220 yards heats, which followed 45 minutes later. Finn felt good. He was in the semi-final of both events and had not extended himself. Finn's next race was his heat of the 440 yards and in this, too, he eased through comfortably. Then was his chance to rest for an hour and sit with his parents and Shirley. H-M approached him, looking worried. "Finn, Symons is feeling unwell and will not be able to run the 880. I am afraid he is very upset – he had a good chance of winning or at least getting a place. I know it is short notice, but how would you feel about going in for the 880 as well as the other three races? I don't want to jeopardize your chances, but I feel you have got it in you, and it would be marvellous if you just got a place, second or third. No Shawbury boy has ever got to the final of four events before. What do you say?" "I'll do it sir, but only if Mrs Black says so. She knows best, and I won't go against her advice, and I don't want to let her or the School or anyone down by making a muck of the whole day." Shirley Black smiled quietly. Finn was the best pupil she had ever trained. She had already advised him about over stretching himself. But now there was a new dilemma. This was not just about Finn, it was about Finn's School, and their honour. She acquiesced, but entreated Finn not to "bust a gut" to win the 880 at the expense of the three shorter events.

There were only two heats of the 880, with four from each heat going into a Final. Finn came fourth in his heat, pacing himself carefully. He had little time to recover before being called to run the 440 semi-final. Here also, Finn ran a canny race, just making sure he was one of the four fastest finishers. He was now in two finals, with the 100 and 220 semis to negotiate. In the 100 Finn made a marvellous start and was two clear yards up at the half way point. He allowed the second runner to close up and with his place in the Final secure, the two breasted the tape together. It was a rotten chance that as the two boys slowed-up , the other lad's spikes caught the outside of Finn's left ankle. Blood immediately poured from the wound and soaked his ankle sock. Fortunately for Finn, the organisers had ensured the presence of the St John's Ambulance. His wound was quickly treated and plastered, but he felt a bit sore and shaken. He had thirty minutes to recover before the semi-final of the 220. Shirley made him lie flat and still on a rug, with another rug over him. "Just shut your eyes and relax. Do some deep breathing. Don't open your eyes. I'll make sure you don't nod off Finn!" Twenty minutes later Finn felt a cool, soft hand on his brow. "Sit up and sip this." Shirley put a small silver hip flask to his lips. "This is rum. It was my husband's. You wont like it, but it will sharpen you up again. Go on, take a sip." The liquid smelled sickly and vile, the taste even worse and Finn could hardly believe the burning sensation in his gullet. But sharpen him, it certainly did, and he was quickly on his feet. "Mrs Black, how could you give me that muck. It's horrible. I will never, ever, touch it again!" Shirley laughed, Finn's mother frowned and Claud smiled discreetly. There was more to Mrs Black than he had realized.

"Finn, the 220 semis are in five minutes. Let's just do a gentle crouching start and see how your ankle feels. I think the plaster will hold ok and I do not think it will restrict you. But I am not going to press you to run if you don't feel comfortable about it. And H-M will not twist your arm either, will you H-M?"

His ankle was sore, but did not restrict him. The runners lined up on the far side of the track from the grandstand, and were staggered so as to allow for the bend. Finn had the worst of the draw, being placed in Lane Eight the outside lane. This meant that he had no sight of the other runners until they straightened after the bend, with only about 80 yards to go to the finishing tape. The 220 is as explosive a sprint as the 100, with little time to make good lost ground. As they entered the straight, Finn realized he was trailing all but two of the other runners; there were five ahead of him, with only two to go through to the final. The leader of the pack was some two or three yards ahead of the next four. These four were bunched, as near as could be dead level with one another. Finn was another two yards back. There was no chance of catching the leader, but he began to close on the other four. With 20 yards to go, he was level with them. With a final lunge he crossed the finish. It was up to the judges to decide who had finished second and thus would qualify for the Final.

The wait was agonising, the pain in his ankle adding to the torment. No photo finishing in those far off days – it was judgment of the eye that decided the issue. Finn knew one of the other four slightly, a boy called Johns, from Rollins School. "What do you think Johns? Was it you or me, or one of the other two?" "Dunno. Too close to be sure, But I don't think it was me, worst luck." The two judges conferred for what seemed like an age, and then, finally, walked over to Johns and Finn. "You dead heated, you two. We could not split you apart, so we have decided that the fairest thing is for you both to run in the Final. Well done."

Finn was in four Finals, an unprecedented number. But being a Finalist meant nothing if one did not win at least one of the distances. Finn's ankle throbbed. A little blood was seeping through the plaster. Slowly, he made his way to the competitors' enclosure. Shirley shook his hand. "Well done, Finn. You left it a bit late though. Still, it is fantastic. You are through to four finals and people are saying that has never been achieved before. The question is, can you run all four? Personally, I think you should retire from one of the events, and I think the one to drop is the 880. By then you will have done the other three, and anyway you were not originally entered for it. Agree?" "I don't know. It seems a waste to have qualified and then not try for the Final, Mrs Black. Can I leave it and see how I do in the three shorter events? But I think I need a fresh plaster on my ankle."

To immense cheers from the Shawbury supporters – and nearly the whole school had turned up – Finn won the 100 yards Final by a mere six inches. Shawbury House had never won this event, in fact they had never had a competitor finish in the first three. H-M was over the moon, every bit as much as Finn himself. "That's one silver pot in the showcase Finn, and one we have never won before. Before you run another yard I am here and now awarding you your Athletics Colours. Congratulations!" there was a Tea Interval before the 220 final. This time Finn was drawn in an outer lane, Lane 6, with only two boys outside him. Finn was aware of the danger, but it was no good. The boy who had won Finn's semi-final was just too strong for him, and won by three yards. Finn could only manage third. It was a big disappointment; He had set his heart on winning both the shorter distances. Still, there was the 440 to come and Shirley Black had always stressed that she thought this was Finn's best distance. She thought he had the speed – that went without saying almost – but also the stamina.

Following the 220, Finn had barely half an hour before this next event. Was it enough? The answer was soon coming. Finn went off fast, perhaps too fast, because the five yard gap he had opened up had closed by the time the runners finished the first bend. Down the far side straight, Finn had slipped back into third place, but not by much; he was nicely tucked in behind the two leaders, who both clearly believed they had to go into the second bend leading, and were straining each other to get there. Finn bided his time. He was in their slipstream and saving his energy. As the final straight was reached, Finn edged closer, and then abreast of no. 2. No 1 was not opening the gap, and with 35 yards to go, Finn knew he could take him.

Perfect timing. Finn breasted the tape by a foot. Not a lot over a quarter mile, but enough for there to be no question who was the winner. Finn was a double champion – and still had the half-mile to come if he wanted it.

The 440 yards was followed by the Hurdles events at 110 and 440 yards. Not Finn's scene. But a precious half hour before he had to decide to go for the double circuit race, or rest on his laurels. The decision was being left to him.

No pressure from Shirley, nor from H-M. A nice situation. It would be the last time he would run competitively this year. 1944 would be a different matter. Very different as it would turn out, but he was not to know that.

At Finn's age, recovery time is fast. He was a double champion, but what a prize it would be to be a triple champion! And if he failed, well, at least he would have tried. But why consider failing? "I'll do it Mrs Black. I've nothing to lose!" "Good, Finn. I never doubted it, actually. Already I am very proud of you, as are your parents and H-M, and I honestly believe that you have a great future in Athletics – always assuming we get rid of Mr Hitler and his cronies. I want to give you a quick leg massage, and you must drink plenty of water. But no more rum!"

The 880 yards was the final event of the Meeting. Unlike in today's era, it was considered unwise for boys and girls in their early teens or younger to run long distances. Time has proved how wrong that belief was, for nowadays it is commonplace for both sexes to run five miles long cross country races at that age. 880 yards is two full laps of the track, For the first lap Finn stayed well in the middle of the pack, but made sure that he was not trapped on the inside. His ankle was still sore, but was not bleeding and did not hamper his running rhythm. He was comfortable. He knew he was running within himself, and thought how nice it felt that no one was expecting him to win a third race. "Nothing to lose" kept running through his mind.

There seemed a reluctance for anyone to take the lead. The boy he had just beaten to take the 440 title had no intention of being caught again by this tall, blond haired boy. He hung back to the rear of the main bunch of runners, but running easily and well in touch with them. A short, broad shouldered lad from Melburn Lodge made the pace at the beginning of the second lap, but with his build would probably lack the finishing burst that might be necessary. He kept looking over his shoulder – a sure sign he did not like where he was and wanted someone else to take over the lead With 200 yards to go Finn eased out, taking the final curve on the shoulders of the five runners in the bunch. The 440 runner-up stayed close – he knew how dangerous Finn was. At the end of that last bend, the lad from Melburn had shot his bolt and receded back into the pack. Finn was now jointly in the lead with two others and " Mr 440 runner-up" was dangerously close on his shoulder. It was now or never for both of them. For Finn there would be the triumph of a third victory, unprecedented at this Championship. For his arch adversary the grim determination to avenge his defeat in the previous race. Both runners strained every sinew, lungs bursting. All the spectators were screaming and cheering, sensing this dramatic climax to the day. Claud, ordered by his doctor to avoid over excitement, forgot all that and was on his feet shouting with the rest of the crowd.

Finn won by a hair's breadth. It could not have been more than six inches. But a win is a win, whatever the margin. He was sorry for his adversary.

That poor lad would go home with nothing. Well, almost nothing. Two Second Places, robbed by inches in two races. Finn went over to him and shook his hand. "Hard luck. I really am sorry. It was so close, wasn't it? Nothing in it. Better luck next year, eh!" Ruefully, came the retort: "Yes, thanks, but I hope YOU aren't taking part. But if you are, watch out. I'll be gunning for you!" They both laughed.

No day in Finn's young life had meant so much to him. He slept for ten hours that night and it seemed that the grin would be there for ever.

CHAPTER 63

If it was a famous month for Finn Browning, it was an infamous one for Adolf Hitler. Success in reading German secret codes, combined with more effective detection devices, were resulting in terrible losses of U-boats in the Atlantic, and in the Bay of Biscay. His navy in the Mediterranean had been virtually neutralised. On the Russian front, Hitler's desperate attempt to progress was blunted by Russian strength. The German offensive against the Russian Armies around and in Kursk was met by an onslaught of Russian T-34 tanks, plus artillery barrages, and the Germans suffered massive losses of men and armour. Having been ejected from North Africa, it was now no longer a question of "If", but of "When" and "Where" Allied landings across the Mediterranean would take place.

The "When" was on July 10th, the "Where" in Sicily. By dawn on that day, 150,000 American and British forces had been landed, with double that number at sea waiting to follow over the next few days. It was the biggest seaborne invasion of the war. Operation Husky, as it was known, worked perfectly. Hitler was convinced that the invasion would take place in Sardinia and in consequence, Sicily was lightly defended, by only two German divisions, plus Italian troops who were poorly led and motivated. It was the Americans' misfortune to meet heavy resistance from the Germans in the south of the island, whilst the British Eighth Army surprised and easily overcame the sleepy Italian forces at Syracuse in the East.

But it was not all plain sailing: storms caused havoc in the air with the supporting airborne assault. Many of the British gliders came down in the sea, and hundreds of soldiers were simply drowned. Fifty gliders landed in wrong areas, and only a dozen reached the target area south of Syracuse. The Americans fared little better, coming under heavy attack from fighters and ground artillery.

By the middle of the month, it was clear even to Hitler, that on the Eastern Front he faced defeat by the Russians. The greatest tank battle in world history had ended in humiliation for the German Panzers. The lighter but more mobile T-34s swarmed amongst the German Tigers and Panthers with suicidal ferocity. There was one account of a Russian driver deliberately ramming a Tiger so that both exploded in a huge fireball. Of the total of 2,000 tanks taking part, more than half were destroyed.

Hitler now had to re-deploy forces from the Russian Front to Italy, to face the inevitable onslaught by the Allies. The Big Squeeze had really begun.

On the 19th July, Hitler paid a surprise visit on Benito Mussolini, the Italian leader, the Duce, after hearing that the Italian Army was at the point of collapse.

Mussolini himself seemed to be a spent force, far from the swaggering dictator of a year ago. It was a wasted effort. The Duce could not be roused from his despair and he returned to Rome to find it smouldering from heavy raids by Allied bombers. Not just smoke, but revolt was in the air. On the 21st in Sicily, the Allies claimed they had taken 45,000 prisoners and controlled almost half the island. By the next day, the US Seventh Army swept into Palermo, the capital of Sicily. Now the final push north to Messina was under way. Messina was only a stone's throw from mainland Italy. The advance up the Boot of Italy would soon begin.

CHAPTER 64

At Shawbury House the Summer Term was over and Finn could devote his time to his non-school activities. One of these was his visits to Headley. No longer did they have to be confined to Sundays. It was long since clear that both staff and inmates at the Convalescent Home welcomed him there, in fact, looked forward to his coming. He was happy to do whatever was asked of him: kitchen work, serving meals to the bedridden, just sitting and talking to the young airmen, listening to their tales, writing letters for the blind, anything that came along. And some of the patients were keen to know what Finn had been up to. He took particular pleasure in recounting his athletics successes (though careful not to do so to one young Spitfire pilot whose knee had been shattered by a Messerschmitt cannon, and would never run again). George from next door went with him sometimes, though not so regularly, and Finn was glad to have his company on the cycle rides from Surbiton.

Now, as well, Finn had time to pay his visit to the Airfield at Wisley. The Commandant had said just to present himself at the Guard House at the Main Gate, but Dad thought it better to ring in advance and make a proper appointment. He was met by Flight Sergeant Bill Owen. And Snarlichops! He may have screwed up courage last time to pat Snarlichops on the head, but Finn still felt very apprehensive. Snarlichops remembered him, however, and wagged his tail and lay down at his feet. "Don't worry lad, even if you bumped into him in the dark he would still know who you were, and purr like a pussycat. You're almost part of his family now. Anyway, it's good to see you again, young man. Now follow me and I'll take you to the Station Adjutant's Office."

The Wellington Medium bomber was introduced into the RAF early in the war, before the heavier, four-engined Stirlings, Halifaxes and Lancasters. It was a versatile aircraft. Not only was it used as a bomber by the RAF, mainly in the Far East, but by Coastal Command, when it was equipped with RADAR and torpedoes to attack enemy submarines and surface ships in the Mediterranean. It was not a huge aeroplane, but to a boy of twelve it would seem so, with a wing span of 80 feet and a height at the tail of more than 17 feet. The Adjutant himself conducted the tour, showing Finn the cockpit and controls, manned by a pilot and co-pilot; the gun turrets (two guns in the nose and four in the tail turret) and the bomb bays and the Bomb Aimer's position (very uncomfortable, lying prone in the nose beneath the nose gun turret.) the adjutant was a kindly man, who had been a flyer in pre war days, but was now too old for active service. "You are a very lucky fellow, Finn

Browning. We certainly haven't allowed any other civilian to go near the aircraft unless they have a working role here, so you are probably the only youngster anywhere in Britain who has actually been inside a Wellington. I know it is hard, but I must ask you not to tell all your friends about this tour. We do not want to be bombarded with requests. However, as a bribe to persuade you to keep your secret, here is a memento of your visit. Whereupon he handed Finn a leather flying helmet. "You can wear that to cycle home in." Finn could hardly believe his luck, but promised to confine to his immediate family the details of his visit.

By this time Douglas had reached Malta safely, but the flight was not without incident. In a straight line the distance from The Solent to Gibraltar would be about 1,000 miles, but such a course would have taken the Sunderland flying boat over North West France and the Bay of Biscay. Enemy territory. The Sunderland has a range of just under 3,000 miles and so was able to steer well clear of Brittany by flying due West into the Atlantic before turning South and parallel with the West coast of Portugal and Spain. This should have been safe from marauding enemy aircraft, but about 350 miles past Lands End and the Isles of Scilly, flying at about 6,000 feet in broken cloud, from nowhere a lone Me 110 caught sight of them. What it was doing out there so far from home will never be known, probably long-range reconnaissance, but there it was, and it saw the Sunderland as a nice, fat, sitting target. It made its attack from below and behind, knowing, no doubt, that the Sunderland had no defence on its under side.. Bullets ripped into the Sunderland's belly even before the British crew realized it was under attack. Immediately the Sunderland banked hard to port and commenced a steep dive. As it did so the Messerschmitt climbed level with its tail. The Sunderland tail gunner had a brief window of opportunity – no more than five seconds before the German was above and in front of him and thus out of range. The five seconds were decisive. That short burst hit the Messerschmitt's starboard engine. From his position by a porthole, Douglas saw the smoke pouring from it, and then the flames. The German had no option. If he was to have a hope of survival he had to break off the engagement and make for land before the fire engulfed the whole wing. Losing height, he limped away. At that distance from France and safety Douglas thought he had little chance. Serve him right! Slow and fat the Sunderland might be, but it still had a sting!

At Gibraltar, divers examined the Sunderland's belly. They found 31 bullet holes. It was pure good fortune that none had penetrated flesh, or vital components. Good old ducks those flying boats. Two days later, Douglas continued his journey to Malta by sea. He remembered his brother Clive's experience sailing to Capetown all that time ago and again felt the fear of going to the bottom. Rather by far to have gone on by air, especially in a Sunderland. His experience had been brief, but he had grown quite attached to it.

In the summer months that followed, Douglas had little time to dwell on that. during the first few weeks he had to undergo a conversion course to Supermarine Seafire fighters, the Royal Navy's version of the immortal Spitfire. A significant difference between the two aircraft was that the Seafire had folding wings, to facilitate storage on board Aircraft Carriers. In general performance and firepower, however, it was as deadly and efficient as its "elder brother". Instantly, Douglas felt at home in it. Its handling characteristics were without equal. It and the Spitfire had been in service ever since the war began and would continue to be the scourge of Goering's Luftwaffe until the war was over. The main role of the Seafire version was to defend the convoys keeping Malta supplied. These convoys were Malta's lifeline, bringing in not only the essentials to the population's survival, but arms and armour, aircraft, oil and personnel for the Allied Armies in the Mediterranean. Day after day, Douglas was in the air. Often, he would return without ever seeing an enemy plane, but there were other days when the sky seemed to be dark with Dorniers and Heinkels, usually with Me109 escorts. During these months he had the occasional success to report, with one Heinkel to his credit for certain and another probably, plus an Italian Macchi MC202 possibly. On one occasion he also spotted a U-Boat on the surface. A tasty dish to rake with his eight Browning machine guns and he was low enough to see several crew members diving overboard for cover. Especially until the Axis forces were finally booted out of Libya and Tunisia, Malta was no holiday resort. There was scarcely a day when the Fleet Air Arm squadrons did not fly sorties in support of the RAF lads, against German bomber raids on the island. Day after day Malta was pulverised. Valletta Harbour and the city itself were the main targets, but the bombers were not too fussy and none of the island was spared, not even nearby Gozo. It was a sickening sight, but it was heartening to witness the way the peoples' spirit and determination, perhaps reinforced by their strong Catholic faith, remained high.

With the invasion of Sicily under way, and after eleven weeks of non-stop and very dangerous operations, the pressure eased a little, and Douglas stood down from combat duties. It was only then that he began to realize just how drained he was, both physically and mentally. The de-briefing by his Station

Commander was short. Commander Jack Stansfield knew only too well the condition his aircrew were in after such an unrelieved stint, facing danger every day. He himself had been there. He had been Carrier based in the early days of the war, flying the old Swordfish biplanes. Talk about sitting ducks! Despite their extraordinary success torpedoing enemy shipping, their losses had been catastrophic. With a maximum speed of only 138 mph, they stood little chance against Me109s capable of almost three times that speed, and even on those occasions when the Luftwaffe were absent, they were a tasty dish for German ships' Ack Ack. Jack Stansfield was one of the few to have survived this long. His DSO was a just reward.

"Douglas, I am giving you 8 days leave. During that time I don't want you even looking at a Seafire, or any other bloody aircraft for that matter. I'd like to get you back home, but it's just not on, I'm afraid. But what I can do is tell you the name of a very nice little beach resort on Gozo. Book yourself in there. Rest up completely for a few days. Lie on the beach and read a book, or do a little swimming. There are a few decent bottles of wine in the mess. I'll tell Cookie to give you a couple to take with you. Oh, and one other thing. I almost forgot" A sly grin creased his face. "A new batch of Jennies arrived this morning from Blighty. One of them has been asking for you. A young lady by the name of Celia Simpson. Well, if she will take the risk of going, you can take her with you, you lucky bugger. You deserve a little R and R. I have organized for her to be excused duties for 3 days. Make the most of them!"

CHAPTER 65

"You fiddled the posting, didn't you? Did your Dad put his oar in somewhere to get you out here? No. on second thoughts he is probably horrified that his little angel is so close to the action. It is no picnic here, Celia."

"I know. And he didn't fiddle it. I fluttered my eyelashes at the Base commander in Rosyth. It's all my own work! I hope you don't mind Douglas"

"Mind? I'm over the moon. I've thought about you every day. Did you get my letters? The post from home is hopeless. I got one letter from you and that was ages ago and you just said how miserable it was up in Scotland. Well you won't have time to be miserable here. Now we've kicked the bastards out of Africa, things aren't quite so bad, but it has been pretty dreadful. I feel desperately sorry for the people here. They've been bombed to hell, and this war wasn't even of their making. It is astonishing how they keep smiling and getting on with things. Honestly, I think I've been safer up aloft than down on the ground. They deserved that George Cross en masse. You know the King came out here and made the award?"

"Yes, Douglas, the papers were full of it, and we know what good work you and your mates have been doing, too. Anyway, we've been billeted well away from the harbour, which is the main target. Now, how about you? You must feel bloody awful after all this time. Have you had any local leave?"

"No, Celia. Not really. There were a couple of short breaks, when they were patching up the old bus, and once when we just had no fuel to fly the damned planes. However, now I have been stood down for eight whole days, and Jack Stansfield has wangled you three days off duties, not that you've even started yet. What is it about you? You must have some magical influence on people! I wondered if you would like to nip over to Gozo. I've only seen it from the air, but I'm told it has some nice quiet beaches and Jack told me about a small guest house that's been commandeered for aircrew rest and recreation. It's the new cure for all ills apparently, this R and R. Would you like to join me? I think actually that you are all the R and R I need. But it might be more Recreation than Rest, my sweet girl."

"Are you making improper suggestions, Douglas? Yes, of course I'll come. All work and no play makes a dull boy. Isn't that how the saying goes? When do we go? Oh, and I'm afraid I don't have much in the way of civvy clothes. Do you mind?"

"God, no. It's summer and bloody hot, and if I have my way you won't need to be wearing much in the way of clothing! That is to say, not if we are down on the beach. There may be another part of the day when you don't need any clothes at all. The nights are very warm!"

"Douglas Browning, I am shocked! I am a Nice Girl. I am increasingly minded to think that you ARE making improper suggestions."

"Perish the thought!" Douglas grinned. "We can cross the Nightime bridge when we come to it. Let's get there first – it's about thirty minutes ferry ride. By the way, I've managed to grab a couple of bottles of Chianti to oil the wheels. That's one thing the Italians are good at, producing decent wine. They're not much good at aerial dog fighting."

Douglas had never been to the Mediterranean in the pre-war era. In fact, he had never been out of Great Britain at all. For the three months he had been in Malta there hade been time for only one thing – waging war. He had hardly looked round Valletta itself, and beyond the city environs not at all. Even the beautiful cathedral had been totally destroyed. He would have liked to spend a few quiet moments there. Not that he was religious. He was not, and even if he had been, that faith would have been under severe strain now. It seemed to him that killing people, even in war, was irreconcilable with the Christian ethic. No, he would have liked to go there just to find peace and solitude for a while, as he had in the little church in Pithiock. Might it have been that he would have seen another little mouse in this Cathedral? But now there were a few precious days when he could put War and Killing to one side. Here on this little island, only four or five miles from end to end, he could turn his back on Death, be it his own or that of others at his own hand, or of the untold numbers of ordinary people all over Europe and the Far East.

And with him to share this time was Celia. Sheer coincidence had brought them together, sitting on a train thudering its way to London. No coincidence that she was sitting beside him now, her hair blowing in the wind as the boat bobbed across the water. She had engineered this. She was no fool. She knew the dangers of coming to Malta and she had come deliberately to see him again. Sometimes events in life creep up on one like a sea mist. He had no doubts that he wanted to share with this woman, to share not just a few days, not just a night in her arms, but the whole of life. A few months ago it was Pamela for a few weeks, then Deidre, or was it Daphne. They were fun, but totally superficial relationships. This was quite different. He saw in this windswept woman sitting beside him a glorious obligation, a destiny, a human that he could protect and guide through life, whatever that had in store.

She turned to see him gazing at her. She smiled and took his hand. "A penny for your thoughts, Douglas".

"I want to ask you something, Celia, and I don't quite know how to put it"

"Oh well, if you are going to ask if I will sleep with you tonight, the answer is yes."

"No, not that". He reddened.

"Well what then you silly boy."

"Will you marry me?"

"Yes you nitwit. Of course. What do you think I came all this way for? But can it wait until we get back to Valletta? I quite like the idea of living in sin with you for a few days first."

CHAPTER 66

With the occupation of Sicily nearing completion, it was only a matter of time before the Allied forces launched their invasion of mainland Italy. The undercurrent of discontent among its people was growing. Secretly, In Lisbon, the Italian ambassador made contact with Allied representatives to pave the way for peace talks. And by now it was clear to the German leadership that not for long could they continue to enjoy the support of Italy's military. Mussolini was a spent force; dispirited and disillusioned. Revolt was in the air. It was no surprise when, in early August, German troops began to pour into Italy to take over its defence. In Madrid, on the 13th, the Italian General Castellano met the British Ambassador to implore the Allies help to dissolve the alliance with Germany. By the 17th, Messina in Sicily had fallen. The cost of the campaign was heavy: the British and Canadian casualties totalled nearly thirteen thousand, and the Americans nearly ten thousand. For the enemy the losses were far worse: killed, wounded or missing amounted to 150,000.

It was a little ironic that the first Allied landings on the toe of Italy took place on September 3rd – the fourth anniversary of Britain's declaration of war against Nazi Germany. The German divisions that had been in the area of Reggio di Calabria had left by the time the British forces came ashore. There was little resistance from the Italians – in fact some of them offered to help unload the landing craft! Meanwhile preparations were under way for the second strike, further north at Salerno, south of Naples. It brought a wry smile to the faces of millions at home when Lord Haw Haw, the British radio propagandist working for Germany, announced that "the final blow will be struck by Adolf Hitler."

By September 8th, Italy was out of the war and General Eisenhower, the Allied Supreme Commander, announced that Germany's partner had surrendered its forces unconditionally. The announcement was also broadcast over Italian radio, just prior to the Salerno landing, thus avoiding any resistance from Italian troops. Germany's reaction to Italy's surrender was immediate German Panzers and Paratroopers occupied Rome.

CHAPTER 67

Douglas and Celia were married by the Base Chaplain immediately upon their return from Gozo. There was no time for niceties, like telling their families in advance, or having a honeymoon, or even a wedding breakfast. No time, even, to share a marital bed – there were no married quarters as there would have been in peacetime. Immediately, each had to report back for duty. There was a change of tactics involving Douglas. The focus now was less on convoy protection, since control of the sea had passed largely into Allied hands. Instead, the priority became the protection of the fleet of American and British destroyers and cruisers, together with the landing craft, that would put men and equipment ashore at Salerno. It was not long before the Seafires were transferred from their Malta base to the airfield at Catania, in the shadow of Mount Etna. Effectively, this provided them with an additional 150 miles range, or 30 minutes of air time, vital for operations in the Gulf of Salerno.

Of course it did not suit Douglas personally – his brand new wife was still in Malta, with little likelihood she would be going anywhere else. War was like that. War was no respecter of individuals, either their feelings or their lives. Celia had a job to do, and so did he. There would be time, he dreamed, for being together after this damnable conflict was over. Then there would be time to have a home, have a family, to see his parents and brothers again, even little Finn. It wasn't Finn's fault that Dad spoiled the hell out of him; he wasn't a bad kid. In fact, he was very accomplished and very kind, too. Perhaps he had been a bit hard on Finn. Well, neglectful certainly. He'd make amends once this damned war was over.

Douglas took off early that sunny September morning. Destination, the beach head at Salerno. He was one of a flight of six Seafires. Objective: attacking the Germans' latest weapon, their Glider Bombs, which were being targeted at British and American warships. These radio-controlled bombs, launched from the air, had already damaged the battleship HMS Warspite and the cruiser Uganda. If the British fighters could shoot them down before they reached their targets, or better still, if they could destroy the German aircraft before they could launch the Glider Bombs, a valuable service would have been rendered to the lads down below. Locating the German launch-planes necessitated flying over German controlled Italian territory. At 16,000feet, Douglas's flight crossed the coast north of Salerno, nearly up to Naples. For a while the sky seemed empty, and they cruised watchfully on a North-South axis, but with no sightings. There were a few puffs of black-brown smoke from German anti-aircraft fire, but hardly a barrage, and rarely within a range that would bother them.

The intercom crackled into life: "Give it ten more minutes and we'll head for home, fellas", the call from Tim Guthrie, his Flight Commander. "If they're having a day off, we might as well do the same!" Mechanically, there was no aircraft more reliable than the Spitfire and its Seafire version. Douglas's plane had always behaved impeccably. Now, without warning, the engine spluttered. The rev. counter dropped, then rose up again, then dropped again. Douglas knew immediately that it must be a blocked fuel line – he had plenty of fuel left. Douglas radioed Tim Guthrie: "Boss, I've got a problem. Engine's on the blink. I'm going to try a steep dive, that might clear the blockage. Over." "OK, Doug, we'll follow you down." Douglas pushed the stick forward. The nose dipped and the aircraft gathered speed. Douglas saw the other Seafires diving with him, two either side. He couldn't see the fifth, but he knew it must be tailing him. The ground below was hilly: he could see little villages nestling between the hills. He wasn't sure how far he was from the coast. At 9,000 feet he levelled out. To his horror, far from firing smoothly, the engine spluttered and died.

"Tim, it hasn't worked. The engine's given up the ghost. I'll have to go down. You'd better get out of here before the bogeymen appear. Let Celia know what's happened, will you. And tell her I love her and always will. Cheers, fellas. Take care. Out.

"Guys, this is Tim. Head for home. I'm going to hang around and see if I can see Doug safely down. OK? I'll catch you up. Out."

The ground rose quickly to meet Doug. He knew he could not lower his undercarriage without power, so it had to be a belly landing. He just hoped he could find a flat piece of land. A field or pastures for preference. Whatever, as long as it was not tarmac or stone. His fuel tanks were still a third full. He did not want to ignite the stuff by setting off sparks on impact. God it would be ironic if he was badly burned and ended up in Headley Court Convalescent Home, with Finn calling in on him! Not likely, seeing as how this is Italy. Concentrate, Doug. The Seafire glided nicely, and with only a couple of hundred feet before he hit ground, Douglas saw just what he wanted: it was near a small village, but a community large enough to have a playing field on its outskirts, with not one, but two football pitches positioned end to end. Silently, with no more than a whisper of wind over its wings, the Seafire skimmed a small barn and hit the turf. He missed the first set of goalposts, but the second snapped like match sticks as his port wing slammed into it. The plane swung on its axis, like some ballerina on ice, and continued its mad slide across the turf, tail first. In seconds, though, with a deafening impact, the Seafire struck a stone wall and came to a halt. Mercifully, Douglas was unhurt. Thank heavens, no smoke, nor flames. The cockpit canopy was intact and slid open easily. In seconds, Douglas climbed out of the stricken aircraft. It was really only half an aircraft now – the port wing had virtually vanished, as had the entire tailplane. "Well, old friend, thanks for the ride, but it is time to say farewell. I'd better make tracks away from here."

He had no chance to do so. The steel-grey Scout Car, with a white Swastika blazoned on its side, screamed to a halt. Four helmeted soldiers leapt out, rifles pointing straight at Douglas's chest. "Achtung, bloody Englander! Hends up! UP!" Douglas raised his hands high above his head. He wondered if this was the end for him. Had the little mouse in Pithiock church felt like this? Maybe, like the mouse, he would survive. One thing was certain though. Douglas would not fly again in this war.

CHAPTER 68

Jack Stansfield watched as one by one the four Seafires taxied to a halt on the apron outside the main maintenance hangar. Four only. Oh God, where are the other two? Who's not there? He checked the numbers on the side of the four Seafires. Of course, he knew them by heart. Tim, the Flight Commander, and Douglas. The four pilots saw their C.O approaching them anxiously as they climbed out of their cockpits.

"What's happened? Where are Tim and Douglas?" "Sir, Tim's OK. At least he was when we left him. Douglas went down, I'm afraid. He wasn't hit. In fact we never saw a bloody Hun the whole morning. Doug's engine just packed up. Died on him. Tim ordered us back and said he was just going to see how Doug got on. He should be here pretty soon."

Tim Guthrie landed ten minutes later and headed straight to Stansfield's Office. "Doug got down alright, sir. He was lucky that he bellied on a soccer pitch. I saw him get out, Germans were there inside a minute. I'm afraid he had no chance to make a run for it. I felt like strafing the bastards, but obviously I couldn't – I'd have hit Douglas as well. So that's it really. His war is over."

"Yes, I'm afraid that's that for the unlucky fellow. Still, at least he shouldn't be shot at, like the rest of us. Not unless he tries to do a runner from some Oflag somewhere. I'll have to inform his wife, poor girl. They've only been married a few weeks. Normally, one would leave her to inform his parents, but she hardly knows them. I'd better write to them, too."

There were daily flights now between the FAA Base in Sicily, and the Airbase in Malta. They were trouble-free, the Luftwaffe were far too busy on mainland Italy, especially now that the Italians had given up the ghost. Jack Stansfield's letter was delivered to Celia in her barrack room by hand. It read:

Dear Mrs Browning,
It is with deep sadness that I have to inform you..." Celia froze. The letter dropped from her hand. Everything went white. She felt she was going to pass out, and sank on to her bunk. He was dead. Her Doug was dead. Not now. Not yet. Oh God, how could you take him from me so soon? Disjointed thoughts flashed and stumbled through her brain. We haven't made love yet, you fool. Well, not since we were married at least! That thought brought her up short. Tears had been welling in her eyes, but she held them back. She picked up the letter... "that your husband Lt.Browning

has been taken prisoner. We believe he is totally unhurt. His aircraft suffered engine failure and he was forced to land on mainland Italy. Tim Guthrie, his Flight commander, observed the landing and saw Douglas emerge safely from the plane. Unfortunately, it seems, he had no time to make a dash for cover. A German scout car was on the scene within moments and he was taken prisoner. I am afraid that is all I can tell you. I am informing Douglas's family whom, together with your own mother and father, will I am sure be a comfort to you. Also, you might like to spend a little time with the Chaplain on your Station. I am informing your C.O of course. Yours regretfully,

Jack Stansfield."

He's alive. Oh, my poor Douglas, what's going to happen to you? For heaven's sake don't try to escape, it's far too dangerous. I'll wait for you, darling.

This bloody war can't last forever., and there's only going to be one winner now, so be patient. Then we will be together again and then, my man, we will never be parted again. And another thing, I want some babies. Okay? Four at least, please.

Her thoughts were interrupted by Catherine Biggs and two other Jennies. "You alright, Celia? You've gone ever so pale. It's not Douglas, is it?"

Celia just sat and nodded, and tried to smile. "Yes, he's been taken prisoner. Of all things, apparently, the engine on his plane just died. I am not sure if it is good luck or bad that he was not over the sea. The letter says he belly landed on a football pitch and the Germans grabbed him. I'm sorry, I feel a bit confused. Can you leave me be for a while."

Jack Stansfield's letter to Mr and Mrs Browning arrived via the War Office. It had been hard for him to find words that did not sound cold and stark, but he had done his best, stressing that his Flight Commander had flown low over the crashed Seafire and had seen Douglas climb out unscathed. It was a terrible blow to Claud and Bobby, and painful for them to sit Kenneth and Finn down and tell them the bad news.

Perhaps for Claud it was slightly less gut wrenching. After all, he had witnessed terrible scenes in Flanders in the Great War. Sometimes, he swore, the stench of filth and death was still in his nostrils. For Bobby, as for any mother, the anguish was not just in the mind, but really did wrench the guts. Poor Celia. She must be agonised too. The Brownings had only just got over the shock of hearing that she and Douglas were married! Now this.

Thus far, Bobby and Claud had only spoken to Celia's mother and father by phone. It had been a slightly formal conversation, though not unfriendly, with a "we must meet sometime" conclusion. With this new development it was time now that they met face to face. Privately, Claud wondered if the Simpsons thought that their daughter had discovered she was pregnant, and that had been why they had married so hurriedly. There had been no mention of it, but these things sometimes happened in wartime. As if by telepathy, the phone rang at that moment. It was Celia's father. "Oh hello, is that Mr Browning, David Simpson here. You've got the news I suppose.

You must be very perturbed. I rang to say how sorry we are, and to suggest that maybe we should meet to drown our sorrow. It sometimes helps. My wife and I know what it is like. We lost our son a while ago, but I daresay you heard that from Douglas. Would you and Mrs Browning care to come to dinner one evening? Say Thursday?" "Well, we are a bit shell shocked, though of course we are relieved it isn't worse. Celia told us about the loss of your son, before she was posted to Malta. We are terribly sorry. So the answer is "yes", we would be delighted to come. Thursday will be fine."

The formalities were minimal, even though they had never met. The common factors of the union forged by their two offspring, plus their shared anxieties and sense of loss, were enough to break down any mutual reserves they might have felt. "Would you mind helping me in the kitchen Mrs Browning, or may I call you Bobby? I am Margaret, by the way. I am sure the men would like to chat on their own. I'm afraid we don't do a lot of entertaining these days, and with the dreadful food shortages it won't be a king's feast exactly."

Claud and the Admiral soon discovered common ground, the latter with his naval career, and Claud with his Army service in the Great War and in Dublin during the troubles in the early 20s. David Simpson was also warmly interested in Claud's Sunday column. It emerged that he had become a devotee of the feature, but had no idea that this "C. Browning" was its author. "Really, writing that must be enormous fun; the research alone must be terribly absorbing. I can see the idea running for ever. It is just the sort of thing I would love to do. Frankly, Claud, I am bored to death with doing nothing for the war effort. Too old, they tell me. Join the Home Guard and go round telling people their blackout is no good, they say. Some contribution to the war effort that would be!"

"Well, why don't you try writing. You must have some wonderful tales to tell from your Navy days. Ever thought of it?"

"Oh, I thought about it, but who the hell would want to read that sort of stuff? People want to get away from the subject of War, surely?"

"I don't think so. Things may be on the turn at last, but we still have a long way to go, David, and I think that what people want is humour, light relief. You must have a huge fund of naval experiences to draw on, and they weren't all about bombarding the Bosch, were they? Give it a try. I might be able to get our Editor Gordon Johns to have a look at it. And don't be shy about embroidering a bit. The important thing is to produce something that raises the public's spirits. That would be a real contribution to the War Effort."

"Well," Simpson replied, "I have to admit I had never thought of it that way, but you are right. I don't know if it is my cup of tea, but it certainly would not hurt to try. Thanks"

Bobby, and Margaret Simpson, busy in the kitchen, found it very easy to find common ground. Children were at the root of it: the one grieving the death of a treasured son, the other in fear for the life of a son, equally valued. There were other things too. Margaret Simpson had joined the WVS and worked in a state canteen, providing lunch for school children and voluntary workers, That was not enough for her, though. When lunches were finished for the day, she drove ambulances taking the sick and elderly to and from hospital. She was fascinated to hear of Bobby's broadcasting activity, and was curious to know if she ever had any feedback from Norway.

Over dinner, Celia and Douglas's marriage was discussed. Impulsive? Rash? Unforeseen certainly. They were both very young still. The Admiral was clearly pleased that his only surviving child should have married into the Fleet Air Arm. The Naval tradition would be maintained. On their brief acquaintance he had warmed to Douglas, but feared privately that in this dangerous world, Celia might be widowed before she had even set up home with her new husband. Ironically, now that he was a prisoner of war, he should survive the conflict. His wife, too, had harboured this fear. For the Brownings, especially Bobby, there was only joy that the flirtatious Douglas had given his heart to this lovely girl. She felt sure the tie would last, and was happy to have at last a daughter, if only "in law". More grandchildren would have to wait until the Nazis had been crushed.

And so the evening passed and new friendships forged, and a promise given for a "return match" as the Admiral put it. It is odd that out of adversity and sadness there may grow a new spirit. Man is a very strange creature. Perhaps there is some unseen puppeteer who can explain it all. Man himself certainly can not.

CHAPTER 69

By September 10th two Allied beachheads on mainland Italy had been established: one to the north and one to the south of the River Sele. The US Fifth Army at Salerno took a terrible mauling, whilst further south, only light opposition was encountered until the landing force had advance some two kilometres inland. A third force, the British Eighth Army, the heroes of El Alamein, had landed at Taranto in the "Heel" of Italy..

On the 12th the Allies captured the beautiful island of Capri, without firing a shot. Far to the east, on the 15th, British forces landed on the Dodecanese island of Kos, close to the Turkish coast, actually assisted by the 5,000 strong Italian garrison, and in the Aegean, the islands of Leros and Samos were taken. It was now some six weeks since the Dictator of Italy, Benito Mussolini was stripped of power and placed under house arrest. By the time of the Allied landings in southern Italy, his whereabouts was unknown. In fact, he was in secret hiding in an Hotel in the Appenine Mountains, the Campo Imperiale. On September 12th, in a daring and carefully planned assault, hand-picked German paratroops crash landed in a glider and rescued Il Duce. A hair raising take-off down a rocky slope in a tiny aircraft and "Musso", as he was not-so-fondly called, was free. He was flown to Vienna and thence onwards to Hitler's HQ. As the month wore on, Allied troops made further landings up the west coast of Italy, at Naples and Bari.

In the Far East, the war against Japan waged fiercely, on land and sea. Japanese forces had pushed up the Malay Peninsula, through Burma and almost to the border with India itself. At sea as well, Britain had suffered grievous losses. But by September 1943, the tide was just beginning to turn in favour of the Allies. In the Pacific, the Japs abandoned the Solomon Islands. Australian troops landed in New Guinea and in early October, a massive US Naval Task force attacked Wake Island.

Closer to home, German Armies continued to retreat in the face of ruthless and relentless attacks by the Russians. Meanwhile, the leaders of the Free World planned the final assault into mainland Europe. The Second Front. Where would it be? Holland? Belgium? France? One thing was certain: all along Southern England, from Kent to Cornwall, British, Commonwealth and American men and armour were beginning to mass.

The day of reckoning was approaching…

CHAPTER 70

"Dad, it is true, isn't it that the war is going better for us now? It seems so from the newspapers you bring home, but I remember you once said that you can't believe everything you read in the papers. So, do you know if things are <u>really</u> better?"

"Yes Finn. But the Germans and the Japanese are still very strong and determined, and it will be a long time before it is all over. It is true that the Italians have thrown in the towel, but the Germans are still occupying Italy, and our troops are getting very bogged down, both by the opposition and now by the weather as well. And the Germans are far from finished on the Russian front. As for the Far East, well the Japs are absolutely fanatical. I don't think they will ever give up. They think it is a disgrace to surrender, and Japanese Army officers sometimes commit hari-kiri rather than be taken prisoner."

"What's hari-kiri?"

"It is a ritual, and not a nice one. These maniacs take a sword and disembowel themselves with it. They think it is the honourable thing to do. They are quite mad, of course. Another thing they have started doing is for their pilots to fly their planes straight into Allied warships. It's another form of suicide, but a very nasty one, as they are taking our poor lads with them – at least if they manage to hit their target! I think sometimes their aim is none too accurate and then they just dive into the ocean. Either that, or they change their minds at the last moment. But when they do hit, they cause terrible damage and many deaths. They are called Kamikaze pilots. The word is derived from the Japanese words for Divinity and Wind. Another thing we hear in Fleet Street, but say little about, is the cruelty the Japanese impose upon our Prisoners of War. It is horrific and I am not going to go into detail about it, son. But if we ever do end this war, it will all come out, and it will not be pretty reading."

"But why, Dad? We don't do that to them do we?"

"No Finn, we certainly do not. The Japanese are different from us. Because they believe that to surrender is a terrible dishonour, they take the view that if their enemy stops fighting, even if he has no chance of winning, he is dishonourable and should be treated mercilessly, even barbarically. You must fight to the death – that is their culture. We should be grateful that even if your brother is a prisoner of war of the Germans, he will not be treated that way, though I'm afraid it won't be very pleasant for him."

"Will they hurt him at all? Oh I hope not, Dad. Will they keep him in Italy?"

"No way of knowing. But they may let him write occasional letters, and we can write to him via the Red Cross. They have access to POWs in Europe, and they should have in the Japanese camps, but the Japs will not give any access – probably because they don't want the Red Cross to see what they are doing. Under the Geneva Convention, POWs can not be made to work, but I am quite certain they are having to in the Far East, so they keep the Red Cross well out of reach. And they don't give a ha'porth what we do to their men, whom we are holding. They say such men should not have surrendered in the first place."

"Will Kenneth have to join up? It would be nice to have <u>one</u> brother still at home."

"Well, son, if the war drags on long enough, yes, I'm afraid, he will have to join up won't you Ken?"

Ken had just entered the lounge where Claud and Finn had been talking. Darkness came early now it was mid-October, and the fire was crackling brightly in the hearth.

"Won't I what?"

"Have to join up like Clive and Douglas. What will you join up into. Have you thought about it?"

"Well, I've got a good few months before I have to decide, and it does not follow they'll take any notice of what I ask for. But I quite like the idea of joining the Army.

With Clive in the RAF and Douglas in the Navy, the obvious thing seems to be to join the Army: game, set and match. Unless I volunteer to be a Bevin Boy."

"What's a Bevin boy, Ken?"

Claud Browning intervened. "Instead of going into the forces, some young men are directed to go down the coal mines instead. Someone has to dig the coal. All our factories rely on it, and we do too to keep warm, unless you've got a source for logs. But you can't operate factories with wood. I have to say it is not something I would like to do. Dreadful conditions and potentially dangerous. It reminds me of 1917 around Ypres. Our chaps started tunnelling under the German lines. The idea was to bury huge quantities of high explosives right under their defences. In fact, the Germans were doing the same thing, though we did not know it at the time. In any case, we got there first. At precisely 3.00am, I think it was on July 31st, all seven caches of gelignite were detonated, blowing hundreds of Germans to smithereens. Actually, all seven did not go off – only five did. The other two are still there to this day, hundreds of feet under Belgian soil. They might get a horrible shock one day, those Belgians, though, as they are under German occupation at the moment it isn't uppermost in their minds. Perhaps after this war they'll get round to doing something about it. Anyway, we were talking about what Ken might do, if he has to join up."

"Well, Dad, it won't be Bomb Disposal, I promise you. Not if I can avoid it. But I might volunteer for the Royal Artillery. I quite like the idea of popping off big guns at the enemy. One advantage is that the big guns tend to be well behind the front line. Might be a bit safer I thought."

"Sounds pretty sensible, Ken. It's worth a shot, I suppose. Oh Heavens, that's a pretty awful pun, isn't it? Anyway, when it comes to it, you'll just have to go where they send you. You can't be that picky".

The three all laughed, just as Bobby appeared. "What's so funny, you boys? Not a crude joke I hope. You English have such a basic humour. We are not like that at home in Norway, I promise you."

"No, Mama, we weren't being crude actually, and if we had been, well, it's not so terrible is it? A bit of light relief in fact."

"Kenneth, I am not a prude, I just do not see the humour in making smutty jokes, so please don't, or at least not in front of me." But there was the hint of a smile, the corner of her mouth twitched an almost invisible fraction.

"Mum", it was Finn speaking, "Do you think this story I heard at school the other day is smutty? Pig Symons told me it: Question. Tell me the name of a tree that does not grow. Answer: a lavatory. See? A lavo tree." And Finn dashed out of the room laughing.

"I'm sorry Bobby. Boys are like that, I'm afraid! It will get a lot worse when he grows up, so you'd better get used to it, if you aren't already with the other two. Didn't Clive and Douglas behave a bit rudely sometimes?" Bobby grinned. "Well, yes, occasionally, when they thought I wasn't listening. That's the odd thing about children; it never seems to occur to them that adults can actually hear, even when they are right in front of them. My father sometimes helped out in what you might call the local Social Club. He used to serve behind the bar and he used to tell us that he heard all manner of confidential conversations between customers standing right there in front of him. It was as if he was invisible. I daresay it's different now, with Gestapo agents skulking about everywhere. People will be very careful what they say , and where they say it.."

Bobby's mind wandered back to Norway, and her family. She wondered how they were coping with the Occupation. It was grim for everyone, she knew, but particularly hard for old people, with the lack of fuel in the bitter winters, and shortage of food as well. She wondered if they were even alive still, her Mother and Father. And what of her sister Eleanor? For over three years she had not heard a word of her. The only contact had been that one time via Lars. And how was he? Was he still alive? She knew how bitter and angry this gentle young man had become. Turned, though through no fault of his own, into a cold killer, destroying human beings as those same human beings had destroyed the two people he had loved so dearly. And in killing Germans he, too, was killing people who had parents and wives and sisters who loved them. But he would go on doing it, even if he hated it, because he must not only take revenge, but rid his beloved country of these monstrous people. And he would not hesitate to kill his own countrymen if they were collaborating with the invaders. Traitors were even worse than the Nazis themselves.

"You've got a faraway look in your eyes, darling. A penny for your thoughts."

"Oh, it's nothing really, Claud. I was thinking of people back home. Wondering how they were all getting on. My parents especially, of course. They are getting very old now. Pa is turned eighty and Ma not much younger. It is hard to think I would never know if they became ill, or worse, if they died. I'm sorry, I did not mean to bother you with all that."

"No, on the contrary, you should. I'm your husband and we are your family and it is right that we share your concern. After all, they are grandparents to our four boys. Our lads have Norwegian blood, remember."

Finn had returned to the room. "I wish I could see Granny and Grandpa Norway, Mum. Do you think they are alright? I can hardly remember them, it's so long ago. And Dad, I don't remember <u>ever</u> seeing your parents. Are they alive still?"

Claud gave a wry smile. "No. Finn, they died a long time ago. But before that, I am afraid they were not actually living together. My father was a bit of a naughty lad and he had an eye for the ladies, and one of them lured him away from my mother. She was terribly upset, and so were we three children, your Uncle Eddy and Auntie Jenny and me. My mother was broken hearted really and even though we rallied round her and made sure she was comfortable, she had little interest in life after that and only lasted a few years. Dad went off up to Burton-on-Trent with that wretched woman and worked running the local paper. We rarely saw him. He died when you were about four, from double pneumonia. The woman he had been living with just vanished off the scene. No idea if she is alive or not. Dad left her a bit of money and the house up in Burton, which she sold, and heaven knows what happened to her after that."

"Come on Finn, it's time you went off to bed. You've got athletics training tomorrow with Mrs Black. You need your beauty sleep."

CHAPTER 71

Finn would be thirteen in January of the following year, 1944. His natural ability at squash dated from his very first encounter with the game as a small boy at Rosedown, back in 1940. By the late Autumn of 1943 his skill had developed to the point where he was able to beat anyone on the Prep School circuit and many of the men at his Club in Surbiton. When time permitted, he would play in the inter Club matches. In times of war these were few and far between, as most of the young players were off in the Services, leaving only those in middle or older age, or in Reserved Occupations who could play. Finn enjoyed these matches. It was the puzzlement on the faces of opponents that amused him. Were they serious, he could see them thinking, fielding a boy not yet in his teens? Of course, it disarmed some of them, and they would stride onto the court convinced they would very soon be off again after giving the boy a 3-0 thrashing. Well sometimes they were off after a thrashing, but it was not the boy who was thrashed. Finn was quite prepared to practise diligently, unlike many others of his age, who would hit the ball around the court for a few minutes before getting bored. Finn would never practise for less than half an hour, concentrating on just one or two particular strokes. His serves were devilish, lobbed high, deep into the back corners.

His drop shots, with a delicate flick of his wrist, millimetres above the tin and right in either corner, broke the heart of many opponents, especially those well-past their youth, who had to race from the back of the court to retrieve. The game being over, the older men would shower, and then make for the Bar and the largest measure of beer they could lay their hands on. Beer, curiously enough, was not rationed. Being largely water and hops, the ingredients were in plentiful supply. Hop fields, it might be thought, would have been turned into grain or vegetable crops. But Government recognized the importance of maintaining public morale, and the availability of beer and spirits were very much part of the policy. Finn did not envy them this "comfort"; he was quite happy to have won his match, and would make a polite exit and make his way home, leaving the men to rue their defeat and turn conversation to the war and its progress.

By the end of 1943, few were in any doubt that the War in Europe had swung irrevocably the Allies' way. It was simply a question of when and where the assault on Europe would take place Speculation centred on France. France was where we had been kicked out back in 1940 in the ignominious withdrawal at Dunkirk. Poetic justice would be a landing there. After all, it was near to the South Coast and that much nearer Berlin, the final goal. And wouldn't it be good to get there before Uncle Joe – Stalin and his Communist cronies? But there were those who believed that the invasion would be further along the coast, in Belgium or even Holland. Scandinavia as a landing place had little support, it was too far from the springboard of the UK. Of course there could be twin assaults. That would give Adolf something to fret about. So Norway and Denmark were not totally out of the reckoning. Then there was the "When". The days were shorter now, and would get shorter still with winter in the offing. A bad time. It would be in May, some thought. Other thought June, when the days were at their longest. Others felt July or August of 1944. Well, none of these guesses was far into the future. We would all know soon enough.

The war in the Far East was another matter all together. It had started later and would doubtless finish later. Emperor Hirohito and his merry men could wait a while. But they too would be vanquished and then there would be peace all over the globe, and we could all get on with our normal, peaceful lives. All those that survived, that is......and so the chatter and the guessing bubbled on.

Finn was not deaf to all this talk. Far from it. He and his peers at Shawbury House were as interested as anyone else. Maybe not so knowledgeable, or opinionated, but intrigued never the less. Finn was not the only one with brothers away at the war. And sisters, too in some cases. Jack Tennison had a sister nursing the sick and wounded in Sicily. Charles Downie had an elder brother who was a Lieutenant with the Chindits in Burma. Mike Sainsbury had lost a brother, torpedoed on an Atlantic convoy. And there were others, fathers and uncles in many cases, some never to return. Terence Perkins had an uncle who had served in the Great War in battleships and was doing the same in this war. On odd occasions he came home on leave, and brought his young nephew a large box filled with chocolate bars: Cadburys Dairy Milk, Fry's Five Boys and Turkish Delight, and Buzz Bars in yellow wrappers. Mike generously brought a few bars to school for friends, but made enemies of those to whom he gave nothing.

Finn still made his visits to Headley Court on Sunday afternoons. The poor lads brought there to recuperate were mostly bomber boys. Back in 1940, 1941 and 1942 the majority were fighter pilots, but with the decline in German air attacks on England and the huge increase in RAF bombing raids on Germany, it was the aircrew of Lancasters and Halifaxes who were suffering the heaviest casualties. Like Finn's brother Clive, no small number were tail gunners, that bit more exposed than their comrades amidships, or in the nose. In many cases these men were recovering from burns. At one time

Finn had dreaded seeing such appalling disfigurements, but now was able to confront them without flinching. Geoff Wheeler was a typical case, though a Navigator, not a Gunner. When the war began, Geoff was only seventeen. He was a Dorset lad, from farming stock, and his main desire had always been to work with his father Ron. Ron himself was third generation on Formington Farm, started by his grand dad in the 1870s. Theirs was a dairy farm with 240 acres of lush pasture and a herd of about 80 Jersey cows. Geoff had been called up in 1940. It had never crossed his mind that he would be drafted into the RAF. His dad had been in the Royal Naval Division in the Great War, a unit set up by Winston Churchill, now Prime Minister and inspiration of the British People. The RND was far from being a seafaring unit. They were soldiers with naval ranks, and served with distinction in many of the great campaigns in Northern France and Belgium. So it was quite a surprise when Geoff's calling up papers instructed him to report for training at RAF Grantham in Lincolnshire. After basic training Geoff was sent on a Navigator's course and then to the Middle East to a Wellington squadron. All was well for a time until one day, as his aircraft raced down the runway for take-off, an undercarriage collapsed for no apparent reason. Screaming along the runway on its belly at over 100mph, the full fuel tanks ignited and engulfed the plane in flames. Minus one wing, the Wellington finally slewed to a halt, a raging ball of smoke and flame. Geoff, terribly burned, was the only survivor. His face was unrecognisable, his hands just bone – all the flesh gone. Somehow, by some miracle, his legs and most of his torso were spared the worst of the flames. Geoff had spent long and very painful months in recovery, with innumerable operations, mostly at East Grinstead, under the care of the great pioneer of plastic surgery Sir Archibald McIndoe. Now, more than a year after the accident, he was preparing for life as a civilian again. He knew it was unlikely that he would ever be able to do much, if anything, manually. He was lucky to have hands at all. Even now, he was unable to use a knife and fork, or even a pen. He had to dictate letters to whoever would write them for him, and this was one task that Finn sometimes undertook. Geoff became very fond of Finn, who was a good listener and liked to hear of his life on the farm, before the war.

Curiously, he knew of Rosedown, and the Hannah family, and was intrigued to hear about Finn's time there in 1939 and 1940.

"I tell you what, young Finn. When this damned war is over, or maybe before even, you could come down to Dad's farm in the school holidays and help out a bit, if you'd like. We'd put you up alright, and there'd be no lack of good grub. I can tell you, we don't go short of good beef and we're awash with lovely milk of course. And there's chickens running all over the place, and Mum has a real nice vegetable patch.. You're a growing lad young Finn, so daresay you could heave a few bales of feed around, and do a bit of milking , why not? Oh and you could borrow a bike and go and see those chums of yours at Rosedown: it's not many miles away. How about that then?"

Oh I'd love it Geoff, I really would. We've not had much time for holidays since the war started, what with Dad's work commitments. Did you know he writes a column in one of the Sunday papers every week, about interesting characters from the past? And Mum does this radio broadcasting to Norway, where she comes from. So its been difficult. Yes, I really would love to come and farm one summer."

And so 1943 came to a close. In the Browning household, Christmas was quiet – a depleted family. There had been no word of Douglas since he was taken prisoner. Clive was still in Rhodesia and letters were few and far between. Kenneth was subdued, anxious about his imminent call-up. They all went to Church on Christmas Eve and prayed for their safe deliverance from this long war – four years long now. There was no turkey on the table, as there had always been before the war, and had been back at Rosedown in 1939. By saving the family coupons and going short in the weeks leading up to Christmas, Bobby had managed to buy a large joint of beef. But strangely, or perhaps not, appetites were thin, apart from Finn's. One bright spot was Charlotte, brought down from London by Philippa on Boxing Day. She giggled happily and raised Bobby's spirits a little. But only a little. Her thoughts kept wandering across the North Sea, and to Rhodesia and to .. where was Douglas now? There would be little to celebrate in any of those far off lands. And she thought of one other person. Lars. Was he still alive? It would be a long time before she knew.

CHAPTER 72

On January 10th 1944, Kenneth became eighteen, one week after Finn became thirteen. They could not then know how indelibly that year would be burned in their memories. On the 15th, Kenneth packed a small suitcase and with a heavy heart said goodbye to his family. Claud knew how his son was feeling: he had been there nearly thirty years earlier, when he had marched in response to Kitchener's famous exhortation "England Needs You". Bobby was full of foreboding for her third son. Twice she had nearly lost Clive. Douglas was in enemy hands. Now, Kenneth was going too. Might she lose him as well? Kenneth said he did not want anyone to accompany him to Surbiton Station. Home was the place to say goodbye. At the end of the street he turned for a moment and waved as they stood at the front gate. Then he was gone, round the corner.

His Travel Warrant would take him from Surbiton Station across London and then on to this odd-sounding town near the Welsh border – Oswestry. In the train there were numbers of other young men, seemingly about the same age, and he guessed they were destined for the same place. But he spoke to no one, lost in his own apprehension for what lay ahead. He remembered his first day at KCS, how fearful he had been, even though on that occasion he had his older brother Douglas for company. There was no company here, except all these other youths on the train, who doubtless were feeling much the same as he. Cold comfort. The Army was not a boys' Public School.

Late afternoon, the train drew into Oswestry Station. It was cold and darkening. The last vestiges of a gloomy day. At least it was not raining. Young men, boys really, tumbled wearily onto the platform. At intervals Kenneth cold see NCOs positioned, one to each coach. "All those for Park Hall Camp, outside and into the trucks. Look sharp now, we aint got all day." The convoy rumbled through country roads and after quarter of an hour turned into the Camp main gate. This would be their home for the next few months. Park Hall was about four miles from the market town of Oswestry, but that was as close as they would get to it for many weeks. It was bleak, exposed to the winds blowing in over the Welsh hills. Row upon row of Nissen huts, which Kenneth guessed were to be their living quarters, were set on opposite sides of the large gravelled parade ground. On the other two sides were the Canteen, QM's Stores, Vehicle sheds, Gun sheds, Staff quarters and Armoury.

Under floodlights, the trucks disgorged their human cargo. Kenneth was dressed in well-pressed flannels and a tweed sports jacket, and tie. Few others looked as smart, or even as clean. "Form three ranks, you miserable lot. Come on, get on with it. God, what a fucking shambles." The Sergeant who spoke was short, wiry, with a face like a ferret. "I am Sgt Harris. You are going to see more of me than you care to in the next few weeks, and you will probably wish you'd never seen me at all. Now, three ranks I said, not thirty-three. Bombardier, get amongst this lot and sort them out. No, wait a minute. Do any of you young buggers play Rugby Football? If you do, form a separate line over on the left. Come on. Look snappy."

Kenneth was intrigued. Why mention rugger? We aren't here to play games. We're here to learn soldiering. But there must be a reason, and at least it might mean mixing with a decent bunch of other recruits. Kenneth fell out to the left of the main group. About a dozen or so others did the same. No explanation was offered for this early segregation. Shuffling and confusion reigned for several minutes, but finally the various groups were marched off, one by one. All in the same direction: the Canteen. The NCOs barked and shouted. It reminded Ken of sheep dogs rounding up their flocks. "Ep I, Ep I, Ep I. Kenneth had the feeling that Sgt. Harris was as nasty an individual as he had ever encountered, and promised himself that he would tread very warily with the man.

They were halted outside the canteen. "Right, you don't deserve it, but you've got 15 minutes to get yourself a cup of tea and a biscuit. Then back out here, in exactly the same groups. Got it? Fall out!" Inside the canteen, long wooden trestle tables were set out, with benches. At one side were food counters, long slabs of stainless steel, behind which half a dozen NAAFI girls in dark green uniforms were dispensing enamel mugs of steaming tea. A queue was quick to form. The tea was strong, hot and very sweet. Along with the mug of tea, each man was handed a biscuit. It was a Cadbury's chocolate biscuit with orange filling. Kenneth had not seen such a delicacy for years. "So this is where all the goodies go!" he thought to himself. He did not know it then, but it was the only chocolate biscuit he was to see during his entire Army service.

The Rugger squad were marched to Hut 14 in H Line, by Bombardier Gingell. Bombardier Gingell was tall, well over six foot. Kenneth thought his hair should be ginger with a name like that. Irrational. It was black. There was no shortage of ginger in the man's manner however. "Right. Get inside and choose a bunk. That'll be your pit for the next sixteen weeks, and let me tell you now that it will be spotless for the whole of that time. One bloody wrinkle or crease, or speck of dirt and you'll be on fatigues, or worse. Fail inspection twice, and you'll be on a five mile route march with full pack.

Three times and you'll be up before the CO and then God help you. Got it? Yes, son. You got a question?" It was Kenneth who dared to raise his hand. "Yes, Bombardier, can you tell us please, why rugger players have been grouped together? Is there a Regimental team or something?"

"Wot's your name, son?"

"Browning, Bombardier. Kenneth Browning."

"Well, Kenneth Browning. There is a Regimental team. But that's for the Permanent Staff. Once in a while, if they run short, a new recruit might be roped in. But even if you are a bloody genius at the game, it's likely you'd be far too knackered after what we've got in store for you. So forget it. As for why you've been put in this troop, you'll find out when it's good and proper that you should know. Got it? Any more smartarse questions? Oh yes, before anyone does ask anything, let me give you Lesson No. 1. In the Royal Artillery, an NCO with two stripes on his arm is called a Bombardier, not a Corporal, as he is in the rest of the Army. And an NCO with one stripe is called a Lance Bombardier, not a Lance Corporal. Remember that. And when you address a Sergeant, he wot's got three stripes, you call him Staff. Don't forget it. Especially don't forget it with Sgt. Harris. He don't like gentlemen who call him Sergeant. Alright? Nah, then, when you've sorted out which bunk you're in, unpack your bags and put your stuff in the locker. Five minutes, then outside and then we'll march across to the QM's Stores and fit you out with uniform and other equipment you'll need. Get moving!"

Kenneth's first evening in the Army seemed endless, and almost was. It was long, tedious hours before all the day's induction was completed. First, the issue of uniform: two tunics, two pairs of trousers, underwear, socks, beret, webbing, brass badge, belt with brass buckle, shoe cleaning kit and, not least, a 0.303 Lee Enfield rifle. And bedding. Then being shown how a bed should be made up, with exact tucks and folds, and how it should be stripped and folded into a particular bundle in the morning. "Then do it you morons, an' then Staff can inspect it." Right. After that we'll show you how to polish yer boots an' yer brasses, until they shine bright enough for you to shave in, that's if any of you are old enough to shave. And if they don't you'll be truly sorry. Oh, I DO mean sorry! Lance Bombardier Harding 'ere will remain to see you get on with it and only when he's satisfied you've done it right, will you go over to the Canteen for a bit of tucker, an' then maybe you can have a few hours shuteye."

It was well past midnight before the work was done, and supper consumed. There had been little conversation. It was only at Lights Out that

Kenneth introduced himself to the inmates of the bunks either side of him. "My name's Browning. I'm from Surbiton in Surrey. How about you?" "Fecking Abergavenny. What's it to you, man! Fecking played rugger at some fecking posh school, did yer? Bunch of ponces by the sound of it." This friendly introduction came from the man on Kenneth's right, in the direst Welsh sing-song voice he had ever heard. It seemed to be all the lad had to say, and did not include imparting his name. The man on Ken's other side had remained silent. He had swarthy skin and greasy black hair.. He was thin and wiry, with eyes darting furtively from side to side, as if expecting to be assaulted. "How about you?" "McVie. Orlando McVie. Glasgow. Dinna play rugger, but it seemed like a good skyve. And doant try anything wi' me laddie, orse I'll carve your face." A single dim bulb was all the light remaining in the hut. By it, Kenneth saw McVie tucking something under his pillow. It was the glint of a sheath knife.

So this was the Army. Kenneth wondered if, after all, he would have been better off to have enlisted like his two older brothers in either the Navy or the RAF.

CHAPTER 73

Four months had passed since Douglas was taken prisoner, without any news from him, or of him. Bobby, so normally cheerful and composed, fell increasingly into moods of depression, and fear that she would never have her four boys all together again. It was a sombre beginning to the New Year of 1944, accentuated by Kenneth's departure to the Army. Now she only had Finn close to her. Finn, and, of course, her husband. Finn was the one child who reminded her of her family back in Norway. His features were her features: the ice blue eyes, the thick mop of blond hair, the tall, lithe frame. Thank God he would never have to don uniform. But the other three had gone. The house seemed empty, and apart from her trips to London to make her broadcasts, her life seemed empty too. Claud spent long hours at the Public Library researching for his column, and if he was not there he was upstairs banging away on his old Remington typewriter. Finn was mostly at school. His life was very full, what with classes and sport and his visits to Headley Court, \not to mention outings with his pals.

It was soon after Kenneth joined up that at long last a letter arrived from Douglas, via the Red Cross in Switzerland. It was brief:

"Dear Mum and Dad and all my brothers, wherever they may be. I am well. I am in a Camp for RAF Officers. I am the only Navy chap here. The Germans do not differentiate – to them we are all just flyers. We are treated fairly, but the life is austere and very boring. Thank heavens for the Red Cross. We have parcels from them about once every three months. Clothes mostly, and very welcome as it is bitterly cold. Right now there is a foot of snow. As well as clothes they contain cigarettes (no consolation for me!) and sometimes chocolate. Oh and playing cards –

very useful. We play poker and so far I have lost ten million pounds! And books, except that mostly they are trash.

I miss you all terribly, but you will understand when I say how dreadfully I miss Celia. We had such a short time together. I have written to her c/o her parents in Wimbledon, but please call them and tell them I am ok.

I hope we will be together again soon. Love, Douglas"

Although she shed tears, Bobby felt a burden had been lifted. There was hope again. Douglas would come home. Not yet, but sometime. A year, maybe. Surely not more than that. If only she could hear from her family back home.

And from Lars…she could not get him out of her head, although she knew that she should. It was odd that the very next day a letter arrived from Clive in Rhodesia. He admitted to having been homesick, but thankful at least that he had been in minimal danger, far from the fighting. His leg, he said, still gave him pain, but it was bearable and he was walking better than when he had left England. He missed Philippa and little Charlotte. How she must be growing, and now she could crawl and nearly toddle. Philippa had sent photos, but they did not really show how big she was, but that did not matter because <u>he was coming home.</u> He could not say exactly when, nor by which route, but fairly soon. And he had been promoted to Flight Lieutenant. Never mind the extra ring on his sleeve, it would be good to have a little extra money in his pocket. He ended by asking if Mum would find out where the Roman Catholic Church in Surbiton was located.

There was a further boost for morale when Kenneth phoned to say he was being given a 72 hour pass. After ten weeks gruelling basic training, square bashing, cross-country   route marches with full back pack, hand-to-hand combat, assault courses, and, yes! Two games of rugger would you believe, there was to be a brief break before switching to gunnery training. In fact, the first session had already taken place – an observation visit to the Firing Camp at Trwsfyneth in the Welsh Mountains. After the leave Kenneth and his mates would be learning how to operate 25 Pounders, a staple light artillery piece widely used by the British Army throughout the war. There was one other piece of news. The mystery of the "Rugger Squad" had been resolved. This had been a simple ruse to identify Potential Officer material, on the basis that Rugby Football was played by "Gentlemen", and "Gentlemen" were likely officers as well! Unlike his chums from Glasgow and Abergavenny, the former having never seen a rugby ball in his life! In a way Kenneth was sad to be parting from them. Both had given him a broader slant on life and society.   McVie in particular, who had had to scrap for everything just to survive.   And "Fecking" from Abergavenny who eventually had revealed that his name was Shane Williams, but was universally referred to as just "Fecking" Williams. It seemed to fit the man.

But it would be good to go to the Officer Selection Board after hands-on artillery training. Hopefully, he would make the grade.

CHAPTER 74

On the Russian Front, 1944 began much as 1943 had ended – with the German Armies in retreat, and the Russians progressively more in the ascendant. Following the monumental German defeat in the tank battle at Kursk, first Kharkov and then Kiev fell back into Russian hands. This was symbolised by the massive increase in output of tanks, guns and aircraft from the Russian factories, and the mobilisation of millions more men and women. In Kharkov German war criminals were hanged in the market square. On January 6th, Russian troops crossed the pre-war border between Russia and Poland. At this rate of advancing – 400 miles in six months –the Russian forces would soon reach Eastern Germany itself.

In Italy, on a dark January night, Allied forces landed at the little port of Anzio. It was uncanny. The little town was deserted and undefended. Within 24 hours some 50,000 men and 3,000vehicles had been landed. Total losses amounted to 13 men, mostly from exploding sea mines. It was a welcome contrast to the terrible losses at Salerno thirty miles down the coast a few months before.

And before the month had ended, the German siege of Leningrad was at last lifted. It had lasted for over two years and had cost a million lives. For eight hundred and more days, its people had been subjected to unceasing shelling and bombing. Many citizens simply starved to death. They even made bread from sawdust. Some ate their dead comrades.

Meanwhile the American re-conquest of the Pacific continued. In early February an American force of 50,000 men landed in the Marshall Islands, supported by cover of a thousand aircraft, most of which were carrier based.

Back in Italy, the Germans counter-attacked at Anzio. By noon on the initial day of their assault, their pounding artillery had killed 1,400 British soldiers. The Allied force was still trapped in their beachhead after ten remorseless days of fighting. Winston Churchill said: "We hurled a wildcat on to the shores of Anzio – all we have is a stranded whale." What at first had seemed to be a glorified picnic became a repeat of Gallipoli.

Claud said nothing, but he wondered how long it would be before Kenneth completed his gunnery training and went to his Officer Selection Board. God let him pass, and go for Officer Training, thought Claud. At least that would further delay him joining a combat unit. What with the ferocious fighting in Italy – at Monte Casino as well as Anzio – and the inevitable invasion across the Channel, there would be a fair chance of

Kenneth being posted to one or another sector, and coming under enemy fire.
At least it was a blessing that he was not an infantryman.

CHAPTER 75

It was not Clive, nor as far as was known, Douglas, nor even Kenneth who next was "in the wars". It was Finn. Not often, but once in a while in the school holidays, Finn was apt to help Mr Hedges the Milkman on his round. Mr Hedges had been a milkman all his working life. All, that is, except in 1914-18, when he had served in the Expeditionary Force in France. He had been lucky. His job had been the training and care of horses. The deep, slimy, sucking mud of Flanders often defeated motorised transport, and then horses had been the only sure way of dragging guns and supplies up to and back from the front line. Casualties were heavy, horses as well as men. Exploding shells and snipers' bullets saw to that.

And many horses just died of exhaustion, their strength failing as they struggled with the mud and shell craters. Yes, Mr Hedges loved horses and although not a vet. nevertheless had the knack of nursing them back to full health. So, after that War was over, what more natural than to resume his job with United Dairies, delivering milk, eggs and butter? His milk float (he never did find out why it was called a float, when it wasn't in water) was painted a bright orange and pulled by "Mrs Kitchener", a fine chestnut mare, standing fifteen hands high. Mrs K was cosseted as no other horse in the whole of England. Brushed and groomed every day by Mr Hedges, and fed with fine oats, which he grew himself on his allotment, Mrs Kitchener revelled in her daily round. And nothing pleased her more than when the children joined in the fun and offered her, their small hands outstretched, a tasty snack. She wasn't too fussy: if oats were not the fare of the day, then a snippet of potatoes, or a handful of carrots were perfectly acceptable. Normally, she was a placid, docile beast, though Mr Hedges did not much care for her being referred to as a "beast". It reminded him to much of the Fritzes back in 1917, who were merciless in shooting the poor, helpless animals as they struggled in the stinking mire. They were the beasts.

Sometimes, Mr Hedges would let Finn, or the other boys and girls, hold the reins while Mrs Kitchener walked unhurriedly the few yards to the next house, or the next street. It was on one such occasion that Finn suddenly had a fit of sneezing. And as he sneezed, involuntarily he yanked on the reins. Mrs K reacted to this not by halting, but quite the opposite, by breaking into a fast trot. Mr Hedges, walking sedately beside his beloved mare, was left trailing. Finn tried his best to bring Mrs K to a halt, but the idea of bit of real exercise clearly appealed to her and far from just trotting, she broke into a fast canter. The milk bottles in their crates rattled and clattered, like some mad glass orchestra. Eggs bounced in their boxes, and then shattered as the float mounted a kerb, and slabs of butter bounced like demented mini-bricks. Finn was terrified out of his wits. He shouted to Mrs Kitchener to stop, but Mrs K was having the time of her life. Beachers Brook would not have deterred her, she would have jumped it, float and all. St. Mark's Orchard curved left and then met a T junction. It was too much for the mare. At full speed she tried to turn right into Berryland road, but without an understanding of centrifugal force. As the mare turned, the float declined to follow, and was hurled on to its side, catapulting Finn into the air and then, with a sickening thud, onto the road itself. Mrs K toppled in a twisted heap, whinnying like the tortured beast that suddenly it had become. Crates and hundreds of milk bottles showered upon its helpless carcass. Puddles of blood were forming on the road, some Finn's, but for the most part poor Mrs Kitchener's., and mixed with the blood, was the white of milk and the yellow of smashed egg yolks.

Lungs heaving, Mr Hedges finally caught up with the catastrophic scene. It was instinct, one supposes, that his first thought was for his beloved mare. The poor creature was in great distress, its legs kicking helplessly as it lay on its side, the pain clearly visible in its agonised eyes. At least one leg was shattered, the bone protruding obscenely. Finn was dazed, but conscious. "See to the horse Mr Hedges. Please help Mrs Kitchener. I'm alright, just scratched and bruised." A long flap of skin, sliced by broken glass, dripped blood on to the road from Finn's right calf.

Blood also dripped from his nose and one cheek. Mr Hedges was no stranger to seeing wounded animals, and knew what had to be done. The mare would have to be destroyed, and the sooner, the better. But how? Passers by were beginning to gather. One did more than just stare, he ran to the nearest house and phoned for the Police and an ambulance. It was only a few minutes before the Police were at the scene, accompanied by an elderly Captain from the Home Guard. He carried a Browning rifle. As the barrel was pointed at Mrs Kitchener's head, it seemed that a look of peace came into the old mare's eyes, as if she knew that her day was done, and she would soon be at rest for good. Finn, still prostrate, looked the other way. As he was lifted gently into the ambulance, he heard the crack of the rifle.

Finn was in Surbiton Hospital for two days. It was not really the cuts and scrapes that kept him there, but the concussion, and the shock of what had happened. It was hard for him to come to terms with the simple fact that a sneeze, an involuntary jerk of the reins, had caused that dear, docile mare to be destroyed.

He did not know, thank God, that before many months had passed, he would witness much worse slaughter of the innocents than that of a horse.

CHAPTER 76

By mid-February, the euphoria of the initial landing at Anzio was now a fading memory. The Allied force had been well contained and badly mauled by the German counter attack and progress in the Italy Campaign stalled. Relief for the Anzio bridgehead was blocked at the little town of Monte Cassino.

Erroneously, Allied Commanders believed that the great monastery on the hill dominating the town was the German defenders' HQ, and its destruction by bombing ordered. The truth was that no German troops occupied it – not, that is, until it was a ruin, when Wehrmacht units DID move in and successfully blocked Allied progress through the valley below. Indian and New Zealand divisions attempted to storm the mountain top and its superb ruin, but were repelled with heavy losses. Again, the monastery and the town below were subjected to heavy bombing, this time by close on 800 aircraft dropping 1,250 tons of bombs. The effect was not only devastating, but counter-productive, as the rubble and craters prevented the Allied armour advancing. It left the infantry to fight on their own. The battle was appallingly ferocious, hand to hand, yard by yard against crack German Paratroop brigades. The scene was reminiscent of Verdun – mud, blood and frustration. The attack was finally called off on March 23rd. and the cost? Killed, wounded or missing were over 20,000 American, over 20,000 British and 8,000 Free French. The gain was Nil.

But this was not the end. Bitter fighting continued for many weeks and it was late May before Polish troops stormed into the monastery. It was deserted.

On March 26th Winston Churchill made a radio broadcast on the overall war situation, and declared that "The hour of our greatest effort is approaching". Amongst the Allied forces in Italy there were many who might have said that the hour of greatest effort had already been attained a good while ago! But Churchill, though not spelling it out in as many words, was thinking of the massive invasion of France that was soon to be launched.

Elsewhere around the globe, the waging of war continued and intensified. In the Pacific, in south-east Asia, in the Atlantic and even in the Arctic Sea, the Axis had not given up the expectation of victory, but inch by inch they were losing strength and ground. Over Germany, raids by British and American bomber squadrons became more frequent, heavier and more devastating, but at appalling cost. One single raid in late March cost the RAF 72 lost aircraft out of a total of 811 that set out. Germany was littered with the burnt carcasses of Lancasters, and their crews, shot down by German night fighters. The chances of a crew member surviving his tour of 30 operations was no more than 50%.

By the end of April, the whole of Southern England, from Land's End to The Wash, was a gigantic armed camp, with vast tank, truck and artillery parks, and innumerable arms dumps, enough to equip an invasion force of three million men. The initial assault would be carried out by the British, Canadians and Americans, but almost every occupied country in Europe would join in "Operation Overlord", the Allied assault against the German fortress of Europe. This included units from Norway, Poland, Holland, Belgium, Czechoslovakia and France. The build-up was marred by a dreadful tragedy off Slapton Sands, in South Devon on 29th April. During the course of a landing training exercise at sea, the American landing craft came under attack from a flotilla of German E-Boats. Over 600 men were lost , though many survivors insisted the number was much greater. News of this disaster was suppressed and only revealed many years after the war was over.

Clive arrived back from Rhodesia on April 16th and after a short de-briefing was granted seven days leave. During the briefing he had pleaded to be allowed to fly combat missions again, insisting that if his leg allowed him to do in-turret demonstrations to the trainees in Rhodesia, then it would stand up to flying missions over Germany. He was refused. He was told that his value as an instructor of air gunnery was too great to be put at risk. His disappointment was tempered by the thought that he would be able to spend more time with Philippa and his darling little Charlotte, who was now walking and talking unstoppably. He might even be able to spark-off a little brother or sister for her.

Although she had said little in her letters to Clive, Philippa felt unease at his decision to adopt the Roman Catholic church. The Hannahs were staunch Church of England. Sir Henry was a Church Warden and he and his lady were pillars of the wholly Protestant community in which they lived. The General was also a student of English History, and fully conversant with the horrors of the sixteenth century. Of course, it had all started with Henry VIII's break from Rome, but it was more his revulsion with Henry's daughter Mary 1st, a devout Catholic, and the retribution she had perpetrated against Protestants in her five years reign, burning hundreds at the stake, that had reinforced his anti-Catholic attitude. His children had followed this line, though far less trenchantly.

Philippa was naturally thrilled that Clive was home again. She loved this gentle man and had missed him desperately. Their reunion was a rapturous moment, and his adoration for her, and now his little daughter as well, filled him joy. But, there was a "but". Other than at Christmas and other odd occasions, neither Philippa, nor Clive had attended church, nor shown much interest in religion of any form. His conversion to Catholicism changed all this abruptly. Now he had a fervour that was alien to Philippa. A Bible and a Book of Common Prayer were constantly at his bedside, and he knelt and prayed before bedtime. He wanted her to follow suit, but she felt embarrassed to do so. He wanted her to accompany him to early Mass, and to bring Charlotte. She protested that his church was not her church and she would be uncomfortable if he persisted. But equally, she did not feel it was the right course to try to cool his ardour – that might have the reverse effect and give it even more impetus. She wanted help, but felt her parents would be insensitive to her situation. They would tell her that it was just something she would have to live with as best she could. That it was a fire that would cool given time, or even fade completely. She turned to Bobby.

Bobby was calm. She would listen and understand another woman's standpoint, even if the problem emanated from her own son.

Bobby did listen, patiently and intently as Philippa poured out her anguish. Then Bobby replied: " Philippa, the primary thing is that you love one another, darling. And I can see that that love is deep. And unbreakable. You must both cling to that knowledge, and if you do, it will see you through this difficulty. With time, he will come to understand that his way is not the only way. You both believe the Christian Story, that is the main thing. He may try to convert you to Catholicism, but he will not risk his marriage in the process. Be patient. Anyway, my guess is that he will try to convert us, or at least his brothers. He'll get short change from them I fear. So don't worry; as you English say: "play it cool"." Philippa was reassured. She thought of how her own mother would have reacted. She could imagine her saying: "Those damned Catholics. What has Rome done to curb Hitler? Nothing. Just sat on the fence in their cosy little Vatican. To hell with the lot of them." She smiled quietly to herself.

Unbeknownst to either Bobby or Philippa, Finn had overheard their conversation. He adored his eldest brother and when, a few days later, he happened to be alone with Clive, he related what he had heard, how distressed was his sister-in-law that she was unable to share Clive's new religious fervour. "I know, Finn, but you should not have listened in to a private conversation. It was not for your little ears, nor anyone else's. I know Philippa feels differently about God, and she and I will have to sort it out. I am sure we can, because if two people love one another enough, they are not going to let anything get in the way of happiness. Don't worry about it, but thank you for mentioning it, you little Worm!"

The night before he returned to duty, Clive took Philippa out to dinner. It was the first time since he left England for Rhodesia, He knew a small bistro in Kensington Church Street, called Chez Gaston. In war-torn London it was surprising such a place could survive, but it and many others, somehow managed to get adequate supplies of food, and with ingenuity produce fine meals. By some miracle, old Gaston, the Proprietor, found a bottle of English wine. There was no chance of anything Continental, of course – that had run out years ago. Clive wore his uniform, proudly displaying his new rank of Flight Lieutenant. There were many who would look askance these days at young men not in uniform, entertaining ladies in such places. "Why aren't they out there fighting the enemy." It was easier not to give their bigotry the opportunity.

It was difficult for Clive to broach the subject of Philippa's conversation with his mother. He was not supposed to know about it, but he decided the best course was to tackle it head on. "Philippa, my darling, that little beggar of a small brother overhead your conversation with my Mum yesterday. You know, about me being all fired up on Catholicism. Of course, he should not have been listening, but he was, and he told me out of the best of motives, because he cares about you and me. Actually, I am glad he did., because I had not realized just how sad you have been. It was bad enough being away from you for so long, and I was so longing for us to be together again. The last thing I wanted was for there to be any tension between us. And least of all about religion."

"Oh, I have tried to understand, love. But you seem to think everyone feels as you do, and how you feel is great. To have your new faith, especially in these terrible times, must be a wonderful strength to you, and especially when you are actually training men to kill other men. That must be a terrible dilemma. But it just isn't me. You know my family is C of E, and that is how I was brought up, except that I have drifted off the path a bit, like so many people. I find it very hard to see why Jesus Christ would let all this killing and cruelty and horror happen, if he loved the world and its people. Yes, I do wonder if He exists, or if it isn't just an ancient fairy story. And yet I don't altogether disbelieve, either. I just don't know. I don't know. I wish I did, Clive. Perhaps in time I will find the sense and reality of it all. But until I do, Clive, you have got to take me as I am. Can you do that?"

Philippa took his hand across the table. "Your mother said one thing that is so true, Clive darling. She said that she could see our love was unbreakable. Unbreakable. Well, if she can see it, so ought we to be able to. I will stay with you, and love you, and give you more children, even if you turn Buddhist or Muslim. It will still be YOU. But you must give me some latitude. Some space. Don't try to shoe horn me into a zeal that I do not feel. Can you do that? For me and little Charlotte?

Clive looked at her. "I've been a bit of a silly ninny, haven't I? You know, I have been so lucky twice in this damned war. First, I was torpedoed and saw my shipmates go down with the ship. Then I almost copped it in the Lanc. If that lump of shrapnel had hit me a foot higher, I would have been a dead duck. But I cannot just put it down to luck. I think there is a greater force at work, and that I must say thanks to Him in a positive way. But not at the cost of my love for you, and my determination to be with you until death. It does not have to be one or the other. I can serve Him and love you. And, by the way, I will take you up on your offer to have more babies. It's getting late. Let's go home. I think tonight would be a good time to see if we can start off a little brother for our daughter. Or a sister would do at a pinch

I suppose." They laughed. They walked home hand in hand through the blacked out streets. They made love.

CHAPTER 77

A further letter from Douglas arrived in April, delivered via the Red Cross. It was brief, written on the torn-out page of an exercise book.

"I am well, but it has been a hard winter here. Snow nearly all the time. In our hut, which accommodates twenty of us, we have one pot-belly stove to keep us warm. We have our uniforms (yes, the one I was wearing when I came down) plus sweaters provided by the Red Cross. Time hangs heavy: cards are a staple pastime. I now owe £5 million at a diabolical game called Brag. This is in addition to my losses at Poker. My creditors say they would settle for a beer or two at their local pub. We get exercise every day, but you try doing press-ups, and playing football in a foot of snow! Sorry to tell you I have taken up smoking cigarettes, provided by the Red Cross. I never dreamt that I would succumb to this foul habit, but I have. One chap in a neighbouring hut has died. No obvious cause. He had not been ill, or ill-treated. Just died. He had been here for three and a half years: perhaps that's what did for him, just could not stand it any more. Longing for this b----y war to end and to see you all again. No news from you. I guess all the letters are blocked. I suppose Ken has joined up now. Not another flyer is he? And how is the Worm. Still beating everyone at squash? Just wait until I get home, young fella, though perhaps by then you'll be bigger than me. Love to you all. Doug."

CHAPTER 78

In late April, Finn began his last term at Shawbury House. In the last few months he had shot up by a good two inches and now stood at 5ft 6in. Level pegging with his mother, all but one inch. Like her, he had a willowy figure – narrow hips and broad, square shoulders. The first signs of male puberty were showing themselves. There was a fair, but distinct down on his chin, and cracks in his voice.

Normally, Captain of School was appointed at the start of the School Year, in September, and this had been the case in September 1943, when Christopher Hollins had been awarded the honour. But at Christmas, Hollins's father had been killed in Burma. His mother, devastated, felt too distraught to remain in their home in Thames Ditton and had decided to return to be with her mother in Wimborne, Dorset. Chris had naturally gone with her. As his replacement, H-M did not hesitate in appointing Finn It would be for only one term, before he left to continue his education at St. Luke's in Dorking, but he was none the less thrilled, and very proud. Now, not only was he Captain of Athletics, but of the School itself. Not many were as gifted as Finn Browning, nor had his capacity for hard work, both in the classroom and in the sporting arena. He had in his short time at Shawbury House excelled in virtually every field. The only weak link was Cricket. He just could not understand how could spend hours standing around a cricket field doing virtually nothing, and when not on the field itself, then sitting on a bench watching others doing the same thing!

But this was a minor matter, and detracted not one whit from his success at other games, especially the battles of last term on the rugby pitch.

So now, with Summer round the corner, Finn concentrated his sporting efforts on Athletics. He had dual aims: one to break every Shawbury House running record in the book, the other to participate at the inter-schools Preparatory Schools Meeting once again, but this time to win all four events from the 100 yards to the half mile races, not just the three he had achieved in 1943. Second places were not something with which he could be satisfied.

By mid-May the whole of Great Britain was abuzz with expectation that the invasion of Northern Europe by the Allied Forces was imminent. Southern England in particular was seething with activity. The Supreme Commander of Operation Overlord was a quiet American, General Dwight D. Eisenhower. Under him, he had redoubtable field commanders: for the US it was General Omar Bradley, and for the British and Commonwealth divisions, the incomparable "Monty". Bradley would squat on his haunches and chew grass as he talked man-to-man with members of the 12th Army Group. Monty, wearing his famous black beret, fixed his men with a steely gaze before making a speech in his clipped military voice. At home in the UK Monty toured munitions factories, too, urging the workers to intensify their efforts. All along the coast, landing craft were assembling, along with a huge fleet of warships.

The Americans were largely assembling in Dorset, Devon and Cornwall, the British and Commonwealth force farther east, in Sussex and Hampshire.

D-Day was originally planned for June 4th. By then, though, a deep depression, with driving rain, strong winds and a low cloud ceiling had approached and entered the English Channel. Monty wanted to go ahead: troops had been crowded into assault craft since June 1st and were tired and cold. He was overruled by Ike and a further delay for 24 hours was ordered. More than that, though, would mean postponement until the end of the month, as the landing, as near to dawn as possible, required a rising tide. Also, to facilitate airborne troop landings and to give maximum air support along the landing beaches, a full moon was needed. It had to be either the 5th or the 6th of June.

D-DAY. JUNE THE SIXTH 1944.

1216hrs British Army gliders land to secure vital bridges on the Caen Canal.

0240hrs British paratroopers drop near the Orne River. The German Commander, Gen. Von Runstedt, decides this is a deception and that the real invasion will be somewhere near Calais, nearly two hundred miles to the east.

0530hrs The British naval bombardment of the Normandy beaches commences.

0630hrs US infantry land on Utah and Omaha Beaches, near to St. Germain and St. Laurent.

0725hrs British forces land on Sword and Gold Beaches, near Arromanches and Ouistreham, and the Canadians on Juno Beach, east of the Americans

1700hrs At his HQ in Berchtesgaten Hitler orders that the Allied force "be annihilated by nightfall."

2300hrs Hitler holds another conference at which he affirms his belief that the Allied landings are a diversionary ploy.

In the whole history of mankind this is, by far, the greatest ever amphibian invasion. On the first day 75,000 British and Canadian and 57,000 American troops have landed by sea. A further 8,000 British and Canadian, and 15,000 American troops have landed by air, either by glider or parachute.

The Allied death toll is put at 2,500, of which 1,000 died at Omaha Beach. 114 Allied aircraft have been destroyed. The scale of the invasion beggars belief: over 4,000 transport vessels, including more than 1,000 carrying tanks and other types of armoured vehicles. In addition there were 300 warships, plus massive aerial cover. Many of the warships were detailed to shell and destroy German artillery batteries and fortifications along the French coast.

The Allies had gone to great lengths to deceive the German High Command as to where the landings would take place. A peacetime actor, Clifford James, with an uncanny likeness to Monty, was sent on a well-publicised tour of the Mediterranean theatre, with the idea that increased activity there would suggest to the Germans that a major thrust would be made in Southern Europe, probably on the coast of Provence. Further confusion was contrived by the assembly of a bogus army with rubber "tanks", on the Kent corner of England, suggesting the shortest route, the Pas de Calais, was the planned landing site.

Finn was woken early on June 6th. Not by his mother for once, but by the deafening roar and drone of wave after wave of aircraft heading South West. They were flying low, at about fifteen hundred feet. There were hundreds of them, as far as the eye could see. Mostly, they were DC3s towing large gliders. Others, without gliders in tow, were carrying paratroopers. From every house, people poured out to watch, craning up to marvel at this endless procession. Vehicles halted. Buses stopped. The milkman put down his crates. The armada continued right through the day and not a living soul had any doubt as to what was happening. This was IT. The Big One. Memories went back four years, to June 1940. Then "our boys" were coming home – tired, bedraggled and defeated. Kicked out of Europe by the German jackboot. Not now. Now it was Adolf's turn. Now it was his arse that was going to get kicked! Finn watched the planes roar over for a full hour, before it was time to go to school. There, everyone was abuzz with what was going on, teachers and pupils alike. There was little chance of any boy learning anything in class. Even if they had been able to suppress their excitement and concentrate, their teachers were far too elated to teach them coherently.

The tugs and gliders were accompanied by squadron after squadron of fighter support aircraft: Hurricanes, Spitfires and American Mustangs.

There were bombers, too, whose task it would be to attack key enemy positions inland from the landing beaches. Mostly, these were American Liberators, but British Mosquitoes – the fastest aircraft in the sky – were there as well in large numbers. By mid-morning, streams of planes were returning – the DC3s without their gliders now, heading back to pick up fresh men and supplies. Finn noticed that one or two were limping with clear signs of damage – tattered tails and wings and in one case a Dak flying on one engine, but still determinedly ploughing its way back to base. Well before midday H-M decreed that it was pointless to try and do any work. Instead boys were given leave to go home and share the excitement with their families and friends.

By the time Finn got home, Bobby had left for London, for the Norwegian Embassy to prepare another broadcast. His father was at home, glued to the radio for news of what was happening. It was recorded that on that unforgettable day, 558 accredited journalists accompanied the Operation Overlord. The BBC alone had 48. They all reported the events with courage and distinction, censored in parts maybe, but in the space of a few hours, the entire world knew of the momentous event. If El Alamein back in 1942 had been "The End of The Beginning", June 6th 1944 was certainly "The Beginning of the End".

Finn joined his father to listen. There was a sparkle in Claud's eyes, an intensity, that Finn had never seen before. There was, too, a hint of dampness in those eyes. Perhaps he was thinking of all the blood that would be shed before final victory. Or perhaps he was remembering further back, to the Somme, to Flanders, to Ypres in 1917, and the waste of life then. And for what? To do it all over again a quarter century later.

"Dad, are you sure this is really the Big Push?" Claud smiled, and placed his arm round Finn's shoulder. "Yes, son. Oh yes, I'm sure. I believe this day will be engraved in the minds of all of us for the rest of our lives. God willing, our armies will push Hitler all the way back to Berlin. And from there to the Hell he deserves. Finn, you are our only son still left at home, the only one not in uniform. I don't think now that you ever will be, and I thank God for that. I've got a large bottle of beer and damn it, what's happening today deserves a small celebration. I think you're old enough to share the moment with me. Fetch a couple of glasses and let's drink to success and an end to this damnable war."

CHAPTER 79

The first Americans arrived in Douglas's prison Camp in March 1944. There were ten of them and Douglas learned that they had been the crew of a B-17 downed by enemy flak whilst bombing Dortmund. In one sense they had been lucky, but not in another. They had managed to crash land on farmland far from any city or township, but not far enough from a nearby Wehrmacht encampment to evade capture. Douglas and the other British prisoners were astonished that they had managed to bring into the Camp, without confiscation, an average of thirty cigarettes each. They said the Germans had searched them and found the cigarettes, but told them they could not stand "Camels" and any American tobacco, so the Yanks had hung on to them. But much more importantly, and undiscovered by the Huns, were the minute compasses secreted in uniform buttons and detailed maps of Germany, printed on thin silk, sewn into the lining of their leather flying jackets. They were a sociable bunch and said they were happy to be out of the firing line. Daytime bombing over the heartland of Germany was a recipe for a very early and sticky death. Even Prison camp would be preferable. Their naivety was astonishing. They seemed to think that life here would be some priced-down version of a Hilton Hotel. They soon discovered that it was anything but, and their complacency about their circumstances soon evaporated.   Before many weeks of incarceration they started making enquiries about the possibilities for escape. Had any attempts been made? Was any tunnelling going on? They did not want to risk their lives reverting to bombing missions from England, but neither were they content to see the war out in this miserable, austere and freezing cold existence, where the only highlight was falling asleep at night – the bliss of unconsciousness.

Their enquiries were met coolly by the British prisoners. First, there was the possibility that one or even all of the Americans were in fact "moles". It was well known that captured airmen were persuaded to turn traitor on their fellow prisoners and betray plans, in exchange for promises of early repatriation, or other favours, which were never fulfilled. Once they had done their dirty work, and the escape plans fed to the Germans, they would probably be shot. Airmen were vulnerable to this persuasion. Unlike Army and Naval personnel, the bomber crews were "At home" every day. They would fly their mission, drop their bombs, and return to their base somewhere in East Anglia. They would be at "The Pig and Whistle", or the cinema or at a local dance next day, or in bed with a local lass if they got lucky, followed by another day of bombing, and never knowing if this was the last time they would make it home. "Home". England, even for the Americans, took on a new importance. It represented a kind of normal life. Safety. Comfort. The contrast was cruel. Thus, the urge to escape was stronger for England-based airmen, of whatever nationality, than for their Army or Navy counterparts.

"Look fellas, none of us want to be here in this hell-hole, but getting out is risking curtains, and even if you get out, the chances of making it back to Blighty are pretty thin. Some of us have been here for years, and some have tried to get out. Only two have succeeded, and we don't know what happened to them. Most likely they were shot as "spies" long before they reached England. This war is going our way now. We know it and you Yanks know it, so the consensus is that we just stick it out until the whole shindig has run its course. It just isn't worth the risk. Just think of the back pay you'll have earned for doing sweet FA."

The Yanks were not convinced. It was not in their nature to settle down to a harsh existence in some benighted country thousands of miles from home. Acquiescence was not the name of the game for these Americans. They began to make plans to escape, both singly or en bloc. They tried to pick the brains of the British airmen, and even recruit some of them, but, although understanding their frustration, the British continued to give them short shrift. If the Americans were undeterred, the British were firmly uncooperative. The Brits must be spineless wimps, the Yanks thought. Douglas and his chums continued to wile away their time. The worst of winter was now over. At least they could get some decent exercise. Not all the guards were cold automatons, and some even agreed to form a football team to play the POWs. To the Americans, football was virtually an unknown sport, and their interests were elsewhere. A slight change in the German guards' attitudes became noticeable. A slight thawing here and there, and even the occasional cigarette was handed over. But this was nothing to do with the weather. This was to do with the way the war was going. Although they had no direct access to news of the outside world, rumours abounded. Occasionally some guard would let something slip: "We are being hard pressed by the Bolshevists. It is not so good on the Eastern Front" Or: "Our people at home are no better off than you. There is no coal to keep warm, and even wood is short in the cities. Out families are making coffee out of acorns." Solid news came if a new prisoner arrived, but this was rare now, because Doug's camp was very full . It was not until mid-May that a downed Spitfire pilot, Peter Edgerton, was brought in. "There is a terrific build-up going on all along the South Coast. From Kent to farthest

Cornwall. Everyone knows we are soon going to cross the Channel: it is just a question of where exactly and when."

This did nothing to dissuade the Yanks from progressing their plans for escape. Their view was that an Allied invasion into France might take years to succeed, or might fail altogether. Soon they gave up tunnelling. It would take too long, and was susceptible to discovery. They could not cut their way out through the perimeter wire. There was an inner and an outer fence, both electrified, plus the possibility that the ground between the two fences was mined. The Camp hardly needed the watchtowers and machine guns! Another non-starter. There was one possibility that might be feasible. Every week, an open truck from Majdanek, the nearby Concentration Camp, was given access to the Oflag for the purpose of clearing waste. The food, often rotting, was taken back to the Concentration Camp for the inmates to eat. It usually came in late afternoon, around dusk. A German Army trooper drove the truck, and a second soldier sat in the open rear guarding the two Majdanek inmates. These two would go to the back of the Staff canteen to collect the large drums containing the waste. They were pathetic figures, living skeletons, dressed in striped pyjama-like tunic and trousers. They could do no more than shuffle about their task, often punched and beaten by their guards. Empty drums had to be unloaded from the truck and rolled to the refuse area behind the kitchens. Each full drum then had to be rolled on its rim back to the truck and then manhandled on to the flatbed of the truck. It was commonplace for this to be beyond the physical strength of the pathetic prisoners, and then some POW would be ordered to assist. The Majdanek inmates themselves would often have to be helped up onto the truck for the return journey to Majdanek and back to the hell of the Concentration Camp. Sometimes, there were a brief few moments when the Majdanek inmates were unsighted from the guards. It was not for long, and it only occurred when the waste drum was in an L shaped angle at the rear of the kitchens

The Americans had watched this activity for several weeks, and had perfected a plan. The proposal was that a diversion would be created in the form of a fight between two or three of the American airmen, somewhere near the kitchens. This would distract the Concentration Camp prisoners' guard, who would try to break it up. During this "sideshow" another three Americans would overpower, strip and tie up the fatigue inmates, and two would don their striped "pyjama" overalls, and take their place. They calculated that they would have no more than ninety seconds, but as the inmates were so weakened from their dreadful privations, they would offer little resistance. In any event, they might well think it preferable to be in a POW Camp, than back at their Death Camp. Another important ally would be the fading light. A third American would hide in the empty drum, and be covered quickly with rotten food scraps by the other two, who would then wheel the drum to the truck and lift it aboard, probably helped by another POW. Once out of the POW Camp, the Americans not concealed in the drum would overpower the unsuspecting German guard and they and their chum in the drum would make a run for it. It depended heavily on the disguised Americans not being recognized as they rolled the drum to, and on to the back of the truck, and being good enough actors not to be spotted as they went through the whole process. The chosen individuals had to approximate in size to the man he was replacing. There were, of course, too many "ifs", and the chance of the plan succeeding was paper thin. Hard as they tried the Brits could not deter the Yanks from making their ill-fated attempt. They were determined. It was worth a try. Or so they thought

The opportunity came on a wet and windy Friday afternoon, early in April. It was a good choice: the Camp guards were not over keen to patrol in soaking weather, and tended to shelter in doorways, in the confident belief that most of the POWs would not be wandering far from their huts. The Yanks had selected Warren, Wes and Louis to stage the fight. The three smallest Americans would overpower, and strip the inmates from Majdanek. These three were Fred Singleton, Bob Friedlander and Sean Goodson, all air gunners. These were the "lucky escapees". At first, it all went like clockwork. Warren and Louis started to shout at each other, and then threw punches. This prompted Wes to intervene, only to be embroiled in the punch-up by Warren and Louis. The Majdanek guard, aided by one of the POW guards, waded in with their rifle butts. It took just under two minutes to bring the melee to a halt.

The Majdanek prisoners were dreadfully weakened, no more than shuffling, mumbling skeletons. They did not resist Fred, Bob and Sean. They couldn't have, even if they had wished to. They stood in the angle, out of sight, and just allowed themselves to be stripped. Bob was the smallest of the three and was able easily to curl himself up in the empty drum. Trying to look as frail and bent as they could, Fred and Sean wheeled the drum on its bottom rim onto the truck. So far, so good. In the failing light, Fred and Sean's impersonation was not detected. Acting the role admirably, they slowly and painfully climbed aboard, followed by the German Majdanek guard. It was nearly dark. The truck rolled forward towards the Main Gate. The gate swung open. Freedom beckoned. The truck gathered speed. AS it did so, suddenly, the Camp Perimeter lights flooded the whole compound, including the huddled figures on the back of the truck. It was Sean who was recognized first. If he had kept his head down on his chest all might have been well. But he did not. The Majdanek guard raised his rifle. Fred moved fast and charged at him, wrenching the gun from the man's shoulder. But for the floodlights, he might have succeeded. The truck driver, unaware of what was happening, drove on, but then heard the piercing wail of the Camp Alarm Siren. The struggle had been spotted from the Watch Tower.

Soon, it was all over. As Fred and Sean leapt from the slowing truck, they were caught like startled rabbits in a car headlight. They never even saw the machine gun that mowed them down. They both died instantly. Bob stayed huddled in the oil drum. He heard, but never saw the commotion, never saw his comrades die. Later, as the truck moved on into the forest, and now in the pitch dark, he emerged from the drum, only to be looking straight down the barrel of the Guard's rifle. The bullet entered Bob's skull through the right eye.

CHAPTER 80

If the whole Camp had not seen what occurred, they had certainly heard it. The British prisoners settled down for the night in sombre mood. They knew from bitter experience that there would be reprisals. And soon. Roll call was normally at 6.00am. It was usually conducted by a junior officer, but today was different The Camp Commandant, Colonel Dieter Hille faced them. He spoke good English. "You will know that yesterday evening an escape attempt was made by some of your American colleagues. We have repeatedly warned you that such attempts will not be tolerated by the Third Reich. You have ignored our warnings, and so it is my painful duty to tell you that an example must be made. At noon tomorrow, the execution will take place of the remaining seven American prisoners. However, we do not think this is enough. We must bring it home to the British prisoners also, that it is futile and dangerous to try to escape. So, seven British prisoners will also face the firing squad.

I repeat, we will not tolerate this kind of activity. That is all. You will reassemble as usual tomorrow at 6.00am. for roll call, and then again at noon, for the executions.

Douglas Browning was asleep when they came for him at 2.00am. the other six were: David Chester, Phillip Forester, John Sims, Gregory Harding, Tim Hicks and Harry Legg.

Fourteen posts had been erected near the perimeter fence. The fourteen condemned men were tied to the posts at the ankles, their wrists were tied behind their backs and behind the posts. They were not given blindfolds. The firing squad also numbered fourteen – one for each prisoner.

Douglas could not control his fear. He urinated involuntarily. His breath came in gasps. His thinking process went into freefall: "Oh Christ, why me? God, spare me. I have done nothing. Celia. My Celia. Pithiock, that was a good time. Oh, little mouse, how brave you were! Now I am the mouse. I do not feel brave, little mouse. Dad, I hope I was a good son to you and Mum. Good bye brothers. Little Finn, I'm sorry. Sorry I did not play with you more."

The rifles were raised. "Take aim. Fire!"

It was over.

CHAPTER 81

One of the most inspired and ingenious designs of the War was what came to be known as Mulberry Harbour. This consisted of huge concrete and steel sections assembled in secrecy on the South Coast of England. These sections were floated across the Channel to Normandy, where they were linked together to form a vast landing stage. Within four days of the initial Normandy landings, more than 320,000 troops, together with 50,000 trucks, tanks and other armoured vehicles, plus artillery, had been brought ashore. Another big factor in the invasion was the Allies air superiority, both in support and protection of the ground forces, and in neutralising enemy oil dumps and other installations. A prime example of this was the daylight Lancaster bombing raid on the concrete pens at Le Havre, which sheltered the German Navy's remaining force of E-Boats. These E-Boats could have wrought terrible damage with their guns and torpedoes amongst the Allied fleet of ships and landing craft, including those ships towing the Mulberry Harbour sections.

It was almost a week after the first landings that the five beachheads: Juno, Gold, Omaha, Utah and Sword, began to join together. It was astonishing that even after these massive landings of troops and materials, the German High Command continued to believe that this was a diversionary tactic, and that the main invasion would be in Belgium or the Pas de Calais. German resistance was ferocious and determined. Progress was slow and costly. The Canadians were grappling with the German 12th SS P:anzer Division, led by the fanatical Colonel Kurt Meyer. At one point, the Panzers had surrounded the Canadian Command Post, until losses forced them to break off the action. The Americans met patchy resistance at first, though some of the opposition turned out not to be German at all, but Poles, Serbs and Russians, whose German officers and NCOs had deserted them! It was a different story when they advanced towards Cherbourg, where flooded fields and thick hedgerows hampered operations. Sheer exhaustion was part of the reason for Monty's reluctance to make a frontal attack on the key city of Caen, an important communications centre for the Germans. Instead, the 2nd Army was ordered to attack Villers-Bocage and Falaise, with the objective of surrounding Caen. Meanwhile, in Central France, near Limoges, the German Army was committing one of the worst atrocities of the whole war, that of the village of Oradour-sur-Glane. Almost the entire population of 642 were massacred. The men were driven into barns and shot. The women and children were herded into the church, which was then set alight. Those who escaped the fire and smoke were maching-gunned.

On the 13th of June, the Germans introduced a new, deadly weapon, aimed at the English capital. The first Flying Bombs, or V1s. In essence they were a robot plane, powered by a ramjet engine that propelled them at 400mph. The engine was programmed to cut out over London or the Home Counties, and the device then nosedived to earth in about 15 seconds, together with its warhead of one ton of high explosive. On June 16th, 73 were recorded as falling on Greater London. In one incident alone, 24 people died when a V1 hit a pub. The demoralizing effect on the public was soon evident. The silence between the engine cutting out and the inevitable huge explosion that followed a few seconds later, was devastating and terrifying. Anti-aircraft batteries managed to destroy a few of these Doodlebugs, as they were nicknamed. But far too many got through. RAF fighters headed out over the Channel and were more effective, sometimes shooting them down into the sea, or exploding them in mid-air, before they crossed the Kent or Sussex coastline. For those that did get through a new technique was developed – highly dangerous, but grimly amusing. The RAF fighter, often a Hawker Tempest, manoeuvred alongside the V1, inching close enough so that one of its wings tucked under the wing of the V1, and then banked sharply, so that the enemy missile was tipped and turned, to head back whence it came – towards the launching ramps in Northern France and Belgium.

Sometimes the technique failed and both the flying bomb and the British fighter collided with lethal effect to both.

The Blitz took place mostly at night, so that during the day more or less normal life could be conducted. Only at night did people settle down in their air raid shelters, or in the Underground Stations. This was different. The V bombs were launched at any time of day. The first people knew one was approaching, was the menacing and unmistakable drone as the missile approached. Ant then the silence. Worst of all was the silence.

Finn was having lunch with Bobby in the kitchen. It was a bright, sunny morning when they heard the distant, deadly drone. It was July. He should have been at school, but had been to the dentist for a filling. Sensibly, they should have hurried to the cupboard under the stairs, but Finn ran into the garden to watch the Doodlebug pass over. But, it did not pass over: as he gazed up into the clear blue sky, its engine cut out. He could see it plainly: it was flying at about fifteen hundred feet. He watched as its nose dropped. As it loomed larger he realized to his horror that it was falling directly towards him. He was transfixed. He experienced an awful fascination as he watched

Death coming for him. Curiously, he did not feel fear. Just fascination. It was rather like watching the snake and its mongoose. There was no doubt its course was directly towards him and no intervention could possibly stop it. He closed his eyes and covered his head with his arms. A futile action, but instinctive. He waited. Nothing. Finally, he opened his eyes again. As he gazed up at the bomb it seemed it was almost an arm's length away. There was no reason why it suddenly banked to its left, but spin away it did and Finn saw it plummet down beyond the rooftops and out of view. The Doodlebug struck an Old Peoples' Home in Pine Gardens – 300 hundred yards away. Finn did not know that at that moment. All Finn saw was a huge pall of black smoke and debris flying high into the sky above the trees and rooftops. There were large black lumps up there: bricks and mortars, and earth, and flesh and bone. Of course in those few seconds it all looked much the same…

As Bobby rushed out to join him, the smoke was still drifting nearer, blown on the westerly breeze. "Oh Finn, I could murder you. You should have stayed inside. Thank God you are all right." "Oh, don't fuss. I'm fine. I'm going to see where it hit. Maybe there is something I can do to help. You coming?"

Bobby knew it was useless to try and stop him. He was thirteen now, and he would never have listened to her. "No, you go. But be careful and don't go too close, or get in the way of the Fire and Ambulance people. Finn, promise!" Finn nodded and ran to fetch his bike from the garage.

By the time he arrived at Cedar Gardens, the emergency services were already busy on the scene. The Police had run a tape across the road some thirty yards from where the bomb had struck. Finn stood and watched. Two houses had been demolished. No. 13, the one with the Old People, and No. 15 next door. The road itself was covered in earth and brickwork, but the houses were just a fifteen foot high pile of rubble. Finn could see pieces of shattered furniture: a bed, a wardrobe, armchairs, window frames. Broken glass and china were everywhere, and incongruous objects: a Teddy Bear, books, broken vases, a lavatory seat. Did old people still have Teddy Bears? He wondered. He saw blood, too. Two old men were huddled together on the kerb, wrapped in blankets. They were covered in dust. One was bleeding from a cut on his forehead. The other's blanket was stained crimson. They just sat, not moving. Not speaking. Nearby, ARP Wardens and Firemen were digging in the piles of bricks, and then a shout: "Found one!"

A policeman came up to Finn and said gently: "Son, I don't think you should stay here, this is no place for youngsters. Off you go home, laddie."

As Finn mounted his bike, he saw two Ambulance men emerge from what had been the back garden. They carried a stretcher, the shape on it completely covered with a white, blood stained sheet. A motionless arm hung from it.

When Finn got home, he was sick.

CHAPTER 82

Kenneth was commissioned into the Royal Regiment of Artillery on July10th, and was immediately posted to 14 Anti Aircraft Regiment, defending Portsmouth. The two main springboards for the Normandy invasion were Portsmouth and Plymouth, and were prime targets for the Luftwaffe. As key Naval Bases, they had been targets throughout the war, but never more than now. 2nd Lt. K Browning had hoped for a more exciting posting, perhaps in the Far East. Command of a troop of Ack Ack guns in Hampshire was not his idea of glamour, but for now it would have to do. At least he was in little danger. He consoled himself with the thought that as the campaign in France progressed, there might well be the prospect of a move across the Channel, and eventually into Germany itself.

Naturally enough, Claud and Bobby were relieved. Already one son had been seriously wounded and another was a POW. And if that was not enough, even Finn had looked down the throat of a Doodlebug. All this seemed to affect Claud more than Bobby. He seemed irritable, snapping at Bobby over trivialities. His sleep was restless, his appetite thin. To add to these worries, his column for the paper was becoming harder to concentrate upon, and he began to miss deadlines. One July day, in the office in Fleet Street, Gordon Johns asked Claud to join him for a lunchtime sandwich and coffee.

"Claud, old friend, you seem a bit out of sorts. Anything bothering you?"

"No, Gordon, nothing specific. Just not sleeping very soundly. Getting old, I suppose."

"Old, Claud? For Heaven's sake man, you're only fifty four. That's five years younger than me!"

"You've not had two heart attacks though, have you?"

"True, but not putting too fine a point on it, I DO carry a heavier load, remember."

"I don't deny it, Gordon. But you don't have three boys in uniform. And you don't have one of them in a POW Camp. I worry myself stiff about him, and now Kenneth is banging off guns too, even if it is only at Pompey. He could be across the water into France at any time.

"Yes, I fully understand, Claud. It's tough. I've got a suggestion. Why don't you work your socks off for two weeks and conjure up enough material for three week's columns. Then take a break. Take Bobby off somewhere quiet and peaceful. You've still got one lad at home, I know, but I daresay he could board at that school of his for a while. Isn't he Head Boy this term? Probably do him a power of good, too. What do you think? Oh, the paper will foot the extra for boarding, if you like. I don't think that will bankrupt us."

"That's very generous, Gordon. Let me think about it and I would need to check that Bobby could get away. These broadcasts she is making seem to be having quite an impact in Norway. The people at the Norwegian Embassy would have to ok it, though I suppose she could do the same as me – work up enough items for several transmissions – they don't have to be related to war events, which is a blessing. I'll get back to you as soon as I can."

It was a relief to Bobby to hear Gordon John's proposition. It was mid-summer and steaming hot. A perfect time to get away. Finn leapt at the idea of boarding for a couple of weeks. Apart from anything else, it would allow him more opportunity to do Athletics practice. With the long double Summertime evenings it was staying light until 11 pm, so he could go out on the field after Prep, when the juniors had gone to bed. The annual inter-schools meeting was at the end of the month, to be held once again at Burns Court, Esher.

Bobby got clearance from the Embassy, so it was just a question of where to go. The answer to that came from the Petersons next door.

"Ever been to the Scilly Isles, Bobby? Do you even know where they are?" Dr. Peterson laughed. "I doubt if one in a hundred English citizens know, let alone people from other countries, and I doubt if one in a thousand have actually been there. But I can tell you this: they are the most remote and peaceful place in England. Fully comparable with some of our Scottish islands, and that is praise indeed. And they are beautiful beyond measure. In all there are about one hundred island in the group, but only five are inhabited. The people there only scratch a living, but anyone there who does have a decent income is quids in, because there is no Income Tax for residents. Just like the Channel Isles, except that they are not under Nazi occupation. I am sure you would love it. I went there a couple of times as a young man, before I got married, just to indulge my passion for bird watching. A lot of migrating birds drop off there and you sometimes see species from as far afield as America, blown off course by the jet stream. If you are interested, I will enquire if you can get there in wartime, but I imagine you can." Bobby had been thinking (and knew that Claud had) of either going back to Pithiock to lodge with that dreadful, whisky-sodden wreck of a man Avondale, or to Rosedown, to stay with the General and his wife. She felt Scilly sounded idyllic, and a complete escape from everything and everybody.

A few days later, Dr Peterson called round. "You CAN get there if you want to", he informed them. "There is a once weekly supply boat, or, if you don't fancy being torpedoed by a U-Boat, you can fly. People of various kinds have to get there for one reason or another. You know, Government folk, business people and of course, military personnel. There is a once-a-week service of DeHavilland Rapides. They use a little airfield near Land's end and I have established that any member of the public can book seats. Have you ever flown? I'm told it is quite exciting. And if you are lucky, you might get an RAF escort.

Apparently, there is a squadron of Hurricanes based on St.Mary's, the main island. Fancy risking it? They've only had one Rapide shot down during the whole war, and that was years ago. Anyway, there are not many Messerschmitts around these days: they're too busy trying to stop our chaps advancing towards Paris, I'd say!"

Bobby's eyes lit up. She had never been in an aeroplane. Nor had Claud.

"Do you think we could risk it, Claud? It really sounds exciting. And if it is as lovely as Dr. Peterson says, it would be wonderful for both of us, especially you. You really do need to get away from everything for a while."

"No more than you, dear. But yes, it does sound very tempting. I'll check it out. I don't think the risk of getting attacked should put us off. The flight only takes twenty or so minutes.

Instinct told Bobby that it was right to go; that Scilly would be invigorating in the physical sense, but more importantly would recharge their minds and spirit. They had not been alone together, not really alone for a long time. Whilst their marriage was on a firm base, there was a staleness to it. Perhaps, she thought, this is normal after twenty odd years, and even more so with the stresses of war. Sex had become a rarity. A perfunctory kiss at bedtime was about the sum of it these days, and not all the fault lay with Claud. Bobby felt guilt. She recalled the many occasions when she had lain awake at night and thought of Lars. Was he still alive? Would she ever see him again? She visualised him sleeping rough in some mountain hide out, a kitbag for a pillow and a rifle at his side. No, Scilly was not merely desirable. It was needed. It was time for reappraisal and renewal, and those distant islands might just be the ideal stimulus.

"Darling, I've fixed it. We can take the night train from Paddington to Penzance. Then a taxi to the airfield at a little place called St. Just – it's not far from Land's End. The aircraft is twin engined and takes seven passengers, and it lands on the Golf Course at St. Mary's, the main island. There is a proper airstrip, but it's for the exclusive use of the RAF during wartime. There is a flight of Hurricanes there, mainly to protect shipping from air attack, and to protect the once-a-week passenger flight, but sometimes to have a go at Jerry bombers scurrying back to France after bombing Plymouth and Falmouth I have booked the flight for next Friday, so we can take the train on Thursday night."

"Goodee, you haven't forgotten to book the hotel, have you? I don't want to sleep on the beach"

"Hotel? Well, no, I haven't actually. I've booked us into a guest house on St .Agnes, the smallest and most remote of the islands. I just thought it sounded more romantic being that much smaller and with hardly any people living there. The guest house is owned by a Mr and Mrs. Trevena, and they sound really nice. They said they'd had hardly anyone stay there since the war started, which was honest of them. I hope that's ok. Apparently St Agnes is very beautiful and we can just walk, or sit on the beach. Mrs Trevena said that although there are anti-tank defences on St. Mary's beaches, no one thought it worth while to bother on such a tiny place as St.Agnes. Only about eighty people live there. So we can loll about or go swimming if we feel like it, or maybe I could borrow a rod and catch a mackerel or two – I haven't fished since I was a boy" Claud's eyes sparkled like a lad who had just found sixpence.

Bobby hugged him. "Marvellous. It will be heavenly just to be alone with you for a spell and not have to worry about finding food for supper. I'm so fed up with the rationing and maybe Mrs Trevena would grill the mackerel for us, if you ever catch one. Perhaps we could try shrimping as well. I love them and you just can't get them these days. I'm going straight round to the Public Library to see what I can find out about the Scillies, and especially St. Agnes"

St Just Airfield consisted of a few tin huts and a camouflaged hangar for the two Rapides. Neither of the planes was visible – too tempting a target for any passing Luftwaffe bomber heading back across the Channel. Their tickets were checked and baggage handed in at one of the huts and then, together with the other three passengers, they were shown to a second hut to await their summons to the aircraft. Tea from a large enamel pot was offered by an attendant, a gentleman well past the first flush of youth, who turned out to be the co-pilot. Bobby could not hide her excitement. Guilt was one emotion. Should she have left Finn? Anticipation of flying for the very first

331

time was another thrill, and even more so with the threat, albeit small, of being attacked by an enemy aircraft. Staying on some remote rocky island out in the Atlantic. Being alone with her beloved Claud, really alone. Would he make love to her? Would they find a lonely spot overlooking the ocean and lose all inhibitions, and make love in the heather? She told herself not to be silly, that she was not eighteen any more. But deep inside, in that secret pit of the stomach, she sensed that delicious agony of desire for him to take her.

They were called to the aircraft. In happier times the Rapide would have been gleaming silver. Not now. It was camouflaged a drab brown and green. Sadly, the windows were painted over too. The pilot apologised for this: "There are things down there that the military folk would prefer stayed unseen, though what I have no idea!" the flight took twenty-five minutes. They flew quite low, at one thousand feet. Claud held Bobby's hand the whole way. Outwardly, this gesture meant "isn't flying exciting?", but for Bobby it meant more than that. To her, it also conveyed a deeper message: "I love you my darling." The plane skimmed over St Mary's Harbour and with a couple of bumps came to rest on the Golf Course.. The pilot turned and grinned: "This is it folks, the most remote airstrip in England. I have to watch out for the bunkers though. There is a squadron of Hurricanes based on the island, so you should be safe enough!" A few hundred yards away, a flight of three Hurricanes and a Coastal Command Anson could just be spotted, parked on the airfield proper. "Anyway, I hope you have a nice stay – Scilly really is a jewel in the ocean."

An old bus drove them down to the harbour. "Old Grenville Stitch should be around somewhere – he'll be pottering across to St Agnes before long" said the bus driver. He knows you are coming, so don't fret – you'll get there all right." It all seemed a far cry from suburban Surrey, and catching the train to Waterloo, but Bobby immediately felt at home. There was little sense of war here, only the tranquility and pace of life of a community that would be not be stirred if they did not feel like it. Bobby was reminded of the old maxim "don't do it today, if it will wait until tomorrow". She felt it should be amended to "If you don't have to do it, DON'T!"

They waited on the stone quay. The sun was warm, the tide full. A few fishing boats were on moorings in the harbour, and a couple of long rowing boats tied to the quay itself. There was the gentlest of breezes, imparting a shimmer to the water. Old Grenville's boat was really an ancient fishing smack, open except for a small cuddy, and its scuppers littered with smelly nets and lobster pots. "Yer can sit where yer likes" he grunted, "yers woan get wet, sea's as smooth as a babe's backside today." He grunted and chewed on his ancient briar pipe. It wasn't alight. "Yers city folk, 'spect?" "Yes, we live outside London" Claud replied. "We thought we would get away from the Doodlebugs for a bit." "Doodlebugs? That's them flying bombs, aint it? Heard about them. Nasty things by all accounts. Still, you can rest easy. You woan find them here, thank the Lord. Though we did have a Heinkel once. Bugger dropped a brace bombs either side of young Herbie, out in Periglis Bay. Blew 'im twenty feet int' air. Made quite a splash comin' down. But he wuz all in one piece, tho' So was 'is boat. Still fishing he is."

Gilbert Trevena met them at Perconger Quay on St Agnes. Almost all comings and goings took place here – a stone finger sloping into the ocean and pointing back at St Mary's. There was another island a couple of hundred yards away, called Gugh, which they learned was connected to St Agnes via a sand bar at low tide. They could see two dwellings there, side by side, with curiously curved roofs, that reminded Bobby of surging waves. She thought she might have seen something like them in Holland, before the war. Very odd. Gilbert was a grizzled old man of about seventy, short and wiry, no more than 5 foot 5inches, but straight as a ramrod. His features were leathery and weathered by a lifetime of sea and storm. His eyes were watery, but still with a merry dance in them. "Pleased t'meet yer both. I'm Gilbert Trevena. And this is Wilhelmina" he added patting the old nag on its flank. "Tis good of you to come so far. Doan get many visitors this far out nowadays. Maisie'll make you at home, though, have no doubt. Get you up in the cart, then."

The track from the quay wound past a boat house, with a steep slipway in front of it, then up hill for a time, running beside a narrow channel on the other side of which was Gugh. "That be Gugh" Gilbert informed them. "If you weren't to know, you'd say it was Gug, like Rug, but hereabouts it's called Gew, rhyming with Hugh. 'Tis a fine and windswept place. As likely as not, you'll meet no one over there, mind, except the gulls – there's plenty o' them, and rabbits. Some fancy bloke built them two houses back in the Twenties —he reckoned the funny shape would wear well in the gales, but there's nowt wrong with the ordinary pitched slate that the rest of us has. They bin there for a couple of hundred years. More in many cases." Round a bend in the track they saw the lighthouse towering above them. It dominated the whole island, with a fine double-gabled house attached to its foot. "Not used now" Gilbert said. "Built way back in the nineties. That's the sixteen nineties. Used to have to drag coal all the way to the top to keep it burning, poor devils. Broke a few backs that did!" The track divided there, one arm going straight on, the other to the right, and down past a little school building, and the Parsonage. One more twist in the track and Wilhelmina came to a halt beside a small granite cottage. "Here we be, and here you be. Tis not a Palace, but tis warm and comfortable, and clean as a new pin. Maisie sees to that." the cottage stood half way down a steep slope, with a fine view across a flat meadow with a large pond and then the ocean, spattered with great granite outcrops. To the north, across the sound, Claud could see two other islands: one he guessed would be Tresco, the other looked deserted. Maisie Trevena greeted them at the door. She was even smaller than her husband. "Come on in, you two. Welcome to Tean cottage. What a journey you must have had. I can't imagine such a trek, but there, as far as I have ever been is St. Mary's. No, I tell a lie. Once when I was a lot younger than now, I ventured over to St. Martin's – but only the once, mind you. Anyways, that's enough o' thaaat. I'll show you upstairs, and then you can come down and Is'll find you summat to eat – you must be starved. Would it best suit you to be called Mr and Mrs Browning, or might you prefer summat less formal? Anyways, you call us Maisie and Gilbert."

"Oh no, Maisie, do please call us Claud and Bobby. We'd much prefer that, thank you."

Their room was cramped: the double bed was hard against one wall and only a foot away from the other. The little sash window was no more than 36 x 36 inches and curiously only about one foot above floor level. To see out, either one had to kneel, or, Claud calculated, you might see a little lying flat in bed. There was one small chest of drawers, and a curtained alcove for hanging suits and dresses. Claud wondered how on earth the Trevenas had ever got a double bed into this tiny room. The bathroom and toilet were downstairs. The bath was an old zinc bath, with just enough room to sit in, with knees well bent. "No room for header tanks in these old cottages" Gilbert told them. "Folk were tiddy bit tiny in those days, living on limpets for the most part, and a few tatties if they could grow them. And the sea spinach of course. Oh, and yer better know now: we only have the electric for a few hours a day. That's with the little jennie running, an' it cost a packet to run a generator – 'tis diesel an' it costs to fetch it here." "Oh, I am sure we will manage just fine" Bobby interjected. "And what's the sea for, if not to keep oneself clean!".

Despite its unpretentiousness, Bobby felt immediately that she would enjoy being at Tean Cottage and that she would enjoy the company of Gilbert and Maisie. After only an hour or two on St Agnes, she felt she had been there all her life. Only a few score of people lived here. Their life was simple and austere: fishing, flower farming (she learned quickly that narcissi and daffodils bloomed several months earlier than on the mainland), a bit of boat building, a few pigs and cows and chickens. Way back an important industry was kelping, the process of slow-burning the kelp seaweed for use in the making of soap and glass, but that had died out half a century ago. There was not much for the Agnes folk, but then they did not need much. They had the sea, a patch of land and each other. It was much akin to being adrift in a lifeboat: they had to help and get on with one another merely to survive.

There were things to learn about life on St Agnes, and Gilbert and Maisie were willing teachers. The first was the Water Situation. Water came from wells and rain collection. There was no mains supply. "I'll need you to be really sparing with water. Will you mind having only one bath a week, please. The toilet and wash boiler take rain water. It's pretty pure, too, of course, 'cos of the eel in the rainwater tank." Claud and Bobby were aghast: "An eel? Surely not!"

"Oh yes", Maisie replied "Bin there since I was a child. Most folk have one. Well known to purify, though what's wrong with plain rain in the first place, I often ask. 'tis only that some people think the gulls mess it up a bit, but what we all say is:

"well, you've got to eat a bit of dirt before you die, don't 'ee." And Maisie laughed like a tumbling stream.

The next thing they learned was that there was no mains electricity. One or two households had a little generator, run on petrol, which they ran for just a few hours a day. It could have been longer, but it was beyond the means of most folk to afford. In winter, heating was by the kitchen range, and open fires in the main rooms. They were coal fed if you could get it, but mostly they burned drift wood off the beaches.

The first night they ate fish pie. Gilbert had caught the pollock that morning, before Claud and Bobby arrived. With it were boiled potatoes and spinach. "Sea spinach grows wild all round the banks, behind the beaches. "It doesn't look like cultivated spinach, but it tastes much the same. 'tis out of season really, but there's still a bit growing down at Per Killier. Full of iron it is. Do you real good. Best of all, it's free, and not on ration!" Again Maisie broke into her delightful laugh. "Puddin 's a problem this time of year. Too early for apples and pears, but we've got a few raspberry canes bearin' well, and a little cream to go with them, so that'll do you wont it? And tomorrow night there ought to be a tasty lobster or crab for your dinner. How would thaaat suit yer?" In Surbiton, lobster and crab was unheard of, and even if the fishmonger ever had them, they would have been far too expensive for the Browning family.

After they had eaten, they strolled down the track and round to Periglis Bay. It was nearing sunset by now. The ocean was still. A few small boats were moored in the Bay. In the distance, beyond a profusion of menacing granite islands and outcrops, they could see The Bishop, the most westerly lighthouse in England. Four miles from shore it stood, perched on a rock and exposed to all the ferocity of sea and storm. Many a ship had foundered there, and many a life lost. Claud shuddered at the thought of manning such a lighthouse. How lonely it must be to live so cut off from the rest of mankind. It must take a special kind of man. To the east, four miles of sea and rock between it and St Agnes, to the west thousands of miles of Atlantic Ocean, until the eastern shores of America and Canada. A mile from where they stood, well short of The Bishop, Claud noticed another island. It was silhouetted in the dying sun. On it stood rocky outcrops that seemed like weird shaped buildings.

Ruined churches perhaps. But in truth they were just carns – rock outcrops shaped by thousands of years of battering by the elements. The island was called Annet. Its population was thousands of birds: gulls , puffins, shearwaters, shags and cormorants. "Oh and a good few poor souls washed up there from the wrecks, of course. The T. W. Lawson went down there in 1907. An amazing ship she was – the only seven master ever built, and twenty five sails.

Many folk were saved, but the cox'n of the St Agnes lifeboat gave his life on that black day." Gilbert knew about all the wrecks. Hundreds of them. "Ay, and a few are buried under where you are standing this very moment, wouldn't be surprised."

Claud and Bobby slept like the dead that night, and awoke to the smell of bacon being grilled. A knock at the door and there was Maisie with two mugs of steaming tea. "Now then, you two, hope you're well rested, but it's time to be up and about now. It's a fine morning and I fancied you'd enjoy some bacon and eggs for your breakfast. 'Fraid I can't promise the bacon every day, though, 'tis just that Gilbert's brother killed one o' 'is porkers a week back. Should be alright for eggs though – no shortage of them, and no ration books required! Olly Higgs keeps a few score hens and keeps us all supplied year round. And chickens too, when we want them. I'll need your Ration Books for other things though, if you wouldn't mind. During breakfast, Gilbert walked into the small parlour, which doubled as both sitting room and dining room. "Morning to you. Hope your bed was comfortable.

Must have been ready for a good sleep after all that travelling. Did you enjoy the aeroplane ride? You wouldn't catch me in one of those contraptions, 'specially with the Jerries after you. Pity you couldn't see out though. I'm told the islands look a real picture from up above. The water in these parts is as clear as clear can be and the colours have to be seen to be believed. One o' my cousins, he's in the RAF, came over in one o' them Ansons, they're called. He said the water round the Eastern Isles is as blue as the brightest sapphire, and when it gets more shallow why, he said, it turns to as fine a green as unripe apples. Well o' course, you can see thaaat from me boat, but he says no, it doan compare. 'Spose I'll need to take his word for it." Gilbert paused for a moment. Talkin' o' boats, don't spose you'd fancy a trip out? Got to lift me pots this morning, if you're to haave a lobster for your tea. Would welcome some company, like. Mark you, it'll take most of the day. There's better part of five dozen pots needs liftin'. It'll be a bit like hard work, so I'll understand if you say no. Anyways, it may well be that that pretty young wife of yours 'as got some plans for you!"

It was plain to Bobby that Claud would love the experience. Two heart attacks did not render Claud weak, nor helpless. Besides, she DID have plans, and they did not include Claud. She had long wished to take up again the sketching she had so enjoyed as a teenager. Then, before she had left her Homeland, she used to go hiking in the mountains with two other girls, one of whom was a talented artist. It was this girl, Frieda, who had encouraged her to try sketching and she had derived great pleasure from her efforts. With marriage, and bringing up four sons, the sketch book had been put away, but she had come across it when searching in a drawer for blotting paper, and had packed it for this holiday. There was so much to take in here: the Lighthouse was one obvious subject, but even after a single short stroll down at Periglis Bay, she could see many others. the Great Pond on the meadow, encircled with reeds and inhabited by all kinds of water birds, was enchanting. The beach, guarded at its far end by a great mound of granite (Maisie told her these outcrops were usually known as Carns). The little fishing boats moored in the Bay, and, jutting out of the sea to the West, the mass of menacing, deadly rocks, like gigantic sharks teeth, that had claimed thousands of sailors' lives through the centuries. All these, and she knew, many other sights, would keep her sketching the whole time if she allowed it to.

Claud gazed at her appealingly. "Oh, go on man, we can be apart for a few hours. Go and enjoy yourself, and help Gilbert in the process. Though don't let him overdo it, Gilbert. We don't want him having a third heart attack!!"

It may have been a guest house, but Bobby saw no reason not to help Maisie with a little clearing up. Apart from helping, it was a chance to learn a little more about the island, and life on it. The first thing she learned was that the whole of the southern half of the island, there were no habitations, just a wide expanse or downland, a glorious wilderness covered in gorse and heather, interspersed with strange, sometimes tortured rock formations, that sloped and tumbled down to tiny coves and beaches. AT one point, Maisie told her, was the Troytown Maze, a spiralling arrangement of pebbles let into the greensward that legend had it had been constructed more than two centuries ago. Bobby promised herself an early visit to see it. Maisie was grateful for a bit of help, but after an hour told Bobby to be off out, it was a nice, sunny day, and not to waste it stuck indoors. Equipped with a flask of tea, her sketchbook, and Claud's map, and a folding stool that Maisie lent her, Bobby set off to explore. First of all, The Maze. "Follow the track down the hill and round to Periglis and just past the Church you'll see a track to the right. Follow it until you reach Troytown Farm. Keeping the farmhouse to your left side, follow the path that curves round to the south on to Castella Down, and there you'll see the Maze. It isn't much really" said Maisie. The path was dry – there had been little rain in recent weeks, apart from one storm early in June, just when they'd wanted to launch D-Day.

The path ran beside the low granite walls that separated each tiny field from its neighbour. Bobby had never seen such small fields, some no larger than her garden at home. She saw no one on the Downs, just the granite outcrops, agonized shapes formed by thousands of years of torment by the sea, the wind and the rain. The grass was a thin mat, no chance to grow long from constant assault by the elements. But there were myriads of flowers; Sea Drift and little yellow Hawkbit. Here and there were Pimpernels, and a tiny red and yellow flower that she only knew as Egg and Bacon. Best of all, to Bobby's mind were the little patches of Sea Holly – blue-grey prickly foliage and purpley flowers. The foreshore was all boulders, no sand could survive this relentless sea. But on it some child, probably, had made a little pyramid of flattish stones about two feet high, no doubt to topple it by throwing stones at it. And there was The Maze.

It was a labyrinth really, about five or six feet across, formed of rounded stones no more than a foot high. No need to follow its nexus of avenues – one could just step over them. Had it really been laid hundreds of years ago,

338

or was that just a tale, the work of a mischievous imagination? It did not matter. It was part of the strange fascination of this magical island.

It was hard to think that a mere hundred or two miles across the Western Approaches, men, guns, tanks and planes were waging the most terrible war, that human beings were being blasted apart, or dying in agony in pools of blood. Yet here she was, in a place that was pure and tranquil, and so profoundly beautiful. How could this be?

Further on, the path skirted a little bay which the map told her was Santa Warna's Cove. Up to her left she saw The Nag's Head, that seemed to be looking out to sea, towards that terrible bedlam across in Normandy. She walked on to Beady Pool and Horse Point. How many times, she wondered, had stately galleons and men o' war passed by this headland, their first sight of England. Sir Francis Drake and Sir Walter Raleigh must have passed in sight of the spot where she stood. And how many ships had foundered in sight of this small island, on those treacherous Western Rocks? She had not yet heard of that terrible disaster in 1707, when Sir Cloudesley Shovell unwittingly led his fleet on to those jagged rocks only a mile away. Nearly two thousand men lost their lives that tragic night. Bobby set up her stool and began to sketch – but not those deadly rocks. Instead, it was the noble lighthouse that demanded attention, past another strange rock formation. Two mammoth rocks, the one balanced upon the other, the two seeming hardly to touch each other, towering up some fifteen feet out of the surrounding gorse. It was as if a tiny push would part them and send the upper stone rolling down the slope to the sea. For a while she sketched, but then the sun began to work its spell and she laid down her pencil and stretched herself on Maisie's rug. Wispy cirrus hardly moving, like strands of hair, cast the thinnest of veils across the clear sky. She remembered that Douglas, darling Douglas, had told her that he had had to learn all about clouds in his flying training. He said these cirrus clouds were sometimes called Mares Tails. How was he, she wondered? God please keep him\safe. It was several months since she had last heard from him She hoped that no news meant good news, like the old saying.

Damn this war! Damn Hitler and his cronies. They had destroyed the lives of millions and, even now that they were facing defeat, they were still tearing the heart and soul out of a whole Continent. Murder, on a scale never known before in the history of mankind. Killing, and oppression, and cruelty and torture, and for what? What drove a man, and a whole people, to perpetrate these atrocities? It defied comprehension and in a hundred years, a thousand years, this question would still be asked and would still be unanswered. Why? For what?

AS Bobby slept, the sun traversed its ineluctable arc, and hid behind a rock pile. She awoke to find herself in its shadow. A cow had meandered from somewhere and was grazing a few yards from where she lay. Far away a dog barked. It had turned five as she gathered her things and headed back to Tean Cottage. Claud had already returned from his fishing trip. His was the face of an exhilarated man. "Bobby, it was a wonderful day. I've never done anything like it and by Jingo, we lifted not one, but seven lobsters, plus a dozen sizeable crabs. One of the little devils grabbed my finger. My God, it hurt, I just could not get it to let go, but Gilbert showed me what to do – he just grabbed my arm, crab and all, and dipped it into a pail of seawater. And that was it! The crab just let go! Just for a break, we set foot on Annet. A strange place. It was so springy underfoot. Gilbert says that's the result of endless years of sea drift just rotting and forming a deep mattress, like rubber sponge almost. And the birds! Thousands of them. We saw puffins and gannets and terns and oyster catchers and others I have no idea about. Oh, and we saw a warship in the distance. Gilbert thought it was a destroyer. One of ours I hope!" He was like a small boy. For now, the war and indeed the whole world, was forgotten. Maisie prepared crabs, and the largest of the lobsters. The four of them all ate together. After dinner, Gilbert asked if the two of them would care to sup a beer at the pub. "Pub? I didn't know there was a pub here! Yes. That would be a great end to a memorable day. Bobby, you'll come too, won't you? Why don't you come too Maisie and make a nice square number." But Maisie smiled and shook her head. "No, I've plenty to keep me busy until bedtime. You three go and enjoy yourselves." And so the days passed. Together, Claud and Bobby explored the island. An occasional shower apart, the weather stayed fine, and warm. One day, they walked over to Gugh at low tide, and in all innocence disturbed the nesting gulls. Once there, they picnicked amongst the heather and bracken near Dropnose Point, and with the help of a bottle of beer from the shop at Rose Cottage, they dozed off, only to find when they awoke that the sandbar back to St Agnes was almost covered by the incoming tide. They had to wade back, laughing all the way. On another day, they found a boat man prepared to take them over to Samson, and collect them again in time for supper back at Tean Cottage. Once, back in the nineteenth century, Samson had a small community. The remnants of their stone dwellings remained, high up on the southernmost brow. To the east, Samson was flanked by the most perfect white beach, facing Tresco across the shallow channel. Not a soul was there. They were totally alone on the island. "Come on, Bobs, lets strip off and have a swim. No one's going to see, and who cares if they do." Though it was a cloudless summer's day, the water was chilly. They splashed and thrashed to get warm and soon they were. Presently, they lay on Maisie's rug to dry off, and Claud took Bobby in his arms. "No one would see if we made love, either", Claud whispered. "Claud, no. There ARE limits. Tonight though. Tonight darling."

They were sad when their time was up. Sad to leave the Trevenas and sad to leave this blessed isle, and sad that they must return to the bustle of wartime suburban life. They made a vow to return when the war was over, and next time, God willing, together with their children, back from fighting it. Each of them recognized, without putting it into words, that it had healed the sour sterility that had invaded their marriage. It was there, in the glow and sparkle in their eyes, as they looked at one another.

CHAPTER 83

The war raged on.

June 11th. D-Day + 5. The British 7th Armoured Division attacks Caen in Normandy. On the same day, in the Pacific, US forces attack Guam in the Mariana Islands destroying or damaging 200 Japanese aircraft.

June 13th. Marshal Stalin in Moscow praises the D-Day landings saying: "In the whole history of the war there has never been such an undertaking."

June 16th A 16" shell from the battleship "HMS Rodney" lands twenty miles inland in Normandy and kills the Commander of the German 12th SS Panzer Division.

June 17th. Hungary. By this date 340,000 Jews have been deported to slave labour, or death camps since the Nazi invasion.

June 22nd The Red Army launches a massive assault on Nazi forces occupying Byelorussia. For this operation, Russia has amassed 1.2 million men, 5,200 tanks and assault guns, and 6,000 aircraft.

June 23rd. Imphal, India. The Japanese 15th Army that invaded India last March has been defeated. Of the 100,000 Japanese who marched from Burma, 30,000 are dead and 23, 000 wounded. The victory was achieved by four Indian Divisions under the command of Lt. Gen. Scoones.

June 14th D-Day + 18. By this date, 750,000 Allied troops have landed in Normandy.

June 26th. The Germans start to destroy all port facilities as the Allied forces continue to advance eastward.

June 27th. A V1 Flying Bomb lands on Victoria Station, killing 14 people.

June 29th. At a conference in Berchtesgaden Hitler refuses to allow his generals to tell him the true situation on the Western Front. Instead, he promises more jet fighters and V-Weapons.

June 30th. London. A V1 lands on Bush House in the Aldwych, killing 198 people.

June 30th. At Auschwitz, the 1,795 Jews from the island of Corfu arrive after 27 days in sealed boxcars, without food or water. More than half have died on the way. The remainder are immediately gassed and cremated.

CHAPTER 84

While his parents were in the Isles of Scilly, Finn busied himself at Shawbury House with his duties of Head Boy. It was no strain. He was well regarded by staff and respected by fellow students, so no great demands were made of him. This left him plenty of time to attend to his two priorities: one to pass his Common Entrance Exam for St. Luke's College, and two to prepare himself for the forthcoming Inter-Prep Schools Athletics Championships. After failing in 1943 to win all four of his races, this year there must be no mistake. It was his last chance before leaving Shawbury and going on to Dorking. H-M was as keen as he was. It would be a fine feather in the School's cap, as well as a huge achievement for Finn. H-M had taken the trouble to delve back over the results since the competition began in the mid-Thirties. No one had won four track events, nor four individual events of any kind. Besides Finn, his parents and H-M, someone else was pretty keen for Finn to succeed. The one person who had devoted more time, far more, than anyone else to helping the boy, was Shirley Black. With H-M's full approval, Shirley came to the School two afternoons a week, plus one evening, solely to train Finn. She was convinced he could "Do the Foursome". She had never encountered, let alone trained, such a talented pupil.

The Championships were due to take place the day after Bobby and Claud returned from the Scillies. The day was overcast and muggy, but thankfully dry. In his role of County Medical Officer for Health, Dr Peterson had a permit to run his car, and offered to take Bobby, Claud and Finn to the ground in Esher. "Not really cheating the system" he assured them, "I have to be there in my official capacity!"

The ground was packed: competitors, adjudicators and officials, school staff, parents, St. John's Ambulance, catering staff for the refreshment tent, and police. Heats were due to start at 1.30pm There was a buzz of excitement and chatter, especially among the young competitors. The chatter died as the faint drone of the Flying Bomb approached. Everyone stood still and stared at the sky. "There it is" someone cried and pointed to the south, the direction of Claygate, a mile and a half away. Half a mile away, over Arbrook Common, its engine cut and its nose dipped a little. It glided towards them. Strange, usually they fell abruptly. If that had happened it would have fallen to earth on the Common. But this one glided down.

You couldn't run from these things, there was never time. Finn was on the far side of the track from the grandstand, with his parents, Dr Peterson.

Shirley Black had walked over to speak to a friend. The bomb exploded as it hit the corrugated iron roof plumb in the centre of the grandstand. Those sitting there were killed instantly and would have felt no pain. Forty-five died like that. It was far worse for those at each end of the stand. They were struck by shattered steel and splintered wood and body parts and flames and just blast. Another twenty-one died like that, and for most of them death was not instantaneous. Debris was hurled on to the track and beyond, together with bodies and parts of bodies, and still living human beings. Bobby had thrown herself on to Finn three seconds before the impact. Claud and Dr Peterson had ducked behind the doctor's car, but the blast hurled the car on to its side. By some miracle it missed Claud, but the doctor was trapped by his legs. He screamed. He just lay there screaming. Bobby was struck in the buttocks by the remains of a lemonade bottle. It just stuck there, looking incongruous, protruding out of her bottom. Her grey slacks were now stained crimson as the blood poured from the wound. She was unconscious, but at least she had saved Finn from injury. The field was a battleground strewn with bodies, many of them naked as the blast ripped off their clothing. One end of the grandstand still stood, but without a roof. The rest was just a jumble of splintered wood and its mangled steel frame. And human beings, some still moving, some struggling to extricate themselves, some moaning, some screaming, some silent just staring. The smell was not just burning wood. It was burning flesh.

Within moments, with smoke and flame still stretching into the sky above this quiet, respectable, middle-class residential area, those who had survived were endeavouring to help the injured. By chance, the St. John's Ambulance caravan had survived, together with several of its crews. They had first aid equipment, but it had been intended to deal with strains and sprains and the odd grazed knee. Not pumping arteries, not smashed limbs, not the burned and the blinded, not men, women and children who had gathered for an afternoon of innocent competition and sport and were now in a state of deep shock and trauma. They needed a hundred stretchers, not the one or two they had brought "just in case". Four men who had been working in the Cricket Pavilion two hundred yards away, lifted the car off Dr Peterson. Lucky man, he had drifted into unconsciousness. Bobby lay on her side, somehow Finn had extricated himself from under her. Claud knelt beside her, cradling her face. He did not know whether to pull the jagged glass from her flesh, or to leave it. He did the right thing – he left it. Just as well, it was preventing her blood from gushing even faster. Ambulances and fire tenders began to arrive. At first, there were not enough of them. Finn tried to stroke his mother's hair, but he did not know really what he was doing. He could not understand why he was unhurt and his mother injured. Shirley Black had not been hurt and had rushed over to check Finn and his parents were alright. She tried to comfort her protégé. By now, the blood from Bobby's wound was spreading all over her clothes – what was left of them – and staining the grass where she lay. Eventually, help came. Face down, Bobby was gently stretchered away, the bottle still protruding. Finn and Claud went with her.

Gradually, the chaos abated. As well the dead, there were thirty nine desperately wounded and some would not survive. Some had lost limbs. Four were completely blinded. Fourteen were badly burned. The split between adults and children was about even. Of the children, three who died had been at Shawbury House.

Clive and Kenneth were given immediate compassionate leave and came home to be with their parents and young brother. Philippa, with little Charlotte, came to Surbiton to run the home, whilst Bobby recovered. She was in hospital for nine days, at first having to lie face down, and then sitting on an inflated ring. They showed her her wound in a mirror. The scar was an almost perfect circle. And it made her laugh, the sheer incongruity of it.

But the wounds of the terrible scene they had witnessed, the Browning family, stayed with them. They never healed.

CHAPTER 85

After the tragedy, there were mercifully only a few days left of Shawbury House's Summer Term. There could be no question of there being a normal end to the School Year – Sports Day and Prizegiving. As well as the three boys who had been killed, two mothers and one father had also died. Then there were the injured. These included several parents and one member of staff. H-M himself had been at the ground and had witnessed the carnage, but had not been hurt, so he had been able to weigh in and help those who had. Vividly, it brought back memories of the blood bath in France nearly thirty years ago. At least there, those involved had been in uniform, fighting for their country's cause, not innocent women and children.

A note went to every boy's home, advising them of the cancellation of the remaining few days of term, but inviting them to attend a Service of Remembrance for those who had died, to be held at Long Ditton Church, on what would have been Prizegiving Day. Recovering in hospital, Bobby could not attend. But Claud was there, and with him were Clive, Kenneth and Finn. And Shirley Black. There were too many to find seats inside - they just stood in the Church porch or gathered outside.

After the service, outside in the churchyard, H-M approached the Browning family group and Claud introduced him to Clive and Kenneth. Then H-M turned to Finn.

"Finn, this is a sad occasion. I had so been looking forward to seeing you run and I felt sure you would have achieved your ambition. Instead, we are here, and your short time at Shawbury House has come to an abrupt and tragic end. I have felt very proud to have had you at my school, and you have been a great credit to it. I am sure you will do well at St. Luke's, and do not imagine I will not be keeping an eye on you! I expect to see you in the College 1st. XV in a few years time, and be breaking all their records on the running track. I think it is inevitable that had we been able to hold Sports Day you would have won the Victor Ludorum, so I have been down to Turner's the Jewellers and they have engraved a miniature of the Cup with your name on it. May I present it to you now. Well done."

Finn took the cup and shook H-M's hand. "Thank you, sir. I just wish I could have earned it on the track. I will treasure this, though" then Finn turned his back on the little group and walked quickly away, because he could not hold back his tears.

CHAPTER 86

"Good day to you all over there in my homeland. This is Bobby calling from London. I am so sorry that I have not spoken to you these past few weeks, but I hope that when I tell you why, you will be understanding. This is not going to be my usual homely chat. No recipes this time! No tips about dressmaking! No tales of how English housewives do things differently from you girls in Oslo or Bergen or Trondheim!

No. I am going to tell you a story of what is happening right now in Southern England to people like you there in Norway. Ordinary people. Peace loving people. Oh, we know how appalling it must be for you, with those German louts on your doorstep day in, day out. We never forget it. We know too, that your misery and suffering will not endure for very much longer. Yes, we are winning the war against those Nazi criminals. Have no doubt about that. they know it, too. But they refuse to recognize it and have not yet given up. So futilely, they still try to destroy our morale here, by killing innocent people in their hundreds.

I will give you an example.

Three weeks ago, in the area where I live, the school children held an athletics competition. Many schools took part. It was for children aged between ten and thirteen. Many mothers and fathers came to watch their sons and daughters take part. And their brothers and sisters came, and their grandparents, and their teachers. All innocent people who took no part in fighting the war. Many of the relatives sat to watch in the Grandstand, whilst the children were out on the field with the officials who were organising this happy event. The first race was to be held at 1.30pm

At 1.25pm in the southern sky there appeared a small black dot. We all knew what it was by the sound it made. It was the beat of an aero engine, a very distinctive sound that we had all heard before. It was the sound of Hitler's latest weapon, the V1 flying bomb. You there in Norway will not have seen, nor heard a V1. It is an aeroplane without a pilot. It is filled with explosive. When the engine runs out of fuel, what happens? The plane falls to earth and there is a big bang. A very big explosion. Sometimes it falls in the fields or on the hills and then, maybe, it kills a few cows or sheep. But that is not Hitler's intention. He wants it to kill people. He wants it to kill old men and women and young children whose only wish is to run and jump.

So, my friends, that little black dot in the southern sky grew bigger and nearer.

And the sound grew louder. And everyone stopped to look up into the sky, hoping that this vile thing would keep going on and over the field where they were, to drop harmlessly somewhere further on. But when it was nearly overhead, the engine stopped and there was a terrible silence. Then this terrible, disgusting object fell upon those innocent people. Sixty six died instantly. Many more died later. Many others were terribly burned. Others lost arms and legs. Some were blinded.

One of those, who lives next door to me, is a doctor. He was trapped under his car which overturned from the blast. Both his legs were crushed and it is unlikely he will ever walk again. When it was inevitable that this bomb was going to fall on us, I threw my son to the ground and covered him with my body. My son was hoping to win four races – he is very fast. He was unharmed, but a very bizarre thing happened to me. A shattered glass bottle embedded itself in my posterior. Yes, in my backside. It must have looked very peculiar, but it was too painful for me and I lost consciousness. And yet, friends, I was lucky. I was not burned and I was not blinded and I did not lose a limb. And now I am here, in London, sitting on my backside and talking to you.

And what I am saying is this. Soon, we will win this war and you will be free. You will be free from the most evil man and the most evil regime that this world has ever known. He has brought death and destruction on a scale never known in the world's history. You have been the victims of this, as have we here. But I want you to take courage. There is a phrase which has become commonly used in the English language. It is this: "Keep Cool" It means be patient and a happy outcome will soon be yours. Do not despair. Do not do anything rash. Retribution for Hitler and his foul associates is coming, and coming soon. And for you Mr Quisling, you vile traitor. If killing little children is all that is left to Adolf Hitler, then he has already lost. And the victors will be you and me. IT IS NOT LONG NOW. I will speak to you again soon, but now, my bottom is hurting a little. Do I hear you laugh? Fine, you've had little enough to laugh about these past terrible years! Goodbye for now. But it won't be long before I return to my motherland, I promise.

CHAPTER 87

Finn was not sure why the tears came in the Churchyard. Probably it was a cocktail of emotions, rather than just one thing: the horrors he had witnessed, first at the old peoples' home and then, far more ghastly, at the Sports Ground. Then there was the loss of school mates in that tragedy. As well, the sadness that war had deprived him of the chance to win those four races. Or even one of them. And then there was his mother. He loved her so greatly. She had always been there, had always encouraged him in all that he did, had always been calm and patient. Never angry. And the Germans had nearly, so nearly, taken her away too. He told himself that he would hate Germans for the rest of his life.

August was an odd mixture for Finn. There were sustained periods of quiet, interspersed with high moments. He was in the limbo of being between schools. Many of his friends were away from home and others he might never see again. Whilst Bobby was in hospital Philippa stayed with Claud and Finn in Surbiton. He had never previously given much thought to his sister-in-law, nor about his little niece Charlotte. Now they were there all the time and he drew a quiet pleasure from amusing Charlotte and feeding her, and chatting with his aunt. Philippa regaled him with stories of her childhood in Dorset, of chasing rabbits, and fishing in the nearby trout stream and of going down to Seatown on the coast and bathing in the sea in the shadow of Golden Cap. One high spot was when his brother Clive managed two 72 hour passes, and on one took Finn cycling all the way to the South Coast at Felpham, near where they had been when war broke out five years ago. It was a shame that they could not go on the beach – still barred by tank traps and obstacles from the old threat of invasion. But they did go to look at Mimosa cottage, where they had holidayed in those memorable years before the war began. To cycle all the sixty odd miles back home on the same day was too much, especially for Clive with his wounded leg, so they spent the night in Bognor Youth Hostel, and returned home next day.

Finn paid several visits to the Convalescent Home at Headley. Now that he was a little older he could help the staff more with the chores and still have time to spend with those recovering from their wounds. On dry days he would wheel those who could not walk around the grounds to enjoy the sunshine and the peace and quiet, and the perfumed roses. One of these men was fit enough to set up Croquet on the lawn and Finn became quite proficient at the game. He promised himself that one day he would go back to Shawbury House and challenge H-M to a game! On another day, he asked his father to contact the adjutant at Wisley, to see if he could make another visit there.

He was met at the Gate House by his old friend, once the ferocious adversary, Snarlichops and his minder Flight Sgt Owen. "Heavens, you've grown, young Finn, you're catching me up". Beside him, Snarlichops lay on his haunches, growling quietly. "Snarlichops, do you remember young Finn? Come on, stand up you lazy bugger, and shake his hand." Whereupon the Alsatian stood and offered Finn his right front paw. "You sure it's alright Mr Owen?" "Yes, he knows you. Take his paw and give it a gentle shake. And you can pat his head if you like, too." As they talked, a Westland Lysander landed and came to rest on the apron outside the Offices. "That's the type of aircraft that flies over to France and lands secret agents behind the German lines. Do you know, Finn, that it can land and take off on the length of a football pitch. Amazing. That's the Station Commander climbing out. I daresay he'll remember you from last time you came to the base. Come and say hello."

Group Captain Tilsley did remember Finn. "Didn't we show you over one of the Wellies, young man?" "Yes, sir, it was great. I hope I may fly one, one day."

"Well, you'll have to get a move on. They're being phased out by bigger and faster bombers. I would love to authorize a flight for you, but I am afraid it would be breaking every rule in the book. However, there might be an alternative that would appeal to you. If you've got time to spare, I don't think there would be repercussions if we did a couple of circuits in this Lysander. It is not an offensive aircraft like the Wellington. Anyway, who's running the show here? It's me isn't it! Have you ever been up in an aeorplane?"

"Gosh, no sir."

"Well, would you like to? I've just flown in from Kenley, the fighter station south of Croydon, and I was going on to Brooklands this afternoon, after lunch. But we could go now if you like and p'haps get a sandwich over there. I used to go and watch the car racing over there before the war. Great fun. They build new, and repair old, war torn Wellies there now, same as here. D'you think your parents would mind? We could call them if you think there is a doubt."

"Oh no sir. Anyway my mother is in hospital. She was injured by that Doodlebug that hit the Sports Field at Esher last month. And Dad is in London. I'm sure they would not mind.

"Where does this interest in aircraft spring from, Finn? Did your father fly in the Great War?"

"No, he was in the trenches, sir. I suppose it is because my eldest brother went into the RAF. He was a tail gunner in Lancasters until he was wounded. Now he trains air gunners instead. Then another brother, Douglas, joined the Royal Navy, but was seconded to the Fleet Air Arm. He was taken prisoner in Italy, though. As far as we know, he's alright, but we have heard nothing for some time now, which is a bit worrying."

"Well, that certainly explains your interest. Now let's see if we can get you fitted out with some flying gear. You're a bit small, but we can probably find something to fit. Did you know, we have young ladies flying now. Transport Command. They deliver planes from the factory to whichever station they are going to be based at. They call them Ferry Pilots, and some of them are pretty tiny, no bigger than you in some cases. Come on."

The Lysander did not reach much of an altitude on the short journey, but it was quite enough to give Finn the greatest thrill of his young life. Tilsley pointed out the Thames over to the right, and Hampton Court Palace, resplendent beside it. Better still, on the return journey that afternoon, Tilsley made a minor diversion and flew the Lysander over Surbiton. Finn was able clearly to pick out the Surbiton Lagoon and the Tennis Club at Berrylands. He was a bit confused by the patchwork of streets and was not sure if he saw his own house or not. When later he cycled home, he was not sure either if the family believed him when he told them he had been flying in a Lysander. It did not matter. He had!

CHAPTER 88

Cherbourg had fallen to the Americans only three weeks after D-Day, but the defence of Caen by German forces was far more stubborn, and Monty came in for heavy criticism from his American counterparts. They accused him of being "unadventurous" and adopting a "they'll be worn down in the end" policy. And General Dempsey's bold attempt to smash through the enemy defences south of Caen was called off due to heavy losses – 5,000 men and 400 tanks.

By the end of July the Americans had made better progress, elsewhere, though with heavy casualties. St. Lo had fallen and they had pressed on southwards towards Avranches, in the Gulf of St. Malo. They were now ready to break out to the West, into the Brest Peninsula, towards Rennes and Dinan, and to the South-East, behind the Germans defending against the British and Canadians in the Caen sector.

Meanwhile, far away on the Eastern Front, the Russian Armies were sweeping westwards into Poland, and by the end of July were on the outskirts of Warsaw.

On July 20th, at Hitler's Wolf Lair in Rastenburg, in the course of a conference, an attempt was made on his life by a group of disillusioned German officers. A brief case, containing a bomb, was placed near to Hitler's chair by Col. Count von Stauffenburg. Unknown to Stauffenburg, the case was inadvertently moved by an officer to enable him to have a better look at the maps on the table. The bomb exploded, but Hitler was only slightly injured. Suspicion fell on von Stauffenburg when an NCO reported seeing him leave the conference in a hurry, just prior to the explosion. He, and the twenty one other conspirators were tried and ordered by the Fuhrer "to be strung up like cattle". They were slowly strangled by piano wire, suspended from meat hooks. Their execution was filmed, and watched by Hitler.

On August 4th, in Amsterdam, a young Jewish girl, who had been hidden from the Gestapo in an attic for two years, was betrayed. He name was Anne Frank, aged fourteen. She was deported, and died, in a Concentration Camp.

After the war, her diary was publihed and became yet another notorious symbol of the horror and monstrosity of the Third Reich.

In Italy also, the German Army was in retreat, and by the beginning of August, had been pushed back north of Florence. The British Army in Italy received a morale boosting visit from Winston Churchill, helping to counter the feeling of "being forgotten, as the focus switched to the invasion of

Normandy. The war in the Far East was progressing more favourably, too. The Allied recapture of the Mariana Islands was completed with the capture of Guam on August 10th. And in Burma, slowly but surely, the Japanese were being forced to retreat by the British "Chindits", under the command of the charismatic Gen. Orde Wingate.

On August 15th, a Second Front in France was opened, when the US Seventh Army stormed ashore on the French Riviera, supported by a force of the Free French Army. The Germans were caught by surprise and Allied casualties were light – only 300 killed out of a force of nearly 400,000 men. Back in Northern France, the Allies crossed the River Seine and advanced to within forty miles of Paris.

In London, reports were published of the liberation by the Red Army of the death camp at Majdanek. Half a million people, mostly Jews, had been

gassed there, and the bodies cremated. The charred remains were pulverized, packed into tins, and then shipped back to Germany to be used as fertilisers.

Claud tried to ensure that Finn did not see these reports, and so pictures never appeared in his scrapbook. But Finn heard of it anyway, via friends. A year later, as the war ended, horrific photos and film of the liberation of these Concentration Camps were published in newspapers and at cinemas. It was not practicable, and not even desirable, that young people of Finn's generation would be shielded from such terrible scenes. The images stayed with Finn and never faded or forgotten, just as the memories of the scenes at the Old Peoples' Home and the Sports Ground could never be erased.

CHAPTER 89

The North Downs run from Guildford in the West to Maidstone in the East, and so link Surrey with Kent. Leith Hill is the highest point of the Downs in Surrey, nearly one thousand feet above sea level, and from there you can see almost to the Sussex Coastline at Brighton. A few miles further east of Leith Hill lies Dorking, nestling in a valley, in the shadow of another high point in the Downs, called Box Hill. It is a pleasant middle class community and an admirable setting for St Luke's College, the red brick buildings blending serenely with the red brick housing estates all around it.

Finn's first term, the Winter Term of 1944, commenced on the first Tuesday in September. Although by then Bobby was back home after her ordeal, it was Claud who took his son to Dorking, on the Greenline coach. Finn was one of some eighty boys, plus parents, who were directed into the Assembly Hall for an address by Donny Doncaster. He did not waste time, nor words.

"Good afternoon, ladies and gentlemen, and new pupils. Boys, this is the beginning of your time at St. Luke's. Probably, unless you make a hash of things, you will be here for four years and when you leave you will be on the verge of manhood. Seventeen, maybe eighteen. In a year or less after that, you will be old enough to serve in His Majesty's Armed Forces. You will be able to vote in a General Election, and you could marry without parental consent. You could also be hanged for murder. I make no connection between marriage and murder!" Roars of laughter, especially from the parents present. Donny Doncaster continued: "Hopefully, by then, you will be fit for purpose. That means you will have enough of an academic armoury, and sufficient general knowledge and common sense, to enable you to survive and flourish in the outside world. Make no mistake: it is a tough, wicked world out there and you will need all the weapons you can acquire at this establishment to make your way through life. The staff here will help you all we can. And so will the older boys. But it is up to you to take full advantage of what is on offer here. Not so far away, in Wimbledon, there is a school called KCS – King's College School. Well, we have KCS here as well. K is for Knowledge, C is for Christian spirit and S is for Sport. Try for all three, boys and you will not be sorry! Now, report to your House Masters, who will be standing out on the Quadrangle. They will be holding up a placard with the house name on it. Go and introduce yourselves. Whilst this is going on, tea will be served for accompanying parents in this hall in about ten minutes time. Oh, boys, I nearly forgot, Housemasters names are: North

– Mr Church, East is Mr West. Don't laugh!. West is Mr Wilks, South is Mr Shaw and Churchill is Mr Meiklejohn. Finally, say goodbye to your parents as you leave this Hall. Get to it!

Finn grinned at his father. "Dad, I am going to like it here, I just know it. I will not disappoint you, I promise." Claud smiled and took Finn's hand. "I know you will son. See you at the weekend." And he walked over to the tea trolley.

"Mr Church, sir, I am Finn Browning."

"Good day to you Browning. Wait will I collect the rest of the intake." Mr Church shook his hand firmly, and smiled faintly. He was a tall man, at least 6'3", with broad shoulders and narrow hips. He looked in his mid-forties and had a short beard going a little grey. He wore a fawn sports jacket and grey flannels. "Oh, I should have said" pointing to the boy standing at his shoulder, "This is David Silk. He is the Head of House." Silk nodded, but looked as though he wished he was somewhere else. There was an air of disdain about him, as though he thought thirteen year old boys should not be here, getting in the way. He said nothing.

The new boys, together with their bags and cases, were led by Silk to the North wing. Here, they were shown the Junior Day Room, where they were each allocated a locker to accommodate school books, tuck boxes (lockable) and other personal items. This was where they would spend such leisure time as was available. Older boys, in the Fifth and Sixth Forms, had their own Senior Day room. The prefects shared separate Day rooms. Silk then led them to the Dorms. Each Dormitory had ten beds. They were black painted iron bedsteads, with rough white sheets and bright red blankets. Beside each bed was a small cabinet and a chair. "Sort out amongst yourselves who goes where" announced Silk. "You are all new boys in this Dorm. Then return to the Day Room and I will show you around the rest of the College. I'll give you ten minutes."

The tour was comprehensive, but hurried and bewildering, embracing as it did, the Class Room Block, the Chapel, Library, the Infirmary, Changing rooms, Ablution block where Finn was dismayed to notice that none of the toilet cubicles had doors ("taken off in 1940 to be made into Spitfires" they were informed), the Indoor Swimming Pool, Squash Courts (yippee, Finn said to himself), Carpenters Shop and Armoury. Confused to a greater or lesser extent, the new boys were led into Hall for tea. Tea was the evening meal, taken at 6pm, after which, on week days other than today, boys were expected to repair to a classroom to get on with Prep. This would normally be completed by 8pm, after which other activities could be pursued until bedtime, which for Juniors was 9pm with lights out at 9.30pm

Finn settled in quickly. For the first few days he felt a little homesick, even though he knew he would soon be home for the weekend. He was not alone in this – most of the other new boys in North were quiet, and confused about who was who, and where was where. Silk remained aloof, loftily indifferent to these "little squirts". After tea on Day Three, Mr Church summoned Finn for interview at his house in the grounds.

"Good evening, Browning, have a seat. Are you finding your way around alright? I know it can be a bit confusing, but don't worry, you will soon get the hang of it. I have had a phone call from your Prep. School Headmaster, and he has been telling me a thing or two about you." Finn remained silent, wondering what was coming next. "He says you were present at that terrible tragedy at the Sports Ground at Esher. You must have witnessed the most appalling scenes, and your mother was seriously injured there, I understand? I hope she is recovering well?" It was said as a question. "Yes, sir. I am trying to forget about it, but it is hard sometimes to put it out of my thoughts. My mother is out of hospital now, thank you and more or less back to normal." "Well, you must be very relieved. Mr Hamilton-Maxwell also spoke about your sporting abilities. Apparently you play squash with the seniors at your local club. Is that so?"

"Yes sir. I learned when I was evacuated at the outbreak of the war."

"Good. I will ensure you get good use of the courts here. H-M also said that you had shown some promise at Rugger. We need some good players in North. We've fared pretty poorly for a few years now. Perhaps you will help us out of the doldrums. There is a House practice for Juniors tomorrow afternoon. I'll see what you are made of then.

Now, is there anything you want to ask me?"

"I don't think so, sir." Finn hesitated.

" Well, perhaps there is one thing. I am a weekly boarder, as you know. I wanted to be a full boarder, but my parents would not agree to it. I think it may have been because I have three older brothers in the forces, and they did not want me to go away as well. So I think weekly boarding is a sort of compromise. Anyway I just wanted to say that I do not want to miss out on weekend activities, especially sport on Saturday afternoons."

"Don't worry, Browning, it makes no difference whether you are full or weekly boarding, or even if you are a Day Boy, All boys must attend Saturday afternoon games, unless there aren't any. Where you will miss out to some extent is on Sundays. That is when boys do all kind of things that do not occur on the other six days of the week, such as Dramatic Society, Music Society, the Railway club and so on. You may also miss out for consideration as a School Prefect, but I shall watch how you get on, and if I judge you are suitable, then you might become a House Prefect That's still an important role. We will just have to see. Anyway, that is several years off. Alright? You'd better cut away now."

Friday House Rugger practice was taken by the Assistant House Master, "Bunny" Weeks. Bunny was only 27, and had been a rugby blue at Cambridge in 1938. In the following winter of that year Bunny had been skiing in Austria and had been caught by an avalanche. He was lucky to have survived. The avalanche had catapulted him into the trunk of a tree, fracturing his skull, six ribs and his right hip. Unsurprisingly he had failed his medical for Military Service.

"Browning, what position do you play? You look like a winger to me."

"I can play there, sir, but at my Prep School I played fly half in my last season. I think I'm best suited to that."

"Righto, well fly-half is all about ball distribution. Dictating the play. We'll give you a go there and see how you get on. Just for fun, we are going to play Seniors versus Juniors, but only touch rugby – no tackling. If you are touched whilst carrying the ball, play will stop immediately. Finn did well, once making a clean break, and several times timing his passes precisely. But fast and elusive as he was, Finn was "tackled" repeatedly, usually by the opposing open side flanker. The fellow was, after all, a School 1st XV player, and in his last year at the College. Finn left the pitch feeling downcast. Bunny Weeks approached him. "Finn, that was a very promising performance and I certainly intend persisting with you. I'll go further and recommend you for a trial in the School Under 15s. You're big for your age and although you are not yet fourteen, I do not think you will be out of your depth. Anyway, it will not be up to me. It will be up to the School Rugby coach, Mr Hanbury. OK?"

This assurance raised his spirits, though not his expectations.

In the class room Finn applied himself to his work, but inevitably some things came easier than others. Languages came especially easy to him, and he was given the choice of adding Spanish or German to the French language he had studied at Shawbury House. Probably it was the young mind's association with the war, and Germany being the enemy that deterred him from choosing German. It might also have had something to do with the fact that the Spanish tutor, Michael Sears, played squash. Sears had heard that

Finn played squash – very much a minor sport at the College, with few boys interested in it – and had asked him if he would like a game.

The first time they played was in Week Three of the term. Sears was short and wiry and wore spectacles, but was very fast around the court. He won the first game 9-2. Finn had not played much during the Summer, and was rusty. In the second game, Sears won again, this time 9-6, a much more even contest and by the end of it Sears was perspiring slightly. Finn edged him 9-7 in the third game and then 9-5 in the fourth, making the score 2 games each. The decider went all the way and those who knew him knew he was a very dogged man, who could never contemplate defeat – especially at the hands of such a young opponent. Sears won 10-8, at the end of which he was totally exhausted.

"Well done Browning. That really was a great effort and I suspect that had your game been honed to its best, you would have beaten me. I fear you will before the end of term, assuming, naturally, that you are prepared to play a return match." Finn could not stop himself from grinning. "Yes sir, I would very much like to, and I will try my best to gain revenge!"

And so Finn settled into life at St. Luke's. It was not all a bed of roses, though. Silk, the House Captain, seemed to take against Finn. It did not go as far as physical bullying, but whereas he was clearly prepared to help some Juniors, he virtually ignored Finn. Except, that is, when Finn became the first of the new intake to be on the receiving end of Silk's cane. All boys were allowed "Down Town" once a week, as long as they went in pairs. It was an opportunity for them to purchase any items they could not buy in the College tuck shop, (access to the tuck shop was controlled by Donny personally – hence the key that always hung round his neck on a coarse piece of string). It was the rule that all boys must be back in College by 3.45pm, in time for late afternoon classes that took place between 4pm and 6pm.

Finn, along with Johnny Legge, had become absorbed in a bookshop and had lost track of time, and was caught returning through the College gates at 3.55 – ten minutes late. A caning offence.

The cane was a thin hazel stick about two feet in length. The regulation was for it to be administered to the buttocks using "moderate force", and in the presence of a minimum two prefects other than the one doing the caning. Three strokes were permitted, but a fourth if the victim cried out. The pain was excruciating, but Finn managed to take three strokes without uttering a sound. Silk ordered him to bend over again, saying: "Browning, you sobbed on the third stroke. You shall receive a fourth for good measure." Finn knew better than to protest. Neither of the two witnessing prefects interceded. Finn at that moment realized that Silk was a man to be wary of, and to be avoided as far as possible. Why, he could not understand.

Silk was one of those boys, verging on manhood, who had risen to a senior position in the College through sycophancy, rather than talent. He had discovered, and practised well, the craft of ingratiating himself with those who had authority or influence, without them realizing it. Throughout his time at the College, he had been at great pains to keep his nose clean. Here he was, Head of House, and he himself had never once been caned. Far too canny for that! But secretly, inside himself, he knew that his talent was mediocre at best. In Schools Certificate he had achieved seven Credits and two Passes, but no Distinctions. Next summer he would sit the Higher Schools Certificate and had little confidence in meeting his parents expectations of getting to Cambridge. At sport he had enjoyed limited success: he had captained the House teams at both Cricket and Rugby, but had only made the College's 2nd XV, and was an irregular member of the Cricket 1st XI. His sole success was in winning the College cross-country title, known as the Boxer, a six mile run over the fields and hills around Box Hill. He was disappointed in himself, and feared his father was too.

In Finn Browning he rightly recognized from the outset a boy who had talent in abundance, and a strong character to go with it. It was ridiculous, but he was jealous of Finn. He knew Browning had played squash with Sears, the Spanish tutor, and knew he had come close to beating him. Silk had played Sears once and lost 3-0, and here was this whippersnapper nearly beating Sears. And worse, Browning had been picked for the School Under 15s rugger team in its first match, against Whitgift School. Silk had watched the game and seen Browning, time after time, ghost past the Whitgift back row and although not scoring a try himself, had made one for his right wing to do so. Silk was almost glad that Whitgift had won the match 12-6* It was a different matter when it came to the inter-House Junior competition. In the first match, against West, Finn scored twice himself and defended so well that North won 15-0. Silk congratulated the team skipper, but could not bring himself to do the same for Finn.

Although Finn was happy to see his parents at weekends, he felt increasingly resentful that he was missing out on weekend activities. He determined that he would say nothing during this first term, but that in the Christmas holidays he would raise the question of becoming a full boarder. Silk, or no Silk.

Finn had made a number of new friends, both in North House and via the sports field. Two in particular were Philip Cummings, the son of a Vicar who lived near Cranleigh, and Ian Bland, who lived at Steyning in Sussex. Philip was in North, and also in the Under Fifteen XV. He was a burly lad who enjoyed the rough-and-tumble of the scrum. Ian was not in the least sporty, but had a huge sense of fun and humour, typically of the schoolboy variety. (He claimed that he could fart into jam jars and "bottle" the vile gas, and seriously tried to sell the product to any one who would pay for it). This appealed to Finn, though he refrained from making a purchase as Ian would have wished. Ian was a whiz on the piano, but also played the saxophone, and Finn liked nothing better than to listen to Ian at practice. But practice took place mainly on Sundays, yet another reason for Finn wanting to be a full boarder. Both these chums kept asking him why he was only a Weekly Boarder, and it was discomforting for Finn to have to explain that "Dad wants me at home because my three brothers are all away in the forces." "Daddy's Boy" was not an epithet that any boy would enjoy. None more so than Finn.

*In Rugby Football at this time, a Try counted only three points.

CHAPTER 90

On September 1st a map appeared in the National Press showing the latest position of the Allied forces. Finn made sure it was pasted into his scrap book. It illustrated the progress that had been made since the D-Day landings in Normandy, and on the French Riviera. In Northern France, the Allies now held the area to the North of a line that included Nantes on the Brittany coast, eastward to Tours and Orleans, then curving round northwards to Reims, Soissons and up to the Channel coast near Abbeville. Paris itself had fallen on August 25th . the Allied forces in the South of France had now pushed West and North, enfolding Marseilles, Avignon and beyond, to within striking distance of Lyons.

At home, the V1 strikes against South East England were now being overcome. Of 94 launched on August 28th, only 4 reached London. As they crossed the English Channel, these missiles were met first by RAF fighters, who were having increasing success, and then by massive anti-aircraft defence. On the French side of the Channel the Allies were capturing the launch sites. The worst was over.

By the 3rd of September, German troops had evacuated Brussels, and next day British tanks entered Antwerp. The Germans were surrounded at Calais, Boulogne and Dunkirk, but were determined to deny the Allies the use of these ports. It was four years since the brave, but humiliating withdrawal of the British Army from Dunkirk. How sweet would be their return!

On September 6th, the Blackout, that had been maintained through out the War, was at last relaxed, and the Home guard – Dad's Army as it had become known, was stood down.

In Eastern Europe, the Germans were in full retreat. Poland had been largely overrun and the Russians were advancing remorselessly into Bulgaria, Hungary and Rumania. It would not be long before they joined forces with Marshal Tito's Resistance fighters in Yugoslavia.

On September 10th an American jeep crossed the border between Holland and Germany at Aachen – the first incursion into The Third Reich itself. Orleans fell the next day, with the surrender of 20,000 German troops.

On September 12th, Allied forces from the South and North of France linked up at Chatillon-sur-Seine.

Defeat for the Fuhrer was now inevitable.

CHAPTER 91

Douglas did not hear the shot that hit him, nor feel its impact into his body. Too instantaneous. Oblivion.

The fourteen men slumped to the ground, and the bearer party approached to take away the bodies. The Commander of the Firing Squad sauntered over to check the corpses. As he glanced at each in turn, one moved slightly. An American. The Commander drew his pistol. A voice over his shoulder spoke. It was the Camp Commandant: "Don't waste a bullet, Hans, it is just a nerve twitching."

At that moment one of the bearers called out to the two officers: "This one is alive, he is definitely moving!" the two officers walked to where Douglas was now moaning in pain, his eyes open, staring with a look of sheer terror. "This is the English Navy flier, isn't it? Shall we finish him?" He raised his pistol and took aim. "No, wait." The Commandant held up his hand. "No. It is the Americans we most needed to punish. The English we wished to discourage, no more than that. Six have paid the ultimate price. It's enough. We are not barbarians. Take him to the hospital unit." He bent to examine Douglas more closely. Blood was pumping from the bullet wound. The Firing Squad had been instructed to aim for the heart, but the bullet had strayed four inches high and five inches to the right – into Douglas's left shoulder. Douglas faded again into merciful unconsciousness.

When a man is wounded, the shock of the bullet tearing through the flesh is sufficient to throw the victim's nervous system temporarily out of gear. His only sensation is that of numbness and an acute awareness that he has been hit.

Full, blazing pain comes some time later in all its pervasive severity. It was so when Douglas regained consciousness. He felt unable to move. The pain made him gasp.

The recollection of what had happened dawned on him. Why am I not dead? Or am I dead? Where is this place? A nurse approached his bed. She smiled thinly from a thin face, but her pale green eyes had light in them, a light of compassion. "Hello Mr Navy Man. Velcome back to zis vorld. You are a lucky man, I tink. Do you need something for ze pain? Ve do not haf much here, but I vill try to make you comfortable. Der bullet has gone, but it has made much damage. It vill take long time to heal, I tink." She smiled a little more fully. "How is my English? It is difficult to say your Tee Aitch sound, and also your Double You sound." She added "Ven ve conquer England, ve vill make you say it our vay, the German vay". She chuckled.

Douglas looked up at her. She was leaning over him, her blonde hair tumbling over her shoulders. "Please what happened?" the nurse stood up straight. "The fool of a corporal missed your heart". Gently, she touched his chest. "Zat is vere he should have hit you, then I vould not need to look after you. But now I vill do my best to make you good again. Maybe there is a god who looks after you. Or maybe a lady at home who vants you back one day!" the nurse leaned close to Douglas again and whispered: "We are in Poland, but zis is a German Military Hospital. My other patients are all Wehrmacht, so I advise you keep veeery quiet, young man!"

It was four weeks before Douglas was returned to the Prison Camp, amid loud cheers from the other prisoners. It was another nine before they heard the distant rumble of artillery.

CHAPTER 92

Field Marshal Montgomery believed the war against Germany could be shortened by several months. before Christmas even, and many lives saved, by dodging the Siegfried Line. The Siegfried Line was a fortified stretch of German defences constructed in the 1930s along the border with the Netherlands. A concrete network of emplacements, bristling with heavy artillery and machine-guns and thought to be virtually impregnable. Monty's plan was to capture bridges beyond this Line by a mass dropping of troops by parachute and gliders. In effect, bypassing it. The operation known as Market Garden, went seriously wrong. It commenced on September 17th 1944 when American paratroops were sent to capture the bridges over the Rivers Waal and Maas. Meanwhile, the British were to land further on, at Arnhem, where they would take the two bridges over the Lower Rhine. The Germans blew up one bridge before the British Paras could stop them, and at the second they were confronted with a strong force at the South End (the Dutch side) Crucially, they did not know that two additional Panzer Divisions had recently arrived in the area. They came under savage German attack and were trapped. Worse still, radio communications were confused and disrupted and re-supplies fell on ground held by the Germans. Though they battled on heroically, many British and Canadian troops went without water for three days, had little food and insufficient ammunition.

The order to withdraw was finally given on September 26th. Of the 10,000 men involved, less than two and a half thousand escaped, many by swimming across the river, others in boats. One and a half thousand were killed and the remainder taken prisoner.. As a result of this disaster, any hopes of ending the war in Europe before Christmas were stillborn.

In England, ten days before the Arnhem debacle, the public were told that attacks by V1 flying bombs were over. Virtually all the launch sites had been captured, although a few were launched by German bombers over the North Sea. In all, it was calculated that 2,300 V1s got through the defences to the Greater London area, destroying 25,000 homes and killing or injuring 21,000 people.

But the V1s were not the end of Germany's attempt to disrupt life and the war effort in Britain. On the 8th September the first V2 rocket fell in West London, and many more were to follow. These huge rockets filled with explosive, were even more terrifying than their V1 predecessors, since there was no warning whatsoever of their striking. Finn swore that he saw one coming down one bright Sunday morning. Though it was not nearby, he saw a momentary, but distinct flash of silver in the direction of London, followed by a double thunderclap.   One was the missile re-entering the Earth's atmosphere, the other as it hit its target.   There was no defence against these missiles.   Only dumb acceptance.   But the British public, and the inhabitants of Greater London in particular, were by now hardened if not immune to the depredations of war.   And they knew that the end was in sight   Winston Churchill's words at the time of El Alamein that "this is the end of the beginning" could now be amended to "This is the beginning of the end."

Notwithstanding the catastrophe at Arnhem, progress was accelerating. News that the German garrison at Boulogne had surrendered, and that Germany had now perforce to recruit boys of sixteen into their front line army, was grist to the mill of rising morale.   A sprinkling of V2 rockets would not undermine that.

Sadly, on the 25th September, one of the great British heroes of the war, Wing Commander Guy Gibson VC, was killed when his Mosquito crashed in Holland.   It was uncertain whether the plane had been hit, or whether it developed   mechanical trouble.   What was certain is that he was flying too low to bail out.

Gibson was the hero of the Dam Busters saga and had   been awarded the Victoria Cross for his bravery during that raid.   He had seemed untouchable. Early in the war he had flown Blenheims at Dunkirk.   He flew nearly one hundred missions and destroyed six enemy aircraft as a night-fighter pilot, before switching to bombers.   As well as the VC, he had also been awarded the DSO and DFC.

Soon after this tragedy, a very different tragedy occurred on the enemy side.   Field Marshal Rommel, the German hero of the North African campaign, received two generals sent by Hitler.   They told Rommel that he had been linked to the July attempt on Hitler's life, but that if he took his own life, his family would not be placed under arrest.   Rommel took poison and died a few minutes after their visit.   It was never established that he had had any part in the assassination attempt.

Such is war.

CHAPTER 93

By the middle of October Finn felt fully at home in his new school and had a growing number of friends. He was getting on well with most of the teaching staff, especially his Housemaster, Philip Church. Also, he had established a regular place in the School Under 15 Rugby team. The classroom held no horrors either, except the Sciences – Biology, Physics and Chemistry – they were just not his scene. In particular, he did not like the idea of dissecting frogs and mice. This early in his young life, he knew one profession he would <u>never</u> follow was medicine. Mathematics did not come easily, especially Algebra, but he could cope. History should have been more intriguing, he thought, than just memorizing a string of dates.

No country on the planet had a more fascinating history and heritage than Great Britain, but the subject just did not come to life for Finn, at least not then. Divinity, in Finn's view, was simply History from an earlier age, and although he held somewhat tenuously to the Christian faith, he lacked the religious zeal of many boys to study the Bible. Where Finn became increasingly engrossed was in two areas of study: Languages and Geography. The English language was the key to so much in life, Finn realized. Even at his young age he was able to perceive that with English, the whole world was open to him. But following close behind were French and Spanish. This was linked, though he did not realize it, with his pleasure in studying Geography, and a determination that when he was old enough, he would indulge his yearning to travel the world and discover what wonders it could yield..

For Finn, Geography was two things. First, there was the marvel of the physical world: the oceans, the deserts, the mountains and forests. At one extreme were volcanoes, at the other icebergs. Huge waterfalls contrasting with cheery trout streams. Jungles contrasting with the gentle woodlands and fields of Dorset and Devon. Raging seas and village ponds. The clouds and the atmosphere. Lightning and thunder and hurricanes at one extreme. The joy of gently falling snow at the other. And then, there were the world's people, the effect they had on the planet and how they used, and sometimes destroyed, its resources. Their nature, some so calm and gentle, living simple lives and some so violent and greedy and ruthless, like Hitler and the Japanese. Strangely in one so young Finn was curious about his own people – the British. A glance at the political atlas showed that some 40% of the globe was pink – the British empire. How could such a small nation have dominated so huge a portion of the world and its people? Was this a good thing or bad? And if Britain could have two fifths, why should not its enemies have the same? And had not we killed and destroyed in order to gain our empire? The more Finn studied and thought, the more he wanted to know. And as time passed, he determined to make his own study of History, to get under the skin of what had happened over the centuries.

He determined to try harder during his history lessons, but to delve deeper than that outside the classroom. Meantime he beavered away at French and Spanish. All boys at St. Luke's were obliged to join either the Sea Scouts, or the CCF, and most joined the latter, including Finn. The flight in the Lysander had made an indelible impression on Finn and what he really would have liked to do was to join the Air Training Corps. But St. Luke's did not have an ATC Squadron. For now, the Army would have to suffice and maybe later, when he was a senior pupil, he could join the 1034 Squadron at Kingston-on-Thames, and attend at weekends and in the school holidays. The College Rifle Club was intriguing though, and although he was not the best Year One shot, he was not the worst either. The College had once been Runner –Up in the Ashburton Shield, the shooting competition for schools, held at Bisley every summer, and Finn made up his mind to qualify for the team that entered for it.

So through that autumn of 1944 life was a hectic affair for young Finn, and he had little else on his mind besides school activities. Except for Master Silk. Silk continued to plague at every opportunity. And then one afternoon Silk made a mistake. It was Parade Day for the CCF. Finn was in B Platoon and took his place in the front of the three lines to be inspected. The Platoon Sergeant was Silk. It was Finn's misfortune that he had forgotten to polish the brass buckle on his uniform webbing belt, and it certainly lacked its usual bright shine. Not something that Silk's eagle eyes would miss.

"Browning, your belt buckle is filthy. Why have you not polished it?"

"I am sorry Sergeant. I agree it is not up to standard."

"YOU are not up to standard, Browning. You never are.!"

"That's unfair, Sergeant. You have never had to pull me up before, have you?" Finn could not think what had come over him. Never before had he spoken back to Silk. He knew all too well that to do so would be to his cost, and instantly regretted that he had lost control of himself now. Silk was furious at Finn's insolence and before he could stop himself, with full force he slapped Finn's face. "You cheeky little bugger. How dare you answer back." The slap caused Finn momentarily to drop his rifle and lose his balance as he stumbled into the cadet standing next to him.

It was quite by chance that the Spanish tutor, Michael Sears, was walking by. Though in no way connected with the Cadet force, he strode across the parade ground and took Silk by the shoulder. "No, Silk. That's not on. You do not EVER strike a cadet under your command. You had better leave the parade here and now. Who is next in seniority here? You, Corporal Sanders? Right, you take over. Silk, go to your study and stay there, whilst I go and see the Head and your Housemaster."

There could be no alternative: not only was Silk relieved of his Sergeant's stripes, but Donny Doncaster had no hesitation in dismissing him as Head of House, and as a Prefect. It was total ignominy for Silk. For the rest of term he never spoke to Finn again, and as he was almost eighteen, he left the College at the end of term. In the following April the sad news filtered back to St. Luke's that David Silk had been killed in action in Germany. The Jeep in which he was travelling had hit a landmine. He was eighteen and three months old. A memorial service was held in Chapel. Finn attended, as did the whole College. Finn knelt and prayed for the deliverance of his soul. "I'm sorry, Silk. I would not have wished that on you. Rest in peace."

CHAPTER 94

With so much success in the European theatre of war, it was not easy for families at home, the Brownings amongst them, to focus on the Far East. But the war there had been, and still was, as vicious and brutal as the war nearer home. However, steadily the tide was turning in the Pacific and South-East Asia, just as it was in Europe.

In Burma, Mountbatten ordered an all out assault on the Japanese holding Mandalay, whilst American forces bombarded Marcus Island in the Pacific.

American bombers attacked the oil refineries at Palikpapan in North Borneo, which supplied a major proportion of Japanese requirements for lubricating oils. Aircraft carriers of the US Third fleet launched an attack against Formosa, resulting in the destruction of more than 300 Japanese aircraft and dozens of Japanese destroyers.

On October 20th General Macarthur kept his promise of the early years of the war, that "I shall return" to the Philippines. He waded ashore from the US cruiser "Nashville" at Leyre in the Central Philippines.. the Japs were taken by surprise and put up little defence. By the end of Day One the 600 ship invasion had put ashore 100,000 American troops.

On October 24th there commenced probably the greatest sea battle ever fought. It was between the US Third and Seventh fleets, and the Japanese First and Second Striking forces. It raged over three days and involved 300 warships in all. By the end, the Japanese had lost their last four aircraft carriers, two battleships and twenty other vessels. Losses to the US Fleet numbered four. But it was during this engagement that for the first time the Japanese resorted to the use of Kamikaze tactics: bomb laden planes deliberately aimed by their suicide pilots to crash on enemy targets.

CHAPTER 95

By November, Bobby's broadcasts to her native country had taken on a dramatically different tone. Gone now were the nice, cosy, morale-boosting items designed to make oppressed Norwegians feel there was someone fighting their corner. The tone now was "Those vile Nazis are on the run. Give them a helpful shove. Freedom is round the next corner – a few months at most."

Every now and then news filtered back to London. All over Norway, secret Resistance transmitters were operating, receiving and flashing back vital information. On rare occasions, written word would reach London, via neutral Sweden. It was a dull November morning that Bobby was handed a buff envelope by Thor Grieg at the Norwegian Embassy. He was grinning: "I think this will brighten your day Roberta.

A certain gentleman made radio contact yesterday and told me that there was a message from him coming to you, but also a message from your mother. I will leave you in peace for a while, whilst you read them." The envelope had one word on it:- "Bobby". Inside there was a single folded sheet and in the fold was another smaller envelope marked Roberta. It was her mother's handwriting and she opened it first. It read:

"Dear Roberta, your father and I are well, as is your sister, so do not worry about us. We know the worst is over and that in a short while Norway will be free of the German vermin. But these years have taken their toll, and we are feeling our age. After all, we had turned seventy before we were invaded! Four years of occupation have seemed more like forty. Food is desperately short and your father would dearly like a glass of Akvavit to wash down the fish diet that we exist on. Thank heavens there still is fish in the fjord to catch! Otherwise we really would starve. It looks like we must struggle through another winter before the Huns withdraw, but hopefully then things will be better and we can see you again, and our English grandchildren. Until that day, take care my darling. Oh, I nearly forgot: we listen to your broadcasts and greatly enjoy them. Well done!

Love from your Mother and Father.

PS We like Lars, this friend of yours. We hope you do not like him too much, though. He is very handsome and courageous. Be careful!!!"

Bobby smiled. They had not mentioned her injury at the Sports ground. She was glad they had missed that broadcast. She had not visited Norway since 1938, more than six years ago. Oh, damn Hitler. Damn him and all those brutes around him. But the day of reckoning is coming soon.

The folded sheet began: "Dear Bobby, I do so hope this reaches you safely. I just want to tell you three things. The first is that I am safe and well – luckily. Just last week we ambushed a German convoy on the road between Skien and Sandfjord. It was dusk, what you call in England "teatime" I think. It was a group of eleven trucks carrying German troops and explosives to Sandefjord. We had managed to mine the road, so that the leading truck was blown up, forcing the others to come to a halt. Before the Germans knew what was happening, we grenaded them and the whole lot went up. Quite spectacular, except that the blast killed three of our men. My hair got a premature haircut – singed very short! My scalp is a bit sore, but otherwise I am fine. The second thing is that two days ago I managed to cross Oslofjord after dark in a small rowing boat and saw your family at Moss. They are ok, thank God. They love your broadcasts, although, of course they have to be very careful about listening to them. It would be death if they were found out. Naturally they do not tell even their closest friends that it is their daughter who is making these broadcasts. I am enclosing a short note from them. I am sorry that it is so short – I could only stay with them for a few minutes. The third thing to tell you is that you are constantly in my thoughts. It is no good pretending that I do not love you. I know you can not reciprocate this love. I know, and accept, that you love your husband and children, and will be loyal to them. But please, dear Roberta, save a little of that love for me. Maybe just 1%! The thought that soon this hellish war will be over and that I may visit England and the friends that I made there, especially you, sustains me at all times. Until then – Lars"

Bobby read this letter twice more. She felt emotionally confused. A mish-mash of thoughts crowded her mind. She should have no feelings for this man, whom she had known so briefly. And yet she, too, had thought about him often and in terms not merely of fear for his safety. Right at this moment she could feel the tightness in her chest. So could her love for Claud be true and total? She had always supposed so, and wanted it to be so. So why was Lars still in her mind? She had no answer.

CHAPTER 96

It was mid-November before Winston Churchill admitted the devastation that was being caused by the German V2 rockets. Since the first one hit Chiswick, in West London, in September, more than ninety had rained down on the capital and surrounding suburbs. They had killed many hundreds of people and homes. These rockets travelled at three thousand miles per hour and rose to a height of over 60 miles. They carried a ton of high explosive.

"There is no need to exaggerate the danger" Churchill said, "The scale and effect has not been significant". Tell that to the people of Croydon, Mr Churchill, which was hit by four of these deadly monsters. There was no warning. By far the most terrible day was November 25th. And tell it to the residents of New Cross. A V2 hit Woolworths and the Co-op at Saturday lunchtime. Both stores were packed with shoppers. 160 were killed and 200 injured. The scene was described by a survivor. "Things were falling out of the sky. Bits of things and bits of people. A horse's head was lying in the gutter. A baby's hand, still in its woolly sleeve, was in the pram. There was a crumpled London bus, with people still in their seats, all dead, and covered in dust. Where Woolworths had been there was nothing, just an enormous gap covered by clouds of dust. No building, just piles of rubble and bricks and underneath it all, people screaming."

Tell THEM Mr Churchill, that there is no need to exaggerate the danger!

CHAPTER 97

It was a quiet Sunday evening at the Browning home. Outside it was dark and windy. Claud, Bobby and Finn were settled in the rear sitting room. Rain splattered noisily from time to time on the windows. Claud had lit the fire and the logs crackled and glowed. Cosy. Bobby was knitting for her little granddaughter Charlotte. She was growing so fast and with clothes rationing it was hard to keep her properly dressed. Claud was deep in a book about Rogues and Villains, looking for items for his newspaper column. Finn was bringing his scrapbook up to date. What a marvellous record of the war that would be in years ahead. "Dad, there is a picture here of Mr Churchill in Paris, with General de Gaulle. Who is he? I mean the General, not Churchill, of course"

"De Gaulle is leader of the Free French. He escaped when France was overrun back in 1940, and now leads the Free French Army, supporting the British and American Forces. He is a very proud man. Very haughty. Self-important I think describes him well. But for all that he is a charismatic character, at least to the French people. I would not be at all surprised if after the war he becomes President of France. What else are you sticking in your book?"

"There's so much Dad. It's really hard to know what to put in and what to leave out. Anyway, most of it is good news now, thank heavens. But the bit I like best is the announcement that the blackout is over and the street lights are going on again after five years. Amazing. I can't remember seeing them actually on before. There is one dreadful cutting though, about the V2 that hit the shops in New Cross. There are several photos of the scene, but I can't decide whether to stick them in or not. It's so dreadful. Should I?"

"Yes, Finn." It was Bobby interjecting. "Yes, put it in. It is no good hiding the truth. It happened, so put it in. One day, perhaps, when you are grown up, you will come across it and remember how those poor people died, totally innocent, just like that terrible time at the Esher Sports Ground. And you may be able to help the world a little to maintain peace, so that nothing like that ever happens again."

There was a lull in the conversation, then Finn spoke again. "It's a long time since we heard from Douglas. Do you think he is alright?"

"I expect so, Finn. I don't think the Germans are so vile as to kill their POWs, especially now that they must know they are not going to win this damned war. We must just keep our fingers crossed and hope for the best. You never know, though, he might be home for Christmas."

Douglas turned to John Stockington, sitting on the next bunk. "Those guns are getting nearer, John. Much nearer. One of the spooks muttered that it was the Russians. He was shit scared and said he thought he and the other Camp guards might just do a runner and leave us to the mercies of the Ruskies. Could be out of the frying pan and into the fire. I don't trust those Ruskies, even if they are on our side. There were pretty dire rumours about what they were doing to the Germans they caught, but worse than that, even, about what they were doing to their own people, especially their women folk."

"Oh come on Douglas. Be positive man. You've survived a firing squad. Surely you don't think your own side are going to do you in. My bet is that we'll be home for Christmas. Bet you a million quid."

It was 2.00am when they heard the bombers going over. And then, two or three minutes later, they heard that terrible scream. STUKAS. The dive bombers must be attacking the advancing Russians. The estimate was that they were no more than seven or eight miles away. That's close! God, was release from this bloody place only a few miles away! Philip Cardew peered out of the hut door. The sky was clear and there was enough moon to see across the compound. The moonlight was augmented by distant flashes. Bombs or shells. Or both. The compound was empty. No sign of any guards. Not even in the watchtowers. It was dangerous to walk out in the open at night. Trigger happy guards needed no encouragement to open fire on prisoners. Cardew kept in the shadow of the hut, then scurried across to the next hut. And the next. No one. Then he saw the perimeter gate. The same gate those poor bastards from the Concentration Camp came through to empty the garbage bins. It was open. Wide open. Not a soul in sight.

Cardew hurried back to his hut. Excitedly he rushed inside. "They've gone. The buggers have upped and gone. The main gate is wide open chaps." "You're joking, Phil. Are you sure?" "Yes, positive, there isn't a soul anywhere." Gingerly, two or three others crept out of the hut door. One of them called out: "anyone there? Oi, you German bastards, are you there?" Silence. "Achtung Fritz, I am coming out into the open. Don't shoot." With their hands up above their heads, Alex Instone and Bertie Ross inched out towards the Main Gate, in full view, with the moon shining brightly and flashes lighting the sky to the East. Nothing. They ran, zig-zagging towards the Main Gate, still unconvinced the Germans had de-camped. By this time , other prisoners had emerged from their huts. It was true: the Germans had deserted, scared shitless at the thought of being caught by the Russians. They knew what that would mean.

"Quiet everyone. Pay attention." It was Wing Commander Bradshaw, the prisoners' CO. "I want everyone out here. Form orderly ranks. Bring your warmest clothes, it's bloody cold. Hurry." Soon, the compound was filled with men. Some were still half asleep, but, grumbling, shuffled into position facing Bradshaw. "Men, it seems to me that we have two choices what to do. Either we leave in small groups and see if we can make our way to the Swiss border. We are in Germany, we know that. Switzerland is one hell of a way off, so you would be taking a big risk. Or, we stay put and wait for the Russians. Personally, I intend waiting here. It's safer and I do not take the view that the Russians are going to mistreat us. You are free to make your own choice, but if you ARE going to make a run for it, you must inform me that you are doing so."

There was an unanimous decision for staying in the Camp. The dangers of running were too great. The end of the war was in sight. There was also an unanimous decision that, apart from appointing half a dozen sentries, they should all go back inside and get a few hours shuteye – always assuming the excitement allowed it. Many could not; the prospect of imminent freedom was too much. Among them was Douglas. Although healing well, his shoulder was still stiff, and ached constantly. In any case, the thought of reuniting with Celia, and his family in Surbiton, kept him tossing and turning until dawn.

It was a little after 8am when three Russian T.34 tanks entered the Camp. Behind them, two armoured cars. All bore the Red Star of the Russian Armed Forces. As the tank commanders climbed out of their turrets, they were greeted by the shouts and cheers (and in a few cases tears) of three hundred British aircrew POWs. It was a day many thought would never come. The euphoria was almost tangible. The Russian soldiers were full of bonhomie – it was a long time since they had encountered friendly faces, too. The handshakes were followed by bearhugs and by cigarettes – dreadful Russian brands, but still welcome. The cigarettes were followed by vodka, even though it was breakfast time. There was only one Russian soldier who spoke English, and fortunately there was one RAF Navigator who spoke a little Russian. These two men accompanied the Russian major in charge of the troop, and W/Cdr Bradshaw to the Camp Commandants office, now deserted, but still with all the trappings of his command: massive leather-covered desk, portrait of the Fuehrer on one wall, and also Hermann Goering, and a large swastika draped on another wall. By the desk, was a steel waste paper basket, still smoking from the ashes of burnt documents.

There was only one topic for discussion, and the meeting was brief. Its essence was simple. Whilst the Russians were advancing, progress had been slow, with bitter fighting, often hand-to-hand. The Germans were far from finished, at least in this sector of the front. There was no guarantee that they would not counter-attack and reoccupy this area, including the Camp. It would be unsafe, therefore, for the British POWs to remain here, but equally it would be difficult to evacuate them. Major Voroshilov would do the best he could to move them East, but it might take time. The only course, therefore, was for them to stay put until evacuation could be achieved. They would have the protection of a platoon of his men. The German guards had left machine guns in the three watchtowers, and another three, plus rifles, could be spared for self-defence if the Germans returned. It was the best he could do. He could not agree to any attempt being made by any of the POWs to make their way out of the Camp. It was in their own interest.

Home for Christmas? It did not look like it!

CHAPTER 98

November 1st. American B.29s attack Japanese -occupied Singapore for the first time.

November 1st. US Army Air Force makes daylight raids against targets in the Ruhr, whilst RAF Lancasters continue their bombing offensive against Cologne.

November 5th. In the Netherlands town of Heusden, retreating German troops force 200 Dutch citizens into the Town Hall, and then blow it up.

November 8th. In Hungary, 38,000 Jews are deported to Extermination Camps in Germany.

November 11th. In Japan, a new Aircraft Carrier is launched, constructed of steel and concrete, designed to be unsinkable.

November 11th. In Paris, Winston Churchill joins in the Armistice Day celebrations, and is cheered all the way.

November 12th. In Tromso Fjord, Germany's last remaining battleship, the Tirpitz, is sunk by a force of 30 RAF Lancasters. The great ship capsizes, trapping 1900 of its crew.

November 14th. US aircraft attack Japanese warships in Manila Bay, sinking one cruiser and for destroyers.

November 17th. The Japanese carrier "Shinyo" is sunk by a US submarine in the Yellow Sea.

November 20th. Hitler leaves his HQ at Rastenburg as the Red Army approaches and returns to Berlin.

November 25th. Auschwitz Concentration Camp. Demolition of the gas chambers begins. Next day, the last privileged prisoners, having completed the burial of their gassed comrads, are all murdered by the guards.

November 29th. US B-29s bomb Bangkok and Tokyo.

November 30th. In Britain, civilian casualties from air raids, nearly all V2 rockets, total over 700 dead and 1,500 injured.

A Government White Paper reveals some fascinating facts about the British War Effort. Output per head of the British population exceeded that of any other nation on earth, though, interestingly, it did not explain how they obtained statistics from Nazi Germany or Japan! However, some of the statistics make interesting reading: For instance, war weapons produced included:

Warplanes 102,000
Warships 722
All ships 4½ million tons

Tanks 25,000
Killed 1 civilian for every 3 servicemen

Bobby answered the phone. It was Philippa. Bobby could hear Charlotte's tinkly voice in the background. "Hello Philippa, is that my little granddaughter chattering in the background? She sounds happy enough."

"Yes, she's fine, and no trouble at all. I can't believe she is so easy going. Well, most of the time. I called to say that I had been talking to Mummy at Rosedown, and she has invited us down for Christmas. She would like you all to come. What do you think? Have you made any plans?"

"Well, no. We were hoping we might see you and Charlotte, plus Clive if he gets leave, and maybe Kenneth as well."

"Well, Clive has got a bit of leave and it really would be great if we could all get together down in Dorset. Shall I tell Mummy you'll come?"

"I'd better double check with Claud, but I am sure he would love to do it. We've never forgotten what a wonderful Christmas we had there in 1939. It would be delightful. So, yes, tell Lady Hester we'll come. If there is a problem I'll ring you back straight away. Claud's round at the library at present, but he will be back soon. Perhaps we can all travel down together. Which day are you going?"

"Not quite sure yet, but I'll liaise with you nearer the time. Must rush. I think You-Know-Who needs to go to the Little Room. 'bye."

The Brownings and Hannahs had not met since Clive and Philippa's wedding, but memories of the time at Rosedown were strong and the gratitude the Brownings felt still endured. Finn was over the moon at the thought of Christmas amongst his old friends down there, and memories were still strong of the times he had spent roaming the hills and countryside. As he neared the end of his first term at St. Luke's, and with the War's end clearly in sight, plus the thought of all his brothers being back home again, Finn could not have been happier. In fact the mood throughout the nation was one of growing happiness. No longer was it "the beginning of the end", it was more like "the middle of the end". This would be the last Christmas before peace returned – at least in Europe, and perhaps the Far East as well.

The Home Guard had been stood down in September. Now, three months on, it was formally disbanded. Twenty-nine contingents took part in a final march past, including an American contingent made up of US citizens living in London. The salute was taken by the King accompanied by Queen Elizabeth., in Hyde Park. In a radio broadcast that evening, the King said: "I believe it is the voluntary spirit which has always made the Home Guard so powerful a comradeship. You have found how men from all kinds of homes and occupations can work together in a great cause. I am very proud of what the Home Guard has done, and I am very grateful."

It all looked good for Christmas and the New Year of 1945. But early on the morning of December 16th, in the snow covered woods of the Ardennes Forest in Belgium, the calm was shattered by the roar of artillery. The bombardment continued for an hour, and then twenty German divisions came out of the mist and fog to attack the sleepy Americans. They were completely taken by surprise. The German objective was the recapture of Antwerp, the key port for the arrival of Allied troops and equipment from Britain.

The sixty mile sector was held by just six US Divisions, approximately 80,000 men. Confronting them were a quarter of a million German troops, supported by almost 1,000 tanks. To a great extent, their success would depend on the fog not lifting. If it did, the vastly superior Allied air power would have a field day. At first, luck was with the Germans. They made rapid and penetrating progress, completely surrounding the town of Bascogne, held by a small contingent of lightly armed US infantry. A courier was sent with a message demanding that the Americans surrender. The reply given was immortal, never to be forgotten. It was one word, scrawled on the German message, by the American General Anthony Mc Auliffe.

"NUTS"

The Battle of the Bulge as it became known was truly on. At first, there seemed to be no stopping the German thrust Westwards. Until, that was, they overstretched their own supply lines. Shortages of fuel and ammunition and stiff pockets of American resistance, began to slow the German advance. Then, the weather conditions began to ease a little and US reinforcements under Lt. General Patton, began to make their presence felt. On December 22nd, the siege of Bastogne was lifted, and also lifted was the fog and cloud that had prevented the German being attacked from the air. On December 27th the German Forces, pounded from the air and on the ground, began to pull back, in the face of Hitler's instruction that they should not do so.

Never again on the Western Front, would the German armies take a step forwards. The die was cast. Only Germany itself remained in German hands – but not for long.

CHAPTER 100

As he had five years ago, Old Herbert met the party at Crewkerne Station. Herbert had aged. He was more bent and, apart from a circlet of white hair at the base of his skull, he was completely bald. But his spirit was undiminished. He saluted Bobby and Priscilla, shook hands with Claud and Clive, and winked at Finn. "Ay, and this must be little Charlotte; she's a little angel, no doubt about it. And Finn, you've become a proper beanpole, young man. I'd hardly know you.

"Herbert, it is good to see you again, and looking so well. We are all so looking forward to Christmas at Rosedown again. It was unforgettable and does not seem like five years ago. It's happier times now though, isn't it. It looks very much as if we've got the better of Mr Hitler at last. Are the master and mistress well?" "Well, ma'am, like all of us, they aint any younger, but I'm sure Mr Hitler will be dead an' good riddance long before the General and Lady Hester." Herbert's weathered old face, as wrinkled as a walnut, broke into a broad grin. "An' I'll do likewise, the good God willing." He turned to Finn. "Finn lad, I declare you be big enough now to save an old man lifting all those bags into the boot. Can you and Mr Clive do the necessary. Then we'll be on our way."

"Herbert, I am amazed the General still manages to run the car still", Claud said. "We had to abandon ours for the duration with no petrol to run it on."

"Well, sir, you may find it hard to believe, but back in 1939 the General guessed what might happen with everything going to the war effort. He bought no fewer than a hundred or more of those big ten gallon cans and filled the lot, and stuck them in a big barn well away from the house, and very well secured as well. Of course, most times we just use the little Austin Seven- more economical, you know. The Rolls has been laid up most of the time - only comes out for very special occasions, an' what more special than the Browning clan! But we get some funny looks from those folk who think we have some special supply, like Black Market."

The journey was different from those years when the Brownings first came to Dorset. Then, it was September and it was still light well into the evenings. Now the lanes were in darkness, and the progress slow, but eventually the car turned into the long, curving drive up to the great house. At this stage in the war, the threat from the Luftwaffe was virtually nil, especially down in rural Dorset, but still lights had to be masked and dim. The General must have heard the car as it drew up, and he and Lady Hester were standing in the porch to greet them. Mrs Hardy was there as well, wearing her apron,. and hands covered in flour. Old Findlay, looking not one jot different, with old flat cap in hand, was there too. Quite a reception committee. The tears welled in Bobby's eyes, but she managed to control them from trickling down her cheeks.

AS always, Finn was in awe of the Great Hall, and the vast, highly polished dining table that stood centre stage. Nothing had changed here, Once more there was a giant Christmas tree, ablaze with fairy lights, and mistletoe hanging above every door and window frame.

Still the portraits of the General and Lady Hester when they were young. They, too, looked older now, but they were in their late seventies, perhaps turned eighty even. Herbert had told him when they were billeted here all those years ago that the portraits had been commissioned when the General received his knighthood, not long after the 1914-18 war. And now we were finishing off another "Great War", only twenty-five years later.

Lady Hester said that she was putting Claud and Bobby in a different room from 1939/40. This one was on the first floor and looked over the walled garden, on the South Wing. Finn could have the attic room to himself. and hopefully would remember that the lavatory was integral with it, not somewhere along the corridor!. Finn reddened, but laughed. He wondered if the deer still coughed in the night, and was the barn owl still there in the trees hooting away the night. Memories flooded back, and he could hardly wait to explore the grounds. Perhaps he could play a game of squash with brother Ken. Better still, he could renew his rivalry with Peter Partridge. They had not seen one another much in the intervening years, but had kept touch by letter from time to time. Peter was now at Beaminster Grammar School. Sadly, his Dad had passed away in 1942, but he still lived with his Mum not far away.

The deer DID cough that night and the barn owl DID hoot, but this did not stop Finn from sleeping soundly. The morning of Christmas Eve was clear and crisp, with a sharp frost. All the Brownings were up early – it was too good a day to waste malingering in bed. Bobby and Claud wanted to spend time with old Findlay inspecting the garden and giving him a helping hand perhaps. Clive, Philippa and Charlotte wanted to walk into Broadwindsor. They were not together much, and a London Park was no match for the lanes and fields of the Dorset country side. Finn asked Lady Hester if he could use the phone to call Peter Partridge. Perhaps he could come over to Broadwindsor and play squash..

If everyone at Rosedown thought that Finn had grown, it was nothing compared with Peter's growth. Although only thirteen, the same as Finn, he was at least an inch and a half taller, but more than two stone heavier. For his age he was a giant, and Finn could hardly recognize him. "Peter, what ever have you been doing to grow so enormous? I can't believe it! But it is so good to see you again and I have missed you a lot. Did you read about what happened at the Sports Ground in Surrey with that Doodlebug? Mum and Dad were there to watch me racing. Dad and I were luckily unhurt, but Mum was in hospital for ages. A flying, shattered bottle caught here in her - Ahem backside. In a way it was funny, but she lost a lot of blood. The whole thing was terrible, with bodies and bits of bodies scattered everywhere."

"Finn, I had no idea. Yes I do remember it. In fact Mum took me to the cinema and they showed it on the newsreel. I didn't see you though. Is your Mum fully ok now?"

"Yes, she is fine. We all are, thank heavens, except Douglas. He was taken prisoner when his plane came down in Italy. We got a couple of letters from his POW Camp, but now we haven't heard from him for ages, so we are a bit worried. Ken is a Lieutenant in the Royal Artillery. He should be her later today. Anyway, how about a game of squash. Have you been playing much?" Peter had kept up his membership of Dorchester Squash Club and . like Finn, had found himself playing with older men. They had a great game and much to Finn's annoyance, Peter squeaked home in the deciding game, watched by the General, just as he had when they first played at age eight.

CHAPTER 101

Evacuation from the POW camp, when it happened, happened quickly, without notice. The frustration the prisoners felt at being free, but not at liberty to leave the Camp, had been in some ways worse than being prisoners. Life was easier in as much as they had slightly better food, mostly left by the fleeing camp guards. And the Russians had conjured up a little vodka and beer, strictly rationed out by Wing Cdr Bradshaw. And they had been allowed to scavenge for firewood in the copse outside the Main Gate, watched over by a section of their Russian "hosts", so they were able to keep warm in the still bitter winter weather. But they had been denied any contact with families back home. This might have been facilitated if the Red Cross had been allowed access to them, but, for whatever reason, this was denied, too. As time passed, frustration increased. They wanted to be back "on side" in time for Christmas

The staff car rolled to a halt outside the Kommandant's Office at noon on December 19th. It was followed by a convoy of closed trucks. The car was a German Mercedes, repainted with the Soviet Red Star. From it, emerged Colonel Ballitsin, followed by a young Lieutenant. An interpreter. W/Cdr Bradshaw greeted the two men on the Office steps, and saluted. Col. Ballitsin returned the salute, and the two men shook hands warmly. Through the interpreter, Ballitsin said: "Wing commander, I have very good news for you. The Soviet Army has continued its advance westwards on German soil. There is no danger to you now and I am pleased to advise you that arrangements have been made for you and all your fellow prisoners to leave the camp. You will be transferred to an airfield some 35 kilometres from here, and then flown to Switzerland. I am not sure how you will get home from there, but no doubt your Royal Air Force will be able to arrange this." He beamed an even broader smile and added "I hope you will get home in time for Christmas. I know how important that occasion is in your country. The bad news is that you must leave immediately. Please inform your men to cease whatever they are doing and to make their way to the trucks. I am afraid there will be very little space for possessions, but then I imagine you have very few!" Actually, it was surprising what prisoners had accumulated during the long years of captivity: diaries, drawings, little wood carvings, and in one case knitting. These things were NOT left behind.

Douglas arrived at Brize Norton Air Base in Oxfordshire on December 24th, at 1000 hours. He took his turn to get hold of the phone. From Surbiton there was no reply. He tried Clive and Philippa's flat in London. No reply.

He tried Celia's parents in Wimbledon. It was Celia's mother who answered the phone. At first she did not realize who was calling. It was a long time since she had seen him, or heard his voice. She was flabbergasted. She felt a little lightheaded.

"Hello, mother-in-law, it's Douglas. I'm back in UK. We got liberated from our POW camp by the Ruskies. I can't raise my family on the phone. Do you know where they are? And where is Celia. Is she still in Malta? I can't wait to see her, or at least speak to her". Douglas could not contain his excitement at speaking to her and the words and questions almost tripped over each other.

Then he heard the Admiral's voice. "Who is this calling please?" Clearly, his wife was struck dumb with disbelief. "It's Douglas sir. I am back in England. The Russians overran our camp in Germany and got us out to Switzerland. I've just landed at Brize Norton. I suppose Celia is still in Malta, is she? I've been trying to call my parents, and Clive, but no answers, I'm afraid."

"Douglas! Fantastic. Are you alright?"

"Yes, I'm fine. Well I'm a bit thinner than when I last saw you, but basically fine."

"Thank God for that."

"I do, actually. I was put in front of a firing squad at one point, but the bastards missed my heart and put a bullet in my shoulder, but it's fine now."

"Are you serious?

"Yes, sir, I am. It was a bit scary, I can tell you. But to be fair, instead of finishing me off, they put me in hospital and treated me really well there. I'll tell you more when I see you, but there is a long queue of ex-Cons waiting to use the phone, so I'd better be brief."

"Right, Douglas. All your people have gone to Dorset for Christmas. It's your sister-in-law's folk – General someone. Your family seem to be developing a taste for marrying into military circles. As for Celia, she is fine and I still have enough clout at the Admiralty to get a message to her, so leave that to me. Off you go, and we'll look forward to seeing you in the New Year."

As Douglas was about to dial Rosedown, a young Sub-Lieutenant RNVR approached him. "Excuse me, sir, are you Lt. Browning? Douglas Browning?"

"Yes, I am."

"Well, sir, I have been sent to request you accompany me to our Intelligence Unit in Pompey. They would like to de-brief you about your

experience as a POW, and, of course, to sort you out with fresh uniform etc.
And, of course, organize a spot of leave and so on.

"You are not serious, are you Subbie? Do you realize I have just arrived
back in England after incarceration by the fucking Huns for heaven knows
how long. I have not even been able to contact my wife and family yet. In
fact they don't even know if I am alive or not. So toddle off back to
Portsmouth and tell whoever sent you that I will be happy to come and see
them in the New Year, and not before, and if they don't like it, they can Court
Martial me for subordination. I would be more than happy to be drummed
out of the service. Have a nice Christmas, young man". No contest. The
Subbie evaporated. The phone had been grabbed by someone else, with
several others waiting. Douglas joined the queue, but as he did so the Tannoy
blared: "Lt. Browning, please report to the Transport Office immediately."

The Transport Officer looked up at Douglas and smiled: "Morning, sir,
I'm charged with trying to sort out onward transport for you chaps. Could
you tell me where you would like to get to please? Can't promise anything,
but I'll do my best." Douglas needed no time to think: "I'm anxious to join
my family in Dorset, if that's possible – Crewkerne would be the nearest
Station." The Transport Officer shuffled his papers. "I've scrounged an RAF
Staff Car for a couple of chaps who want to get to Bournemouth. You could
share that, and I could give you a Rail Warrant to get yourself on to
Crewkerne. It's leaving in ten minutes. Want to give it a go?" Douglas did
not hesitate. "Yup, I might just get home in time for the turkey, though I'm
not sure my stomach could accommodate such luxury after the muck of that
POW Camp!" "Well, good luck sir. It's marvellous to see you chaps back in
Blighty. Here's your Rail Warrant and we are issuing everyone with £20 in
cash, to tide you over till your back pay turns up. That must amount to a tidy
sum, eh."

When Douglas emerged from Crewkerne Station, the last light had faded,
but the stars offered a dim glow. By luck, a taxi was waiting. "Do you know
Rosedown, near Broadwindsor, driver? Good, as quick as you like." He lay
back in the rear seat, and in seconds was asleep.

CHAPTER 102

Douglas awoke as the taxi came to a halt on the gravelled drive. "You're here, guv. Rosedown. That'll be two shillings and sixpence, please." Douglas took a deep breath and pulled the bell handle. It was Mrs Hardy who opened the door. "Yes, sir, can I help you?" the figure confronting her was tall – Douglas had reached six foot since she had last seen him five years ago – and slightly dishevelled in a RAF greatcoat over navy blue trousers and much in need of a shave. "Mrs Hardy, it's Douglas Browning, remember me? I suppose it's not surprising you don't recognize me. You might remember my family were evacuated here back in '39 and '40."

"Oh my God, can it really be you, Mr Douglas? We heard you were in a prisoner of war with the Germans." "True, Mrs Hardy. May I come in, it's rather chilly out here, even with this army coat on." "Goodness, of course, sir, come in the warm. All your family are here. They are getting ready for dinner, sir. My, what a surprise. I can scarce believe I'm not dreaming. They'll get a shock sir. I'll call them immediately.

At that moment, Bobby entered the hall. For a few moments she stood stock still and stared at the figure in front of her, transfixed. "Hello, Mum. Don't stare like that. It IS me. Douglas. I'm not a ghost! I thought I would drop in for Christmas.!"

It was too much for her. She felt she could not breathe. She could not control her movements. She sank to the floor, on her knees, and she sobbed and sobbed. "Oh Mum, come on now. I know it's a shock. Upsy getsy." Gently, he lifted her to her feet and hugged her. Discreetly, Mrs Hardy slipped away to find the General and Lady Hester. "How?" she gasped. "How did you get here? We've heard nothing for months We were frightened something awful had happened." "Well, it did actually. But that's a long story. I'd better save it until the others appear. I tried to call you as soon as I landed at Brize Norton, but no answer, so I got on to Celia's Dad and he told me you were here. Are you all here. Dad and Finn?" Bobby nodded. "Yes, and Kenneth, and Clive and Philippa and little Charlotte, everyone except Celia, she's still in Malta, but I expect you already know that. Did you know you were an uncle? I can't remember, I've lost track of time" Gradually, Bobby was regaining her poise.

At that moment the General and Lady Hester appeared. "Good God, Douglas. How on earth?" the General had the right priorities. "Hester, go and pour the man a very large Scotch dear, will you. It's clear he needs one. And one for me as well, there's a dear. Oh, and instruct Mrs Hardy to raid the cellar. This calls for a bottle or two of our best Taittinger. I've been saving it for far too long!" Lady Hester did not respond. She did not say a word. She came to the now seated figure of Douglas Bowning and did something that had rarely, if ever, been seen before. She bent forward and deposited an enormous kiss on his stubbly cheek. "Thank God", she said. "He DOES hear prayers after all, that good Lord. Now I will fetch you that drink, and it will be Henry's very best."

Moments later, the rest of the Browning clan trooped into the Hall. Claud, with Kenneth and Finn. Then Clive, with Philippa and little Charlotte. It was a scene of many emotions – amazement, disbelief, pure joy. Handshakes, hugs and kisses, questions, bewilderment and after all that. laughter. Little Charlotte wondered who this strange man was and why all the fuss and so hid behind her mother. Presently, practicalities took over. Lady Hester took command. "Douglas, you need a bath. A long, deep one, with my favourite bath salts in it. And a shave. Clive, lend the man a razor and a clean shirt, will you, you're about the same size. We'll delay dinner half an hour, Mrs Hardy." No one protested. This would be a very memorable dinner and a very wonderful Christmas.

It was past eight before they all sat down to eat. Refreshed, and in clothes borrowed from brother Clive, Douglas told them the full, horrific story, beginning with his forced landing in Italy, and then those interminable months in the POW Camp, the foolish attempt by the American airmen to escape, and its terrible sequel in front of a firing squad. He omitted the unutterable terror he felt, standing tied to a post, and his inability to control his bladder. But he told them of awakening in the German civilian hospital and the decent treatment he had received. Then the thrill of finding that the German guards had vanished during the night and the frustration of having to stay in the camp, even after the Russians had liberated it, and finally the frantic journey back to freedom in England.

"I do not know, son, how even to imagine facing a firing squad and knowing that in a few moments, for sure, you are going to die." It was Claud Browning speaking. "After that, you must think you could face anything, survive anything.." "It's odd, Dad, but I had help of sorts from a mouse. A baby mouse at that. Do you remember that holiday we had just before I joined up? I told you I was scared of going down with my ship. You suggested I went into the church next door to the pub, and try to rationalise my fear: pray perhaps. I did. I was sitting there in one of the pews, in the gloom, when a baby mouse scuttled along the to top if the pew in front of me. When it saw me it stopped. We just stared at each other, and I thought "well, if that tiny creature can sit there and not be frightened of a being hundreds of times bigger, why should I be scared of going to sea. The mouse really helped, and I tried to think about it when those rifles were pointing at me. I am very grateful to that mouse. Sadly, a cat's probably had it by now!"

There was silence round the table for a few seconds. This was a family, in fact two families, coping with war. Claud had certainly seen the horrors of the trenches in the last war, as had the General. They were lucky, and had survived to live full lives. Now it was the turn of the next generation. Clive had had two lucky escapes, first at sea, then later over Germany. Even Bobby and Finn had narrowly averted death from the Doodlebug at the sports ground. But Douglas's experience capped all of this. Only Kenneth had " a clean sheet", and there was still time for him to face danger – the war was far from over yet.

"Douglas", the General spoke, "It is the Hannah custom to go to Midnight Service in Broadwindsor on Christmas Eve. I think in view of what we have just heard from you, we all have some special thanks to offer the Good Lord this year. But you must be whacked out, so don't feel you have to come. We'll quite understand if you have an early night."

"No, sir" Douglas replied. "I'd like to come. He deserves my thanks for getting me here. By rights I should be pushing up the daisies in some very foreign field! It may be His birthday we are celebrating, but I feel rather as if it's my re-birth."

CHAPTER 103
CHRISTMAS EVE - 1944

The first ever raid by jet propelled aircraft – German Arados – successfully attacked targets at Liege, in Belgium.

In the English Channel, the German U-boat U486 sank the American troop carrier "Leopoldsville". 819 American soldiers lost their lives.

Thirty-one V1 Doodlebugs were launched from the air by Heinkel bombers. They were aimed at Manchester. 17 reached their target, killing 32 people and injuring many more.

In reprisal for an attack by French Resistance in September, German troops murdered all men between the ages of seventeen and thirty-two in the village of Bande.

HAPPY CHRISTMAS!

CHAPTER 104

Finn was awe-struck by Douglas's adventures. Hitherto, he had proudly related to his friends how Clive had survived his ship being torpedoed, incarceration in an Argentine jail and finally being seriously wounded in a raid over Germany. What a hero! But Douglas had gone one better – if that was an apt description. First he had crash –landed his fighter plane in enemy territory, and been taken prisoner, and if that was not enough he had faced a Firing Squad, and lived to tell the tale. How many men could claim that?!

So here were two brothers, each with ugly scars. The one, jagged wound on the thigh, the other even more dramatic – a neat round scar where the bullet had entered his shoulder. Four inches down, and left a couple of inches, and it would not have been flesh, bone and sinew that would have been so painfully torn. It would have been his heart, pierced and blown apart, and certain death.

Quietly to himself during that Midnight Mass in Broadwindsor Church, Finn thought "There must be a Guiding Hand Up There. A Saviour. Was it Jesus who spared my brothers?" The priest administered the Sacraments to most of the congregation, whilst Finn, not yet confirmed, stayed sitting with Clive. Now a Roman Catholic, Clive could not take the Host in an Anglican Church. Of course, he could attend a Protestant Service, he could joyously sing the hymns and carols, and murmur the prayers. But he could not bring himself to kneel at the altar rail. How crazy that was, he thought to himself. Was Jesus not everyone's Jesus? It was the same Man who gave his life on the Cross – a life surrendered for all mankind. Devout as he now was, Clive felt that both Catholicism and Protestantism suffered from this silly schism. It was like children squabbling over who was right and wrong. But for now, he had no choice, he just had to sit and watch this most sacred act of worship, in this sweet little country church.

For Douglas, this was a precious moment in his life. Here he was, in the heart of rural England, amidst all his family, in this church aglow with a hundred candles, with the local children's nativity scene set beneath the stone pulpit, with old and young alike singing the Holly and the Ivy, all wrapped in their winter coats and scarves and gloves. Only Celia was missing. His thoughts drifted back to that frozen and hostile land. A week ago, he was shivering in the snows, somewhere in Eastern Germany, with all his comrades. Just waiting. Free from incarceration, but not free to go home, killing time with games of cards and foraging for firewood. Then further back: facing those fourteen rifles and staring certain death in the face. And why had he and the other thirteen been chosen, and then why had HE been spared by the tremor of a German's hand and the others had all died? Was there a God orchestrating all this? With these questions raging through his mind, his head slumped on to his father's shoulder and he slept. He dreamed, but it was not dreams of horror and fear, it was of a young Wren in a railway carriage, sitting opposite him and smiling.

Kenneth's thoughts in that Church were quite different. His mind was not really on Christmas, or his family, or friends. It was on the War. Ken had worked hard to gain a commission, and he felt his training should be put to better use than sitting around defending Portsmouth. In the whole time he had been stationed there they had seen not a single German aircraft. The Luftwaffe, what was left of it, had for more urgent business to attend to close to home, as Russians to the East, and the British and Americans to the West, pressed on remorselessly. For him, his khaki uniform and the brass pip on his shoulder, meant that he should be doing something positive to prosecute the war. Oh, he was enjoying being here with his family, and especially now with Douglas back home and safe. But Christmas would soon be over, and then he would have to return to the dreariness of his barracks in Portsmouth. A waste of time. He wanted action. He wanted to stand tall with his two older brothers who had done so much. He promised himself that he would ask his CO for a transfer to a unit across the Channel somewhere, or to the Far East.

Claud was not really religious and never had been. It wasn't that he did not believe the New Testament story. It was just that since that birth in Bethlehem and Jesus's crucifixion thirty or so years later, 1,900 years had gone by and the only thing that had happened, it seemed, was that Man had killed his Fellow Man, frequently in the most bestial of ways. If Christ was to come again, as he had said he would, then it was high time he did so. And in the meantime, the World just went from bad to worse. So how could anyone really, deeply believe the storyline? One could hope for better things, but to Claud hope was not conviction, and far from having conviction, Claud had little hope to console himself with. So here he was, in this charming little church, amidst this congregation of good, well-meaning Dorset folk, almost as an observer. He went through the motions of taking Communion, as a formality that was expected of him. Not to do so might be seen as some kind of protest against Christianity. But as he lacked conviction about any Second Coming, so also did he lack conviction of the futility of believing to the point of openly showing it.

"God Rest You Merry Gentlemen Let Nothing You Dismay" rang through the church and Bobby sang it with the rest of the congregation. But as she did so her thoughts turned to her family, those here and those others in Moss.

Joy that right here beside her was her entire family of Claud and her four sons. Two of them a bit battered, but all safe and here. But her joy also flew across the North Sea to her parents and sister. They , too, had survived the devastation of five cruel years of occupation. Soon they would be liberated and she could see them again. What a marvellous moment that would be, to hug her old mum and dad, and to embrace her dear sister. She loved them all dearly, and had missed them deeply, and feared for them for too long. And what of Lars? Still she could not forget him. She had to face the truth that much as she loved her husband, she needed to know that Lars was safe and well, and even more than that, she had to admit to herself that she wanted to hold him in her arms and not let go.

The Service ended with Silent Night. There was a resonance to it this Christmas of 1944. It brought back memories of that Christmas all those years ago, when the Blitz was at its most intense, when they had prayed that it WOULD be a silent night, that the sirens would stay quiet for once, and the night sky would not be lit by searchlights and exploding bombs and shells, and the bright vermilion of burning buildings. They had been spared then, and now those grim days were surely past. A bright New Year beckoned, but this time the brightness was of Peace.

CHAPTER 105
THE FINAL YEAR

On January 2nd 1945 the Browning family went their separate ways. Claud, Bobby and Finn returned to Surbiton on an early afternoon train. Finn had a last game of squash with Peter Partridge, and a pact made that each would spend a week with the other in the next Summer holidays. Clive had a few more days leave and decided to spend it at Rosedown, with Philippa and Charlotte. Kenneth returned to duty in Portsmouth, determined to press on with getting a posting overseas. Douglas was sure there would be no repercussions over his refusal to report to RN HQ at Portsmouth immediately he had landed in Britain, and did not much care if there were. Sure, the Admiralty would wish to conduct interviews about his experiences as a POW, especially about his brush with the firing squad. Probably they would want to hear about his hospital treatment., and check his medical condition. Then, they'd damned well better extend his leave, if not actually demobilise him altogether! The idea of active service again was anathema to him. He had had quite enough of combat flying. There was also the matter of Celia. God, how he needed to see her. Before leaving Rosedown, he called the Admiral in Wimbledon to ascertain if he had spoken to her. He had. He had done more than that. He had pulled strings and got an undertaking from the Admiralty that as soon as he was fit, Douglas could resume ground duties in Malta for the duration of Celia's posting there. With a new lightness of step, Douglas set out for Portsmouth. It would be nice to have brother Ken nearby. There should be the chance of a beer or two with him. And then Malta. And Celia. In his arms. Better still, in his bed, warm, sweet smelling and yielding. At the thought he felt a throb in his groin. It had been a long time

In the Far East, the New Year began with promise. Promise of victory for the Allies. and promise of defeat for Japan. Mainland Japan was now threatened. Aircraft from more distant outlying regions were being withdrawn to help defend Japan itself.

Control of the air had now been ceded to the Americans and the Japanese Navy had been decimated. More and more Kamikaze attacks were being used, a desperate measure, but there seemed to be no shortage of young Japanese pilots ready to commit suicide in this horrendous way in the service of their country. In utter desperation, even submarines were being used to ram Allied shipping.

In South East Asia, Japanese Armies were in retreat. In some of the Pacific Islands, they had merely been bypassed – left to wither, without reinforcements or supplies or air cover. In Burma, the British and Commonwealth troops under the command of General Slim had planned to bring the enemy to battle on the Swebo Plain, only to find they had already retreated across the Irrawaddy River. A British Officer recaptured the town of Akyab single handed, the Japanese having fled two days earlier. In some sectors, however, the Japanese continued to fight fiercely and fearlessly. On January 4th one Kamikaze succeeded in sinking the US Carrier "Olmmaney Bay", and on the 6th, in Luzon in the Philippines, with only 35 airworthy aircraft left, Kamikazes attacked US warships and killed 150 American sailors.

In Europe, there was further progress, but it was not all plain sailing for the Allies. The Luftwaffe mustered a force of an estimated one thousand aircraft to attack airfields in Belgium and destroyed 150 Allied aircraft.. In doing so, they lost 220 of their own. It was probably the last hurrah for the Luftwaffe, but hearing of it made Kenneth redouble his efforts to get across the Channel. His CO, Lt. Col. Mark Fenton, replied courteously to his request by saying that although he understood the young officer's desire, it was the impetuosity and ill-judgment of youth and with the war drawing towards its successful conclusion, he should see sense and stay safe. He was unwilling to forward Kenneth's request to divisional HQ. "For heaven's sake Kenneth, simmer down. In a few months you will be back in Civvy Street. You are still in your teens, man. You can go home and do some studying and get yourself to University, or some professional qualification. There's a good chap."

On the Eastern Front, by the end of January, the Red Army was through Poland and well into Germany. The Russians made astonishing progress, advancing westward at a rate of one hundred miles a week. In the North, by the 20th, the Russians had torn a 40 mile wide hole in the East Prussian defence zone and were 30 miles into Germany itself. By the 27th Marshal Rokossovsky's forces had burst through to the Baltic, and cut off the German forces in East Prussia. The Russians were now within 100 miles of Berlin itself. On that same day, Russian troops entered Auschwitz-Birkenau Concentration Camp. It was the biggest of all the Nazi extermination camps. As they entered, they saw living skeletons moving slowly and agonisingly in a landscape of corpses. The Germans had already left a week earlier, driving with them on foot some 20,000 inmates sufficiently able to be moved. The few hundred left behind, too weak to walk, many with typhus or diphtheria, had mostly been shot. Gas chambers and crematoria had been blown up in a feeble effort to conceal the truth of what had been happening.

CHAPTER 107

By the beginning of February, despite dogged resistance and occasional successes, it was perfectly clear that Hitler's regime was doomed. The question was: how should Germany be administered once the surrender had taken place? To determine this, Marshal Stalin, President Roosevelt and Prime Minister Winston Churchill met at Yalta, in the Crimea, and after almost a week of talks and bargaining, spelled out what they had decided on February 11th. Germany was to be split into four administrative zones: one each for the three major powers, and a fourth for France. They also announced that a further meeting should take place in April, to establish a charter for a new United Nations Organization. This would succeed the failed post Great War League of Nations. Not made public at this time were certain other decisions, notable of which was that Poland's eastern boundaries would be moved to enable Russia to annex Polish territory.

By this time, British and American bombers virtually had freedom of the skies, both by day and by night. On the 7th of February Bomber Command raided the Dortmund Ems Canal, and the towns of Goch and Cleve. On the following night it was the turn of Politz and Krefeld. And as the three leaders were meeting at Yalta, USAAF bombers, with heavy fighter escort, attacked Berlin, setting on fire a major area of the city. An estimate of civilian casualties was 1,000, dead and injured.

American bombers also raided Vienna, but suffered heavy losses from enemy ack-ack.

Then, on the night of February 13th, there occurred probably the most appalling act of sheer, cruel terrorism perpetrated by the Allies up to that time – though worse was to follow. On that night a force of Lancaster bombers attacked Dresden. Until that night, Dresden was one of the most beautiful cities in Germany, with peerless architecture. It had no military value. But its population of 700,000 had been swelled by some half a million refugees from the East. The weather conditions were perfect and the Pathfinders dropped their marker flares exactly on target. The attack was merciless. The first wave of 200 Lancasters dropped H.E. bombs and followed this with a deluge of incendiaries. The city was soon ablaze. The second wave numbered about 500 bombers and they dropped more than a thousand tons of bombs. One description went as follows: "then a firestorm followed. People were sucked into the inferno like leaves into an autumn bonfire. Many took shelter in cellars, only to die of suffocation." Its purpose was twofold. Firstly , it was intended to demoralise the German civilian population and thus hasten the end of the war. Secondly, it was a political act, to be seen as an encouragement to the advancing Red Army. Despite some American opposition to the plan, they nevertheless weighed in with a second attack, the next day sending in a force of 300 B17s to drop a further 700 tons of bombs on the smoking embers of this beautiful city. It was an annihilation on an unprecedented and indefensible scale.

Cinemas throughout Great Britain showed newsreel pictures of the raid, but these gave no conception of the true extent and horror of what had taken place. Only later, after German surrender, could the full extent of the desolation be revealed to the world at large.

As the days wore on, German resistance became more frantic and forlorn. Women, who until now had only volunteered for war service, were now drafted into the Volkssturm. Boys as young as fifteen were also recruited. Doctors and nurses were diverted to the front, rendering medical facilities for the civilian population totally inadequate. On the 19th Himmler met Count Bernadotte of the Red Cross and made overtures for peace talks with the Western Powers.

Since the war began over five years ago, Britain and its Empire had by this time lost more than 300,000 men. Additionally, British civilian casualties amounted to 60,000. It was a high cost, though nothing compared with the loss of human life in mainland Europe, and the rest of the world.

And the conflict, the hate, the cruelty raged on. This bloody war would claim many more lives before peace returned to the world.

CHAPTER 108

"It's time this bloody war was over, Claud. I: just wonder how many more human lives have to be destroyed. Did you know that British losses, counting in the Aussies, Canadians and the rest of the Empire, total over three hundred thousand. And that's without the civilian casualties – another sixty or more thousand. Then just think of all the widows there must be to add to that lot. It's horrendous."

"Gordon, it's no good railing on about it. You of all people. There are a lot of people who look to papers like ours for moral uplift, you know.

"Yes, I DO know, and of course I don't talk like this publicly. But we've known each other a long time. We are the same generation. Same background. You know – 1914 and all that. It was even worse then. No, I correct myself. The military casualties were worse. But there was not then the murdering of millions of Jews, and Gypsies and the mentally retarded, and everyone else Hitler didn't like the look of." Gordon Johns looked old and haggard. He had carried the paper right through the war, had done so much to bolster the staff's spirits, and, via the paper every Sunday, a large chunk of the British public as well.

"And I wanted to say another thing, Claud. You've done a damned fine lot for reader morale with that column of yours. Consistently it has been first class stuff and has lifted the gloom in many households. There are a lot of people who should be grateful. And one other thing, old friend. It may not sell newspapers, but your missus has given the people across the North Sea one hell of a morale boost. I've listened in a number of times. She really has a knack of coming out with the right stuff. I loved that piece she did after the V1 put her in hospital."

"Thanks. I'll tell her, Gordon. By the way, you didn't call me in just to tell me that, did you?

"No, I didn't". Gordon stood up behind his huge desk, grinning. "I wanted to give you this" He held out a white envelope.

"God, that's not my leaving notice, is it?"

"Don't be damned silly. Just open it. Here's a paper knife."

There were two pieces of paper in the envelope. The first was an invitation to Mr & Mrs C Browning to spend a 3-day weekend, all expenses paid, at the Grosvenor House Hotel in Park Lane, courtesy of the Sunday Gazette. The second was a cheque for £500.

"What on earth is this for, Gordon? Five hundred pounds! That's half a year's salary. What on earth would the Chairman say if he knew?"

"Look at the signature, Claud, he signed it. It was his idea, although I planted the seed, perhaps. It's our view of the contribution you have made during this blasted war, both to Gazette newspapers, and the reading public. Go off and enjoy it. And the Hotel. I wish I could afford to stay there! And when you get back, there is still a war to polish off. Then we can all relax a bit. Now it's time to broach that bottle of twenty year old Bruichladdich Single Malt Scotch. I've been saving it for years. I said I'd wait until the Armistice is signed, but we'd better check it's drinkable now, don't you?"

Claud was a little late getting home that evening.

CHAPTER 109

Finn was happy to go back for his second term at St. Luke's. Whilst Christmas at Rosedown had been memorable, especially with Douglas appearing out of the blue, he was eager to be back amongst his new found friends at the college, and back to his widening range of activities and interests.. Silk had gone. He was history and thank heavens for that. The new House Captain was Maurice Cashmore, a fellow who would not stand any nonsense, but was fair and square. Finn was fully aware that some "pretty-boys", usually first or second-termers, unwittingly attracted the unhealthy attention of "seniors". Cashmore would not countenance any of that unhealthy behaviour. At fourteen, Finn knew all about "the birds and the bees". It was an annoyance to him that thoughts of the feminine sex sometimes intruded on more important matters, such as sport. Even worse, there were occasions when the thought of girls generated a disturbance of another kind, which might be visible to the casual observer. One dreadful manifestation of this was when travelling on a bus, when almost invariably, the bus's vibrations triggered a swelling in his trousers, to the point where he had to make sure he had a newspaper or bag that he could carry to hide the offending bulge. Some boys bragged about their sexual development and one of his dormitory companions once smuggled in the monthly publication of the Naturists Society, called "Health and Efficiency" which contained pictures showing totally naked members of both sexes (though the genital areas were blanked out!). This lad charged two pence for a look-see, which earned him enough to go into town and stuff himself with custard tarts from "Miss Lily's Bakery".

Without question, at this stage of his young life, the idea of having a girl friend had no appeal whatsoever. They were a nuisance, it was that simple. Of course, there was Diane, who lived a few doors away. In the holidays he could scarcely avoid her. Like Finn, she was tall for her age and had hair as fair as Finn's. She had always been friendly, and a bit tomboyish, and had once invited him two or three years ago to play with her in her parents' air raid shelter at the end of her garden. But her suggestion that he pretend to be a "patient" and her a "nurse", had immediately palled when the young lady further suggested that he should remove his shorts, so that she could give him "a medical examination" No thanks nurse, I would rather do some athletics training! It never occurred to him that reversing the roles might be interesting: he the "doctor" and she "the patient"!

He enjoyed life at St Luke's. All that is, except the food, which was bordering on the atrocious. Of course, there was still rationing, and it was no less restrictive because the tide of war had at last turned in Britain's' favour. There was still a threat from U-Boats, though much diminished, and Britain depended on shipping for so much of its food. Grain, in particular,\nearly all came across the Atlantic, either from Canada or the USA, and much of the meat came from South America. Vegetables were more plentiful, but then it was a matter of how they were cooked. Usually too much in Finn's view. His particular hate was spinach, boiled always until it was a dark, slimy sludge. Similarly, meat at College was normally boiled, until all the colour and flavour had drained from it. Why it had to be boiled Finn never discovered. The residue liquid was served as soup, perhaps with a little Bovril mixed in, or an Oxo cube. Puddings were a bit better, but not much. Rice Pudding was fine, but not when it was a case of grains floating in an opaque, watery liquid, or when all the liquid had been boiled away, leaving a solid mush. Then, there was the Flying Squad. This was the team of boys detailed to clear the tables and clear away the debris to the kitchen, and after that, lay the tables for the next meal. This duty rotated from one House to the next, and was the preserve of first year pupils, supervised by a prefect. Flying Squad duty carried the additional handicap that the post-lunch opening of the Tuck Shop (by Donny Doncaster with the key that always hung round his neck) was too brief for flying Squad members to attend it.

This apart, life at St. Luke's could be a lot worse. Finn was clearly popular with his contemporaries, many of whom envied his sporting ability. Rugby in the Easter Term was played for only the first six weeks. Thereafter, boys had a choice of other games: Fives, Squash, Cross-country Running, Tennis or Hockey. News of Finn's now-regular squash matches with Michael Sears had spread throughout the College and invariably attracted an audience in the gallery, most of whom rooted for Finn, except for those few hoping to ingratiate themselves with Sears. And Sears was far too streetwise to be taken in by that.

Finn was still disappointed that his father would not yield to his plea to become a full boarder, but at least it left him able to pay visits to the Convalescent Home at Headley. The Home had been established by the RAF, but since the invasion of Normandy, a growing proportion of "customers", as the staff called them, were Army personnel, recovering from gunshot or shrapnel wounds, or in some cases burns or amputations. It was when mentioning this weekend activity to Michael Sears, that Finn learned that he had been invalided out of the RAF early in 1942. It emerged that he had been a Hurricane pilot escorting bombers on a daylight raid on the U-Boat pens at Le Havre, when his aircraft came under attack from an Me109. He had taken a cannon shell in his left arm, but diving for cloud cover, had managed to nurse his plane back across the channel and land it at Tangmere Fighter Station, near Chichester. "I was lucky, Finn. I was hit where my beautiful features were not disfigured, unlike some of those poor devils at Headley" he joked. He was also lucky that being right-handed, the damage did not affect his squash. After two months in hospital reconstructing the shattered bone, he had applied to return to flying duties, but had been refused, as his left arm had only limited usage. He was given a choice of ground duties, or the option of returning to civilian life, though not before being awarded a DFC. The thought of being grounded and watching young men taking off to "have a go" at the enemy, and never coming back, was too much. "I thought I would be more useful returning to my old job of teaching young layabouts like you! Anyway, young teachers were in short supply, so here I am."

Finn enjoyed Sears's Spanish lessons more than any others, partly because of his admiration for the man. As well as the beautiful cadences of the Spanish language, he enjoyed the insight Sears gave his pupils into the art and literature of Spain. He learned to appreciate the work of Velasquez and the Cretan born El Greco. And there was a line from a Spanish poet that stuck in his mind for the rest of his life:

"Toda la vida es sueno, y suenos suenos son." "All life is a dream, and dreams are but dreams." Sometimes Finn wondered if this was true, that all his experiences of those war years were just a dream: all the fear and the horror of it. Seeing the glow of London burning during the Blitz, seeing the stricken German bomber over Home Park and watching the crew member baling out and his parachute not opening, the hypnotic sight of the V1 plunging onto the grandstand at the Sports Meeting and the carnage that followed and now, more recently, the ghastly stories and pictures of the Concentration Camps. Surely THAT was unreal, a dream? In his more pensive moments Finn wished that he could lose himself reading Lope de Vega or Juan Melendez Valdes, and put the war out of his mind altogether. Well, at least the end was in sight. And all his family had come through – battered and scarred in three cases, but ok. So that was good. Perhaps if the war did end this year, the family could all go off for a holiday somewhere. Mum and Dad had raved about the Scilly Isles – perhaps they could all go there, especially now Dad had been given a huge bonus!

CHAPTER 110

The war raged on and now Finn had to start his third scrapbook. This latest one had a picture on its first page of the Stars and Stripes being raised on Mount Suribachi on Iwo Jima, a small island four miles by two miles, lying 600 miles south-west of Japan itself. Iwo Jima was a key stepping stone for intensifying American bomber attacks on the mainland of Japan, and the Japanese were well aware of it. Twenty one thousand troops defended it, dug into an elaborate network of tunnels and caves, that had survived two months of intense aerial bombardment. It was probably the most bitterly contested lump of rock in history, and it took four days of intense, hand to hand fighting before the Japs were finally subdued. "You know, Finn" Claud told him "Iwo Jima is about the same size as St.Mary's in the Isles of Scilly, which has a population of less than two thousand people. Can you imagine IT being defended by 21, 000 troops, resisting a vastly superior number of attacking troops, supported by massive air and sea bombardment as well. It's incredible!"

In the Baltic, millions of German civilians were being shipped westward, to escape the Red Terror of the advancing Red Army. The Russians were inflamed by propaganda exhorting them to wreak revenge on the enemy by killing the men, then raping and killing the women. There was no mercy. To escape, these terrified people left all their possessions behind and tramped across the icy wastes to reach Danzig and board ships to carry them, they hoped, to safety. But the sea itself was a danger – from mines, submarines and aircraft. Even that was better than facing and falling prey to the dreaded Red Army.

On March 1st, US troops captured the town of Munchen-Gladbach. Next should be Dusseldorf and Cologne.

Next day, 850 British bombers raided Cologne and the German army began to retreat from the Rhine.

Half way round the world the last pockets of Jap resistance in Manila, Philippines were mopped up, and twenty thousand Japanese troops died defending the city.

On the 7th the US Army crossed the Rhine at Remagen, after heroic attempts by individual Germans to blow up the bridge ended in failure.

In London on the 8th of March, a V2 rocket killed 110 and injured 123 when it hit Smithfield Market in London.

The raids on Dresden which so shocked the civilised world, with an estimated fifty thousand dead, were dwarfed on the night of March 9th/10th when a massive force of American B29s Super Fortresses attacked Tokyo. The estimate of dead lay between 80 and 120 thousand, with bodies piled high on roadsides and bridges, and in the canals. A further one million were estimated to be homeless. Incendiaries, fanned by a stiff breeze, ignited the mainly flimsy wooden homes and buildings. Sixteen square miles of industrial areas of the city were flattened, with hardly a building left standing. The effect on Japanese morale was devastating. And yet, and yet, these doomed enemies of the free and civilised world fought on. But was "civilised" an appropriate description to apply to the Allies who perpetrated these horrors? There were those who said that they had sunk to the same, depraved inhuman depths as those they strove to defeat. Though inevitably acutely aware of the events of war, nevertheless Finn's world was the world of a young boy. It takes a man, perhaps even an old man, fully to grasp what a hideous cataclysm Mankind was turning his planet into. It was a process that showed no hint of slowing down, let alone reversing, even after the end of this appalling conflict.

CHAPTER 111

Trains out of Waterloo were disrupted. No one seemed to know why, there were just hundreds of people milling about the Station forecourt. The Departures board displayed the simple and unhelpful words: "To Be Advised". Bobby was lucky to find an empty seat in the Cafeteria at the south end of the concourse. It was 6.15pm on March 16th. She had been at the Norwegian Embassy making another broadcast on Free Norway, and doing some preliminary work on the next one.

She had to be careful, now that the end of the war was near, not to overplay the euphoria. Not whilst her listeners were still under the Nazis control. It was tiring and she had eaten little during the day. Too bad that the cheese sandwich was tired as well. She shared the table with a couple who were clearly in love with one another, staring dreamily into one another's eyes, and clutching hands. What was their story ,she wondered. Was he in the Forces? Couldn't tell; he was wearing a sports jacket and grey flannels. He looked to be about 35, she a few years younger. Bobby noticed she was wearing a wedding band on her fourth finger, left hand. But the man was not. She speculated. Maybe they married recently and he was leaving her to return to military duty. Probably wildly wide of the truth. Her thoughts drifted away from them. Her Svengali! She loved Claud. Would never leave him, never betray him. Claud loved her, there was no doubt of that, right from the moment they had met in Dublin those many years ago, just after the Great War. The war to end all wars, they had said. What a joke! God, it would soon be their Silver Wedding – 25 years together. Of course it was not all plain sailing with Claud. At times it had been extremely difficult. Sometimes, for no discernible reason, he would fly into a rage. Almost always about the most trivial thing. Even nothing, sometimes. He was better now, but on one occasion in the early years, he would hurl some object across the room. She remembered once, at Barnes, he had hurled a sherry glass (a present from her parents), straight through the open window onto the stone terrace outside. He had spent the next half-hour clearing all the glass fragments. That had calmed him down a bit. He was really sorry. Ashamed. But then there were the tender moments, too. She must not forget those. He would stroke her back in bed with the most delicate of touches. His fingers would trace the vertebrae of her spine, then down into the lumbar hollow and then on to the curve of her buttocks. It sent delicious shivers through her whole frame. And what a lover he had been. God, he knew how to arouse her. He was like the conductor of an orchestra, willing, teasing, enticing the musicians to a crescendo. Oh and what a crescendo!

This "Lars business" was ridiculous. For heaven's sake, she had only met him once, apart from the initial rebuff she had handed out at the Recreation Ground. Sure, he was handsome – far better looking than Claud, and a whole heap younger. And he was Norwegian, like her. Was that part of his appeal? "Appeal?" There had been far too brief a connexion with him to say there was any appeal. Whatever it was, she could not forget him. And did not want to.

At long last, the Station PA sprang to life to announce that the blockage on the line, at Queen's Road Battersea, had been cleared and that passengers should consult the Departure Boards. Bobby rose, only to see that her next train would not leave until 7.35pm. She still had nearly three quarters of an hour to wait. She found an empty phone box and called home. Claud answered. "Darling, the trains are running late. Some trouble on the line. I'm at Waterloo still, but I should be home soon after eight. Don't wait supper, please. Had a good day?" "So, so. It's quiet without you, but I have been working on my column. Like me to meet you at the station?" "Oh, no need. I'll walk up the hill. The exercise should do me good. See you at eightish. Bye"

Bobby felt like something a bit stronger than coffee, and made her way to the Buffet. "I suppose you couldn't manage a Gin and Tonic" she asked the elderly barman. "Madam, have you forgotten there is still a war on?" He lowered his voice to a whisper. "But I do have a secret bottle of Gordon's, that I save for special people, so I think you are in luck." It was fortunate that he kept his voice low – he did not want the whole crowded bar to hear him. Then, in a louder voice: "Your tonic water, Madam.", and he winked slyly at Bobby and drifted away to serve a customer further along the Bar. Bobby found a corner seat and was soon lost in thought again. Not Lars this time. Nor her husband. It was her homeland, her beloved Norway. It was six years since she had set foot there, and been in the mountains and fjords of her childhood and youth, and smelled the pine forests and listened to the waterfalls. How had her family survived? And her many friends there? Had they survived at all? And her Mother and Father, what of them? Elderly now, almost certainly physically less able. She vowed to herself that she would return as soon as the war had ended. Not long now. Not long before Hitler and his mob faced a firing squad, as her son had done. No, that's too good for them – better to hang them from the highest tree and let them rot there.

Thank God all her sons had survived. But in two cases only just. It had been bad enough thinking of Clive's narrow escapes – torpedoed in the Atlantic, jailed by the Argentinians, then shot up over Germany. Still, he was out of the firing line now. And married and a father to boot! She loved Philippa as if she was her own daughter, the daughter she had always longed for. And now she had a granddaughter as well.

Little Charlotte was a pet, and growing up so fast. She had the Norsk fair hair, just like Bobby herself and her uncle Finn. Same pale blue eyes as well.

But Clive's survival was matched and surpassed, if that was the right term, by his brother Douglas. The terror he had faced was beyond comprehension. To look death in the eye, to know that in a few moments he would for certain be shot dead, to hear the order "Take aim" and then hear the rifle bolts slam the bullets into the breech, and then the order "Fire". If it was possible to die before death, then Douglas had died. Nothing could be worse than that. Douglas was not the same man who had left for Malta to take on the Luftwaffe. Then he had been self-assured. Bright eyed and immortal, and eager for combat. Not now. Now he had aged. Already his hair was receding, but that was a triviality compared with the change in his personality. He was quieter now and grim-lipped. There was a steeliness about him. Celia had returned from Malta a few weeks after Douglas's repatriation, which was far better than Douglas going to Malta as had at first been the plan. He brightened a little then and smiled a bit, but there was still the hauntedness about him, as if he was thinking of that terrible moment in his life. "Why don't you go off to the Scillies? You both have a bit of leave", Claud had suggested. They had done so, and stayed in the same little cottage on St.Agnes that she and Claud had told them about. They had wandered out on the wind-swept Downs. Of course, it was early in the year, so the weather had been chilly, but the sun had shone most days and the daffodils flooded the fields like a golden patchwork on a green quilt. They had found a sheltered spot, in the lee of a great rock, and had made love there, even though it was wintry. No one to see them out there! Celia had tried to take him out of himself, but she knew, she could see, that the nightmare kept flooding his thoughts, and then he would fall silent, brooding, and be miles away.

Eventually, like Michael Sears at Finn's school, Douglas had been offered demobilisation, but he had refused. He wanted revenge for what the bastards had done to him, and to his mates in the Camp, who had been less fortunate than him. Innocent young men who had died for nothing other than to deter others from trying to escape. He, Douglas, wanted to take aim and fire, but not just one bullet. A hundred, a thousand, ten thousand and, with each one, to kill a German. But life had not been that easy. After Christmas he had had to be medically checked. That was okay; the bullet in his shoulder had done no irreparable damage. The psychiatric people had reservations, though. It was a question of whether his hate and the sheer malice he expressed, could override cool judgments in the face of his enemies. Recklessness was no good for this young man, nor the aircraft he was flying and worst of all, for the safety of the colleagues he would be flying alongside. In the end, they decided that Douglas needed time. Douglas needed re-familiarisation with the latest Mark of the Seafire. This would take until mid March. He could then be posted to the Far East to join the S.E. Asia Fleet, based at Colombo in Ceylon. If by then he was considered fully "airworthy" he could have a go at the Japanese. That was if the war was still not won. Celia's parents had set aside a room for the couple at their home in Wimbledon, and had discreetly found reasons to "be seeing friends in the country" whenever the pair could be there, leaving the house conveniently clear.

"I suppose you could not find another "Tonic Water" for me, barman?" "Of course, madam, just like the last one?" He winked, there were still twenty minutes until her train.

Bobby's thoughts turned to Finn – her "baby". Finn had been a great comfort to her through these years of anxiety and stress. Now fourteen, and growing taller every day, it seemed that he had developed in more than just physical terms. He had displayed a sensitivity rare in one so young. He cared about people. Especially, he cared about those poor men at Headley, and gave freely of his time to helping them and raising their spirits. And he brought a smile to the faces of Bobby's women friends, seeming to understand the female psyche, making these ladies feel that they were not just boring housewives and widows. With gentle, innocent flattery he could make them smile and laugh a little. As she sipped her second gin and tonic, Bobby pondered what Finn might do with his adult life. University would be a sensible launching pad. Whilst not a genius, he had a good brain and applied himself readily. He had settled well at St. Luke's, and his first term report had been very gratifying.

Kenneth was pretty bright too. He had a level head, just occasionally impetuous, and sailed through getting his commission in the Royal Artillery.. Thank heavens that it looked unlikely that he would be involved in any combat at this late stage of the war, unless the Far East campaign dragged on. In civilian life she thought, the City might attract him. He had always shown an appreciation of money, and certainly the Post War financial world would provide opportunities. It was strange, she thought, that none of the boys seemed interested in following their father's profession of journalism. She could be wrong, of course.

So lost in these thoughts was she, that she had to hurry to the barrier at Platform Eleven. Claud met her at Surbiton Station, despite her having assured him it was unnecessary. They walked up St.Mark's Hill and he held her hand all the way home. That night they made love. He was very gentle, just as he had been in her thoughts at Waterloo. Bobby slept until eight next morning.

CHAPTER 112

"Browning, we are putting you in the Senior Squash team on Saturday, against Holmbury Hall School. Congratulations! Actually, we have checked back on our records, and by a mile, you are the youngest boy ever to play for the St. Luke's Squash team. Mark you, don't let it go to your head, we only started playing inter-school squash in 1937, but none the less it is very creditable. Now, make sure you win your rubber." Michael Sears smiled, and shook Finn's hand. A squash team consists of five players , and it is the usual strategy to field the weakest player first and the strongest last. Without notifying the St. Luke's, Holmbury Hall reversed their order of play – probably wanting to get off to a flying start by winning the first rubber, and possibly the second as well. Not sporting. There were smirks on all the Holmbury Hall faces as their star turn took to the court, and found he was playing a fourteen year old. To everyone's astonishment, after losing the first two games 5-9, 5-9, Finn proceeded to win the next three 9-7, 9-6, 9-7, after forty seven minutes. By the time St. Luke's had won the match by three rubbers to two, the Holmbury Hall smiles had turned to looks of shamefaced embarrassment. Sears was delighted: "Well done lads, and especially to you Browning. But keep your feet on the ground chaps, Holmbury Hall are not the greatest opponents we will encounter. Oh, and by the way Browning, I think it safe to say you will be picked again and maybe a little higher than Fifth String.

The next morning, the whole team were clapped into Assembly.

CHAPTER 113

On March 6th, advance units of the American First Army entered the cathedral city of Cologne. In the southern suburbs, they came across retreating remnants of their dispirited German opponents. Only about one quarter of the city was still standing, but miraculously its beautiful Gothic cathedral had survived the bombardment, even to the extent that regular services had been held in the vestry. Only 150,000 of Cologne's peacetime population of one million remained.

An extraordinary statistic was recorded by the RAF around this time. It was the dropping of the biggest bomb so far used in the war. It weighed 22,000 lbs, or almost ten tons. This involved modifications to the Lancaster bomber that carried it: strengthened undercarriages, cutaway bomb bays, and more powerful engines. To save weight, two of its normal crew of seven, were dispensed with. At the instant of release (scoring a direct hit on the Bielefeld Viaduct) the Lancaster shot up some five hundred feet!

In Germany, Adolf Eichmann declared: "I shall go to my grave happy in the knowledge that I have helped kill six million Jews. Rudolf Hoess (not the same as the Deputy Fuhrer Rudolf Hess who fled to England), former Commandant of Auschwitz, declared that he had gassed two million Jews between 1941 and the end of 1943, on the orders of Heinrich Himmler.

By the end of March, the Red Army was preparing for its final thrust – the assault on Berlin itself. The Russian Commander, Marshal Zhukov, had by now crossed the Oder river and had taken Kustrin – his last obstacle before the capital. Berlin itself was only 35 miles away. To the West, Monty and the American General Patton continued their advance. Monty's aim was to push across the north German plains, whilst further south, Patton secured the Ruhr, the heart of Hitler's industrial powerhouse. With one and a quarter million men and five thousand artillery pieces at his command, Montgomery's assault was unstoppable.

By the 20th of March, in Burma, Mandalay had fallen to the 19th Indian division under the command of General Peter Rees, at only five feet high, he was known as the "Pocket Napoleon". As March turned into April, resistance to the Russians in the East, and the British & Americans in the West was weakening – especially in the West. It was simply a question now of who would enter the German capital first. Would it be the Russians, who were only 30 or so miles away, or the UW & British who were nearer 200 miles from Berlin? Eisenhower, the Supreme Allied commander, ordered his forces not to advance beyond the Elbe. He stated that he was not prepared to risk the lives of his men for the sake of a political advantage over an Ally. He had many and powerful critics: the British, Canadians and Americans were by now meeting little resistance, whilst the Russians were fighting fanatical SS Units, more than willing to dog it out to the bitter end.

April began. In Paris, the Arc de Triomphe and the Eiffel tower were floodlit for the first time, since war broke out six years ago. The German Army in the West was disintegrating under the impact of Allied columns racing for Bremen, Hamburg and Hanover. The roads were clogged with long columns of German prisoners plodding westward into the Allied Prison Camps. German towns and villages were passed, bearing no sign of war, other than white flags hanging from the windows.

Simultaneously, in the Pacific, American forces had landed on Okinawa, a mere 300 miles south of the Japanese mainland. They were surprised by the lack of opposition, as the Japanese were known to have 100,000 men there. Okinawa is to be the springboard for the invasion of Japan proper. But the Japs have stationed few men on the beaches in order to save them from the massive naval bombardment that preceded the landings. They were there all right, but had established strong defensive positions further inland, beyond the range of naval gunfire. Okinawa would not fall lightly.

On April 12th, President Roosevelt died suddenly at the age of 63, whilst sitting for a portrait. Roosevelt was the only US President ever to be elected four times. He was instantly succeeded by the Vice President, Harry S Truman. Minutes later, Truman was informed by the Secretary for War that the US had developed a new explosive of incredible power.

It was called an Atom Bomb.

As the end of term grew near, so the excitement swelled. It was always so at boarding schools. The end of "incarceration", a few weeks of heaven, which in most boys' minds equated to a) no more tedious lessons and homework, b) lying in bed all the morning, c) having a hot bath instead of tepid showers (even if you were only allowed five inches of water in the bath), d) keeping out of trouble with the Staff and, most important of all e) some decent food. Oh, and reuniting with the family. But this end of term was different. For weeks, the buzz about the war's progress was everywhere, on everyone's lips, Staff included. Morning Prayers now included an appeal to the Almighty "to end it soon and deliver our loved ones safely home again."

In the Great War, lads of seventeen and even younger, had hurried to serve their King and Country, often tricking the authorities by lying about their age. Many of these same "lads", now in their late thirties or early forties had again taken up arms in this conflict. The losses had been many times greater than in this War, and yet there were three major differences that made this time seem worse. The first was that this time the war had come to the towns and cities of Great Britain, and indeed Germany as well. Tens of thousands of innocent civilians had died, often in their own homes. Only God knew how many more had been injured: limbs lost, sight lost, bodies burned, minds shattered. The second difference was that every single person had SEEN the horrors, and not just the ones on their doorstep. Few had failed to view the cinema newsreels. The scenes of devastation in terms of human lives and property, throughout Europe and now, if that was not bad enough, the sickening sights of the concentration camps that were being liberated. The third difference was that, horrendous as it had been, the Great War had lasted only four years. This was in its sixth and still raging.

And so to term's end.

"Cheerio, Harry. See you in May. It'll be over by then, daresay."

"'spect so, Andy. Fingers crossed. Wonder what they'll do to old Adolf."

"Finn, s'pose you'll be looking forward to your brothers coming home?"

"You bet I am, except that they'll start bossing me around again, worst luck. Either that or they'll totally ignore me!"

"Johnny, isn't your Dad out in Burma somewhere?"

"Not sure where he is right now. But he should be ok, as long as the Japs call it a day, and I'm sure they will once the Germans put their hands up."

Finn had been home for two weeks when news broke of what had been discovered at Bergen-Belsen Concentration Camp. The British Army negotiated a truce with the local German Commander, which enabled them to enter the Camp peacefully. On entering they were confronted with a pile of naked female bodies, four feet high, thirty yards wide and eight yards long. "You can't see any faces, just bony elbows, knees and buttocks, or twisted hands and feet." With the British in full control, the Camp Commandant was arrested. His name was Josef Kramer. He and his men were put to work burying the estimated ten thousand bodies lying dead. About thirty thousand victims were still alive, but many died from starvation, typhus and dysentry before they could be saved.

Later in the month at another Camp – Dachau – American soldiers found mounds of human bodies and were so enraged that they summarily executed over one hundred German guards who had surrendered. At yet another Camp, this time Buchenwald, it was too much to take for even the toughest of men. Generals Eisenhower, the Supreme Commander, and his aide General Bradley, burst into tears. General Patton, by common consent the most battle-scarred of all the Allied leaders, was so overwhelmed by the sight and stench of the piles of human bodies, that he bent down and vomited.

Among those found in the prisoners' huts there were tens of thousands of slave labourers, mere skeletons, too weak to move. Among them were many of Europe's leading intellectuals, from Austria, Poland, Hungary and the Netherlands, as well as Germany itself.

The extermination of Jews and other "Undesirables" became known as THE HOLOCAUST.

It was beyond understanding

It was beyond reason

It was beyond forgiveness

It was beyond the depths to which humanity, in all its long history, has ever before degenerated.

If, at age fourteen, Finn still retained vestiges of childhood, they evaporated as these scenes unfolded. These revelations shocked the whole world. Numbness. Disbelief. Disgust. Fury. Sorrow seemed too anaemic an emotion to feel. These were emotions and reactions for which there were no words.

In the Browning household, few words were spoken. For several days Finn did little but stay in his room, just coming downstairs for meals. Some of the time he pasted in pictures of the scenes at these Camps into his scrapbook. He did not turn away from these terrible revelations, but neither could he really grasp them Nor could he bring himself to discuss them to his mother and father, because what was there to say? There was no salvation, no easing of the mind and spirit, no explanation possible.

When finally the holiday was over and the new term began, Finn was glad. Though he could not know it at the outset, the new term, the Summer Term of 1945, was the last during which the War would still be waged.

CHAPTER 114

By late April it was nearly over. By the 23rd, the Red Army had broken into the outskirts of Berlin from the North, the South and the East. Russian shelling was destroying western and central areas of the city, and overhead their aircraft strafing over the rubble to subdue any lingering resistance. Next day, German forces heading east from the Western front to help relieve the capital, were bombed by the RAF. By the 25th Berlin was completely encircled, and doomed. There was no way out, no escape. Government buildings in the Wilhelmstrasse were under fire from Russian field artillery. By the 27th Russian troops were advancing house by house and street by street. They are brutal, looting and raping as they go. All that is left to the Germans is a garrison three miles wide and ten miles long. They are running out of food and ammunition. Russian troops were infiltrating through the subways and even through the sewers. Risking instant execution by the fanatical SS, German soldiers were nevertheless surrendering to the Russians. On the 30t$^{h.}$ the Reichstag fell after heavy bombarding by Russian guns. Late that evening the Red Flag was hoisted over the building. The battle for Berlin was over.

Deep in his bunker, Adolf Hitler married Eva Braun, his mistress. Next day, after lunch, Hitler and Eva retired to his quarters. Goebbels and a few other faithful followers heard a shot ring out. Nearby was the body of Eva Braun. She had taken poison. On the 1st May, Goebbels poisoned all his six children and then asked an SS orderly to shoot him and his wife Magda in the back of the head.

On May 4th, a team of German Generals and Admirals, led by Admiral Friedeburg, entered a tent on Luneberg Heath and signed the surrender of all German Forces in North-West Germany. The terms of capitulation were read out by Montgomery. He denied the Germans' request that he accept the surrender of German forces fighting the Russians, insisting that they must surrender to the Russian Commander. Fighting continued against the Russians for a few days, but that was the end.

"The Third Reich will last for a Thousand Years", Hitler had claimed. It lasted barely twenty.

On May 8th, Claud, Bobby and Finn caught the train to London. They were met at Waterloo by Clive, Philipppa and Charlotte. Then they all joined the vast throng gathered outside Buckingham Palace. Loudspeakers broadcast Winston Churchill's statement from 10 Downing Street.

"The German war is at an end. Advance Britannia! Long live the cause of freedom. God save the King! Until that announcement the crowd had been expectant, but subdued, awaiting those words. Now the pent-up feeling burst loose. There was dancing in the streets, people sang and blew whistles, and climbed lampposts. Clive, in his RAF uniform, was embraced and kissed by total strangers. At the Palace, the crowd began to chant. Bobby and Claud and Finn and Clive and Philippa and even little Charlotte took up the cry: "We want the King!" "We want the King!" Soon, the King appeared on the balcony, with the Queen and the two Princesses, Elizabeth and Margaret Rose. It was the first of eight appearances the King made that day. Churchill made a formal announcement to the House of Commons: "Finally", he said, "Almost the whole world was combined against the evildoers, who are now prostrate before us. But let us not forget that Japan, with all her treachery and greed, remains unsubdued and her detestable cruelties call for justice and retribution."

Churchill appeared later on the balcony, with the King. He waved his hat as the crowd, undiminished in numbers, sang "Land of Hope and Glory".

"This is your victory. In all our long history, we have never seen a greater day than this.

On the way back to Waterloo, the Brownings encountered a Fish and Chip shop. They ate out of newspapers bearing the date of the last day of the war with the greatest enemy that Britain had ever faced. They should have kept that newspaper as a lasting memento, but did not think to do so. Anyway, there was still the Japanese to finish off. Finn's War was not quite finished. Not quite.

CHAPTER 115

After the euphoria, it was back to business.. For those fighting the Japanese, the happy events in Europe were of small comfort. The Americans fighting in Okinawa were meeting ferocious resistance from their fanatical enemy. From the air, US troops on the ground were attacked constantly by Japanese airmen hell-bent on suicide. Hundreds of these Kamikaze pilots also struck at the Allied naval task force supporting the ground operation.

Elsewhere, British destroyers have success in the Straits of Malacca, sinking the Japanese heavy cruiser "Haguro", whilst Australian troops capture Wewak, the last enemy held port on the mainland of New Guinea Air attacks on the Japanese mainland continue with fierce incendiary attacks on the port of Yokohama, the bombing of mainland Japanese targets is in preparation for the final land forces assault upon it. But Allied leaders are well aware how fanatically it will be defended and know that losses on both sides will be heavy. Their hope is that if Japan is bombed sufficiently heavily, and continuously enough, then surrender will be forced upon them without recourse to a land invasion. And so the bombing continues. On June 1st a force of B.29s drop 3,000 tons of incendiaries on Osaka and on the 5th drop a similar quantity on Kobe. By the 12th Japanese forces on Okinawa have been forced into a small pocket of a mere square kilometre and start committing suicide in preference to being taken prisoner.

Phone lines to the Occupied Countries of Europe were soon re-opened, and as soon as they were, Bobby called her parents.

"Mama, it is Roberta. Can you hear me alright?"

the voice that answered had changed in six years, but was still clear and firm. "Roberta! Is that you, Roberta? Really you?"

"Yes Mama. It is really me. How are you and how is Papa?"

"Well, we are alive. And that is a bit of a surprise, I suppose. It has not been easy here. Some terrible things happened, but it is best not to talk about them. Not now.

We listened to your broadcasts. How wonderful they were. Many people listened. Of course, we did not tell them it was you. Too dangerous that would have been. We were so proud of you! But you were wounded last year. That was terrible. What a tragedy at that place, with all the children there too. Is it really all right now, your – you know where. I do not like to say the word!" Bobby heard a little chuckle from her mother."

"Yes Mama. My back side is fine. No trouble now. The English have a rude word for that part. They call it their BUM.

Bobby heard another small laugh, then; "Tell me, Roberta, about Claud and your boys. Are they all alright?"

"Yes, mama, Clive was flying in Lancaster bombers. He got wounded, but not too badly. Also, Mama, he is married and you have a little great grand-daughter. She is sweet and called Charlotte. Douglas was a fighter pilot in the Royal Navy. He came down in Italy and was taken prisoner in Germany." Bobby decided to say nothing about his facing a firing squad. It would have been too great a shock, she felt. "But he also is married, to a lovely girl called Celia. No children yet, but I hope, I think there will be soon. Kenneth joined the Army, but he did not have to fight, thank God, and of course Finn was too young. He is as tall as me now, and he has the look of a Norwegian boy. Eyes like ice, and lovely wavy blond hair. He is a fine athlete"

"Oh, it all sounds so marvellous, darling daughter. How I have missed you. I hope we can see you soon. How is Claud?"

"Claud is fine now, but he had another heart attack a while ago, so he does not exert himself too greatly. But with four strapping boys, he does not need to do heavy work. Just a little golf now and then. Now, Mama, let me speak to Papa. Is he there?"

Bobby spoke too her father for a short time, and he too, sounded different. Older. The voice had a slight quaver to it. Bobby knew that she should do everything possible to get to Norway as soon as she could....

CHAPTER 116

The Summer Term at St. Luke's was sheer joy for Finn. He revelled in all the activities he was now involved in. Apart from sport and the class work, Finn had taken up carpentry, and spent happy and productive hours in the workshop. He also developed an interest in birds, and when ever time allowed, he would cycle out to White Downs, Box Hill, to see what he could spot. At the White Downs one early evening it was not a bird that caught his attention, but cubs emerging from a badger sett and he spent half an hour just entranced watching them. At St. Luke's, little emphasis was given to Athletics as a sport, but a Sport Day Competition was held nevertheless. Finn took a full part and it came as a surprise to no one when he won the Under 15 220 and 440 yards finals. But on the debit side of the balance sheet, he just could not get fired up about Cricket. The best he could do was make up the numbers for his Junior House Eleven. North House made the final that summer, but Finn could only score seven runs, all in singles, and make one running catch at deep fine leg.

At weekends he still went to the Convalescent Home at Headley. The war in Europe might be over, but that made little difference to the terrible injuries that had been suffered by the men there. Finn was now near totally inured against the appalling sights that he was confronted with. On fine, warm days he would escort some of those able to leave the wards and sit or stroll in the gardens. He would chat about what he was doing at school, or about the birds he had seen and nests he had located. In those days skylarks were still plentiful and he would just sit with the patients and listen to their magical song high in the sky.

Everyone at St. Luke's was now intent on listening to the news bulletins whenever possible. There was a radio in the Junior Common Room and the news on the Home Service was a must at 9.00 pm, last thing before getting ready for bed. After lights out the gossip still continued, until a Dormitory Prefect called out: "Shut up you lot. Settle down. The war will still be on in the morning." The Prefects had a sneaking sympathy for the youngsters chatter, for they, too, would be indulging just the same in an hour's time when they settled down for the night.

The days passed. The tension and excitement grew. Again, just as it had back in May in the Easter Holidays, expectation was a little greater each day. But weeks passed and still the Japanese fanatics fought on. To a Japanese soldier, defeat and surrender were unthinkable. It would bring dishonour on them individually and on their proud nation. Far better to die with honour.

On July 16th history was made when the United States tested their new, secret weapon in the bleak, desolate New Mexico Desert. Robert Oppenheimer, the director of the laboratory responsible for this terrifying act, quoted the words from Bhavagavad-Gita: "If the radiance of a thousand suns were to burst into the sky, that would be like the splendour of the Mighty One". It was the first Atomic explosion.

Exploding with the force of 19,000 tons of TNT, it fused sand into glass and sent a mushroom cloud 40,000 feet into the sky. It was visible for a distance of 125 miles. Two weeks later, and knowing the appalling loss of life it would cause, the US President, Harry Truman, nevertheless gave assent for this terrible weapon to be dropped upon Japan.

At 8.15 on the morning of the 6th August, a single B.29, named "Enola Gay" dropped the first ever Atomic bomb upon the Japanese city of Hiroshima. The exact number of fatalities would never be known, but in a city of some 200,000 people, at least half died instantly, and, within five years, double that number had died from radiation burns and sickness. People died in many different ways. Some were just vaporised. Others were burnt to cinders where they stood. Others' eyes, intestines and brains just burst from their bodies. Some of those vaporised left shadows - imprints – of themselves on the scorched earth or stone. And yet, Japan did not surrender that day.

Three days later, America unleashed a second Atomic Bomb on the city of Nagasaki.

Five days later, on the14th August 1945, Japan surrendered unconditionally, bringing to its final end, the Second World War. In London, the announcement was made on the radio at midnight by Clement Attlee, the new Prime Minister, who had defeated Churchill in the July General Election. It had been a cruel blow for Winnie, who had so inspired the nation through the dark years, but that was politics. That was life.

By then, the School Term had ended. Finn had taken the offer of one of the patients at Headley, to help out on his father's farm in Dorset. Finn stayed up late to listen to Clement Attlee announce the final end of World War Two. Next morning, August 15th, Finn helped pull in the corn harvest. It was a fine summer's day, the sun beating down. A gentle breeze whispered through the golden wheat. As Finn toiled happily away he could hear a lark singing high in the blue sky. He thought to himself: It was a day like this when we sat round the radio at Mimosa Cottage. The Third of September, 1939. We listened to Neville Chamberlain tell us we were at war. But there was no lark singing that day. For a moment Finn paused, then sighed.

Finn's War had ended.

THE EPILOGUE

CLAUD

During the years following the War, Claud's health gradually deteriorated. Basically, it was bronchial, rather than his heart. The Great War in the trenches in France and Belgium had been a major contributor, as had those years of Fire Watching on the Office roof during the Blitz. Breathing became more and more laboured and physical exertion more difficult and tiring. At the end of 1948 he was compelled to give up all work, and spent his days just sitting in his favourite high-winged armchair in the lounge, reading the daily paper, or sometimes a book. Gone were the days when he could, or even wanted to potter in the garden. A small greenhouse had been built, and on warm days he would sit in it, but only to do a little dead-heading. Bobby took over care of the flowerbeds, but she did not really have her heart in it. By then the three older boys had all fled the nest and only Finn resided at No. 18. In the summer of that year, Finn left St.Luke's and in the Autumn went up to Jesus College, Cambridge. A sadness, an emptiness descended on the house.

On November 11th 1948 Claud went to bed early, saying he felt tired. Bobby remained in the lounge reading for a time, and listening to the ten o'clock news on the radio. When finally she went upstairs, Claud was lying on the bed, still dressed except for his jacket and his shoes. His hands were folded on his chest. Peacefully, he had died. Curiously it was exactly thirty years since the Great Armistice was signed at Versaillies – November 11th, 1918.

BOBBY and LARS

In the Spring of 1946, Bobby had made the journey back to Norway, to reunite with her family. Though still alive, her father and mother were in their eighties, and frail.

Clearly, it would not be long before they passed on. Whilst there she met Lars, who had written to her regularly (and of course directly, now that the war was over). His letters had always been carefully worded, so as to give no hint of his true, and undiminished feelings towards her. Lars had survived the German Occupation of his country unscathed by his daring exploits against German installations and personnel, and sustained by his anger towards those who had murdered his wife and son.

They met at the Norseman Hotel in Oslo on a grey morning in April. Since their last meeting all those years ago in Surbiton, Lars had grown a beard, a beard as fair as his wavy hair, though this was now flecked with grey at the temples. For a moment, she did not recognize him, sitting in the Hotel Lobby in a smart, two-piece grey suit. Lars saw her approach, rose, and smiling took her outstretched hand. To Bobby, it seemed a slightly uncertain smile. "Hello, Bobby. Last time it was a teashop. Peggy Brown's I think. I remember at the time I thought the name was so similar to your own – Bobby Browning! Perhaps now we could chance something a little stronger than tea?" She laughed. "Yes, of course. It is a very special moment. I feared I would never see you again. Nor should I have wished to, being so happily married, but now I am glad. And glad that you are alive and well. May I have a gin and tonic?"

During lunch he told her some of the things he had been able to do to undermine the Germans, and the anguish it had given him, knowing that his actions would trigger dreadful reprisals against innocent fellow citizens. He was keen to know about Bobby's war, and how her sons had fared during it. Especially he asked how Finn was doing with his Athletics.

Later, as they parted, Lars took her hand and shyly pressed it to his lips. Almost involuntarily, Bobby raised her face to his and kissed him on the cheek. "Will you come to England one day? This need not be goodbye." She whispered. He nodded. "Yes, I will come whenever you ask me" he replied. She smiled, turned and left him. Then turned again and called out: "Good. Make it soon, then". She laughed.

Between that first visit and Claud's death in 1948, Bobby visited her parents twice more, and each time she saw Lars in Moss, in the same Hotel. They lunched together and the friendship became firmer, but never was there a question of a physical relationship.

Lars used his wartime experiences to good effect. He founded a retail business selling skiing and mountaineering equipment and clothing, binoculars and telescopes, fishing rods and tackle, and hunting rifles. It flourished and he prospered. He also lectured and wrote about his life and adventures during the German Occupation, and in the course of this met numbers of beautiful women. But it was Bobby, no longer young, but still radiant and for him alluring, that he yearned for.

Then, in the Summer of 1949, only seven months after Claud's passing, Lars came to England, and asked Bobby if she would marry him. It was so soon after her loss. Whilst her conscience, the feeling of guilt said "No, it is too soon, he is hardly in his grave", her heart said "Yes". Finn would soon be gone, following his three brothers into that independence that all sound men attain. The emptiness, the thought of years of loneliness and solitary old age, were too much to contemplate. And she genuinely loved this man – so very different from Claud. Her final moment of indecision passed when all four sons urged her to "Go for it Mum – be happy", and Clive said that he would insist upon walking her up the aisle, and Charlotte wanted to be her Bridesmaid.

The wedding took place in September 1949, in Moss, where she had been born and raised, with all her family present. Bobby and Lars lived out their lives joyfully in Rygge, south of Oslo. Lars died of cancer in 1973, and Bobby died in her sleep three years later. She was 77.

KENNETH

Kenneth, disappointed that he had never seen action, or gone overseas during the war, was demobbed in August 1946. Before settling into a career, he decided that he would like to see something of the world. During his Army service he had bumped into a couple of Kiwis in a bar at Chandlers ford, near his base. They were officers in the NZ Navy. They raised his curiosity about life in New Zealand, and Ken made up his mind that he would go there and see for himself as soon as he had saved sufficient funds. For a year, he worked in an Insurance Broker's Office in Leadenhall Street in the City, and late in 1947 he bade au revoir to his family and embarked on a freighter heading Down Under.

One of the Kiwis, Mark Finnegan, had given Ken his parents address in Browns Bay, on the Auckland North Shore, where they ran a haberdashery business. They and Mark made Ken welcome and showed him the sights of the city. They gave him the names of friends in various parts of New Zealand, and Ken spent six weeks touring North and South Islands, until money began to run low. Returning to Auckland, he took a clerk's job with Isitt and Partners, Insurance Brokers, doing similar work to what he had been doing in Leadenhall Street. By this time, Kenneth had completely fallen in love with the Land of the Long White Cloud. Here was a country the size of Great Britain, but with a mere three and a half million people. Space, the feeling of openness, the relaxed outdoor life, the absence of "class" which he had detested in England, completely won him over. He adored the miles of empty beaches, the deserted lakes, the mighty mountains and glaciers, the tortured shapes of the volcanic hills, the fjords, tranquil and majestic. He was beguiled by it all, and warmed to the friendliness and openness of its people.

After a few years, and still in his early twenties, and now with his own modest apartment, he had enough experience and confidence to strike out on his own. He had noticed that certain sectors of the life insurance industry were under-exploited – particularly in two areas: Permanent Health Insurance and Personal Pensions. Ken took the plunge and opened a small office in nearby Takapuna, a burgeoning , middle-class district. He prepared a leaflet, a mailshot on these two subjects, ten thousand copies of each, for door-to-door delivery all along the North Shore communities, offering personal advice and help. The response was better than he had dared hope, and very soon he had to hire help to field all the phone calls and make appointments for him. The "help" was an attractive and intelligent young girl, called Alana. She soon showed that she could handle enquiries with charm and persuasiveness and sympathy where needed. Business flourished. So did Kenneth's fondness for Alana, and in 1951 they were married in a civil ceremony. Her family attended in strength, but none of the Brownings could make the long journey. However, Bobby's first grandson was born a year later, and christened Edmund, and for that ceremony Bobby and Lars did fly out, taking three days each way .in a Lockheed Super Constellation, stopping at Bombay, Singapore and Brisbane en route.

Ken opened more branches: in Hamilton, Napier and Wellington. Alana bore him three more children, all girls. Eventually, Ken sold the business whilst still in his early fifties, and retired to a small estate he had bought on the shores of Lake Taupo, in central North Island. He became an accomplished sailor, and loved nothing better than to sail his own forty foot catamaran to the islands of the South Pacific. He never returned to England. He could see no point in going back to a country that had become increasingly crowded, congested and riddled with class. As air travel improved and became so much faster, Bobby and Lars used to visit him, though towards the end of her life, the journey became too taxing. Edmund loved sport, especially Rugby Football, New Zealand's passion. He was a strong lad, stocky and quick off the mark. Ideal for a scrum half. In 1973, aged only 21, he was chosen for the All Blacks and won his first cap in the Second Test at Christchurch, against South Africa. Sadly, in 1974, a ghastly break and dislocation of his left ankle brought his career to a premature end. His three sisters all married, and live not far from their parents, one in Taupo itself and the other two in Napier.

Ken is now 81 and Alana 78.

DOUGLAS AND CELIA.

After the war, many pilots turned their back on the whole notion of Service Life, particularly flying, either civil or miltary. Douglas was different. He took the view that the nation had gratefully trained him to pilot aircraft, but had been deprived of his services because of a silly engine failure over enemy territory. He still wanted to fly. He felt he was meant to – some kind of destiny, perhaps. He applied for and was granted a Short Service Commission and soon was appointed Lieutenant Commander.

By this time, Celia and Douglas were the parents of two fine boys, Peter and James, and the owners of a spacious four bedroom house in Alresford, near Winchester. In 1950 with the erupting threat of a conflict in Korea, Celia pleaded with her husband to leave the Service. She dreaded a repetition of those terrible years when Douglas was a POW. If he was captured again he might this time face torture and death at the hands of the North Koreans. Douglas acceded. The stories filtering back made his flesh creep. Once had been enough.

After resigning, he applied for training as a pilot for the burgeoning national airline BOAC. It meant tedious conversion to multi-engined passenger planes, like the Viscount and Constellation, but it was a whole heap easier for him, than for raw recruits with no aviation experience at all. Better still, some of the training was at Hamble, on the Solent – only half an hour's drive from home. In time, Douglas graduated from the propeller aircraft of the 1950s, to jet powered aircraft: first the Boeing 707, then later to the Jumbo 747, on long haul to the Far East and Australasia. He was a frequent visitor to brother Ken and his wife and family in New Zealand, initially on his own, but eventually with Celia and the kids. They, too, loved New Zealand and nearing retirement they bought a "Batch", a small holiday home on the shores of Lake Taupo. Here they would escape the cold and dreary English winter. Douglas retired in 1980, but kept up his PPL and when in England spent happy summer weekends at the Lasham Gliding Club, both towing-up gliders, and flying them himself. Douglas died in 2001, aged 76. Celia, now in her 80s, is still alive today, and divides her time between Alresford, and the little house on Lake Taupo.One of the boys, Peter, is a successful solicitor in London and the other, James, followed his father and captains Airbus 320s for British Airways.

CLIVE AND PHILIPPA

Clive and Philippa's marriage survived the stresses placed upon it by his fervent devotion to the Catholic faith. After long and fruitless years of endeavour, he finally abandoned hope of "saving" Philippa, or any of his brothers. He even relented in his desire that Charlotte should be brought up a Catholic, or Henry, who arrived in the summer of 1948. "The door", he said, "should be open to them, but it is up to them to decide whether to pass through it."

Philippa had always received a generous allowance from her father, Sir Henry, but this did not preclude Clive's need to find work and earn a living. After the RAF had released him, he realized that he had no firm notions about what he wanted to do. Civilian life seemed insipid after the adventures of the war years. He knew he was not the Brain of Britain. He could not persuade himself, and Philippa could not either, persuade him to go through the grind of University or Professional qualification. Finally, after wallowing, and doing nothing, Claud found him a position as a cub reporter on the Gazette, reporting on Sport. The trouble was that he had never emulated his brothers' enthusiasm or abilities. "Clive has got two left feet" Kenneth cruelly used to say, and this showed in his reporting. It lacked all passion, or flair.

During the terrible winter of 1947, Philippa received a phone call from her mother. It seemed sir Henry's health problems were becoming more serious, and his doctor advised that he needed a warmer, drier climate. After carefully considering the options, they had decided to purchase an apartment near Funchal, in Madeira. They were sad to be leaving their beloved Rosedown, but they would be infinitely sadder if the old house were to pass out of the family. Philippa's brother had been long settled and successful in British Columbia for a number of years, and had made it clear he had no interest in returning to England, and even less in taking on Rosedown. Would Philippa and Clive agree to take it over, lock, stock and barrel. In any case it might avoid Death Duties at a later date, provided the General and Lady H. lived long enough. Of course, it was a wonderful surprise, and came precisely at the moment when Clive's career as a journalist was clearly faltering. The problem was, how to make it a paying proposition. Not on Clive's meagre salary, not even with the allowance from Sir Henry. That was certain.

It was Philippa who had the bright idea. "Clive, there is a new idea taking hold. It is called Time Share. People buy a period of time, probably a week or two, in which they are entitled to live in a particular property. The same week for so many years. It varies, but typically twenty or thirty. We could do that with Rosedown. We will never need to use it all, and I thought, why not let off the South Wing. It would easily divide into several self—contained units. The Nouveau Riche are buying timeshares in Spain and

Portugal, and places where they can get a winter or summer break for a week or two. But I think some of them would just like a break in the English countryside. You know, all those people grinding away in the City and so on. We could throw in use of the Walled Garden and the Squash court, and if things worked out, well, we could build a swimming pool and a tennis court as well. What do you think, darling?"

Clive leapt at the idea. "What about your parents Philippa. Do you think they would mind? We'd have to clear it with them, but if they were happy, then let's go for it. It will mean taking out a sizeable mortgage to fund all the construction work, and fitting out each unit. But with luck we could handle that on my present miserable job, plus you allowance." A little to their surprise Philippa's parents were not only in favour, but said they would fund the conversion work. "It's only your inheritance in advance, dear daughter, and if the project is successful, well, we can always buy a timeshare in our own former home. There's a curious thought!"

The South Wing converted into four totally separate units, each with its own entrance. They advertised in "Country Life" and "Field", and contrived to get articles in magazines and newspapers. After a few years, not only summer weeks were taken up, but the shoulder months as well. And to their amazement, all four units were bought for the Christmas season – a really unexpected bonus. In later years, revenue was such that they could not only install an all-seasons swimming pool, but by purchasing land from nearby farmers, they constructed a 9 hole golf course, complete with a Professional, and a Pro's Shop.

Today, Rosedown is still a flourishing business, managed ably by their son Henry and his son Andrew. As for Clive and Philippa, they retained a small apartment, just so they could monitor the business ("no interference, kids, just like to know how things are going"). They winter in Madeira, in the apartment bought all those years ago by Sir Henry. Clive's profound faith never wavered, but he was deeply saddened by the scandals that surrounded the Church of Rome. He was especially mystified and disillusioned by Papal unwillingness to condemn, or even challenge, the hideous barbarism of Hitler's regime, and more recently, the barrage of stories about Priests' abuse of young children.

Now in his eighties, Clive still walks round Rosedown Golf Course, and in summer swims a dozen or so gentle lengths of the Pool. Philippa occasionally joins him, but more often just sits and watches him, sometimes recalling that moment long, long ago when she lay in the bath, eyes closed, day dreaming, when Clive silently bent over and kissed her breast. Long ago it may have been, but the moment is still bright in her memory, and brings a faint smile to her lips.

FINN

Finally, in his last year at St. Luke's, Claud and Bobby relented and allowed Finn to become a full boarder. At the College there was no doubt in anyone's mind that Finn was an outstanding pupil, if not academically, then in most other ways. In September 1948 he was made Captain of the School. His first act was to plead with the Headmaster – still Donny Doncaster – to abolish corporal punishment, except by the Headmaster himself. He succeeded, to the approval of Staff and boys alike. Finn also became Captain of the First XV. He set a fine example of attacking Rugby. His swervy, raking stride beguiled many an opposing back row defender, and inspired his team to play an open, flowing style of play. His maxim was simple: the ball travels faster through the air than anyone can run, so move it quickly between players as much as possible.

From St. Luke's, Finn went to Jesus College, Cambridge, to read English, and graduated in 1951 with a 2:1 degree. He gained a Blue for rugby and a Half-Blue for squash. Up to this point in his life, Finn had never travelled overseas, except to Norway to see his Norwegian grandparents, and a one-week College trip to Paris. He determined to see what the world had to offer, just like his elder brother Kenneth. He obtained a position with the P & O Shipping Line as a Cabin Attendant. For a year he cruised the oceans, visiting the Middle East, India, Singapore, Australia and New Zealand. Ken's children adored him and implored him to tell them bedtime stories about the places he had visited. When this was exhausted he found he had a flair for making up fictional tales about animals and children's' adventures. It encouraged him to try writing for children and much to his amazement found favour with a London publisher with his first anthology of children's' tales. The book sold well and he then tried his hand at a full length book for children, based on a character called Henry George Tinker. More by accident than intention, writing children's' books became his full-time career. It gave him enough income to travel the world (occasionally piloted by his brother Douglas) and he began to write travel articles and guides for a variety of papers and magazines, in addition to his children's' novels. Later, with TV broadening its scope, he also produced holiday and travel programmes for the BBC.

Finn married late, at the age of 33. His bride, Susan, was the daughter of a diplomat, Sir Paul Finch, British Ambassador to Thailand. They had only one child, James. Like his father, James was a tall, fair-haired boy who also excelled at sport, especially golf, at which he became a successful Tournament Professional.

By this time in his late Sixties, and no longer as active physically as he had once been, Finn decided to write the story of his childhood during the war. For many years he and Susan had lived in Shropshire, in a beautiful Elizabethan manor house. Finn loved the countryside there, especially the hills to the south of their hamlet: Caer Caradoc, The Lawley and Long Mynd, and the gentle fields of corn, and tiny, winding lanes. He loved also their two acre garden, so lovingly cared for by Susan. But she had always longed to live near the sea. As a child in the early days of the war, her family had evacuated to Bude, in North Cornwall. The place had left an indelible impression upon her and she would often refer to her time there. The sea was like a magnet; she felt drawn to it. She would say "The Shropshire country side is beautiful, but it doesn't move. The sea is changing all the time. I yearn to be by the sea again and to take in all its moods and changes." Eventually, recalling Finn's parents visit there in 1944, she and Finn were prompted to visit the Scillies, and stayed in a little guest house on St Agnes. This tiny island, the most remote habitation from the English mainland, was, to Susan especially, an enchanting place. Immediately, she sensed it was her destiny to live there. They knew no one there, nor did they have the faintest conception of life there, of the rhythm of existing in such a small, tight-knit community. But what is life if one never takes a chance, a leap in the dark? A long lease came on the market for a pretty little fisherman's cottage. It was built of granite, painted white with bright blue doors and windows, and it had stood close to the beach at Periglis Bay for three hundred years or more. Susan loved it. "That would see us out, and probably James as well. Shall we go for it darling?

Just sell up here in Ryton and bury ourselves in island life?" Finn nodded. "Yes" he said. Nothing else, just "yes"

They moved to St. Agnes in 1998. They are still there today, fully integrated with the tiny community of 75 souls, with no desire to return to mainland life, except for the occasional shopping trip, or perhaps the rare visit to New Zealand to see Finn's brother and his family. Susan tends her little garden. Actually, there are two gardens: the back garden which is very secluded, and the front garden, crammed with semi-tropical rarities, which visitors stop to admire, and sometimes photograph. Finn looks after the Church next door. Every Sunday the priest comes from St Mary's to conduct Holy Communion. Finn prepares the altar and collects the priest from the quay, and runs him back afterwards. He still writes the occasional children's story, just to keep his hand in, but his itchy feet have long since calmed down. All the peace and beauty in the world are on his doorstep, and he will surely see out his time there with his beloved Su. He says he will die with a smile on his face, from knowing that some poor sod will have to dig his grave. And the graveyard, after three feet of earth, is solid granite!

THE END